POISONOUS WHISPERS

by

JANA BEGOVIC

To my dear friend
with lots of
love
Nenna
xxx

www.RoanePublishing.com
Copyright ©2016 Jana Begovic

ISBN-13: 978-1540641953

Content Editor: Lynne Street and Kathleen Marusak
Cover Artist: Bill Oliver

CHAPTER ONE

David

The knock on my door is so soft I'm not even certain I heard it. My first thought is Mrs. Knight has come back to retrieve something she'll have forgotten in my office. It seems she never ends a session with me without leaving something behind, be it her reading glasses, gloves, or a scarf. Last time she even left her purse. I shake my head at her forgetfulness. At the same time, feelings of anger and irritability rise up in my throat, leaving the taste of bile. It catches me by surprise as for a long time I have been lulled into thinking I had gained the upper hand over such outbursts. After all, didn't I psychoanalyze myself to exhaustion? One should never underestimate the tenacity of inner demons.

"Come in." The door opens and to my surprise I see Dr. Springfield in the frame. Her expression is somber, and there is a strange fire burning in her eyes. She and I have had very little contact since I came to work at this hospital eight years ago. I have always had the feeling she is a bit suspicious of me, and not only because I combine psychoanalysis with hypnotherapy, the latter eliciting snide remarks from her, as I'd learned from another colleague.

"Please, come in, Dr. Springfield. What can I do for you?" I get up from my chair and stand, feeling awkward with this unexpected visit.

For a few moments she is silent. Her serious expression is replaced by a shadow of what looks like mild embarrassment. She hesitates before she speaks. Her voice is whisper-like and I strain to hear what she's saying.

"I was wondering…I was wondering if I could talk to you if you have a few minutes. And please, call me Leandra. May I call you David?"

"Yes, of course…yes, we can talk. My last patient's just left. In fact, I thought it was her coming back for her scarf, purse, or glasses. She always forgets something in my office."

"Oh, you must be ready to go home. It's almost eight o'clock, but I know on Tuesdays you work long hours. I shouldn't be imposing on you like this, unannounced. I did mean to call, but then I had second thoughts, and in fact, it was on impulse I knocked and…." I can sense her unease. It is almost palpable, piques my interest, and suddenly I'm alert.

"No, in fact, I'm on call tonight and decided to stay and work on a paper, so please, make yourself comfortable."

"I saw Mrs. Knight on her way out. Is she doing any better with the new medication? In our group meeting you mentioned you changed her meds, didn't you?"

"It's too early to say. Her husband certainly doesn't think so. He had to call the police again after she threatened to kill herself in front of the children. Unfortunately, her bi-polar disorder seems to be particularly resistant to medication and psychotherapy."

Leandra lets out a deep, pained sigh. Her blonde hair looks a bit disheveled and her green eyes suddenly well up with tears. She's obviously distressed, and again I start feeling uncomfortable in anticipation of what she might reveal. Why would she possibly want to talk to me? I've never seen a more composed, level-headed or brilliant psychiatrist. Her competence is only matched by her amicability and the genuine interest she shows in her patients' stories. Her articles are always insightful and instructive, and her presentations at conferences always interesting, engaging and laced with humor—sometimes self-deprecating, which makes her even more endearing. Why have I shunned her in the hallways? Probably because I found her attractive but was afraid she might see it if she looked into my eyes. She must be at least fifty years old, and yet there's something youthful, timeless and energetic about the way she moves, talks and smiles.

She sits down with another sigh and starts twirling a strand of hair around her finger. Whatever is plaguing her seems to be serious. I wonder if it has anything to do with her family. I'd heard nurses comment that her daughters live in Europe, attending university. I also met her husband at our last Christmas party. A good-looking and fit man, but too aloof for my taste. I also didn't appreciate his sarcastic, negative comments about most of the topics we discussed that evening. But I should remind myself again not to be judgmental. Perhaps I was just jealous of his good looks. I look at her again. As a single childless man, I've always envied those who were able to realize their career aspirations and manage a happy family life at the same time, and Leandra certainly seems to have it all. What could be wrong with her? And what caused her to come to see me?

"I've heard you sometimes use hypnotherapy with your patients?" she begins gingerly.

I wait for her to continue, but she looks at me unblinking, waiting for an answer.

"Yes, that's true, when I reach an impasse with more orthodox ways of treatment, I resort to hypnotherapy. If I may say so, I have been made aware of your skepticism. If I recall correctly—in one TV interview you gave you made a reference to hypnotherapy, and especially past life regression, that was somewhat, how shall I put it, derisive. Didn't you say it was a bunch of hocus pocus?" I catch the acerbity in my voice and her resulting wince.

She lowers her eyes and her voice comes out cracked with contrition. "Forgive me, but yes, I had considered hypnotism as quackery, and especially your claims you've had success with regressing patients to past lives and affecting healing through regression. I must confess, I could never conceive how a serious psychotherapist could believe, or rather use his belief in reincarnation as part of his treatment. But I've changed my mind in the meantime."

"What made you change your mind? Have you also come across instances indicating evidence some of your own patients could have had past lives?"

"No, nothing like that…," and then she breaks down in tears.

I'm so taken aback I'm rendered speechless. I can find no words of comfort or any words at all. In the few relationships I've had, a woman's tears would always fill me with dread, guilt and powerlessness, and even anger. But what is it about this woman I've found so disarming, even though I've never had a chance to get to know her? I cannot tell.

Silence falls between us like a black velvet curtain. Almost in fascination, I watch her tears drip onto her lavender blouse, leaving tiny wet spots and a thin trail down the silky fabric. I notice the well-tailored and form-fitting navy blue suit she's wearing. She's always dressed professionally and yet fashionably. The color of her suede pumps matches her blouse and earrings, and I admire the coordination of her apparel. The shade of her lipstick is a hue that reminds me of lilac blooms.

"Please, Leandra, would you like a tissue? A glass of water, maybe? How can I help?" I detect a slight stutter in my voice, a stutter I thought I'd never have again after the two years of intense therapy I underwent as a thirteen-year-old.

"I want you to hypnotize me; regress me to a past life and…."

Her voice is still a whisper and I'm straining again to understand what she's trying to say. This whole conversation seems disjointed and incoherent, and that's how I sound to myself.

"Hypnotize you? What's the reason behind this unusual and unexpected request, may I ask?"

"I want you to hypnotize me and suggest to me while I am in the hypnotic trance that when I wake up I will not remember certain things, or rather a certain person. Or if you regress me to a past life, and I learn he's been my soul-mate and I've known him before, I might be able to understand better what happened to me and get over him. Sorry, I'm very confused, and distraught, as you can see." She expels all that in one breath, and for a moment it seems relief washes over her face.

"I'm willing to help you deal with whatever is distressing you. But, before we decide on any course of action, let's start from the beginning because I don't quite understand what you're after. I'm not even sure I understood what you've just said. Tell me what's wrong. Why are you here? And who is this 'he' to whom you're referring?"

Tears still stream down her face and she seems unable to find her voice. Streaks of mascara smear below her eyes which are getting red and puffy. Her cell phone rings and she answers. She manages to sound calm when she speaks.

"Hello." She listens attentively and says, "Sorry, honey, I have to stay late tonight…I've just been called to the ER…we have a case the on call resident can't handle. I should be home in an hour."

She's a smooth liar.

She finishes her conversation and looks at me as if reading my thoughts. "Yes, I've turned into quite an accomplished liar, deceiver, and betrayer."

Again I find it hard to find words as the evening is becoming more and more surreal. Outside, the sky has turned dark, and the first raindrops start pattering against my office window. I get up to close the window because all of a sudden I feel a chill.

"Why do you want me to hypnotize you?"

"I…I'm in love and don't want to be—and cannot be, because I'm married…and because he no longer wants this relationship…and because I have to accept it's over…and I have to let go. But I haven't been able to let go, no matter how hard I try. In fact, the harder and harder I try, the more difficult it seems, and most of my waking hours I'm in pain."

"Are you telling me you are having an affair?"

"I *was* having an affair, but it's over now. I mean…we broke up. But as I said, I'm having difficulty letting go, even though it's been six months now. I'm aware the relationship was hopeless and it was a matter of time before the end would come. But for me time has stopped, and I'm stuck in the past when I was still with him. I think about him often—that's an understatement. I'm obsessing about him and am having difficulty focusing on work. My husband looks at me in puzzlement and tells me I sometimes look like an alien, and he has no clue what the hell's wrong with me. I can't go on like this. I'm tormented, I dream strange dreams, I dream of past lives in which I knew him and loved him. I often feel we're still together. We are connected by…I don't know…like astral bodies in astral space connected with soul energy, or energy cords. I'm losing my mind, and I need help.

"I keep re-reading the stories he wrote about us. I'm re-reading his love letters, or emails, and my husband and daughters must never find out what I did. I betrayed them, I betrayed myself and my principles. But strangely enough, I have dissociated myself from the feelings of guilt…I'm not remorseful…and if he called or texted, I'm sure I'd get sucked back right into the affair. That's why I need you to help me get over him and forget, not forget completely, just rid myself of the pain, and learn to treasure beautiful memories."

"Leandra, do you remember the article you wrote about infidelity after Dr. Braunstein's patient, Mrs. Lazar, attempted suicide for the first time? You're probably aware I respected Dr. Braunstein and still wish he'd postponed retirement by another couple of years. Sorry, I'm digressing. But, in his long career it was the first case which left him feeling helpless as a psychiatrist, and yet it seemed to be so simple. Her lover left her, she became depressed. I remember you quoted Galsworthy during our monthly meeting when Dr. Braunstein presented her case. What was that quote again, something about grief—"

"'There's no grief that does not sob itself out with time.' I did think Mrs. Lazar would recover from love sickness in a couple of months, and I later believed she'd had serious mental problems, and didn't kill herself because of her lost and unrequited love, but because she'd suffered from depression. As for her poor husband, who patiently let her grieve her lost lover and is now grieving her, I felt both pity and contempt for him, because I just could not relate. I laughed at the thought of Adrian letting me grieve my lover. He'd never forgive me.

"And yes, I wrote an article for 'Modern Psychologist,' but at the time I wrote it, theory and abstraction were my motivation. I wrote the article with a cool head, and logic drawing on the latest brain research that presented love as a biochemical reaction and painted love stemming from affairs as a romantic illusion, a chimera that springs from the fecund soil of secrecy and sexual infatuation, a castle in the air built by two people taking a flight from reality. My thinking was always science-based and driven by logic. Some might even consider it linear." She sighs again, and I can't help noticing the heavy heave of her chest.

"Was the affair you had anything more than a romantic illusion?"

Again, her voice comes out as a whisper. "I'm no longer able to think because I am tortured by the strangest dreams, and because I still feel connected to him. I'm sure I'm being delusional, because he must be over me by now. I have moments when I no longer know who I am, because for a year and a half I was someone else, and before that I had been a completely different person. I feel splintered and fragmented and disoriented. Lately, I've tried to incorporate every piece of advice I have ever given to a patient going through the same nightmare of trying to fall out of love. And I've had a couple of patients who were so distressed after breakups they contemplated suicide. I could not comprehend such power of emotion and obsession with another person. And now, I've found myself in the same black hole of despair and my heart is rebelling against reason. It has its own irrational beliefs, it's still in denial, it does not accept the end, and wants him back. My thinking is impaired. I'm aware affairs can be as destructive as earthquakes or tsunamis, and anyone with any sense would run away and never look back. That's why I'm asking for your help. If you can help people quit smoking with hypnosis, maybe you can help me erase this experience and reclaim my sanity." She starts crying again.

"Do you want to tell me the whole story?"

"Yes… But where do I start? I never thought I would need psychiatric help for being desperately and illicitly in love. The reason is simple: before it happened to me, I felt morally superior to those so ensnared; I considered myself as someone who could never succumb to temptation, who was above human fallibility of that kind. My Dr. Jekyll simply did not have a Mr. Hyde. I was no frigging Madame Bovary or Anna Karenina, God forbid! The friend I confided in said, 'You're the last woman I would think capable of infidelity. If it happened to you, it can happen to anyone.' But, David, I'm sure you'd agree, life often finds ways to prove us wrong and teach us humility, and to 'never say never.' I now believe even the strongest of characters may fall prey to temptation, if that temptation is intense or lasts long enough. Have you read anything by Somerset Maugham?"

"Only his novel, *The Razor's Edge*. I'm not much of a fiction reader, I'm afraid."

"There's a wonderful short story he's written… I forget its name, but in it this married missionary is trying to convert a prostitute into an honest woman, and instead succumbs to her charms. One thing's true, though. Love affairs don't just happen, you don't just fall in love, you allow it, allow the affair to spread its wings and fly out of control. For me, it was a conscious decision to engage in a game of mutual seduction. And I don't any longer believe infidelity can only be ascribed to something being wrong in a person's marriage. Crossing that boundary may originate from the need to escape temporarily the frustrations of an unsatisfying marriage, but it could also arise from curiosity, from a lust for life, the desire to try something adventurous, potentially dangerous, like an extreme sport.

"In my case it could also have been a sign of menopause when I realized youth had left me for good, and I was now denying that stage of life by grabbing onto something so rejuvenating in every sense. I still don't know what my reason was, but it certainly was not marital unhappiness. But then, perhaps….

"Over the years Adrian and I had lost our emotional closeness, or the need to be romantic, to seduce each other again, to add sparks to our marriage. I just don't know."

"Where did you meet him?"

"You've met him, too." Suddenly she appears to be nervous, restless, and impatient with herself. "Listen, David, I shouldn't be wasting your time with a story you'll probably find shallow, frivolous and certainly in no way unique, when you have patients with serious problems…people ravaged by anxiety, depression, suicidal thoughts, shattered lives. Here I am simply lamenting I've lost a lover I never really had in the first place."

"Please, go on."

A dreamy haze mists her eyes.

"I saw so much beauty in this illicit relationship, in the feelings which developed out of the blue. Now I believe it was probably just an attempt to justify something unjustifiable. But I did feel spiritually elevated, ennobled and enriched. There must be millions of stories like mine, both in real life and in works of literature, and art, and stories sung in innumerable songs. While it lasted, this love was thrilling and exhilarating, mysterious and sparkling, and special in all its illicitness. Now I'm sure all lovers feel this way about their love and find it unique.

"And David, let me tell you something. If I'd seen a fortune teller before my trip to Boston, where you and I attended that truly extraordinary conference, and if that psychic had told me I'd meet a man to whom I would feel irresistibly attracted, and with whom I would fall head over heels in love, and moreover, with whom I would reach erotic bliss of the kind I had never dreamed of, and to whom I would write not only love letters, but erotic stories… I would have laughed in utter amusement, and have forgotten about such nonsense in no time, regretting having squandered money on something as banal as a visit to a psychic.

"God, I've made you blush! But anyway, you may wonder why I would've considered this as completely ludicrous and unrealistic and as likely as getting struck by lightning on a clear and sunny day? First, I was at an age and a point in my life where romantic love was not the object of my desires, or a perceived or conscious need. I believed I'd already met the love of my life, and it was my husband. I've been married for many years. You met my husband last Christmas.

"By the way, he told me he enjoyed speaking with you. Before that fateful conference, I had lived a tranquil and content life, convinced that most things were in their proper place, and in the mosaic of my life there were very few missing pieces. No life or relationship is ever ideal. In every marriage romance ebbs and wanes, but is replaced by something deeper and more substantive. I've always been grateful for what I have, and not unhappy with the aspects of my life that still may be lacking in some way. What I expected at that stage of my life was to experience the first signs of menopause rather than a '*coup de foudre*.' And the unimaginable happened."

"Now you've piqued my curiosity. I wish I could guess who it was. Probably not that pompous ass, Dr. Nielsen, from Denmark."

"Are you kidding me? He was intolerably overbearing with his know-it-all attitude. I was tempted to generalize and think all Danes were weird." A smile lights up her face, momentarily dispersing the clouds of pain from her eyes.

"It began on the second day of the conference. I'd just finished my presentation on the clinical effects of a new anxiolytic I had studied. If I recall, you were the first presenter that day. Anyway, my presentation was followed by a coffee break. When I stood up to leave the auditorium, I locked gazes with a man I'd seen at a conference a couple of years before. I remembered him because of the compliment he'd paid me and for which he later apologized. He told me I looked stunning. It was at a formal dinner so I'd worn a very tight black dress. At the time, I thought it was strange he felt compelled to apologize for a comment I'd found flattering and in good taste. Before I left for Boston, I'd noticed his name on the list of attendees and remembered him, and then a few moments later forgot all about him."

"I think I know who it was because I saw the two of you talking at lunch and thought he seemed inordinately interested in you. He has a very strange first name, Wey-something? I remember—Weylin. He explained it was an old Celtic name meaning 'son of the wolf'."

"Yes, and whenever I touched a patch of hair on his lower back, I would think of wolves." Her eyes turn misty again. It must be longing which colors one's eyes such a deep hue of heartache. "I like wolves…

"But back to the beginning. What was unusual about the moment when I caught his eye was, the distance between us was at least fifteen yards yet I clearly felt a force of attraction at play. As soon as I thought he was looking at me, I dismissed that idea as a figment of my imagination, thinking I might have been unconsciously looking to flirt or craving male attention. Later, during lunch, I saw him again casting a glance at me, and once again I attributed the exchange to a coincidence and my imaginings. However, I felt irresistibly drawn towards him, like the tides under the magical pull of the moon.

"The next day, during the sightseeing tour, we exchanged furtive looks which left me wondering if I was really imagining an attraction between us or we were falling under the spell of some mystical force. That evening, we happened to be in the same group of people who'd decided to have dinner in a pizzeria. I don't remember if you were with us or if you went out in another group. On the way back to the hotel he and I engaged in a somewhat strained conversation talking about our backgrounds and schooling. He told me he was from Dublin, but then again, I'd known he was Irish."

Leandra's eyes are sparkling as she reminisces about Weylin. In them I can almost see his reflection, and at that moment I wish I had someone in my life who would love me with eyes full of sparkles.

"Do you remember Weylin? He's tall and dark-haired, with piercing green eyes and an age I couldn't determine. How old do you think he is?"

"I can't say because to tell you the truth, I didn't pay much attention to him. I read a couple of his articles and found them well written; however, he appeared so nervous and jittery during his presentation his delivery ruined the high quality content."

She sighs and her green eyes take on a deeper hue.

"I agree he's not a good public speaker. I couldn't even say he's charming, but his presence and proximity stirred up an emotional storm in me. As we were crossing a street that evening, I felt his hand touch my back, intensifying my discomfort because he was still a stranger encroaching on my space. I felt exposed and vulnerable due to the attraction thickening between us. At the hotel, he offered to buy me a drink, and again his physical presence in the bar unsettled me. I didn't flirt with him; I did nothing whatsoever to encourage him, yet at the same time I was acutely conscious of what was happening between us without my wanting it.

"Suddenly he placed his arm around me and asked me if I wanted to leave the others and go somewhere with him. Touching me like that was highly inappropriate and I would've normally recoiled in shock; however, the attraction between us was so palpable I understood he probably couldn't resist the urge to touch me. I was also aware I must have been sending signals of being attracted to him, without any volition on my part. Then he did something even more shocking. He groped me…he reached down under the table and squeezed my calf. Imagine the brazenness! I said I was leaving and wanted to go to sleep, and that was all I managed to say, as my normal eloquence and ease with which I chat when among friends and colleagues had evaporated.

"I could not believe he would grope me like that. Imagine; he squeezed the calf of my right leg. So strange! The next day I didn't see him and thought he was avoiding me after he'd realized he'd overstepped the line of propriety.

"On the last day of the conference I approached him and his Irish colleagues and asked them if they would be able to help me with a further study involving the same drug. I did need help with that study. But, it was also a pretense to talk to him again. Weylin asked me to explain to him what data I was seeking, so I explained the details, excited at finding a common thread between us that would ensure future contact.

"That evening a group of colleagues took a cab to a restaurant and Weylin and I sat in the back, our legs touching, and jolts of electricity flying between us.

"At the restaurant we sat opposite each other, stealing glances and then averting our gazes in order to avoid being conspicuous. I felt spellbound and couldn't eat, or drink even one glass of wine. On the way back to the hotel we again sat next to each other. All of sudden I felt his hand on my thigh and he asked me if I wanted to spend the night with him. I told him I didn't do that. He told me I was very attractive, and I replied he was also attractive, but it was irrelevant. Once we got out of the car, we started walking toward the hotel together and I felt his arm around my waist, and at the same time my arm, as if with a will of its own, wrapped itself around him. The next moment, we disengaged and I wondered if our colleagues had noticed this display of utter indiscretion and folly, and I was in disbelief the magnetism between us was so strong it rendered us powerless and unable to control ourselves.

"The next few hours we spent at the hotel bar, continuing to exchange glances. I knew I should have left the bar to try to get a few hours of sleep before my early flight back home, but I couldn't move. I just sat opposite him, transfixed. What was happening to me? Yes, I know, people are often attracted to others, especially at conferences. They have one night stands, they have extramarital affairs, but that was always other people, not me.

"It shouldn't have happened to me! I am strong—morally, spiritually, professionally. Other women have reasons for infidelity and I don't. I could not be tempted. There's nothing I need to look for outside my marriage. How can everything you believe, all the values you think you have and would never betray…how can things change so quickly and so completely?

"I decided to leave the bar to go to my room. I hugged and kissed my colleagues one by one, and when Weylin stood up, he held me in his embrace for what felt like a very long time, and whispered, 'Infatuation'!"

"'Drop me a line,' was all I could say.

"The next few hours were like a dream. I was reeling from the experience—every cell in my body seemed to be aflutter with excitement, this unexpected feeling of being moonstruck. I wanted to see him again, I wanted him to write.

"As soon as I was back in my office and opened my work e-mail, my heart skipped a few beats. There was an e-mail from him—he said he trusted I had a good flight and he hoped to see me again. He also said he'd obviously misread some cues from me. I replied immediately, saying my memories of Boston would forever be colored with the spoken and unspoken moments we shared, and that he hadn't misread me. I added I would write back concerning my request for help with my study by gathering information from his patients. I finished with, 'Keep in touch.' I didn't know at that moment my whole world was about to change."

She is crying again.

Suddenly, she looks up at me and says, "I'm certain I'm going through withdrawal; this is how addiction feels. I'm suffering from love addiction and it feels like mental illness. Almost. But I will heal, there's no other option but to heal. I still want you to hypnotize me."

"All right, I'll hypnotize you tomorrow after I've seen my last patient. Are you free at five?"

"I'll make myself free. Thank you." And as unexpectedly as she had walked into my office she leaves, closing the door softly behind her.

I sit bewildered, and in that bewilderment I sense a spot of jealousy. What's so special about Weylin that he could make a woman like Leandra lose her composure and emotional stability, and fall in love so deeply? I remember him as rather withdrawn, ill at ease in new company, someone who looked as solitary as a lonely wolf. The name does befit him. Leandra and Weylin. Who would have thought?

CHAPTER TWO

Leandra

I leave David's office dazed and in disbelief I've actually sought a colleague's help over a broken heart. But a glimmering of hope warms my heart. Perhaps I will be whole again. Perhaps I'll be able to give my husband the energy which my falling in love with another man has shifted from my marriage. Perhaps my sexual desire for my husband will reawaken and Weylin's face will fade into oblivion never to reappear. Thank god for David! He's like a straw at which I'm now clutching desperately.

I look at the watch and realize it's nine o'clock. Adrian might already be in bed after an exhausting day in court. As a prosecutor his work is demanding and tiring, and he often works long hours. It occurs to me I've never thought his coming home late more often than not meant he might be having a love affair with a legal assistant or colleague. He's also always trusted me in that respect. If he only knew what I'd done, and what I'd do again if Weylin contacted me.

When I walk into the house I realize he's already in bed asleep. He must have come home drained after a year-long trial prosecuting a pimp who killed a prostitute. In the kitchen, I find cheese and a bag of cold cuts left on the table. He obviously had a sandwich and forgot to put the food back into the fridge. I also feel exhausted and after brushing my teeth I slip into bed beside him. Our cat Meeko is sleeping at Adrian's feet and snoring lightly. I'm afraid of falling asleep because of the dreams I've been having lately. I remember David saying once 'dreams can represent fragments of past lives'. I've never believed that.

However, lately, in my attempt to find meaning in the events which have unfolded over the last year and a half, I've been hoping to find in my dreams some symbol or message or a sign telling me I'd be reunited with Weylin. After all, he and I made a wish—one day we'd end up together, in conditions under which we wouldn't hurt anyone in our intertwined lives. I cannot imagine how that might happen unless our spouses left us or died, God forbid! My dreams also frighten me because they've been so

14

bizarre and so painful—every one of them ends in our parting. Parting from him has been more painful than the childbirth I endured.

As I'm drifting off to sleep I see before my eyes a beautiful snow-covered forest. I am floating above it and all of a sudden I hear a voice whispering softly in my ear.

"If you continue wandering through the Forest of a Thousand Whispers on this particular December night, you will stumble upon a small, hidden lake and the scene before your eyes will look like a picture in a fairy tale, and you will have to stop in awe bedazzled by the beauty of the winterscape."

I turn around trying to see who is talking to me. Perhaps it's a voice in my head…I might be losing my sanity. I see a lake with a breathtaking scene. A wind awakes and skips across the lake's ice- and snow-covered surface as small snow squalls start forming in the cold December air. It's the night of winter solstice—two days before Christmas Eve. I don't know how I know that. It also doesn't make sense because it's April. I'm also aware I am lucid dreaming, which feels like being awake within my own dream.

As suddenly as it has risen the wind dies down and with it, a lonely cloud vanishes from the ink blue sky and gallantly allows moonlight to cascade down creating bright bluish tinsels over the white treetops to paint them an effervescent silvery hue. The lake is enclosed by huge cliffs, flanked by a dark evergreen forest that seems to keep perpetual guard over the lake. Silvery snow glistens and shimmers in all directions; the lake's glassy surface reflects the softly tumbling moonlight, the snow-covered rocks jut into the lake, and the night is enveloped by the velvety dome of the endless sky lit with millions of starry lights. Magic reigns at this midnight hour. The beauty around me makes me breathless. All of a sudden I realize I should be feeling cold, but I'm not.

In the middle of the lake I see a tiny island, or rather, a huge, barren rock. I also notice an almost imperceptible movement on its surface which appears as a bouquet of colorful sparks. Around the sparks, there's movement of some dark substance. All of a sudden, both the sparkling and the dark mass transform into columns that start coiling themselves around each other; the columns change shape into what looks like human silhouettes whose arms enmesh, and whose heads look as if they were locked in passionate kissing. Sounds reminding me of insouciant and happy human laughter reverberate in the air.

The silhouettes disentwine and lower themselves at the edge of the rock. Watching them closely, I can see they keep transforming from moment to moment, looking at times like two resplendent female and male humans, and at other moments like glittering and formless masses of interwoven lightness and darkness. The figure woven from light which shines like brilliant cut diamonds extends what looks like an arm, and makes a sweeping move over the frozen lake. Both the light and the dark figures bend over the picture appearing on the lake surface as clearly as in a mirror.

I hear the same voice whisper to me, "Look into the ice mirror." I lean forward and peer into the surface of the frozen lake, and see the reflection of a hotel room. I lean closer and see the only light in the room comes from two half-burned green candles. On the bed, a man and a woman are making love. Both are slim and tall and have light green eyes of almost identical color. It is easily discernible they are deeply enamored, and utterly drunken with desire for each other. As an unintentional, but now curious voyeur, I observe they view each other's body as a cornucopia of the sweetest of pleasures and erotic delights. They are pouring wine over each other's bodies, thirstily licking it and lapping it up, infusing the scene with sensuality. Through their gazes, their throbbing souls are rushing toward each other's spiritual embrace to create a union. There is so much intensity in their erotic play I wonder if these two people are trying to condense an inordinate amount of lovemaking into a few brief hours, because time seems not to be a luxury at their disposal.

And then I gasp, and scream, because I recognize Weylin and myself in that man and woman. But they are much younger versions of us; they do not look older than thirty. My heart stops. This is us, had we met some twenty years earlier. We might have been happy together. Longing fills me and my throat and chest constrict. I look at them again and hear him whisper, 'Don't you ever forget about me…' and my heart lurches into my throat because Weylin whispered that to me when we first made love.

I turn around again, trying to see who had guided me to this place, but see no one. I want to wake up, but I can't, and I feel I must remain in this place until I have seen more, or learned something.

The shape made from lightness changes slowly into a woman shrouded in flowing hair which looks as if made of innumerable tiny crystals. The dark shape assumes man-like features with shoulder-length black hair, piercing obsidian-black eyes and a handsome chiseled face.

Now comes a surprise, because I hear sounds coming from these two unearthly entities. I wonder who or what they are, and if they are indeed talking to each other, or if that is music coming from celestial lyres and harps, suffusing the air with their song. But I realize it is not music I hear; it is a conversation between these two specter-like figures. My curiosity is now piqued and I'm wondering what they're talking about.

Again, that voice starts whispering to me, "If you could understand the language of pagan deities—yes, you heard rightly, for that is what they are, even though you are probably laughing derisively at such a preposterous suggestion—you would know their secrets. Nevertheless, you seem intrigued; you want to hear what they are discussing in this world of the gods. So listen carefully, and suspend belief for at least the duration of the winter solstice. After all, you are the subject of their conversation!"

With what we would consider a pensive look, the female is watching the hotel room scene. "Despite the cobweb of unpropitious circumstances, these two humans are falling ever more deeply in love. Perhaps it is the barriers they cannot break asunder which bolster their feelings for each other. Human behavior is such a source of mystery and amusement," says the goddess.

"When we created conditions for them to meet again, and when we breathed between them a great force of attraction, you still believed she would not succumb to the type of love humans consider inappropriate," says the male deity with a tone of mockery in his voice.

So even at a younger age Weylin and I would not have been free to love each other. After all, I was married before I turned thirty.

Mesmerized, I look more closely into the eyes of the goddess and detect a tint of empathy. "She knew not her own heart and soul, or her own unconscious proclivities, caprices and frailties. From the first flutters she felt in May, by summer solstice she was in love and hid the self-revelation deep in her heart," says the goddess.

The god raises his hand and makes two sharp movements over the hotel room, and the scene vanishes like vapor, replaced with a new picture.

I am so engrossed with the story of Weylin and me that I keep leaning forward, straining to discern the new revelations in the lake mirror. I'm looking at the same couple who are now separated by an ocean stretching into infinitude. We always lived on two different continents. Our eyes reflect depthless longing as we're writing love letters to each other.

Watching the scene the gods created, the goddess comments, "I see such disproportion between their infinite longing and the modest gains of such fleeting bliss, happiness and pleasure. I thought one of them would have left these impossible circumstances by now, suffered through the pain and tears of parting and emerged healed after a number of seasons, or what humans call time."

So she doesn't know we have parted, I am in so much pain. Did they do that to us? How many times have he and I met?

The male figure makes another swift movement with his hand and I now see a restaurant which looks like the interior of a home: bookshelves, comfortable sofas and armchairs, landscape paintings on the wall, the atmosphere warm and cozy. I see a couple sitting at a table for two. Oh my God, it's us again, and this was our last meeting. This was when we broke up, when he said he could no longer maintain what we had because he felt so mentally and emotionally depleted from the affair. He buckled under the pressure of his parallel life and the fear his wife might find out, leave him and he would lose his children for whom he lived.

Two glasses filled with wine sit before them, as well as a platter of bread, cheese and olives, but both the food and the drinks are left untouched. It's a strange feeling to look at the woman whose eyes are overflowing with sadness, and who has difficulty swallowing as she is trying to speak—and to know the woman is me. The man's face is distorted with intense sorrow. She starts crying soundlessly, yet a piercing wail of pain is reflected in her eyes.

As an observer, my heart is now clenched in the vise of deepest aching because I am a silent witness to my own final goodbye and descent into grief and suffering. Why did I have to relive the stormy agony in a dream? My heart is veiled in the blackest of desperations and I try to wake up and escape the anguish, but feel imprisoned in this nightmare.

I'm trying to decipher who is saying the obstacles hemming them have only multiplied, and the time has come to part for good as there is no other choice left, but I'm not able to discern that. In my dream, I'm despondently wondering how, in colliding with indomitable fate, we all lose; how finite love, life, the whole world, our dreams are; and how the only thing left to one is to make a truce with the inevitable. I plead with the deities for mercy, and at that moment, I feel relieved the goddess blurs the scene with a look of reproof and says, "There shall be no such ending yet. You shall not decide their fate…if their hearts are false and fickle, then love will disintegrate on its own without any doing on our part."

Hope leaps in my heart. Maybe 'the ending' was just temporary and this dream is telling me he will contact me and we will make up.

"Fickle should be another name for the mortal heart," says the male deity with a truculent tone. "It is pain they shall reap from what they have sown." His voice is vitriolic.

"They have not sown pain around them; therefore, they shall not reap it," comes the female deity's retort. She metamorphoses again into that mass of light, brighter than before, and now levitates above the lake. Blinding shiny sparks fly off of her in what seems like rage. They fall on the icy lake surface, lighting it, and in that circle of light a new image starts to emerge.

I am mesmerized, incredulous, and I think—even for a dream this is too much. But I'm now drawn to this new image in hope a new segment will show us together again.

What I see now is a magnificent city, with buildings and edifices boasting breathtakingly beautiful examples of a variety of architectural styles, such as the Romanesque, Baroque, and Neo-

POISONOUS WHISPERS

*Renaissance. It's a warm summer evening and the streets are
filled with people. Among them, I recognize the man and the
woman from the previous moving tableaus. The contrast is
striking.*

*Unlike a few minutes ago, when they looked forever
destroyed, they now look blissfully happy, reflecting the brilliance
of each other's gaze. The woman is wearing a formfitting, black
dress (a sweetheart neckline, and spaghetti straps cross in the
back). A simple diamond pin in the shape of a dragonfly is the only
adornment on the dress. She looks elegant, with her hair up, and
in black open-toed sandals with high, gold-studded heels. In her
hand she carries a green velvet evening bag and a shiny black
shawl.*

*The man is wearing a black suit and a snow-white, V-cut T-
shirt underneath. He looks handsome and chic as he walks hand
in hand with the woman. Alongside a number of other people, they
move toward an imposing building. All of a sudden I know this is
Vienna and the building is the Viennese opera house. In front of
the entrance, a large placard shows "La Traviata" is playing that
evening. Oh my God, Weylin and I look so beautiful and happy!
Perhaps, one day we will visit Vienna together!*

*I see them now on the Grand Staircase, which is indeed a
grand marble structure lit by an impressive chandelier and
accented by statues. They find their box and sit on comfortable
red velvet chairs. The woman leans forward to watch the
spectators as they are seated, and to admire their evening attire.
She turns around and kisses the man, smiling at him with her
eyes.*

*The man is not an opera aficionado, but gladly fulfilled the
woman's wish to see one of her favorite operatic pieces. Again,
where does that knowledge come from in my dream? I don't know.
Looking at them, I'm filled with more knowledge—before they
came in, she had briefly described the tragic story to him.*

*The curtains open, and they marvel at the elaborate and
lavish scenery of Act One. After a few minutes, they both notice
the boxes around them are empty. As the tenor playing Alfredo
starts singing the famous "Drinking Song", she feels the man's
hand on her thigh, his gentle caress through the thin fabric. As
always, one touch is sufficient to draw a moan from her. He*

moves his chair closer to her and leans over to kiss her. What begins as a superficial kiss turns into breathless, long and deep kissing—a clear overture to lovemaking. For a few moments they lose all sense of where they are. She rains down fiery kisses on his eyelids, licks his ears, his neck, and then she stops, flustered, and whispers to him they have to stop behaving like teenagers in love.

They are enveloped by semi-darkness illuminated only by tiny floor lights and sconces on the outside walls of the boxes. Her brain is inundated with intoxicating opera music, making her think she's walking through a dream. She squeezes his hand hard, never wanting to let go of him. She rests her head on his shoulder and he kisses her hair, whispering he loves her. She feels awash with the feeling of connectedness to him, of such deep and lasting love that the music now sounds distant, and the physical surroundings themselves seem to fade, and all she hears is the throbbing of their hearts in unison. At the moment they look into each other's eyes, they realize Act One is over and people are bustling outside the boxes. They embrace each other and exchange sweet and soft smiles filled with promises of everlasting fidelity.

As suddenly as it appeared, the opera scene vaporizes and I realize the male deity has wiped the ice clean with his breath. I see him swooping over the lake surface as if he is painting a new picture. I'm now aware the deities are trying to impose their will upon each other, playing with us unsuspecting humans as pawns in a game of power and of sheer entertainment. I'm entranced with this game, and want to see who will emerge victorious. I'm in awe realizing there are gods pulling the strings of my earthly destiny and determining my weal and woe.

A new picture develops, showing the man from the opera box sitting in front of a computer screen. The screen is as empty as the void of his gaze. I don't have much visual evidence, but I feel the man is suffering from extreme lugubrious moodiness; he appears to be in self-dictated seclusion and is weary and aged— but not from naturally passing years, but from a ruptured heart. I realize the god has prevailed over the goddess and, more importantly, Weylin is in as much pain as I am over our break up.

The male deity looks triumphantly at the puzzled female goddess. "Where is she?" she asks accusingly. "Is she dead, sick...did she forsake him?"

"Here she is."

Another picture appears showing the woman, now barely resembling the effulgent and elegant figure from the opera. As she moves around in a kitchen, she looks aimless, and somehow torn and fragmented. The flame once in her eyes is now extinguished which seems to reflect the hollowness of her soul. I recognize myself again, and pain wells up in me anew.

"Why did you do that to us?" I shout, but the deities cannot see or hear me. I feel crestfallen, and ponder how human history abounds with broken hearts, romances gone awry, loves lost. He and I are two insignificant specks in a universe filled with pain.

The female goddess turns to the male god and whispers, "I shall let it end your way. I am going back to the lake where I belong and shall never surface to meet you again. The only purpose behind your dark and baneful designs is to thwart mortal love and desires, and to woo them toward destruction."

As she turns to leave, the male god suddenly changes his tone and says with a conciliatory note, "Can't you see they have just been dreaming their life away by building love castles in the air, and those castles will soon become evanescent and crumble to dust—with or without our interference? But I am willing to change their fate, because I want you to stay. Without your brightness, I am all gloom! Tell me, what fate do you see as desideratum for Leandra and Weylin?"

So finally they speak our names. I don't dare to breathe as I await the goddess's reaction. She breaks a long icicle off a fir tree, and using it as a paint brush, she starts creating a new picture. I cannot wait to see it.

A beautiful house is shown in the ice mirror. It is of gray-colored stone, covered with ivy and climbing roses, which are in full bloom. The house looks new, and has large windows through which light streams unhindered. The backyard is crisscrossed with flagstone walkways alongside which blooming shrubs make the air fragrant with the sweetness of summer. A willow tree stands in one corner of the backyard and under it is a stone bench.

Butterflies and dragonflies glide through the air and birds whistle, trill and chirp in this paradise-like setting.

I hear peals of laughter inside the house. I peek through one window and see the same man and woman, this time in the kitchen. Now they both look the same age as Weylin and I actually are. His arms are around her while she playfully tries to extricate herself, pointing to the clock. She holds a wooden spoon and wears an apron. It seems she's been busy preparing a huge meal—there are dishes and various delicacies cooling on granite countertops, and the large dining room table is set for ten.

What started as laughter suddenly transforms into sighs and moans of erotic wanting. Their kisses turn feverish and thirsting, but she pushes him gently away explaining they have just enough time to change before the guests arrive. Kissing her softly on the lips the man turns and walks through French doors into a spacious room filled with bookshelves. A large computer desk sits in one corner of the room with two piles of books atop it. He takes one from a pile and lowers himself into a big, comfortable armchair.

Through the open window, a dragonfly flies in and alights on the man's face. The woman comes into the room and stops, in wonder. The man smiles and very gently plucks the dragonfly off his face and places it on the windowsill. It lingers there for a few seconds and its wings glisten in sunlight. Then it flies away to live out its short-spanned fate.

The woman comes to the man and says something, laughingly pointing to his shorts. She takes him by the hand and leads him upstairs. It seems she is insisting he change his casual clothes before their guests arrive. Walking up the stairs, they kiss and wrap their arms around each other's waists.

I'm curious to see whom they are expecting for lunch, family or friends, but suddenly the picture vanishes; the same house reappears, but now it is night. A soft summer breeze is swaying sheer white curtains on the second-floor window; the air is imbued with the monotonous chirping of crickets, and all is still. I don't know how, but I'm able to peer through the curtains on the second floor. An incredible feeling washes over me.

I am looking into my own life, or a scene of what might happen one day or could have happened had fate taken another turn. As my eyes try to adjust to the darkness I hear a voice say with utmost tenderness, "Good night, my lovely dragonfly lover, I love you."

A male voice replies, "Likewise," but his words are lost in a clap of thunder which startles me with its suddenness and leaves me trembling.

The thunder shatters not only the stillness of the night, but also dissolves the picture of the house. I try to penetrate the darkness left in the lake mirror, but there is not enough light left in the place where the stone house had stood. Perplexed, I avert my gaze from the lake and search for the deities, hoping for an explanation or a definitive end to the story of Leandra and Weylin.

The male god has a strange glint in his eyes as he raises his hand in what looks like an attempt to draw another tableau depicting another vicissitude to which the couple will be subjected. From his facial expression I try to read his intent but I cannot divine it.

But, before he has a chance to influence the life path of Leandra and Weylin, the goddess, now metamorphoses again into a column of flashing sparks, flies right through him and for an instant I see a hole in his body her burning rage has made. The hole disappears in a flash and the god, now in the shape of a column of dark mist, flies after the goddess. In the distance I see their shapes entwined again in what looks like a struggle at first, but soon turns into what one might describe as a dance of love. Just when I detect an awakening of hope that the winter solstice will extend its magic to us, I am flooded with realization—mortal destiny will always remain veiled in inscrutable darkness.

I wake from this strange dream drenched in sweat and sobbing loudly. My husband is awake and strokes my hair.

"It's just a dream, Lea, sweetie, just a bad dream."

I hug him, shaking uncontrollably. I am being comforted by the man whom I've betrayed. I must be a horrible, horrible person. Something is so wrong with me. I feel the urge to vomit and barely make it to the bathroom. My stomach is heaving, and I'm covered in cold sweat. Adrian holds my head over the toilet bowl. Retching, I feel as if I'm about to die and spit my guts out in the toilet bowl. Once I stand, I feel so utterly exhausted I have no strength to speak. I want a sleeping pill but cannot manage to unscrew the bottle.

Adrian leads me to the bed and helps me lie down. I'm now shivering, convinced I have a fever and am coming down with the flu. Or I'm simply dying from a broken heart, because apparently, that's quite possible. I remember reading in Márquez' "*Love in the Times of Cholera*" that when an autopsy is done on those who have died from a broken heart, crystals are found in their hearts.

My heart must be full of crystals.

Adrian brings me a glass of water and helps me change into a clean nightgown. I want to cry, but I'm too tired; I only hope for a few hours of dreamless sleep. Adrian lies beside me and puts his arm around me. I feel safe and comforted, and guilty at the same time. How could I have done this, and how can I still love someone who no longer wants to be with me? Sleep only comes at dawn.

CHAPTER THREE

David

I've just swallowed the last of my sandwich when my office door opens and Leandra walks in. She may have knocked, but I didn't hear. As usual she's dressed impeccably, her hair well styled—but she looks tired and despondent.

"Is it still a good time for you to see me?"

"Yes, of course. Please, sit down."

She sits with a sigh. "I can't help feeling I'm wasting your time."

"Don't worry about that. How are you feeling?"

"I had a bad night and am still reeling from a strange, multi-layered dream. I could imagine people who use hallucinogenic drugs have such strange dreams. I'm also still in disbelief of what I've done and still in denial it's over. I feel torn, pulled in every direction. I want to get over him, but I feel I'm just spinning my wheels."

"Tell me about the dream."

She recounts her dream to the very last detail, and I'm impressed with the vividness of the picture she paints. It is a strange dream which, it seems to me, might contain fragments of past lives or even a prediction of what's to come. I'm a believer in the symbolism found in dreams and also in reincarnation, unlike Leandra and a few other colleagues who are more oriented toward cognitive therapy as a means of effecting changes in their patients' thinking and behavior. Over the course of my career, I've regressed enough patients and collected enough evidence to believe in the mysterious, and to weave it into the scientific.

"The dream felt so real, David, it frightened me. What if there *are* gods who play games with us mortals?"

"It's a very seductive thought given the unpredictability of our lives. Perhaps we'll find some answers during hypnotherapy and you'll regain peace of mind."

She starts shifting her weight in her chair. "You know, I find this situation very embarrassing. Weylin and I did the right thing and we broke up before anyone got hurt. But I feel so weak

26

wanting to hear from him and start our affair anew. And I despise that weakness. I never want to be so vulnerable again. Before this happened, I'd always considered myself as strong as the Rock of Gibraltar; now I'm anything but."

"You aren't weak; you are just another fallible and imperfect human like the rest of us, and by falling in love illicitly, you've been forced to face your own fallibility and vulnerability."

She laughs nervously and with a self-deprecating expression on her face, continues. "I once had an obviously delusional thought I might get close to the state of the highest good which Kant discussed, and by being morally virtuous I'd be perfectly happy. I'd hoped most of the decisions I'd make in life would be morally worthy."

"But Leandra, Kant himself realized there is no moral perfection, and virtue does not ensure happiness or wellbeing. Sometimes we make morally dubious decisions in order to attain happiness. And by attaining temporary happiness—I'm assuming the relationship made you happy—you've violated your own moral convictions. Because you're now suffering so greatly, it may be that your relationship with Weylin was probably a mistake. Have you analyzed what may have been missing in your marriage to make you open to an affair?"

"But I was happy in my marriage. Or I thought I was happy before this happened to me. I'm sometimes tormented by the idea that I've given up my moral convictions for erotic pleasure. And at other times, I just know this love I still feel for him defies reason and logic. It should have flamed out by now considering the physical distance and time that's elapsed since we broke up. Why am I still resisting the fact that the break-up is final? I can't explain why I'm not completely letting go of the idea we'll be together again."

"Letting go of someone or something is a process we all need to exercise."

She looks at me with a wan smile and says "That's true, because I've not learned how to let go of him. I've counseled so many patients on the art of letting go of their past, and I know all the theories on how it should be done, and yet I'm so helpless. I just can't reconcile myself to him no longer being a part of my life. It doesn't even matter that both of us broke all our moral principles. Morality would be easy to maintain if we could just rid ourselves of desire and turn into Buddhists striving for enlightenment, reducing expectations to a minimum and living in a state detached from real life!"

"But, Leandra, morality is also relative. What's immoral in one society may be quite acceptable in another. Homosexuality used to be considered a sexual aberration and deviance; today I'd like to think that, at least in our society, it has become accepted as something genetically predetermined and simply a variation of normal. Therefore, Kant's *a priori* established norms of morality cannot be cast in stone, because concepts, beliefs and social norms evolve, and change, and there are very few absolutes."

"I'm grateful you're not judging me negatively. And when I think back, I can see I simply succumbed to desire; I succumbed to seductive magic I thought resided in this relationship. Now—I'm ready to be hypnotized. I want to reach the deepest recesses of my soul and my memory and see if I can find Weylin there."

"Very well. In preparation, I want you to sit in that armchair. Last night's dream reveals there's a possibility you'd known Weylin in a past life, and we will explore that. But before we start, I'd like you to tell me more about how your relationship unfolded after the conference in Boston."

"We'd been exchanging e-mails for two months before we saw each other again. This exchange turned out to be a wind which fanned a wildfire of amorous feelings. We quickly became virtual lovers, connected in thought across an ocean, valleys and mountains. Our love—forbidden and socially unacceptable—grew in spite of our physical absence and impossible circumstances. His e-mails would take my breath away, and I would tremble with intoxicating passion; they had the effect on me of a narcotic. What happened between us was so beautiful and intense, I want to enshrine it in words and immortalize it, so it doesn't become a faded memory."

"Writing is therapeutic and cathartic as you well know, and I do recommend you put that experience on paper. But, please continue."

"In the first few e-mails I sent I didn't reveal too much, even though I was experiencing all the symptoms of falling in love; butterflies in my stomach, my heart lurching upon seeing his name pop up in my inbox, a deep sense of disquiet when his e-mails wouldn't come for a few days. Even though the first e-mails had a rather innocuous content, I felt an enormous erotic energy behind Weylin's words. That energy was fully unleashed after I replied to an e-mail in which he, in the form of questions and answers, allowed me a glimpse of himself by revealing facts about his love of reading and travel, and his disdain for poetry and philosophy. One of the questions asked how many tattoos adorned his lanky body. The answer was none. I wondered whether I should say something about tattoos knowing my comment might provoke a strong reaction. I wrote something like, 'Even though I've decided to trust you when you say you have no tattoos on your body, I wouldn't expect you to protest too vehemently if I insisted on verifying the truth for myself.' And his reply was swift and feverish."

"What did he reply?"

"He said if I had asserted I had no tattoos, he wouldn't take my word for it either, and would want to check by inspecting my body most meticulously, removing my garments one by one and turning me over and over again. I replied, saying my comment on tattoos had obviously sparked a whole frenzy of fantasies. He replied I had no idea what wicked fantasies my e-mails provoked on the other side of the Atlantic. Our exchange continued for a couple of weeks, and then I asked Weylin if there was any chance he could attend the upcoming conference in Barcelona.

"He said he'd check his schedule, and a couple of days later he confirmed he would, and wrote he was looking forward very much to seeing me there. In my reply I explained I was also looking forward to seeing him again; however, that I also felt a great deal of trepidation over Barcelona. I added I felt as if I was suffering from temporary insanity, and that not only was I playing with fire, but also with the power of a seething volcano. Weylin replied that he wanted to feel me erupt. That sent such erotic ripples through me I doubled over in my chair reading it."

"The attraction and infatuation were obviously deepening…?"

"Oh, yes, I was falling more and more deeply into the quicksand of illicit passion. In his next e-mail, Weylin wrote about his sadness over losing a young patient. The patient had suffered from depression and committed suicide. He asked me if I'd ever lost a patient.

"In my reply, I said I'd never lost a patient to suicide; however, I also remember philosophizing about the moments during which human pain and grief are of such immeasurable magnitude as to elude rational thought, yet they still have to fit into the smallness of the human heart. I wrote about my own experience of losing my father, and witnessing depthless grief when a colleague's nine-year-old child (to whom I'd donated blood because we shared the same O-negative type) died of cancer. I will never forget those moments of complete silence in the house of my colleague when I came to express my condolences. I will never forget his wife who, struck with grief, held her head in her hands and never raised it to acknowledge the presence of people in her home.

"There was nothing to say during those moments; no words to soothe that pain. As I looked mutely at the mother in grief, I remember thinking of what Wittgenstein had said: *'What we cannot speak about we must pass over in silence'*. That was applicable to this situation, because there was nothing to speak about; it was the kind of grief words can neither describe nor console."

"I've witnessed such ineffable losses myself, and can relate to that. What was Weylin's reply?"

"I ended by saying I'd been day-dreaming about him and feeling butterflies in my stomach. And then, two days later, I opened my e-mail expecting more of his musings on the subject of death and loss. However, in the subject line I read, DD number twenty four, an acronym for a daydream. What followed was an explicit daydream of his in which he described an erotic scene between us. In disbelief, I read the first line, in which he was describing himself exiting the bathroom with a towel wrapped around his hips, and watching me lie on the bed pretending I was asleep while soft sunrays were frolicking on my naked skin. He started kissing me and his tongue began to travel down my body, finding first honey in my navel and then slithering between my thighs, his licks becoming deeper, his breathing heavier, until his towel fell off and I, now stirred to a full state of wakefulness, matched his passion with my own.

30

"Sorry, David, for going into such detail. I never wanted to embarrass you and make you feel uncomfortable."

"No, that's all right. Go on." She looks at me quizzically and I wonder if she notices my blushing. I couldn't help envisioning the scene she's describing, and couldn't help wishing I were Weylin. She looks away and continues dreamily.

"He concluded by saying he thought he would explode with longing while he was writing it. At that moment it became clear to me I had a lover, albeit a virtual one. I felt confused, embarrassed, scared, and doubting whether I should even go to Barcelona and risk turning a virtual affair into a real one. I felt possessed by demons and wished they could be exorcised. I couldn't bring myself to reply to that e-mail for a couple of days. I replied by sending him an erotic fantasy of my own.

"Can you believe it? That I would succumb to insanity like that? To lose my mind so quickly and completely, and with such abandon without considering the consequences! Anyway, I have it here printed out if you want to read it. I want you to know the details, because I believe you'll be better able to counsel me, and help me escape this insanity, this...this obsessive thinking which keeps my mind in a vise."

She hands me a printed paper and I read the short story she'd written for her lover. Reading it, I feel again envious of Weylin, envious he could attract so much love only to let it go so easily. But, it is also understandable that his devotion to his family would and should prevail over the infatuation of illicit passion. As I enter the world of her erotic novella, I wish someone had written it for me.

CICADA SONG
The room is washed in soft and flickering candlelight; moonlight is seeping in through the wide open windows creating dancing shadows on the warm-hued hardwood floors. The bed is high and wide and has gauze-like fabric stretched across the canopy and the four ornate posts crafted in inlaid wood. A man and a woman are on the bed. He is leaning comfortably against large and crisp white pillows. He is bare-chested, and part of the white bed sheet covers his groin; he's sipping wine, and seems to be absorbed in thought. The woman is wearing a long, white

sleeveless cotton nightgown discreetly adorned with lace and violet flowers. Her face looks serene as she slips into slumber.

Unexpectedly she lets out a small, almost imperceptible gasp as if taken by surprise by an invisible force. She feels the erotic tide swell up in her again even though she had thought the wanting must have already been quelled. As new ripples of lust start sending electrifying quivers through her body, she turns toward the man, takes his wine glass from him and places it on the night table. He smiles at her with his eyes, recognizing instantly what her look reveals. Slowly, still gazing into his eyes, she moves her fingertips across his lips, and then touches them with a kiss so gentle and tender, he thinks a dragonfly has brushed against his mouth with its translucent wings. Her next kiss is hungrier and deeper, and he feels a slight stirring in his loins. His sigh is as light as the rustle of weeping willow leaves under the caress of a summer breeze.

She takes his hand and dips his fingers into the wine glass, and then licks the wine drops off his fingers, making swirling motions with her tongue. He lets out another sigh when the sensation he feels in his fingers suddenly ricochets through him. The woman drips a few more wine drops on his lips and licks them off with quick and precise flicks of her tongue. She continues by pouring wine on his chest and his belly, lapping it up slowly. Some of the wine slips off his body, staining the bed sheets. A thought shoots through her mind that it will be difficult to remove those stains unless she pours white wine over them to neutralize the red. In the background, music scores from love movies emanate from a CD. "Orfeo Negro," one of her favorite instrumentals, is playing, mixed with the hypnotic song of cicadas coming through the windows on this hot, summer night.

Now, the woman's blonde head is between the man's legs. She smiles seeing how fast he is able to transform from a state of flaccidity to one of full rigidity. The air in the room is permeated with the scent of honeysuckle. The fragrance seems to be everywhere, in her hair, in the bed linen, in the gossamer fabric enveloping the bed.

She now mounts the man while removing her nightgown. Giddy, insouciant and inebriated with the mystery and magic of the moment, she takes the bottle and pours the wine over her breasts. The man sits up while they are still joined and starts licking the wine drops off her. Their breathing is heavy. He murmurs in a language she doesn't speak, but can somehow still understand. It sounds like old Celtic, and its sound fans her passion and love for this man whom she's stealing. His eyes glaze over with desire as he lays her on her back and merges with her in an Eros-inspired dance of two bodies in complete accord. They pulsate against each other, dissociated from the real world.

Once the wanting starts to ebb, they lie quietly, holding hands. The touches they've branded on each other's skin seem to be etched in their minds and souls. One day, they will have to find a way to erase them, but not just yet.

"It's a beautiful and sensual tale," I say, aware of the hoarseness in my voice. "It's easy to imagine how it would spark feelings of love in any man who would be the recipient of such passion-laden words. What's his marriage like?"

"He told me his marriage was bad, loveless and sexless. A cliché every married man offers his lover. He has two sons and a daughter he adores. He has tried for many years to improve his relationship with his wife, but his efforts have proved unsuccessful. At least, that's what he said. From her perspective, everything's right between them; obviously, he expected and wanted more than she could give. I always wondered what she would tell me about him if we were friends. Who knows what needs she has which he hasn't fulfilled. And maybe, like most people, he's been focusing on what he hasn't been getting, rather than on what he hasn't been giving."

"I'll want to find out more about you and Weylin, and to read something he wrote to you, to get a sense of him."

"He wrote erotic tales for me, too. I have them on a flash drive in my purse, zipped away in a pocket I've hoped no one would ever find. Shall I leave them, for you to read later?"

"Yes, please."

She rummages in her purse and produces a blue flash drive. She gets up and moves to my desk and I stand to let her sit in my chair. After a few minutes she gets up again and says she has saved three of his stories on my desktop.

Once she is back in her seat she exhales deeply and says, "I'm ready for hypnosis if you are."

"OK, let's begin. I want you to relax and try to empty your mind of all thoughts."

CHAPTER FOUR

Leandra, and Jilleen

I sit back in the comfortable suede-covered armchair and exhale deeply. Because I'd not slept much the night before, I worry I might fall asleep instead of going under hypnosis. Exhaustion is helping me loosen up.

David goes to pour a glass of water for himself, and I watch him as he walks to the water cooler. He's about six feet tall and rather thin; his face has a nice oval shape, and his eyes look as black as onyx. His lips are full, and when he smiles a set of perfectly straight white teeth gleam in the light. His hair is black, streaked with grey. It's tied in a low ponytail giving him an artistic look. It also strikes a contrast with his pale skin. He looks like someone who never goes out in the sun and who spends too much time indoors. He could even pass as handsome, and that's the first time in eight years since I've known him that such a thought crosses my mind. What I like best about him is his calm nature and composure; he looks as if nothing could ruffle his feathers or shatter his peace. His mere company has a soothing effect on my pain, and I sense he will be helpful during this difficult time I'm experiencing. Oh, what have I done to myself!

He sips from his glass, sits back in his chair. "We'll begin our session now. I will be recording our conversation, and will give you the recording afterward so you can listen to it and discuss it with me the next time we meet. I will also add music in the background to help you relax."

The next moment, I recognize the first notes of the soundtrack from 'Braveheart', an instrumental I could listen to over and over again.

"I want you to focus on your breathing. Take a few deep breaths. Inhale…exhale. Now, as you are inhaling, imagine you are being bathed in effervescent white energy. It is enveloping you and it is protecting you. Imagine you are breathing it in, and see it infuse you from within and spread to every cell of your body. You are relaxing more and more deeply; every muscle in your body is loosening up; any stiffness in your neck, shoulders, lower and upper arms is draining away steadily, and you are now feeling completely relaxed and completely safe.

Your awareness is now fully attuned and a sense of deep serenity fills you. The energy you have breathed in still surrounds you like a bright, white light; the light connects you to the spiritual energy of the universe in which all living beings are interconnected. This energy is soothing and healing, and this healing will continue after you wake up. I am now going to count from ten to one, and on the count of one, you will disconnect from this physical space and go back to a previous life and explore its scenery. Ten, nine, eight…you are going deeper and deeper, entering a past life…seven…six…five…four…in that life you will pay attention to every detail, to the colors, smells, textures…three…two…one…."

David's soporific voice seems to come from afar as my eyelids start feeling as heavy as lead and I find myself in a world which at first I don't recognize. After a few moments of disorientation, as I try to absorb the sight before me, distant memories struggle to surface in my consciousness from some dark recesses of the Freudian Id.

"Where are you?" I hear David's voice come from a great distance. It feels as if we are separated by many layers of time and space, and yet I know he is close, and I feel safe with him.

"I'm not sure where I am…perhaps Ireland."

"What makes you think it's Ireland?"

"The scents are so familiar…everything smells so green and lush…I am not sure where this knowledge comes from."

"What year is it?"

"It is sixteen thirty five…or sixteen twenty eight or…I'm not sure."

"Tell me what you see and what you are doing," David's calm voice instructs.

"I see huge blocks of white stone, arranged in a seemingly perfect circle. At four points in the circle, a rectangular stone stands on top of two stones, creating the look of a gate. It looks like Stonehenge, but it's not Stonehenge. There are four gates. In the middle of the circle there's a large, flat, round stone with five white candles burning. Wan moonlight is struggling to penetrate a cloud shaped like a wolf's head. I'm all alone, but I'm not afraid. I feel excitement and joy, and great anticipation."

"What are you anticipating?"

"Something important…a long awaited encounter…someone special is meeting me here tonight. I'm trying to remember."

"How old are you and what do you look like?"

"I'm nineteen. I'm tall, my hair's long, brown and curly—so thick and curly it's hard to tame. My eyes are green; my husband, Aidan, tells me they are the color of a gleann in springtime."

"What are you doing while you wait?"

"I'm not afraid, but I am nervous and biting my lower lip. I can taste a drop of blood my bite has drawn. I still don't know why I'm so excited and restless."

"What is your name?"

"Jilleen."

"Do you have family besides your husband?"

"Yes, I know I'm married, with a son. He's two years old and I love him so, so much. I had a brother, Aengus, but he was killed in a war. He was my step-brother. My heart's heavy thinking about him, like a part of me is missing. I have two sisters—I mean step-sisters. Both are married to noblemen. I know somehow neither of them is happy in their marriages. My father is a Protestant priest sent here from England to convert Catholics to Protestantism. He and his wife adopted me when they found me on the doorstep. We never found out who'd abandoned me as a baby."

"Are you happy in your marriage?"

"My husband's a good man, a protective man, and a kind man. He's a chieftain and even though I consider him kind, I know he is feared and most probably hated by many. But with me he's as tame as a house cat. He's always been very good to me, and has given me lots of freedom. When I accepted his proposal I did it under the condition he let me preserve my ways, the ways many people here find strange."

"What is so strange about you?"

"I've always liked to roam in the woods and meadows, in sunlight and in moonlight, in rain and in snow. I like to walk barefoot and feel the healing power of the earth beneath my feet. I worship stones and rocks, and feel spirits everywhere; trees talk to me, but I don't reveal that secret to anyone. I love animals and nurse them back to health…even snakes don't fear me, nor do I fear them. I find holiness in all life forms. I can spend hours lying in the grass and gazing at the clouds and divining fortune from their shapes.

I know the servants gossip about me riding out alone, roaming the fields and climbing the hills, but my husband tells everyone he wants a happy wife, and not one subservient to his every whim. I love him because he cares about my happiness, unlike most men who look at their wives as possessions, prized or not so prized, and keep them caged, in servitude, and beat them-- even kill them. I always used to say I would not marry anyone, and my father was afraid no one would want a wife who roams like a wild beast for hours, and when she is not roaming, she wants her father to teach her to read and write, and then let her read all his books."

"What do you do when you wander the fields and forests?"

"I collect medicinal herbs. I talk to trees and animals, but don't tell that to anyone. That's my secret. Some people think I'm crazy, or I'm a witch, because I make potions from the herbs I pick. My grandmother, who came from England with my father and his family, taught me the art of healing, but also always warned me to be very discreet about my gifts. Knowledge, especially if possessed by women, is considered a sign of the devil. She also told me people would be grateful if I help them and cure their sicknesses, but they might also hate me, mistrust me and ascribe evil powers to me. I don't think anyone hates me, because everyone welcomes me warmly into their homes, and they let me hold their babies. They also tell me that when I touch them, my hands shine heat and that heat alleviates their aches and pains. Perhaps they don't really love me, but they tolerate me because I help them, and because they also fear my husband. I cannot be sure. I often think that I understand the animal world much better than the world of people."

"Are you ever injured during your wanderings? There must be evil people around who could harm a solitary young woman."

"I fear nothing when I roam; I feel my spirit guides protect me. A wolf also follows me around and makes me feel safe. But people have warned my husband that harm could come to me wandering about unprotected. They also say it is indecent for a woman to behave as I do and that my husband, who is feared by many, has not been able to tame his wife. But, as I said, I have no fear because I believe I can make myself invisible. I can summon mists to envelop me and hide me from potential danger. At least, that's what happened once when a group of horsemen appeared out of nowhere just as I exited a grove of trees. I felt fear at first but then I closed my eyes, spread out my arms and spoke an incantation my grandmother had taught me. When I opened my eyes, a mist was hovering all around me, and the horsemen rode by without even looking in my direction. I don't know who they were."

"Do you love your husband?"

"I think I love him, I am happy with him. I feel lucky he chose me when he could have chosen any girl he wanted. I married him for love. It was the kind of love you feel toward someone who is kind to you, and who lets you be free. I would feel like a bird in a cage if it were not for my husband's generosity and kindness. He knows I desire no jewels or gold or expensive dresses…and he gives me what I crave most—blue skies, and grasses scented by summer, and treetops bedazzled by moonlight. I love him, but not the same way I love…"

"Who is it that you love differently?"

I find myself struggling to respond as distant memories dance before my eyes like wisps of fog.

"I loved my husband and was happy and content until…"

"Until what?"

"Until I met Kieran. It is Kieran whom I am awaiting. It is because of him I'm so excited, and yet I often feel so torn, and so guilty of betraying my husband and his goodness."

Upon uttering Kieran's name, I feel excitement infuse every cell of my body.

"Where did you meet him?"

"I am trying to remember…my memories are slowly rising and taking shape as if through a vapor. I met him during a summer solstice celebration, but before I set eyes on him for the first time around a blazing bonfire, I had met him many times before in my dreams where I surrendered myself with complete abandon to his love. Every time I would awaken, the dream would linger with me for days, and I would feel a soft burning on my skin left by the gentlest, yet most fiery touch of fingertips. It took many a dream for me to finally see his face clearly. He has a narrow face; full, sensual lips; green eyes; and curly hair the color of ripe wheat, and as soft as a duckling's down. His body is sinewy and muscular and exudes strength and endurance."

"What do you remember from that meeting?"

"Seeing him on the other side of the bonfire with a goblet of wine in his hand made my heart stop with recognition. When our eyes met, I knew he had also recognized me. In a trance-like movement, we started walking toward each other not averting our gaze for a moment. When we came close, so close we could feel each other's breath on our faces, my fingertips lovingly touched his lips, his eyes, and his cheeks. A tree shielded us from the other revelers, and he lowered his lips toward me and kissed me. In that moment of instant recognition I knew I had found the lover of my dreams.

As he embraced me, we wordlessly exchanged knowledge of each other; not only did our bodies carry a remembrance of each other inscribed in every cell, but our souls rejoiced in the long-awaited union. Oh, I remember everything now. I also remember that at the moment we met I forgot I was married, I forgot the danger of being seen and discovered because at that moment, everything around us seemed to disappear and we felt like the only two people left in the world."

"Describe that evening."

"It is embarrassing to talk about what we did that evening. If we had been discovered, we would both have been stoned to death, because he is also married. But, we will not be discovered…I seem to have some special powers to protect us and make us invisible."

"Tell me what happened that night when you met him."

"I placed my hand on his chest and unbuttoned his white shirt. My hand travelled to his heart and its beat felt like the flutter of a dragonfly's wings held captive in the palm of a hand. He took my hand and led me deeper into the woods behind the clearing where the revelry was taking place. The night sky was aglow with blue moonlight and a star-emitted incandescence; his hair and eyes seemed to catch and reflect the silver splendor of moon rays. He lowered me down on the moss-covered ground and I started to shiver and sigh with erotic wanting. His nimble fingers began to undress me slowly and sensually. He first kissed the laced-up front of my white dress. The bodice of my dress—it was trimmed with delicate pink rose buds. The dress had drop sleeves made from mesh lace fabric. The back of my dress had a low v-cut, also laced up. My husband paid a hefty sum in gold for that dress.

Kieran unlaced my front first, and then the back as I lay turned on my side toward him. While unlacing my dress, he was kissing and licking the nape of my neck while whispering that now that we had found each other, I was not allowed to ever again forget about him." I pause, remembering more.

"Why are you silent?"

"I'm thinking about that night. I want to remember every detail, but I cannot…"

"Let us leave that memory for a while. I want you to take another look at your present surroundings. Describe the place to me and try to remember why you are meeting Kieran tonight. Is that the place where you usually meet?"

David

I am observing her under hypnosis. She appears enraptured and I know that look emanates from her love for Kieran, Weylin, or who knows what names he's had in all the lives when they've met. Again, I feel an arrow of envy pierce my heart. I wish I were loved like that, illicitly or otherwise…it would not matter. Witnessing the depth of her love and passion, I start inventorying my own love experiences, and none of them can measure up to this kind of devotion. I have had a tepid love life and never suffered much after break-ups.

My work held such interest for me that my feelings of longing would fade inordinately quickly. My last relationship ended in intense acrimony. Myra accused me so many times of selfishness, emotional unavailability, anger and irritability, and an inability to meet any one of her needs. She left abruptly after calling me a cold-hearted bastard. I should have felt hurt, but for some reason I didn't. Perhaps she was right.

Perhaps I am capable of giving only a limited amount of love, an amount that could never satisfy any woman. Perhaps my mentor was right when he told me during the psychoanalysis sessions I took as a resident that my cold and composed demeanor was too thin a facade for my simmering rage over unresolved family issues. From that day on, I strived to maintain a cool and almost expressionless affect for fear that someone might notice my intermittent inner upheaval.

I look again at Leandra. Her eyes are closed and a faint smile dances on her lips. She is describing the world to which I have regressed her, and her description of the scenery is so vivid I can visualize the stones in the moonlit night. As I am following her story, I feel hypnotized myself. She is now describing looking at the stones again, walking among them and touching their rough surface.

I close my eyes and find myself in the stone circle. Like whispers, Leandra's words are swirling in my brain and through her words I see the moon, in its full silvery splendor, rise against the deep Cerulean sky and paint the stones a luminous shade of white. The air has a sweet and fresh vernal scent as if it had been un-breathed before, and the starlit landscape around me appears un-trodden.

At the moment the stone circle is kissed by moonlight, a wolf howls and there is infinite solitude echoed in its sound, and it seems to have howled her name. Is the wolf really howling Jilleen's name and if it is, what does it mean, what does it forebode? It sounds almost like a warning. Is the wolf her spirit guide warning her of her lover Kieran's advances and their import?

Jilleen is standing still like a statue. Her white dress moves ever so softly in a light breeze. Behind a stone, a wolf emerges and pads toward her. She reaches out and pats him on the head and then kneels and takes his head into her hands. She looks deeply into his eyes as if reading a secret message. The wolf's eyes glimmer in the night, a bright yellowish color. He licks Jilleen's hand and trots away. Slowly, she gets up and turns toward the stone gate facing south, and sees a man approach her. It's Kieran. Her eyes light up as the sight of him fills her stomach with wildly fluttering butterflies, and her heart lurches with palpitations of depthless love. I can feel all of that happening in her as I observe her with my spiritual eye. Kieran is slim, straight and tall, and his hair creates a halo of golden locks around his narrow face. His stride is slow and measured as if he is in no hurry to fall into her arms.

"What are you feeling now, Leandra…Jilleen?" I want to know what she is feeling. At the same time I'm not feeling like a professional psychiatrist trying to help a patient in distress, but rather like a voyeur feeding his sick imagination with other people's love stories.

"Oh, how much I love him! I want to be with him, but I cannot," she exclaims. "My husband would banish me from our castle and take away my child. I am so torn I sometimes wish to die to escape this torment."

Kieran's eyes are like two red-hot coals burning a path into her heart and soul; his lips are warm and moist and his kisses make her blood boil with unquenchable desire for him.

"Are the two of you alone?"

Leandra's voice becomes hoarse and raspy as she answers my question. "It is the night of Beltane celebrations and I hear unbridled revelry in the distance. But I know he and I did not come to this sacred place to revel with the others. We are here for a reason, but I don't remember what. It is not just to meet in secrecy; there is a reason why we are here."

"You will remember; don't try too hard. Look around you again."

"Kieran is saying she will come, but I don't know who she is."

"Ask him why the two of you are there."

There is silence during which her eyelids flutter.

"He says we are to undergo a pagan ritual of spiritual unison officiated by the high priestess. The ritual is not widespread or known, but offered only to the chosen few whom the priestess deems worthy of the secret act. It is also punishable by death because it is a pagan ritual and the priests call it heresy, and the punishment is stoning. I'm so afraid all of a sudden. Why am I risking my life? What will happen to my son if I am caught in adultery and a ritual considered witchcraft? It hasn't happened often, someone being accused of witchery, but there is always the danger of it happening."

"What happens next?" I am filled with an impatient curiosity to learn how Jilleen and Kieran's story will unfold.

"Hand in hand, my love and I walk around the stones. I am now trembling with fear and excitement. I want this and yet I fear for my life. I also fear for his life because he is risking everything to be with me. Every now and then I turn because I believe I see the wolf's shadow. I have met this she-wolf many times in my life, and always at the crossroads of decisions or whenever I was in need of solace and comfort. I have always believed she was my guardian and beacon. If only she could tell me what to do, or not to do."

"Why are you silent? What do you see now?" I continue to probe.

"I see the high priestess."

"What does she look like?"

"She's tall and wears a long white, billowing dress. On her head is a crown of willow twigs and her hair is waist-long and blonde; the blueness of her eyes penetrates my soul and I feel peace and love. In her hands she carries a ritual knife, a chalice and a few weeping willow twigs. She beckons us to follow her outside the circle, and then leads us to the first gate. Seeing her, my fear dissipates."

"Do you know her?"

"Yes. I recognize her. She is a healer and her name is Ailionora. Many people believe she is a witch. Many women avoid being seen with her. I like her. She is kind and understanding. I confided in her my love for Kieran. She did not say it was a sin against God. She said it was meant to be and our purpose on earth is to love and be loved."

"Where is she taking you?"

"She beckons us to follow her. We are now following her, and pass through the first stone gate. The gate faces east and symbolizes air. How I know this is a mystery, but my mind is illuminated with the light of understanding. As we are entering the gate, she asks us what our wish is and I reply my love and I want our soul energies to be joined in air so we may meet again in the times to come. We are now exiting the circle and re-entering it through the south gate, symbolizing fire, and the priestess asks us what our wish is. My love replies that we wish the flames blazing between our two hearts and bodies never turn to embers and dust, and constancy forever reigns in our hearts. The next gate faces west and water is its symbol. Our wish is that water may sweep away all obstacles before us. The last gate through which we step is that of the north, representing earth, and our last wish is its steadfast stability will so imbue our love with strength that it may survive in the now and in the future."

"Where are you now?"

"She leads us to the round stone in the middle of the circle. Onto it she places the silver chalice and the ritual knife, the bejeweled handle of which sparkles in a multitude of colors. From her pocket, she produces two blue candles and places them in the middle of the circle made of white candles. Their light falls on the stone and its surface looks like azure-colored stardust. She takes our hands and places them on the stone. She tells us to close our eyes and open our hearts and minds. Then she starts to chant."

"What is she chanting? Can you make out the words?"

"Her chant is whisper-like. I can discern fragments such as 'perennial love,' 'light and laughter,' 'in deep love and perfect trust,' and 'may nothing set you apart while you love each other'. After each verse, she ties our hands with a willow twig until our hands are tied fivefold. The priestess is telling us, five is our lucky number. She then brings the chalice to our lips so we may both drink of it together. The dark liquid in it is covered with gardenia petals giving off the sweet scent of May. With eyes closed, we drink the nectar-like liquid and feel immortal with the knowledge we will always find each other, no matter our circumstances.

We open our eyes and we are alone. The sweet drink we drank burns on our tongues and I feel bolts of fire starting to float through my blood. The warmth spreads through my body like an unstoppable wildfire and I feel wetness drench the hidden place between my legs. I feel out of breath as my lover takes me in his arms and pushes me against the stone altar and then lifts me up on it. In his eyes I see the voraciousness of a wolf who has found his one perfect mate. The candles are still burning and the chalice is still on the stone.

Gazing into my lover's eyes, I dip my fingers in the chalice, and they come out viscous with a honey-like substance that still smells of gardenias in full bloom. I put my hand between my legs and gently mix the nectar on my hand with my wetness. I am so hot I tear off my dress in one quick move. With one sweep of his hand, my lover pushes the candles off the stone and their flickering light dies in the soft grass. I am now sitting naked on the stone and my lover's head is between my tremulous thighs. Like a cherry blossom, I feel myself open up to his tongue and lips and the sweet pleasure permeates my every pore and turns my blood into a flaming river of molten lava."

"What happens next?" Again, I detect hoarseness in my own voice as Leandra's words set my blood on fire. I want to move over to her chair and shower her with hot kisses as I become Kieran. Her voice penetrates the haze in my head and I hear her continue to describe the love scene between her and her lover.

"My lover rises and presses his lips fiercely into mine. We kiss and bite each other's lips and explore each other's mouths with insatiable hunger. I dip my fingers again into the chalice and wet his lips with the sweet liquid and lick it then from his lips. I slide off the stone and lie on the grass pulling him towards me. My hands travel down his sweaty back to the place on his lower back that's covered with a patch of hair. In my dreams, I had often touched the luxurious coat of my guardian the wolf, and my lover's hair has a similar, coarse texture. Tonight, as always, his passion is unbridled and uncurbed and when he enters me I scream and cry out, and his name, Kieran, escapes my lips like the softest of sighs. In my delirium of pleasure I can barely make out the words he whispers in my ear.

'Don't you ever forget about me.' How could I ever forget about him! We make love until we fall exhausted over the stone, which is still warm with candle wax."

Before I let her continue, I decide it's time to stop the session, as two hours have elapsed and I do not want to exhaust her. I am also shaken by her story and by the intensity of emotion she has stirred within me. I feel confused and uncertain about my feelings and actions. She's a colleague, and a patient, to whom I am now feeling attracted. Or, I may be attracted to the story of love and passion which has spanned more than one lifetime. I believe only exceptionally strong soul-mate connections emerge across lifetimes with the purpose of teaching those involved important life lessons. I'm still feeling like a Peeping Tom, and am considering telling her this is posing a conflict of interest, and she should seek someone else's help; but I know I will not do that. I know I will continue this exploration of her past lives.

Gradually, I bring her back from the state of hypnosis. Like a shadow, a look of bewilderment dims her eyes as her gaze crosses from one object in the room to the next. Then she looks at me and in her gaze I recognize hope and expectation.

CHAPTER FIVE

Leandra

I open my eyes and look at David, not recognizing him at first. He seems flustered and almost uncomfortable. I ask him what's wrong and if he was able to hypnotize me, and if I was able to reveal anything which could explain why I have been feeling so strongly I have met my former lover in a life before this.

Without speaking, he presses the button on his recorder and time stops for me as I listen to his questioning and my answers. I am astonished—I can remember most of it, and even additional bits and pieces I had not even revealed to David. The feeling of listening to my own voice describing scenes from some past life fills me with awe, and yet a cold dread. I notice my hands are trembling, and pain wells up in me like a wave threatening to drown me. I am crying and shaking, as the memories of the scenes my voice is describing are trying to push themselves to the forefront of my consciousness.

"How is it possible?" I ask him, sobbing. "Does what I've said, and what I seem to remember constitute any proof I have lived before?" David hands me a tissue and I wipe my eyes.

"Although many people think these are false memories created by one's imagination and there is no proof for reincarnation, I believe I have regressed you to a past life in which you knew Weylin, that is, Kieran."

"David, I am feeling so shaken I'm unable to process what has just happened. But I want to continue with this and learn more. When can you see me again?"

"Next Tuesday, but only at seven in the evening, if that's not too late for you."

"It's not too late. Nothing's too late. I need your help. I can make it." I try to get up to leave but feel so weak and queasy I sit back again. David rises instead and brings me a glass of water.

"David, is it normal that under hypnosis I, as Jilleen, am using words or concepts Jilleen would not have known…or should people under hypnosis speak only in the vernacular of the time where you regressed them?"

"Not necessarily. Some may speak, let's say, ancient Greek, and others will use their present-day vocabulary to describe their life five centuries ago. And they will also use modern day concepts in their descriptions. There is no set formula."

I am still trembling and don't want to go home.

"Take a few minutes to compose yourself. I understand this kind of discovery can have a very unsettling effect."

"I can stay a bit longer. Adrian's in LA for the next couple of days and the cat should be all right alone."

"You said you'd met with Weylin several times in different European cities."

"Initially I met him at the conference in Barcelona. That was the first time we made love. I didn't know if I'd be able to go through with it, and texted him that I'd like to talk first. He'd arrived before me. When I arrived, I showered, changed into a new summer dress and instead of calling him to arrange for a meeting to talk, I just went to his room and knocked. I will never forget the look of delightful surprise in his eyes. I put my arms around his neck, and he pinned me against the door. We kissed slowly, panting and gasping for air...then we undressed, peeling the clothes off each other. He whispered, 'This is how it should be, with love and passion. You are an ideal partner for me.' During the daytime, we didn't spend a lot of time with each other, not wanting anyone to suspect we were lovers. During dinners, our feet would touch under the table, our gazes would lock in meaningful exchanges of passionate longing; it was unforgettable.

"The last day we spent alone in a park, walking hand in hand, enjoying our newly discovered illicit love like two teenagers. We also had a very special moment in that park. It was a warm summer day and all around us dragonflies were flitting in the air. At the moment when I told him how much I liked dragonflies, one of them landed on his face and stayed there. I called him 'my dragonfly lover,' and thought such a moment of synchronicity must be a good omen. Remember, in my recent dream, a dragonfly also landed on his face. I wonder now what it signifies."

"What does it symbolize for you?"

"I don't know, perhaps passing beauty, summer, sunlight, the brevity of life, and most of all perhaps fragility and impermanence."

"Did Weylin reveal much about his life?"

"He confided lots of things to me. He said he was abandoned by his biological parents as a two-year-old boy and was raised by his maternal grandparents. His parents left him and went to India in order to 'find enlightenment'. They joined a cult and the first few years sent postcards and letters regularly. Then their writing became infrequent until one day his mother reappeared in his life. His father had left his mother because he'd fallen in love with an Australian woman who came to India to practice meditation.

"His mother came back very embittered, and soon started changing lovers. She remarried, and Weylin found a nice step-father in her new husband. He was very attentive to him, took him to rugby games, and spent time helping him with his school assignments. Unfortunately, that period of emotional stability ended when his mother fell in love with a man fifteen years her junior. He was, in fact, only five years older than Weylin who was then twenty and in his first year of university. When his step-dad discovered his wife was cheating on him, he left them, so injured by her betrayal he no longer wanted anything to do with Weylin either. So he was abandoned by two fathers. His mother always seemed to care more about her love life than about being a mother to him."

"That sounds like an untypical mother."

"But because her travel bug never left her, she took Weylin travelling all over the world and infected him with the love of travel."

"I assume he must have felt unlovable and unworthy of love with a mother like that, and those fathers. He must have experienced a sense of abandonment more than once."

"That's one of the reasons he went into psychiatry, wanting to understand the human psyche and through that, heal himself. His marriage is, according to what he says, loveless, and he stopped trying to turn it around a long time ago. He said he started noticing how the chemistry changed between him and his wife when she got pregnant for the first time and suffered a miscarriage. One day in her office, she just started bleeding, and her colleagues took her to hospital.

"Losing that child was extremely painful for both of them, but after that he felt she no longer loved him as she once had. Over the next few years they had three children. However, he could never reconnect with her emotionally or sexually, as she remained distant. Whenever he would try to talk to her about it, she would say everything was all right, and she didn't really understand what he wanted or expected. He told me that at one point he even contemplated suicide, but the thought of his children needing him helped to dispel that idea. But I've already told you that, I believe. In a way, he's a fractured man, who worries a lot, who's filled with anxiety and fears, not only of heights but also of illness.

"Because of the role his mother played in his life, and because of the way she involved him in her love-related problems—she would talk to him about her love life and her disappointments—because of her focus on herself more than on him, he has always tried very hard to please women and win their love. While he was in hot pursuit of me, he was clearly assuming a subservient role. You see, David, he readily revealed all his vulnerabilities to me, his social anxiety and his general feelings of inferiority, and those revelations made me want to heal him and make him whole, the way most women have this urge to fix and repair broken men. As a psychiatrist I know it's often impossible. As someone said, by trying to fix others we just cut ourselves on the shards of their broken souls."

"Everyone is fractured to some degree, and everyone is capable of healing. If people were not fractured, we'd be out of business, right? You will also forget this and after a while the pain will dissipate, and you will probably wonder how you could have even believed you were in love."

"David, I don't know how I'll feel tomorrow, but today, I'm still as devastated as I was half a year ago when we broke up. I'm still in pain, and not even close to starting to forget. I remember one moment very clearly. During our first lovemaking, he whispered in my ear, 'Don't you ever forget about me!' And I also heard that sentence in the dream I recounted to you, and I've also heard it on the tape a few minutes ago. It makes me wonder if he has hexed me or cursed me with that whisper. During sleepless nights, I sometimes think this whisper was like poison he poured into my ear. He must have cursed me, because I have a feeling I won't be able to forget him for the longest time, perhaps not ever. It's like I'm under a spell."

"I have no doubt you *will* forget him. This was an earth-shattering experience for you because of its nature, because of infidelity and because you've now discovered you might have known him in a past life. We'll pursue the route of hypnotherapy until you find all the answers you're seeking and can to let go of the past, and move on by directing your energy back into your marriage. When did you see him next?"

"After Barcelona, I saw him again a few months later. I visited my older daughter in Freiburg, and I met up with him in Glasgow. I told my family that while in Europe I wanted to see some of Great Britain. Adrian never asks too many questions; that's why I've been able to get away with this."

"Tell me about that encounter."

"David, I'm not able to talk anymore. I'm exhausted and slightly nauseated, and the cat needs to be fed. Because I knew my memories would inevitably fade, I wrote them down in order to capture the moments of all our secret rendezvous before they vanished. They mean too much to me and I don't want to lose them, ever. I've chronicled all our encounters, and I can leave my flash drive if you wish to read them. But I warn you, they are explicitly erotic because I also wanted to freeze those frames forever with words.

"You will have so much to read now, not only what I 've written, but also the stories Weylin wrote for me. It became a habit for us to exchange erotic tales. Anyway, the file name is Glasgow. I'll leave the flash drive with you. I could have done so immediately when I gave you the first story I wrote for him. Perhaps, as an objective reader, you'll be able to gain more insight into this love affair, even though I'm sure that most affairs are very similar, or at least they share a lot of commonalities."

I hear myself sigh and continue. "One thing I cannot get over is, how is it possible that he loved me as much as he said he loved me, but then things changed overnight for no apparent reason. The only reason I can see is, at the last conference in

Berlin, the one you didn't attend, a woman from Norway flirted with him quite openly, and all I could do was watch helplessly as she shook her black mane of hair while drinking beer with him at the bar. And when she went out to smoke with a couple of other delegates, he followed her out. For the rest of the evening, she never left his side, and he never left hers. I felt jealousy, and told myself it probably didn't mean much. I also heard her say she would write to him. She is very lovely, and I'm sure he felt attracted to her. But what kind of man would love one woman one day, and leave her for someone he finds attractive a couple of weeks later? How could he have loved me with such passion one day, and after a few days break up with me? Who can do that?"

"A man who cheats on his wife can also cheat on his lover, or shift his interest to another woman. Why would that surprise you? Why would you expect integrity from him toward you if he has none in his marriage? Do you think you had enough time to get to know him well, to become acquainted with all his demons, all his secrets and flaws, his lack of character?"

David's words have taken a caustic tone and they hurt me, because through the fog in my head I can detect a certain truth in them, or at least a potential truth. It's as if the veil of fog has parted for a heartbeat to let a ray of truth in before it encloses my mind again. I look at him and in his glance I read displeasure or perhaps annoyance. For a moment I see a chink in the armor of his calm composure, allowing me a glimpse of another David, a stranger I have yet to meet.

But I abandon that impression, thinking that what he sees in my eyes must be utter naiveté and gullibility. He is probably surprised by his discovery that a mature woman, a renowned psychiatrist with a wealth of knowledge, is acting like an inexperienced teenager who's just swallowed the bitter pill of love and wonders why it tastes so acrid. No wonder love is considered insanity!

I get up and leave with a curt goodbye, eager to get back home and slip under the covers. It will be another night when I will need a sleeping pill.

CHAPTER SIX

David

As soon as she leaves, I open the files on her flash drive and find the Glasgow folder. Again, I feel like a voyeur peeking into the life of a woman intoxicated with love and glimpsing the most intimate part of her. Moreover, to help her deal with this, I don't really need to know what happened between her and Weylin. I have enough information already to know what turmoil this illicit love has stirred up in her. I am still fascinated by so much passion because I have never before believed, based on my own experiences, love could be so fiery, so consuming, so potentially deadly and destructive. She should feel grateful they didn't wreak more havoc than they have; they chose to engage in an illicit relationship and as a consequence, they have suffered great emotional pain, at least she has. He may already be over her and onto a new illicit relationship which will make him feel better about himself.

I find it strange that I am thinking about Weylin as if I knew him, as if I had a clue about the contents of his mind and heart. I also find it surprising and highly worrisome that when I think of him, I become angry, as if he had somehow transgressed against me. I suppress the unsettling thought and with trembling hands, I click on the file. It opens and I plunge into the world of forbidden love.

* * * *

The plane's engines are roaring—the final touchdown. I'm returning from a visit to my daughter, Cassandra, and making a stopover in Glasgow for the sole purpose of meeting my lover. My family believes what I've told them—I want to see as much of Europe as I can when I cross the ocean. To arrange this amorous encounter was simpler for me than for Weylin. The web of deception we spin is becoming more and more complex; however, deception has been an integral part of our Modus Vivendi, and in my case is now causing fewer and fewer instances of burning compunction.

I arrive at the hotel and go to my room to take a nap. Weylin will be arriving the next day, and the longest evening and night stretch before me like the boundless and most desolate desert landscape. I still don't dare believe we soon will be together, so I shoo away excitement, fearing I might somehow jinx our weekend if I allow joy to overwhelm me. After a nap, I head to the pool, but the water is too cold for me to venture in so I return to my room and watch endless reports of alarming economic and financial woes in Europe. I fall asleep before nine o'clock and rise with tumultuous expectation at seven the next morning.

He should be at the hotel any time after noon and gradually, trepidation, thrill and joy flood my heart with a suddenness almost too much for a mortal heart to bear. I shower and wash my hair, spending an inordinate amount of time styling it. A flight status check on the computer shows his plane has landed on time and I start to quiver and tremble. The mere thought of him appearing in the doorframe sends throbs of aching longing to my heart and soul! In an attempt to quiet my wildly beating heart, I read a few pages of the book I brought with me. Still, I feel as if I am treading the fine line where dreams and reality mingle. I manage to calm my heart rate, but realize my hands are still shaking as if I had overdosed on caffeine. His knock will open the doors to a deluge of love; it will disperse the shadows of my painful waiting, it will ignite wildfires of desire which will finally be sated, and I will temporarily lapse into a slumber of contentment.

When I hear the knock, I feel myself turn pallid with anticipation. I get up from the armchair with a start and open the door and there he is, standing and smiling, wearing the white and red checkered shirt in which he looks so dashingly handsome. I cannot tell if I smile, if my eyes are aglow with love, if I am able to utter a word, whisper his name, or if I greet him with stunned silence, or even if I look like a wraith caught between two worlds. Was it even necessary to say anything; had not love existed before words?

I fall into his arms and our kisses reflect our greed of dizzying intensity. He pushes me against the closed door and his hands start travelling over my body. I cannot get enough of his touch and of his lips that leave mine feeling almost bruised. I am awash with a sensation of languishing and fear I might start feeling unwell; however, I compose myself and anchor myself in every moment I so desperately want to ensnare forever in the nets of memories. I slowly unbutton his shirt and sweep my hands over the black T-shirt he is wearing underneath, with a craving to touch his sun-gilded skin. Our thirsting hands and eyes drink deep of each other's effervescent love. With each pulse and each breath our desire grows and blossoms like a meadow awakened from winter's slumber by the sweet breath of spring.

A few moments later, we are on the bed caressing each other and exhaling sighs, drunken with love and lust. I'm on top of him, pulling the belt out of his pants and then pulling his pants down, until he is in his underwear—which is bulging invitingly. The moments that follow are filled with erotic frenzy as our bodies fuse into one, moving in perfect tandem to the ethereal music of love only we can hear.

The next day is a string of the happiest and most magical moments which will remain etched in our hearts and souls for eternity. We walk hand in hand, we embrace and kiss every few minutes, we enjoy the local food and we come back to our candlelit room with a renaissance of erotic wanting. Our erotic play reminds me of sheer fantasy; we are transported to a space-less and timeless dimension in which only we exist, with our minds and bodies entwined, a sparkling love bubbling up within. As I look into my lover's green eyes, and as I stroke the hair on his lower back, I suddenly see a wolf's eyes and I am at a loss as to why a wolf would appear before me.

Do I have a wolf spirit guide? Weylin's facial expression is contorted into a grimace of voracious and yet tender wanting; his look is feverish, and an erotic inebriation wells up in me making me feel faint again. I don't know what I want…no, I want everything…to feel him in my mouth, to feel him rub his throbbing erection against my nipples.

I want him to suck my nipples and lick the chocolate and wine on them, to feel his tongue again between my legs and his fingers slide in and out of my wetness while I am sitting up engulfed by a whirlwind of sexual waves making me writhe and convulse as if I were about to take my last breath. I am almost unaware of the candlelit room, of Adele's raspy and plaintive voice singing longingly 'Someone like you'. He finally raises himself and when he enters me I cry out in absolute ineffable pleasure as I wrap my legs around him. We each instinctively seem to know what the other wants and our erotic play is spontaneous and creative. We are both in disbelief that lovemaking like this is even possible, that two bodies and minds can vibrate on such identical frequency and be so synchronized, so attuned, so in love with each other.

As everything in life exists in duality, there is a price to pay for our love and this relationship. When, after a simple supper of bread, cheese and tomatoes, he embraces me tightly, a stream of tears runs down my cheeks. I feel a frosty foreboding of an imminent farewell and an upcoming sorrow. Thoughts of pain enter my mind and I fight them, not wanting it to eclipse and sap the joy we have shared. He kisses away my tears and whispers, 'Leandra, I cannot leave my children, that would kill me. If it was only my wife, I wouldn't think twice.' I tell him I would never want him to leave his children for me.

I would never leave my family or husband for him, but I don't say that. I hope he doesn't misinterpret my tears for expectations he should make such sweeping, life-altering decisions. He cannot change his circumstances and I cannot change mine, and we must master the art of living despite the frustrations of being apart. Our love is simply enisled in a sea of impossibilities. Albeit deeply passionate and genuine, the nature of our love is such that it lacks the spirit of purpose and holds no promise of 'they lived happily ever after'. The story of us exists in and for the moment only. It just is. Even though I am aware of this, I also shiver at the thought that our love story might die as suddenly as it has begun, and be covered with the frost and snow of oblivion.

His kisses of solace suddenly undergo a metamorphosis and tints of passion color them. It takes only a few moments for us to light the flame anew with desire as if our lovemaking has taken place in the distant past. His fiery breath and his branding kisses disrobe me of my sorrow and sadness, and I plunge into the sea of heavenly pleasure that drugs all my senses and creates in my mind the sweetest nebula of fulfilled dreams. This time, our lovemaking takes on a hue of despair and an undertone of hidden grief, a desire for the embrace to never be broken. Despite the sorrow that just moments ago had felt like a knife being plunged in my heart, Weylin and I spend the rest of our time together joyfully joined in sinful pleasures. I fall asleep in his arms wishing to stay in his embrace for a much longer time than this one brief night.

The next morning we drive to the airport together. We don't know when we'll be able to steal more time for ourselves. As I leave him in the airport lounge, I hope that from one encounter to another, from one stolen kiss to another, our love does not wane. And once again our hands are apart, and once again sorrow etches a new crack in our hearts.

* * * *

I finish reading her account of their meeting in Glasgow and cannot decide whether such love is a curse or a blessing. Probably a curse, under their circumstances. No wonder they broke up. Who can sustain such intensity, such longing, and the realization that to change the circumstances would multiply the hurt! I also wonder if by hypnotizing her I am prolonging her agony. I should, instead, try to help her get over him and heal, turn her attention back to her family and work. I plan to talk to her tomorrow about taking a different approach. But before I meet with her I am curious about what he wrote to her. I open the next file in which Weylin writes a story for her. She said that it was based on one of his dreams about her.

* * * *

I watch the stars on the clear moonless sky above us. I am behind you, hugging you. 'I never get tired of watching them.' My voice is low. 'It's like a portal into the past. All the objects we see are really images of the universe long ago, sometimes millions of years ago. We are actually watching the past! That is so cool.' You do not answer, simply reveling in being here with me. We're standing on black smooth rock surrounding a crystal-clear lake. Although it is night, I have the distinct impression the water will be azure in the daytime. My hands are on your breasts now. You are wearing a light knee-length summer dress cut low in the back; without a bra, the thin fabric allows the heat of my hands to penetrate your skin. I feel your nipples harden and you lean back into me. You can feel I want you desperately; I press my arousal into the small of your back and buttocks. My hands slide up under your dress, caressing your cheeks inside your panties.

I whisper unintelligible sounds into your ear and lick you. You turn around and we kiss, unrushed and lost in our exploration. You take off my T-shirt and let your hands run down my body. I love the way my swelling presses into the soft area between your legs. You let the straps of your dress drop down over your shoulders, so that it falls to the ground with a faint whisper. While you are looking into the void above us, I worship your breasts and kiss them, using my lips to softly bite your nipples. You gasp with pleasure. 'Let's do it,' I say and take your hand. We start wading into the cool water in front of us.

I watch you from behind. Your lithe body is reflected in the water's dark surface, illuminated by the millions of tiny specks of light above. When the water reaches your panties, they immediately become translucent. I take pleasure in watching the way you move. We swim for a while, wash each other, kiss. I go ashore to get the big towel.

'Come here, Toro,' I call to you, making matador-like movements with the towel. You laugh and gradually step out of the water. You walk towards me, exaggerating the swagger of your hips, like a model on a catwalk. How beautiful you are, how utterly mesmerized I am.

'Thank you,' you say with eyes gleaming, without my having uttered a word. Having slung the towel behind my back, I hold it open to you and you walk into it like you would step into a tent. I close the towel behind you, wrapping it up to your neck, and we are mummified, standing close together, waiting for the combined heat of our bodies to kill the slight shiver we both feel. Our tongues meet and it feels as if electrodes are attached to my body, only it's wonderful. You reach down into my shorts and carefully take out my erection, sandwiching me between our stomachs so that I point to the stars.

I am pulsating against your skin. I make a sound in my throat like a purring cat. The feeling is so intense, filled with passion and love and desire.

'Time to go back,' I whisper. The black rock surrounding the lake is slippery, but as soon as we reach the lush moss-like grass the footing gets better. It's like walking on a cloud. Fireflies light the way back. When we come to the sheet-sized white blanket secured with pegs in the corners, there is a wine cooler containing a bottle of white, two glasses, and a bowl of assorted berries. Our bodies are dry now; there is no trace of the cold we felt after the swim in the lake.

I look into your eyes. I feel wonderful and wanted. The warm air is like an aphrodisiac, licking our bodies. You look so sexy wearing only panties. I kiss your neck and you move into a crouch, kissing me back and moving down my body. I look down at you, spellbound. I take off my shorts and bounce all over your face. I feel self-conscious. You giggle, not derisively, but happily and in your eyes are smiles.

'You are lovely,' you say and ever so softly fondle the base of my hardness. Then you kiss it, let your lips embrace it, and swirl your tongue wantonly around it. I moan with lust, wondering briefly if anything I do to you will ever feel half as incredible. I want time to stop right here and now, the sensation is so intense. I caress your hair while you continue to taste me; you make sounds that indicate you are enjoying me. After a while you stand. You know very well that my ears are highly erogenous zones; so while you aspirate your words more than usual and make sure to let your tongue flick inside me, you whisper, 'I'm so hungry. Feed me.' You lie down.

'Yes, Ma'am,' I croak, hoarse with longing.

I pour you a glass of wine. We sip the rich red liquid and look up into the incredible stellar show on display. I dip strawberries into my wineglass and feed you. Occasionally I let a few drops of wine fall onto your face and kiss them off. I place blueberries on your stomach and raspberries on the mound between your legs. Slowly I bend down over your body, picking berries up deftly with my lips. When I come to your navel I pour a stream of wine over you; it spills onto your panties. My hands are all over you. You open your legs for me and my head goes down; I taste the wine on the lace covering you. My hands creep inside your underwear, each hand on a buttock. I kiss the inside of your thighs.

My tongue is like a small animal, wandering all over you, making my loins ache with lust. I lick your thighs right up to the area covered by your lace. You wiggle, impatiently trying to guide my tongue inside you; but I tease you and lick the fabric hiding your wetness. I pull down your panties, and I can feel you can no longer wait for my tongue to go inside you. When it finally finds the spot you have been craving me to find, you let out a cry and arch your back. My tongue is making love to you, and I sense you are about to erupt. I make that purring sound in my throat again. I stop and move up to kiss you, making sure my erection sits restlessly in the moist area between your legs. I gently take your arms and let you know you should keep them above your head. I then kiss your neck, your ears, your armpits. I am then back between your legs, driving you crazy. My hands are on your breasts, your stomach, between your buttocks.

When I enter you I make a sound like a wounded animal, filled with intensity and uninhibited pleasure. You wrap your legs above my back, to force me closer and deeper. My body is like a coiled spring, moving slowly and rhythmically inside you and on top of you. You squeeze me while I am inside you and I gasp. Our kissing is hungry, greedy, a mad endeavor. We roll over and you are on top of me, rocking in a trance-like way. I sit up and we continue moving, looking into each other's eyes. When we climax, our world explodes. For a moment there are fireworks inside my brain and the darkness of the night lights up. We remain sitting joined like that for a while. I can hear and feel your heartbeat. I lick the sweat off your chest and breasts, and kiss you. We lie down, looking up at the sky, listening to the cacophony of insects. Just before I fall asleep, I can feel your hand stroking my hair.

* * * *

After I finish reading Weylin's account of his dream, it is clear the sexual attraction between them was of volcanic magnitude. Because my head is cool, I can also see how easy it would be to label lust as love and how such magnetism between two people could quickly make them forge an emotional bond. Under the power of such force how easily people forget their wedding vows, and the fact they have families to whom they now must tell lies. It is probably for the best that the affair was over before it was discovered by either of their spouses. I wonder if all affairs are just about white hot sex, or does true love ever develop under such clandestine and deceitful circumstances.

I want to explore this story further, and am interested in what more she might reveal under hypnosis.

CHAPTER SEVEN

Leandra

I had another sleepless night in spite of having taken one milligram of Lorazepam. During the short time I was able to sleep, I was tormented by another strange dream. Looking at myself in the mirror this morning, I didn't recognize the woman with dark bags under her red-rimmed eyes through which an anguished and tortured soul was peering. A bout of anger welled up in me and I felt like smashing the mirror.

What the fuck is wrong with me? There is so much loss and tragedy in the world, and I'm grieving the loss of a lover who probably just fell out of love after he'd had his sexual fill of me and satisfied his curiosity, and who now might already be in hot pursuit of someone else. What are the stages of grieving and in which one of them am I stuck? My head is foggy and my thinking impaired from the effects of the sleeping medication. Will I also need anti-depressants soon?

I take a shower, which doesn't clear my head. I am considering phoning in sick and cancelling my appointments, but to deprive people dealing with mental illness of my help because of my trivial problems is not an option. If my patients could only see me; if they could see the person they obviously admire and respect spiraling down into self-destructive behavior over a lost lover. I laugh out loud and my laughter sounds so shrill, forced and phony it startles me. The next moment I notice tears streaming down my face. I feel useless, irrational, and embarrassed for obsessing over a failed love affair. Hypnotherapy might have been a bad idea; it seems only to have intensified my confusion and anguish.

The coffee tastes awful this morning. The white pants I pull on hang on me as I've lost a few pounds. Nothing helps you lose weight like anxiety and unquiet following the initial shock of being dumped. I try to enjoy my cereal, and then toast, but I can't swallow more than a couple of bites. I look at the clock and realize I have to leave if I want to be on time for my appointment with David. I wonder what he thought while he was reading my explicit chronicle of our encounter in Glasgow, and Weylin's dream about us.

I'm so distraught and drained I'm unable to feel any shame over my writings, and sharing them with a colleague. I'm glad Adrian is away on business, because I'm afraid he might start questioning me about my strange behavior, and I might break down and admit what I'd done. That would ruin my life completely.

I arrive at the hospital five minutes before my appointment with David. I have just enough time to stop by my office and check with my receptionist Fiona on any changes in my appointments.

"Good morning, Dr. Springfield." Fiona is new and for some reason finds it hard to call me by my first name. Her cheerful tone lures a forced smile from me. "Is my first appointment still at ten?"

"No, Mr. Davis called to cancel. He apologizes deeply, but he's come down with flu and had to reschedule. He left a message last night."

"No problem. I'll be in David's office discussing some cases. I don't wish to be disturbed for at least an hour."

I notice a flicker of puzzlement in Fiona's eyes. She is a most observant young woman, and I'm sure she finds my spending time with David out of the ordinary, but she makes no comment. It would be funny if she thought an affair was brewing behind our meetings in his office. I need another affair like a bullet in the head. Or, on second thought, a semi-affair might help me get emotional detachment from Weylin and sever the cord keeping me captive.

As I knock on David's door I feel my heart skip a few beats. What strange world am I going to plunge into next in my search for answers?

David smiles as I walk in. For the first time I detect there's true warmth in his eyes. He puts an empty pipe in between his teeth and drags on it, inhaling non-existent tobacco smoke.

"How are you doing, Leandra?"

"I'll be better soon, I'm sure." My voice sounds firm and there's a faint glimmer of hope in my chest prophesying that I will, indeed, get better. Dying of a broken heart is an unacceptable option.

David's wearing a blue shirt with a black collar that reminds me of the types of shirts Weylin likes to wear; however, it does not stir up any emotion in me. All of a sudden I feel like getting to know him better, asking him about his life, the scars love has etched on his heart. But I know this is neither the time nor the place.

He puts on his glasses and flips though his appointment calendar.

"My next appointment is cancelled, if you wish to stay longer."

"Is that synchronicity or what? Fiona has just told me my ten o'clock has also been rescheduled, so yes, I'd love to stay the extra time, especially if we are continuing with hypnosis."

"Leandra, are you sure you wish to continue with hypnotherapy? Shouldn't we try something more orthodox to deal with your grieving process? You are experiencing a lost love, and it makes no difference that it was illicit, perhaps impossible, and more a fantasy than a real relationship. You know, many people think love affairs are not even relationships."

"No, David, let's continue with hypnosis. It hasn't made me feel better yet, but I'm convinced some of the answers I'm looking for can only come by delving deep into my subconscious, or by being regressed to a past life. You may think a case like mine is simple and straightforward: A woman experiencing a midlife crisis falls in love illicitly; suddenly a whole new world opens up before her, a world of intense erotic feelings, intoxication, a world of new possibilities to explore life, to live it intensely. She experiences a heightened sense of aliveness because the affair is forbidden and the excitement dizzying. And yes, she plunges headfirst into this fantasy, believing it.

"She obviously needs excitement because her married life has grown stale and routine. Her marriage has lost luster, and the raspberry zinger has turned to vanilla. Due to their busy schedules, she and her husband have disconnected emotionally and drifted off in different directions. Although the sex is still regular, even super regular, considering the number of years they've been married, it's no longer love making. It's devoid of romance. If a woman like me came into my office for counseling, this is what I would tell her. And I would talk to her about illusions and self-delusions, and the need to let go of him and re-invest her efforts into her marriage. I have excellent solutions for others, but none for myself. That is why I need you to help me."

David sighs and looks at me with empathy. "I enjoyed reading your Glasgow story. You have a knack for erotic writing, did you know that?"

"No, I didn't. I've never thought about writing something erotic. I was also never much interested in reading erotic stories. An unknown aspect of my persona has surfaced." I find it strange how I can say all of that without blushing. "What did you think of Weylin's dream?"

"His sexual fantasy about you is as explicit as it can be. The lust between you is obvious, and also the way he writes would certainly have an effect on a woman thirsty for romance. I can now see how you would have become attracted to the world he painted for you. But how are you feeling? You look tired, as if you'd had a bad night or perhaps experienced more strange dreams?"

"Yes, I did have another unusual dream. David. I can't believe this. I'm going through psychotherapy with you because a lover dumped me." I hear myself sigh heavily as if a ton of bricks were lying on my chest. David leans back in his chair, crosses his arms.

"Stop beating yourself up about seeking my help because of a broken heart. People can die of that; at least, that's what I read up on last night. So, I'm listening. Tell me about last night's dream first, and then we will try another session of hypnosis. Dreams are as revealing as past life regressions. So together we'll see if more stories are buried deep in your unconscious mind and if their revelations bring you any closer to the answers you are seeking."

I breathe a long sigh, thinking of the dream that left me feeling puzzled. I was also apprehensive of being hypnotized again, remembering how shaken up I was after having listened to my recounting of the story of the pagan ritual and the wolf. Since that session, I have often imagined a wolf's eyes were watching me, and I often see clouds in the shape of a wolf's head. Again I think, perhaps the wolf is my talisman and my animal protector. Am I becoming superstitious, abandoning my firmly rooted beliefs in scientific explanations? All I know is, I've lost myself as the person I'd known myself to be, and I must find or at least redefine my new self—and it cannot be anything but a painful process.

"What I dreamed was strange, because it was a dream within a dream, meaning I was lucid dreaming again. In the dream I heard voices, and they sounded like those of the pagan deities from the first dream I shared with you. This time, however, I did not see them as the same shapes of light and dark or as the human forms they earlier assumed. The first thing I remember is a faceless voice asking, 'How much longer can this love continue?'

A whisper from another voice echoed, 'Just a little longer.'

The first voice then asked, 'How much is a little longer in human days?'

The reply from the second voice was, 'Two weeks to two eternities.'

The first voice said that was confusing; it was the voice of the female deity from my first dream. In my dream I realized she had given up fighting the male god's resolution to destroy the relationship I had with Weylin.

"David, at first I wasn't even sure I was dreaming because the voices sounded so real, and so close. I realized I was dreaming the moment I recognized them as the voices belonging to the two gods playing with my fate."

"What happened next?"

"In my dream, I saw a flutter of blindingly glittering tiny wings touch my face and disappear into the darkness. Disoriented and not knowing whether I was still dreaming, I thought of fireflies flying over meadows. It must have been their light I saw, I thought, but then again, how could it be so dazzlingly bright, and why were the voices the same as those in the previous dream? The tiny lights flickered again and I thought I was hearing peals of insouciant laughter coming from one corner of the room.

"All of a sudden, stillness shrouded the room and filled my racing heart with undefined anticipation. I dared not breathe or move, waiting for something magical to happen. A soft sigh reminded me I was not alone in bed. Yes, I was in my bed at home and thought Adrian was sleeping beside me. But, when I looked, it was Weylin sleeping peacefully beside me. In that dream I had a sense of foreboding, of the imminent demise of our illicit love story."

"So you were dreaming of an imminent break-up even though in reality the two of you broke up months ago, right?"

"Yes, it will be a year in November."

"Go on."

"In my dream I felt something fly across my face and brush against it with a feather-like touch, and I stifled a scream. I could feel my eyes open in wide disbelief as I took in the sight. A tiny fairy or a dragonfly had landed on my chest and was peering into my eyes with what could only be described as curiosity. What was even more astonishing was my feeling I was no longer a woman, but a fifteen-year-old girl who still believed in fairies, fairy tales and undying romantic love between princes and princesses.

"Suddenly, I saw myself leave the body of the sleeping woman, stand at the foot of the bed and scrutinize the bed scene with the eye of a dispassionate observer. The couple stirred in their sleep and the woman wrapped her arm around the man, facing him. I was startled with the realization the woman was a future me, and the man was her lover with whom she would be in a relationship for another two weeks or two eternities.

"How could I have physically detached from that woman and gone back to the time when I was a teenager? Which was the present moment if I was simultaneously experiencing myself as a young girl and a mature woman in the future? Confusion drenched my brain, yet at the same time I noticed I felt no fear, despite the strange contradictions of the situation. I must have been still asleep."

"That dream reveals your conflicted feelings over your affair. The young girl is your subconscious telling you that you've departed from the values you had built over time: that you would fall in love, get married and remain faithful. I'm amazed you remember your dream in such great detail," David says.

"I wrote it down quickly as soon as I woke up."

"What happened next?"

"I remember asking myself in the dream what the meaning of it was. I kept looking in awe at the sparkling creature whose shape kept changing from a damselfly to a resplendent tiny fairy."

"Leandra, how in the world could you discern whether it was a damselfly or a dragonfly?"

"I have no idea. I just seemed to know in my dream." I hear myself reply laughingly, and my laughter is sincere this time.

"Anyway, I asked this creature to tell me who I was and who the man beside me was and why I was with him."

"What was the answer?"

"The answer was '*All the answers to all your questions lie within yourself, and you should still your thoughts and mind. Behind that gate you will find the real you, and the time when your blood was mingled with his*'.

"The voice also told me our soul-mate energies had mixed many times before and they would mix again unless I learn the lesson inherent in the dream. I asked what the lesson was. Was the lesson all the pain and suffering I've endured? Was the lesson that true love can conquer impossible obstacles? Am I to hope we would be together again? But the creature looked at me and said I would soon learn what I need to know to grow."

"Your dreams seem to indicate we should dig deeper. So I think we should continue with hypnotherapy. How did the dream end?" David asks.

I close my eyes and go back to the scene in my dream. I hear myself continue in a soft, languid voice reliving the scene. "I'm watching the couple in bed. The man sighs again in his sleep and moves closer to the woman. She softly moans and presses her body into his. Under the thin cover, I can see his hand start sliding down the woman's thigh and hear her let out a louder gasp, turn towards him and open her eyes. Her eyes sparkle like gems infused with fiery joy and love. Their lips meet and a muffled, 'I love you,' reverberates in the warm summer air.

"I look at the couple in wonder. There is something lyrical in their lovemaking, like fluid poetry, and it brings tears to my eyes. And yet, even though the man and the woman are deeply enamored, as an innocent girl in love with the concept of unadulterated love, I resent that a future me has been placed, albeit of her own volition, in the role of 'the other woman.' In my dream I ask myself how I allowed myself to fall in love with a married man. If I had lived before, did I always have to share him with another woman?

"I ask the fairy this question and at the same time, I am awash and disturbed with the knowledge I am married, too, and my lover is 'the other man' in my life. I ask the fairy if she can show me how this story will end. I look back at the couple, and see the man's lips trace a trail between the woman's breasts and her stomach. Through the curtains, dawn is shyly peering in and its pale light is eating away at the darkness.

"I look around and I'm back in the woman's body feeling unable to grasp for a moment my identity. It feels as if that knowledge has vanished on the wings of the fairy or dragonfly which had entered the room a moment ago.

"And that is it, David. Another confusing dream! Why, even after so much time has elapsed, have I not been able to move on? Why am I so stuck in the past? We were together, no one got hurt, no one found out. I should be able to close that chapter of my life and recommit to my marriage, but I can't. I find this situation very embarrassing.

"I'm wasting public health money using your services when there are so many people on your waiting list suffering from serious mental diseases, going through terminal illnesses, devastating divorces, the deaths of their loved ones, their children…the world is riddled with problems, famine, poverty, injustice, animal cruelty, true suffering! There is a sea of tragedy around us and I'm here wasting your time, playing some kind of 'regress me to a past life' game as if neither of us had anything better to do. Sorry, David. What the hell's wrong with me? This is not normal behavior. I should know better than to pine after someone who no longer wants me. Have you ever had a bad break-up?"

"I've had quite a few break-ups and that's why I am an old bachelor." He laughs wryly.

"Bachelor, yes, but old you certainly are not," I say.

He smiles again. "I've never had an extra dramatic break-up, except maybe the last one. I've been dumped a few times because my girlfriends felt I was devoting more time to my studies and other interests than to them. In hindsight, I've never experienced love or lust of the intensity you have been describing, and, if I may say so, I envy you for that. I wonder if I would even be capable of falling in love head over heels. Or does it have to be illicit, to be so intense and thrilling?"

"No, it doesn't. When I fell in love with Adrian it was even more intense. I had frequent periods of very brief blackouts when he'd embrace me. The sexual connection was very strong, and stronger than with Weylin. And I'm sure everyone is capable of falling in love deeply if they meet the right person, and experience that explosion of sparks between them. Tell me about the women you loved. Who was the greatest love of your life?"

"I'm still hoping to meet her. The longest experience was my relationship with Myra. We lived together for two years. She was a biologist. We met at a lecture. I liked her initially, she was witty, well-read, a good cook, and I thought we got along well.

"I was surprised when she started complaining I was neglecting her and spending most of my free time reading scientific journals, writing papers and doing anything else but paying attention to her. She also mentioned my flare-ups of anger and impatience over her constant nagging. In the end she stormed out of the apartment accusing me of being a cold-hearted and ill-tempered son of a bitch who made her feel invisible. I must say I had noticed signs of dissatisfaction in her, but had attributed them to all kinds of things—except problems in our relationship. She wanted kids, and probably expected I'd propose, but I felt no need to change our relationship, and I certainly had no desire for marriage or family."

"Did you experience much pain after the break-up?"

"I missed her for a while, but was soon over it. She called once to ask if we could talk about a possible reconciliation, but I declined. And that's it. Before Myra, I dated several women, but had no serious relationships. One of the women was a single mother of two who had hopes we'd get married. I had a feeling she was looking for security for herself and her kids. I couldn't feel much love and passion from her, but then again maybe she'd say the same about me. Anyway, my love life never reached the amplitudes yours did. I may have been too mistrustful of letting anyone get too close'.

"But, on the upside, I've never gone through much love-related angst. Even though by listening to you I wish I had, or I could experience a love of such depth; however, if it were offered to me at the cost of the pain you endured, I don't know if I could accept the terms."

"When you're plunging into something like this, you aren't aware of any constraints, or strings attached, even though logically who in their right mind would expect a happy ending under such circumstances? Shall we begin another session of regression?"

"Would you like a drink before we start?"

"No, thanks, I'm okay, but if you need a coffee or a break, I can wait."

"Give me a few moments. I'll be right back. I do need some coffee. I also had a bad night. Perhaps reading the account of your Glasgow rendezvous and Weylin's dream about the two of you shattered my normally peaceful sleep. And the genre was a significant departure from what I normally read at bedtime." He winks at me mischievously, and I feel my face turn crimson.

He notices and quickly says, "Sorry. That wasn't very professional of me. Forgive me. It's just…I feel we are transcending our relationship as colleagues, or the doctor-patient relationship, and becoming friends who can joke about all this."

"All's well, David. I do feel embarrassed by sharing everything with you, but that's what I want. I also feel we are turning into friends. After all, we've been colleagues for so many years. Why wouldn't I have a psychiatrist who's a friend and a colleague, too?" I laugh and all of a sudden I feel awash with relief. It is such a welcome feeling to know I have found a friend in my psychiatrist. My smile reflects my mood. I feel sheltered in this office cluttered with books, papers and furniture that has seen better days.

"Hypnotize me. I'm relaxed and ready."

"Hold your horses. I'll be right back," he says and leaves the office.

Alone, I look around his office and notice there are no photos. I had just felt friendship flow between us like a current of electricity, and yet I know so little about my new friend. I know he lives alone. It also seems he doesn't allow any past lover to walk through his dreams and thoughts, disrupting them with aching longing. Does he have a pet which shares his solitude? I want to get to know him better and I plan to do just that. David interrupts my reverie by coming back into the room.

"Where's your coffee?" I ask.

"My secretary, Wendy, made me an espresso, which I gulped down. Let's not wait any longer, and begin our journey into your past lives. So, close your eyes…breathe deeply. This time…focus your eyes on the paperweight I'm holding in my right hand. As you affix your attention on it…you are starting to feel more and more relaxed…"

The monotone of David's voice is growing distant. Unlike the previous session when it took me a long time to relax and leave this plane of reality, this time I feel as if I were falling headfirst down a bottomless well, and the darkness around me is splintered with tiny multi-colored bursts of starlight. I hear David's voice break into my thoughts.

"Where are you and what do you see?"

"I'm in what looks like a cell in a jail. Through a tiny window, a ray of moonlight is licking the floor, right at my feet. I strain my eyes and see a contour of what looks like a straw bed right under the window. I'm wrapped in a dark brown cloak made of a soft and fluffy fabric. It provides some warmth and comfort. I have a feeling someone who loved me made it for me, because its touch feels like a loving caress."

"Describe your feelings," David instructs me.

"Something brushes against my feet and sends a jolt of alarm through me. I realize it's a rat, but for some reason, once I know what it is, all fear leaves me. I don't fear animals and expect no harm from them. I fear people—the seed of evil sprouts and blossoms in them, and not only evil, but the darkest darkness lies within them, the darkness ignorance creates, preventing the light of reason, mercy and tolerance to penetrate."

"How old are you and what do you look like?" David's voice reaches me from afar.

"I can't tell, but I think I'm young, perhaps about twenty. My hair is dark and hangs down my back in a heavy braid. It smells of honeysuckle, and I wonder how long it will still smell so sweet before the musty and rotten smell of the cell becomes all pervasive."

"Why are you incarcerated?"

"I don't know."

"What are you thinking now? Tell me your thoughts as they come to you." David's voice sounds so, so far away.

"I'm trying to remember. Slowly, images of angry faces shouting obscenities at me flood my consciousness and I gradually comprehend. I've been accused of being a heretic and a witch. They saw me visit Ailionora a few times, and someone overheard me say to her that every stone and every flower and animal had a spirit, and nature around us was the source of divinity. My father, the town priest, had often warned me not to question God's intentions, and not to reveal before the common folk that I've read all his books, and I write as well as he does, and enjoy most of all eavesdropping on conversations he and my husband have with the other important men.

"My parents' fervent desire had been to marry me to the most powerful man in the region, and I bowed to their wishes, but I also liked Aidan. After all, my husband is an attractive man exuding strength, courage and resolve, and he makes me feel safe. I also love him because he is good to me. And he has allowed me freedom to romp through the pastures, fields and hedges around our castle, collect herbs, visit people and help them with my healing knowledge. I enjoy his company and his sense of humor. Because he is so feared and so powerful, I don't understand how I wound up in this cell. Oh, oh my god, a horrible thought.

"Perhaps he has learned of my secret encounters with Kieran and this is his punishment! He will not want to save me! I will never see my son again! What will happen to my boy if I am killed? My heart is frozen with dread thinking my husband might have discovered my adultery. I'm replaying in my mind the last few days, trying hard to remember if anything in his behavior toward me might have indicated he knew the truth, but I realize I've not noticed anything unusual. My husband will surely try to save me; he was in England when they captured me. He will come back soon and save me. After all, he is one of the most influential men in the country. He has even earned the respect of the king of England.

"How is it possible that people who admired me two days ago could now see me as a heretic and a witch? I helped so many of them with money, kindness, and work that saved families from the most abject poverty. And where is Kieran? Is he seeking me frantically? No, he's not. That thought makes me feel crushed, because even though I deeply love Kieran, I'm also aware cowardice and fear reside in his heart, and he will not risk his standing to save me. He is afraid of losing his family and his life.

"How can I love a man who does not possess the qualities I most admire? Love is a mysterious force that attracts us to very unlikely objects of desire. And now that I find myself in such a predicament, I see my lover in a less flattering light. I'm so afraid of what might happen to me, I push everything else out of my consciousness and feel myself transform into survival mode. I've always refused to witness people being dragged to the jail and executed, because the mere thought has made me throw up in horror, imagining any living creature dying such a horrendous death…stoning, or burning at the stake. Many have been killed for lesser crimes than mine. Oh, I can feel their pain and terror. This cell is filled with the energy of suffering.

"I also remember now—one of the accusations of witchery was my sight; not my ordinary sight, but my ability to penetrate people's minds, to sense if they carry around them an aura of illness, goodness, or evil; my ability to see their immediate future.

"Cold dread fills me as I realize…at dawn I may be executed, drowned, stoned to death or killed in another gruesome manner without a trial, without a chance to defend myself, a chance to expiate the sins of which I have been accused."

"What are you doing now?' David's voice is almost inaudible. I am talking, but I do not know if he can hear me.

* * * *

Jilleen

I cry out as I hear a key turn, and the door creak. A weak light follows the silhouette of a man dressed in black. My heart beats wildly in my throat, and fear is making me feel dizzy. A rat scurries across my feet and I yelp in terror. Still sitting on the hard, cold floor, I raise my gaze to meet that of my visitor. Under the light produced by his torch, I sink my fear-filled gaze into the blueness of his eyes, in which I recognize a glint of curiosity. Suddenly, I become self-conscious of the way I look. *Is my dress too soiled, is my hair too disheveled?* At the same moment, I reproach myself for allowing myself thoughts of vanity when my life may be hanging in the balance."

"You are Jilleen, right?" His voice is soft and sensuous, tinted with kindness, and faint hope flutters in my chest.

"Yes. And may I inquire who you are?" My voice is tremulous, and I sound like a stranger to myself.

"I am an inquisitor, passing through your village on my way to Kildare. I have been asked to preside over your case in two days, but I must leave tomorrow as another trial awaits me. I am here to interrogate you and establish how grave your sins are. It seems you do not remember me. I am Faolán, the boy you played with when you were eight years old."

"Faolán," I gasp. "Of course I remember you. You used to visit us with your father, and while our priest fathers were engaged in serious discussions you and I would play in the attic, and by the river. Remember when you waded into the river thinking it was shallow, and you almost drowned when the water suddenly engulfed you?"

"And even though you were a small girl, you had the strength to grab me by the arm and drag me out into the shallows. You probably saved my life. But why are you in this dungeon? What is this talk about you being a witch and saying blasphemies?"

"I don't know. I thought no one wished me any harm as I've never wished any harm upon anyone. My father told me many times I might get into trouble because I think differently, ask strange questions, nurture sick animals back to health, spend time reading, roaming the fields, gazing at the night skies. I'm married, and have a boy who is my life, and I hope my husband is now looking for me and will get me out of this horrible place. I am *not* a witch, please believe me."

"You have been accused of witchcraft and heresy."

"Witchcraft and heresy! But I believe in God. I see God everywhere; I see his spirit in every bud, leaf, kitten, cloud and stone. He is in every moon ray, in every drop of rain, in every beat of my heart and yours."

"That may be part of the problem. They find your behavior strange and accuse you of bringing the hailstorm that destroyed most of the crops."

"I brought no hail. I just felt something terrible was going to happen and expressed my concern to a few neighbors. I...I sometimes see what is going to happen, but bad things do not spring out of my heart and soul, they come from...I know not whence."

While I'm speaking, our gazes are fused and some strange warmth starts coursing through my blood. Instinctively, I feel he will want to help me; as a boy he was fascinated by me and told me we would marry when we grew up. Now, I feel he is pulled toward me and I want to survive this horror so much I am willing to do anything to extricate myself from this predicament. I unwrap my cape and let it fall to the ground. I am wearing a simple, long-sleeved white dress with a lace-up front; underneath I have a white shift, so my skin cannot show through the lace opening.

I feel my face go crimson under his unwavering stare, but if I have to surrender to him in order to see my child again, I will do it. Kieran will never know and even if he finds out, he will surely understand. I enjoyed Faolán's company when we were children, but now as grown-ups, I have to get to know him again. Oh my lord, I am going through a tempest of emotions ranging from confusion, fear, panic, and most terrifying of all, I'm feeling guilty for my thoughts of seducing him in order to save myself.

"Am I going to die? Are you going to condemn me to death before the village council and a bloodthirsty crowd? Am I going to burn?"

His hand is suddenly on my face, and his fingers are tracing my jaw line, my cheeks, and my neck. My skin is burning under his touch. In the blueness of his eyes, tiny flames flicker, illuminated by the light of the torch he is holding. I feel weak, but realize at the same time fear is leaving me. *Forgive me, Kieran, I am letting another man touch me, and I do not find it unpleasant.* He is still a friend and I dare expect him to help me, even though I am aware he will be risking his own life doing so.

"I will help you escape."

Was he reading my thoughts?

"This is what we will do. Tomorrow, I will pronounce you a witch, and order you not be burned at the stake, but thrown into the river to drown. I remember how as a child I envied you your ability to swim. I was convinced you were not a girl, but a fish which could turn into a girl. I never told anyone of your ability to swim, and I now hope you've also kept that a secret—because it will be your lifeline."

"I have always swum in secrecy, and always sat by the river hiding a book in my dress sleeves. I even kept my ability from my father, never revealing I had taught myself to swim, or that water has always had a magical pull on me."

All of a sudden I feel Faolán's lips on mine and I do not flinch because they taste of sweet wine, and because that kiss holds the promise of my salvation. It is not Kieran's kiss, but at this moment it is the kiss of life, a kiss that will take me back to my son, and I feel gratitude and a sisterly love toward him.

"I think I now know for the first time how it feels when one is falling under the spell of love," he whispers, and again a pang of guilt shoots through my heart, because just as when we were children, and I enjoyed his adoration and his desire to fulfill my every wish, I'm using his weakness for me.

A memory of him and me as children suddenly flashes through my mind. I see him picking blackberries for me, going deep into the brambles, and bringing them in his handkerchief; me eating them oblivious of the scratches on his hands, arms and legs. I remember him tending to injured or abandoned wild animals because he knew I could not stand animal or human suffering. How did we ever lose sight of each other? Why did he move so far away? I ask him and he tells me a nobleman offered his father the position of a priest in a very rich village on the other side of the country. He and his parents and five siblings had a good life there.

"I will have to leave you now, but you can trust I shall not betray you. I shall order you be thrown off the Meagher Bridge at midnight. The moon is almost full, and tomorrow night the bridge and the river will be brightly lit by moonlight. I shall say it is now preferred to throw witches into water at night, because as they dance and cast their evil spells in moonlight, it is under such circumstances their guilt or innocence is most easily proven. No one will dare question my order.

"I will also order you wear only your chemise. It will not hamper you from diving and swimming. Once you find yourself in the water, dive deep, close to the weeping willows. There are so many of them, and their branches hug the bank so closely and densely they will make you invisible. To be safe, you must swim all the way down to the Faery Grove. I will walk along the bank with the crazed mob to the Great Oak, and will then pronounce you have drowned. It will be my directive that everyone return home.

"I will have to go back with them, but fear not, you shall see me before daybreak. Tomorrow morning, I will ride down to the Grove and hide a bag of dry clothes and some food and water for you. But you must promise not to leave the Grove before I come to fetch you. I am going to save you and keep you safe."

"Where will you take me?" My voice is trembling and my body is all a-shiver. I feel his arms around me, but his warmth does not reach me.

"Will you trust me; will you place your life in my hands and do as I say?"

"Yes, I shall." My words are a whisper laced with fear. "I shall do whatever you say. My trust is in your keeping and so is my life." Through my constricted throat these words sound as if they belong to someone else.

I suddenly remember how close we used to be, but we were only children and many seasons have come and gone since I saw him last. And now, that shy blond boy of my childhood has grown into a handsome man with the power to save or take away lives. Before him, I feel so small that I disappear in my own eyes. I also wonder what made him become what he is now, and I also wonder how many innocent people may have been killed after his judgment sealed their fate.

Again, I shudder, but chase away the horrible thought that a murderer may be saving me from death. I slump down on the floor as my knees give way. Through a fog of renewed fear, I see him extend his hand toward me and I grab it as he pulls me up from the floor. He raises my chin and I sink my gaze into his eyes not knowing what it is I hope to find in them. With pounding in my temples and in my heart when he lowers his lips onto mine, I try to suppress feelings of repugnance and shame of selling my body and soul so I may live. I also feel a sense of weightlessness, as if I've left my body and am now observing this scene unfold before me without my control over it.

POISONOUS WHISPERS

I might wake up any minute and find myself in my bed beside my husband and my son who often sleeps with us. Or, upon waking, I will find myself in Kieran's arms, hidden under our willow tree, after we engaged in lovemaking that has me suspended and hovering over the earth in ecstatic delight. When I regain my senses, I see him smiling.

"I have to leave you now, but I will see you early in the morning. Trust me, please. Let me be your savior."

After he leaves, I drop to the floor and weep in utter despair. I feel abandoned, I feel punished by God for my sins, for loving a man who is not my husband, for leaving my child with our servants so I can meet my lover in the secrecy of night. I feel guilty for being different from what is expected of a woman. I writhe on the floor in agony and wish I could die and escape this torment. I start retching and vomiting—and then there is blackness covering me in my oblivion.

CHAPTER EIGHT

Jilleen

A tiny streak of pale light is cascading softly down the cell window and making a shy sliver in the veil of darkness. I open my eyes, disoriented. I don't move; I don't dare even blink until I get my bearings. Then I remember, and freeze in horror. I sit up, aching all over my body, with cold dread in my heart. Instinctively, I try to disentangle my matted hair with my fingers, but it is hopeless. All around me, I smell mold, decay and death. How can I survive another day in this hole? The sound of the door opening with a screech makes me jump in terror.

The gaoler walks in; a heavy set of keys dangling and jingling in his hand.

"Come. You're being moved in preparation for tonight's execution. A verdict was reached."

I follow him. We climb a steep staircase. Below us, I hear moans and yells, and what sounds like the death throes of those hopelessly lost to the world and forgotten by justice, compassion and mercy. Again, I feel dissociated from the event of my calamity; I see my body walking, but my soul is not in it, and indifference of what might happen floods me. Death is not the end. Death offers me salvation from pain, from the torment of living a human life.

We leave the gaolhouse and enter the house across the street from the village inn. The inn owner, James Bourke, looks at me with hatred and disdain. He also always hated my husband because his wife had hoped my husband would marry her. She was in love with him, and when he married me she tried to kill herself. James married her later, but has always known she never stopped loving my husband.

The gaoler takes me upstairs to one of the guest rooms and locks the door behind me. The room is wide and clean even though sparsely furnished. The bed is large and looks inviting and I realize how exhausted I am. On the bed is a white, thin chemise and I immediately understand this is what I will wear tonight when I am pushed off the bridge, into water which is cool even on the hottest of summer days. Will I have the strength or will to swim and save myself?

What surprises and almost delights me under such grave circumstances is a bathtub in the corner of the room. There is steam rising from it and I immediately undress and slip into it, relieved to be able to wash off the dirt, the grime, and above all the horrible stench on my body. I rub myself raw trying to clean my skin. Washing my hair is more difficult because at home I have servants who help me with bathing, dressing and undressing. I have been spoilt by marrying a man of wealth and power. Where is my husband now? I crave his protection. If Aidan saved me now, would I give up Kieran? Would I give up love in order to live? I surmise I would.

After I have bathed, I feel more exhausted than ever. At the same time, I realize I've not eaten for over a day, and devour the plate of bread, cheese and apples ravenously. As I am eating, tears stream down my face; they are tears of silent despair and hopelessness. My chest is heaving with pain and I have difficulty swallowing the last few bites. I throw myself on the bed believing my weeping and sobbing will continue forever, but I fall asleep.

One would think my dreams would be filled with the terror of the situation, but instead I dream of Kieran. In my dream I accuse him of being a weakling, of not fighting for our love. He just looks at me sadly and his eyes are filled with tears of powerlessness. He's also saying something in his defense, but I don't understand his words. I wake up feeling a sharp pain stabbing my chest and I gasp for breath. I feel I am suffocating. I take a sip of water from the pitcher on the floor and the pain subsides. Outside, the moon is peering out from behind a cloud and I realize I've slept through the whole day. It is time to get ready for a new chance at life, or for death.

I use the chamber pot and wash myself again with the bath water, no longer clean. I tie my hair into a braid and pin it up. If I had scissors, I would gladly cut it off so it cannot weigh me down once the cool river takes me in its wet embrace.

I sit on the bed waiting for my fate to open the next chapter of my life. I don't understand why I'm suddenly so peaceful, and I cannot be certain if it is tranquility or resignation which has filled my heart.

I have no reaction when I hear the key turn in the lock and see the homely face of the gaoler appear in the doorframe. He is carrying a large red candle, and in its light his toothless smile appears eerie and foreboding.

"Are you ready, my lovely, to face the savior? I must say 'tis a shame to see such a nice body go to waste and be eaten by fishes and snakes. But you're not the first or the last wretched witch this village has put an end to."

His laughter is broken by a cough that must be tearing up his insides. It's so strong it overwhelms him and he has to bend down to cough out something awful that seems to have been stuck in his throat. What a horrid man! I dread the thought of being held against his smelly and sweaty body. His black hair falls in thin wisps over his bumpy forehead, and his eyes are two obsidian-black beads glinting with cruelty. Now, I just want to breathe fresh air again and face whatever fate awaits me.

The street is deserted, which surprises me. I had expected the usual crowd crazed with anticipation of a spectacle that will end in someone's death. Now it is my turn to serve as amusement for the villagers.

The moon is high in the sky and its silver lights up the night. Stars, like countless tiny torches, blink innocently and indifferently at our weal and woe. As soon as we turn the corner behind the church, I see silhouettes of people standing on the bridge and looking in our direction. And then, shouting breaks the night quiet…and wild chanting. 'Kill the witch,' thunders in my ears. Only two days ago, all these people smiled at me and thanked me for helping them with food, with work, with medicine and other kindnesses. What did I do to now deserve a death sentence?

Just as I feel a sharp stone graze my cheek, a thunderous voice roars at the crowd, "Drowning is the punishment for this witch, and you shall not harm her in any other way. Anyone who throws stones at her is acting against my orders, and will answer to me. Move away, and let her step onto the bridge."

The crowd cowers before Faolán's authority and I cannot but wonder at how imposing he looks in his long black robe and red hat. At the same time, I wish I had the means to save myself and not need to depend on any man; I wish I had the powers of which I have been accused. And I also wonder how I am unable at this moment to see what my future holds; my second sight has abandoned me. But it has always been useful in predicting the fate of others, and not so much my own.

The river is flowing quietly and indifferently. It sparkles in the moonlight. Under the bridge, the water is at its deepest, and I need its depth to hide me. I am afraid the bright white of my chemise will be visible under the water and people will immediately discover my ability to swim, which will be further proof of my witchcraft and guilt. As if reading my thoughts, Faolán comes near me.

"As a witch, your soul is black! You shall wear this black chemise to your death. Take off the white you are wearing and put on this."

He spreads his robe wide, shielding me from the stares of the mad mob. The black chemise he is holding is beautiful and woven so finely one can almost see through it. It will be easier to swim in it, not only because of the color, but also because of its light weight. He then hands me a black scarf to tie around my hair. He is doing everything he can to camouflage me so I may slip under the water unseen and reach the willows which will keep me hidden until I am able to swim out at the right time onto the river bank.

I have no more time to be fearful—this is a time to survive. The gaoler comes close to me, ready to push me off the bridge, and he is waiting for Faolán to give him a sign. Faolán looks at me and I imperceptibly nod my readiness. At this moment, I am eager to plunge either into a new life or death, as all fear has left me. I am placing my fate in the hands of the Goddess mother in whom I believe without having ever openly admitted to anyone my faith follows a path divergent from that followed by most.

The push I feel in my back comes so suddenly and painfully as the gaoler's fist slams into the small of my back. My feet lose their grip on the bridge and my drop into the water is almost instantaneous. I should feel lucky a stone was not tied to my ankle to ensure my drowning.

I do not even feel the cold of the water once it envelops me. I touch the bottom of the river briefly and immediately flip my body head-first trying to stay as close to the bottom as possible. It is dark and murky as moonlight cannot reach this depth. The current is strong enough to propel me downward toward the weeping willows.

Because I did not have a chance to breathe in before I was pushed into the river, I now fear I will have to surface to take a breath, and be seen. If that were to happen, Faolán would have no choice but to have me burned at the stake as that would be proof I am a witch.

I am carried by the fast-moving current, becoming disoriented, and can only hope that by swimming to the right I will soon be able to surface safely among the willow branches. There, I can rest and listen for the presence of those looking for me.

My lungs are burning, ready to burst, and I am forced to swim upward not knowing where I will find myself. As soon as I break the surface I feel enclosed by willow branches. I grab a branch and try not to gulp in the cool air too loudly. All is quiet around me except for the intermittent chirping of crickets. I feel exhausted, but I know I must swim farther down the river to the place where I can find some safety, and where Faolán said he would leave dry clothes and food for me.

As soon as I hear voices approaching, I know it is time for me to move on. I do not need to dive but rather just swim, close to the bank where the shrubs offer shelter from those who seek me. No one has come to the river, and it will probably take them another half hour before they reach the place where I now am. Faolán promised he would order everyone to turn back after a while, telling them I must have drowned as I knew not how to swim.

I swim faster now to reach the grove as soon as I can. With my head above the surface, I can now orient myself and know it will not be much longer before I can climb out of the river. I wish I could go back home immediately, but I cannot be certain if my husband knows of my adultery; or if it was he who ordered my arrest. Is there anyone I can trust now? Kieran is with his family and even if he knew I was in trouble, I would not expect him to defend me as he must see to his own protection.

I see the grove, and push myself to the limit to reach it. My knees are shaking as I drag myself from the water and stand. Even though the night is moonlit I can still barely discern the trees, and wonder how I will find the bag Faolán has left for me. Staggering from exhaustion, I try to get my bearings, but I give up and drop. I am shivering from cold, with no strength left to move.

I cannot tell how much time I have lain on the ground before I hear a horse neigh and the sound of horse hoofs muffled by mossy ground. I hear someone softly call my name and I recognize Faolán's voice.

"Here!" My voice is feeble, yet he hears me and is by my side in what seems like an instant.

"Are you all right, Jilleen?" I feel something warm around my shoulders and I wrap his cloak closer around my shivering body.

"I am fine...I think. I couldn't find the clothes you left." I'm trembling as I speak. "What is going to happen now? Where do we go from here?"

"I am taking you to my friends' house. You will be safe there. But take off your wet chemise and put this on. I realized you didn't find the bag when I saw it hanging where I'd left it."

Shaking, I undress myself and he helps me put on the dry clothes. I cannot even feel ashamed of my nakedness. Once dressed, I start feeling less cold.

"But I cannot stay there long! I want to go back home." I am crying now, exhausted and desperate.

"You cannot go back immediately. It is too dangerous, and besides, you don't yet know if your husband will want you back after being accused of witchery. But do not worry; I will take care of you."

"Your life is also at risk if word gets around you are harboring a witch."

"My friends are loyal and would die for me. I have saved their lives and there is nothing they would not do for me. Let us leave this place. I ordered everyone to go back home, but I cannot be certain I was not followed."

CHAPTER NINE

David

It takes me longer than usual to bring Leandra back from hypnosis. She is so ghastly pale I'm concerned. I'm again filled with doubt about my ability to help her. I've always thought healthy individuals should get over break-ups in a few months, but perhaps my expectations are biased by my own lack of experience with deep and passionate love. To me, that kind of love drama belongs in fiction, be it literary or film based.

She opens her eyes and looks at me without recognizing where she is. Once recognition flickers in her eyes, she asks, "Did I reveal a lot this time?"

"Yes, you did." I hand her the cassette.

"You're so old fashioned. No one uses cassettes anymore; it's all digital now."

"I'm old-fashioned in many ways. But so are you because you still own a cassette player."

Her smile is wan and reflects her fatigue. "The only reason I own one is because Adrian is a hoarder. He still has a gramophone in the basement and old records. David, when I look into your eyes, I see your impatience, telling me you're probably thinking, by now I should have regained my senses and stopped pining after Weylin. After all, don't we tell our own patients their thoughts create their reality, and they have the power to change the way they think and thereby change their life circumstances?"

"Yes, because it's always easy to give advice to others as we can have a clearer insight into their life circumstances than into our own, as you're well aware, and you don't need me to tell you the obvious. And as much as I hate to admit it, a streak of impatience does run through me. I guess it takes another psychiatrist to notice it because I do my damnedest to hide it from my patients and the rest of the world."

"Please tell me what I revealed in this session. I do remember some of it, but still want you to tell me all of it so I can compare your version with mine. Also, I'd rather you tell me than listen to my own voice. I feel safety in your company. You have become not only my psychiatrist, but also a friend, and I hope I will someday be able to repay you with…I don't know what…advice, kindness, friendship," says Leandra, with much warmth in her voice.

"I have a suggestion. Why don't you take care of your next two patients and then come back, and we'll go out for lunch. I'll recount your own story back to you. It's quite fascinating."

"It's a deal." She gets up and says, "In fact, I'm starved and plan to have a big lunch. I haven't had much of an appetite lately; I'm losing weight rapidly, which is not good. Being too skinny adds years to my appearance and my vanity protests."

After about two hours, she is back and looks refreshed. I get up from my desk and tell her I've made a reservation at 'Taste of Heaven,' just a block away from the hospital.

We walk to the restaurant in silence, but the energy is palpable between us. I'm relieved that what I'd feared was physical attraction to her has turned into friendship. It would be embarrassing if I were to fall in love with a colleague and a patient. I may even start to love her as a sister. What she has awakened in me is a sense of protectiveness. I want to help her and protect her, because her vulnerability is so disarming.

The word 'sister' flashing across my mind brought back memories of the twin sister I lost when I was nine. She went on a canoeing trip with her classmates while I was home sick with flu, and fell out of the canoe. They pulled her from the water quickly, but she was already dead. The subsequent autopsy determined she'd had a congenital heart disease which contributed to her quick drowning.

"A penny for your thoughts?" says Leandra.

We enter the restaurant and as soon as we are seated I tell Leandra about my sister, Victoria. I had been suppressing the memory for so many years, unable to deal with the pain of loss that left me emotionally crippled. But I find it so wondrously easy now to relive that sorrow before Leandra.

"Perhaps that loss, from which I've never healed, has prevented me from loving anyone deeply, with a heart fully open and committed. What do you think?"

"Perhaps you've just never met a woman able to unleash the full power of love in you. When that happens, it feels like a volcanic eruption which cannot be reversed or suppressed or diminished in its intensity and voracity. Under the right circumstances, that's the ultimate blessing the universe can bestow on us. In my case, it often feels like a curse or an evil spell cast over me to rob me of peace and sanity. How did your parents deal with the loss?"

"They divorced after about a year. After the funeral, it felt as if an eternal silence descended on our home. My parents stopped talking to each other. I could see them go through the motions of getting up, cooking, cleaning, and going to work, but they operated like robots. My father moved to our guest room. Even at meals, there was hardly any conversation and when they would address me and ask me about school or what I did with my friends, the questions sounded forced and perfunctory. My mother, who had never been religious, started going to church obsessively trying to find solace and a reason to continue living.

"Apparently, I was not reason enough because I could not detect any joy in her my presence should have brought. At the time, I started to stutter, which brought me huge embarrassment at school and a lot of taunting by my classmates. I also displayed uncontrollable outbursts of anger. During one such episode I smashed all the religious figurines my mother had assembled on the mantelpiece. My mother took me to a speech therapist and a child psychiatrist and I saw both for two years. As I said, about a year after the tragedy, my father moved out and my parents divorced. He remarried and gradually severed all ties with us. He and his new wife have two children, but I've not seen them or heard from them for many years."

"How did that make you feel?"

"Abandoned, and punished for a crime of which I was not guilty. And angry beyond measure. I did not cause my sister's death, and yet I was punished by losing both parents. It was such a lonely world at home I tried to spend as little time there as I could. Most of my after-school hours I spent at my best friend's place. During the times spent outside my home the demons of my anger would loosen their grip on me. Eventually, with the help of therapy, my angry outbursts went into complete remission.

"Did your dad ever send you birthday cards or presents, or did you spend any time at his new home?"

"For the first couple of years I would visit him every second weekend, and then it was once a month and then every couple of months—he would always find some reason it was not convenient for him and his new wife to have me over. Gradually, they stopped inviting me to their home."

"I've always found it strange that some parents can cut off ties with their children from previous marriages. I find that both cruel and cowardly. The more people you have in your life, the more love around you. Did you ever try to get in touch with him?"

"I did in fact, after I graduated from med school. I wrote to him and we got together over lunch, but our conversation was forced and strained and it was clear that any father-son bond had dissolved long ago. I remember sitting at the table and clenching my fists under it trying to put a lid on the anger seething within. I felt like getting up and punching him in the face and knocking his teeth out, but was able to restrain myself. Once I calmed down after gulping down a double gin, all I could sense was the great gulf between us, and neither of us had any desire to cross that chasm. We had lost each other for good.

"After that, neither of us made any attempt to reconnect. I figured if he didn't want to see me anymore, why should I want to see him? By cutting me out of his life, he probably wanted to obliterate all painful memories. Little does he know, the more you suppress pain, the more easily it finds a weakness in your soul and gnaws at it, corrodes it.

"In fact, there is no real oblivion, no matter how deeply you bury your painful memories. Pain always finds a way to ooze out when least expected. So, I don't believe my father was able to close that chapter of his life."

"Have you forgiven him?" Leandra asks.

"I used to feel so angry with him, but for many years I haven't thought about him. If that's forgiveness, then I have forgiven him. But what has always disturbed me was a fear I might have just displaced that anger and redirected it toward some of my girlfriends."

"It does appear you might still have some lingering anger issues, if I've observed correctly."

"It's disappointing to admit I haven't emerged completely victorious from my battle against anger. From time to time it still

90

erupts out of the blue. It's required a Herculean effort to subdue it and appear unperturbed at all times…I'm surprised I'm talking so openly about my feelings."

"Was your anger the reason you went into hypnotherapy?"

"Yes, because the psychoanalysis I underwent as a resident uncovered it, but didn't fully resolve it. To my disappointment, hypnotherapy was no more successful, since the hypnotherapist was unable to regress me. However, I learned from him and became fascinated with the technique and his successes with many of his patients. Even though I didn't directly benefit from it, I saw the potential in the treatment and recognized the reason behind my anger. Emotional and physical abandonment."

"That's something you share with Weylin," she adds. "Abandonment by a parent. That is why Weylin is a wonderful father. And if you'd had kids, you might have also become a model dad. But it's still not too late for that. While I was with Weylin, I always thought that if I were to become his second wife, I would love his children as if they were my own. I can't imagine myself being possessive of him to the extent of excluding everyone from my husband's previous life. That's why I can't understand your dad's new wife didn't insist he be a good dad to you. How did it make you feel when you realized you would never have him back as a father?"

"I suffered through a long bout of depression. But depression seemed to act like a damper on my anger, so those bouts of fury didn't plague me, at least for a while. The meeting with my father coincided with the break-up of a relationship which had lasted for nine months. I didn't really feel I missed her. I guess what I really missed was that sense of predictability, coziness, and trust, and of regular sex for the first time in my life. I can't say it was thrilling by any stretch of the imagination, not even close to what you have described transpired between you and Weylin, but it was still pleasant enough and exciting."

Leandra's face is crimson all of a sudden and she laughs nervously. "I still *cannot* believe I shared the most intimate moments of my life with an almost total stranger."

"I've been meaning to ask you if you've ever shared the story of your infidelity with anyone."

"Yes, with two good friends and my sister," Leandra replies, picking at her salad with an obvious lack of appetite.

"How did your sister react?"

"With understanding and advice to cherish that experience and not let my husband ever find out. Why were you never tempted to marry?"

"I never believed two people could stay happy together for a long time. My parents were my example. I often wondered if they would have split up even if tragedy had not struck our family. But enough about me! My own life story is ruining my appetite."

She appears pensive and gazes out the window. The salad on her plate remains untouched and I urge her to eat, reminding her she'd said she was starving.

"Tell me what I revealed under hypnosis. I still find it less scary hearing it from you than listening to my own voice."

I start recounting her terrifying experience as a proclaimed witch. As I retell the story, her eyes grow wide, and clear disbelief floats in her blue eyes. Again, I feel tenderness for her filling me, and I want to protect her from the pain of discovering the tumult in her past lives. How her life has taken a turn for the strange and bizarre, and the painful and the unpredictable! But would she have chosen differently had she known where the path was leading? I decide to ask her. Her reply is swift.

"I would have chosen the same path of illicit love, because the passion I have experienced and the feelings of such ultimate physical and emotional intoxication have overshadowed everything else I've known, including motherhood. Of course, there are few people to whom I would say this. I have friends who've always told me the love they have for their children cannot be compared to anything else; but I know I haven't lived in vain, because of the enormity of this love, a love even more enormous and significant because it seems to be tied to my previous lives. I've accepted my own suffering as a gift given to me by the universe. I know this may sound to you like self-abuse, but I'm grateful for all I have been allowed to live through because it has enriched me...it has changed me...it has deepened my understanding. You have no idea how much I miss Weylin, how hard it is to let go, and...I don't want to let go.

"I know what you must be thinking. If I had a patient like me, I'd tell her she's developed a very unhealthy pattern of thought, and has to discard the burden of the past and move on."

"Leandra, it may come as a surprise to you, but I almost envy you your feelings, because they create a deep sense of being alive, and the information you've accessed through the hypnosis bears witness to the depth of your feelings. I wouldn't be surprised if Weylin—my god, what a weird name—anyway, is also going through some tough times, perhaps even more painful than your experience if he has no one to confide in. Also, it's important for you to allow yourself to feel all your emotions and feelings linked to him. Your relationship is a karmic one that has perpetuated itself through maybe several lifetimes and yet, has never been resolved. You cannot think yourself through this healing process, but must feel your way through it until you are healed, or until you have understood and extracted the lessons this experience with him has taught you.

"And I don't only mean this recent one, but also all those in the past. By allowing yourself to delve into your past lives, you are also allowing your intuition to shine through, and I also believe you're not delusional when you say you feel the two of you are still connected by love. It's your intuition revealing that simple truth. Break-ups do not mean the end of love; they just mean circumstances do not allow two people to continue their relationship."

"Does all of this mean he is my soul-mate?"

"Yes, I firmly believe that. Soul-mates often hurt each other as much as they love each other. You did well to release him from the bondage of illicit love. He will come back to you if you haven't taught each other all the lessons you need from this bond. If not in this lifetime, then in the next. So trust your intuition. I assume it's telling you not to contact him, right?"

Her sigh is the color of suffering and the light in her eyes dims.

"You're right. My intuition tells me I shouldn't contact him, yet at times I want so much to send him a text and tell him nothing has changed and I want to be with him again. But I remind myself I cannot do that…I have no right to shatter his peace, and I have no right to expose myself to more distress. And I feel stuck in this quicksand of tumultuous feelings, but I cannot let go of this love story in which I played a main role. I cannot let go of the erotic romance and fantasy he and I co-created, for fear I'll never experience anything like it again. When you reach a pinnacle and have to come down, you must accept experiences of such magnitude are no longer possible.

"Maybe I shouldn't even want them. I should be happy. I have a loving husband and a good marriage, and I should be rejoicing in the successes of my children and my work. But I can't, at least not presently, because this love story of mine has consumed all my thoughts and feelings, overshadowed all my interests. I wish I could see him, and realize I no longer love him, that what happened between us was infatuation which blazed through our hearts like a meteor shower across the night sky and then burned out. But, tell me what I revealed to you under hypnosis. Did I survive the plunge in the river?"

I tell her every detail I can remember, and I also tell her although I'm looking forward to further exploring her past life experiences, I don't want these sessions to be too frequent as they may have an adverse effect on her.

"You need to regain your physical and mental strength. We've both seen what unrequited love and broken relationships can do."

"Don't worry. I'm already feeling much, much stronger, much more myself. I won't die of a broken heart."

"Do you still have feelings for your husband?"

"Yes, of course. We get along great, but after so many years of marriage the flame of romance is nearly extinguished. And now, feeling love for someone else has constricted my heart, even shut it down; the only romantic or erotic love I can feel is for Weylin. But we need to go back. I still have five patients to see this afternoon, and then I'm on call this evening. When can we continue with our sessions?"

"How about next Friday? My schedule is light around four."

"I'll re-arrange my bookings so I'm done by then. Also, are you free Saturday evening? I'd like to invite you for dinner. If my friends' opinions are to be trusted, I'm apparently an amazing cook. My sister will be in town and I'd like you to meet her. It's not

94

a set-up because you are single and she might be headed toward a second divorce. No long-term luck in love. Who has it, anyway?"

Her laughter is charming and I eagerly accept the invitation. It certainly sounds more appealing to have some company on a Saturday night than spending the evening alone with another journal or book. And as I've never been interested in cooking, I could certainly do with a home-cooked meal for a change. I suddenly realize how lonely I've been for the past couple of years. In fact, I felt lonely in almost all the relationships I've had. However, with Leandra, it's different. What is almost palpable between us is this pervasive sense of warm friendship and trust.

It takes us a few minutes to get back to the hospital and as soon as we reach our ward we notice an unusual commotion.

"Is something going on?" I stop Samantha, the head nurse who was on her way to jet by me.

"Oh, I didn't see you. We have an emergency. The patient in room thirty two, who was supposed to be discharged tomorrow, you know? Dr. White's patient, Emma Reed, tried to kill herself. They are stitching her up now...she cut her wrists with a blade."

"Has Dr. White been contacted?"

"He's on vacation until next Monday. Dr. Bilic is with her. She's conscious and hasn't lost too much blood, but it shocked us all because she was doing so well."

"Did she say why she attempted suicide?"

"She said her boyfriend left her by sending her a text message. She said she was hoping they'd patch things up once she was discharged, but he didn't want to give it another try. She said she couldn't endure the cold finality of his words."

"Today's generation! Breaking up with a text message! How weak! He could've had the decency to visit her one last time. What was the message...did she say?"

"The usual shitty platitudes guys use when they want to ditch girls. He never meant to hurt her; it's him, not her; he wants to stay friends; he's willing to wait until she's ready for friendship; he's deeply sorry—the usual crap."

Samantha's voice is so laced with bitterness I can't help thinking she must have been dumped in a similar way and her personal experience speaks through her acrid words.

"Dr. Springfield's on call tonight and she can check up on her." I look at Leandra who has not said anything for the past few minutes, and who suddenly seems even paler than before. Perhaps, by trying to help this girl deal with this sudden loss, she may actually help herself.

"Of course, I'll talk to Emma as soon as I'm finished with my patients. By that time, she'll have been transferred from the ER back to the ward. As if she needed a broken heart on top of her other problems!"

Leandra's deep sigh reveals how shaken up she is with the news. I give her a reassuring smile before I hurry back to my office in an attempt to arrive there before my next patient. On the way to the office, I notice how dark and menacing the sky is. I close the window and feel a slight shiver as a childhood memory floods my senses out of nowhere.

When I was eight years old an exceptionally violent storm shattered the window in my room and sent me screaming into my parents' bedroom. Ever since then, I have been terrified of thunder and lightning. What kind of doctor am I? Filled with fears, unfulfilled in love, trying at all costs to stay in control and to never let my shield down, lonely and trying to help others deal with their demons. *Who am I kidding*?

My patient comes in. It's Mr. Dawson, a wealthy businessman suffering from an obsessive compulsive disorder. He's a *germaphobe* in a constant fight against bacteria. He doesn't even want to touch his wife for fear of getting infected. His office is more sterile than any intensive care unit and the level of cleanliness he expects of his staff members has resulted in a very high turnover rate in his company, as few people can take longer than a couple years of his tyrannical demands for an aseptic environment.

I've tried the usual therapy of exposing him to his fears of germs, and we've already had fifteen sessions of psychoanalysis, but I've seen little improvement. All of a sudden I feel weary, like someone who's been trying too hard to make a difference in the lives of so many sick and unhappy people. Doubt in my own competence seeps into my brain. Perhaps my own father could see I was lacking in many ways, and he no longer wanted me as his son. No, that's an unreasonable assumption. I snap out of these self-defeating thoughts and focus on Mr. Dawson.

The session goes well and I do see some progress. He tells me he went out to dinner last night and was able to control the urge to wipe all the plates and utensils with sanitizing wipes, and was even able to enjoy the meal. I see three more patients. After the last one leaves my office, I call Leandra. Her secretary tells me she has just left her office to visit Emma. I thank her and head to the ward to join her, hoping Emma feels better surrounded by people who care about her well-being.

As soon as I enter the room, I notice Leandra looking at Emma with eyes full of compassion and tears. She's holding Emma and rocking her gently like a child. Emma is talking, but as I come closer I realize she's half drugged from the sedatives. But even through the sedation, her distress is visible. She must be hallucinating under the influence of Demerol. Her wrists are bandaged, her hair matted, and her eyelids swollen.

"How is she? Has she spoken with you?"

"No, she's only been partially conscious and I'm concerned about her delirium. The dose of painkillers she was given doesn't explain her ravings."

"What did she say?"

"It's hard to make out her words or connect what she's been trying to say to something logical and coherent. She's obviously talking about her boyfriend. She said they'd had a soul connection, but he ruptured her heart with his lies, and left her walking on shards of her shattered dreams. She speaks poetically, obviously has a talent for writing. She must be an intelligent and educated girl."

"She is a poet in fact, and her work has been published in a few literary journals."

"How do you know?"

"I heard some nurses talking about it. She's a librarian as well."

"Oh, I didn't know that. Poor girl! Broken heart right after the depression we had just brought under control! What else can befall her? She also said all the color in her life has been dimmed forever, all her smiles erased, the sparkle in her eyes extinguished never to be relit by another love, and so on. It sounded like she was reciting a poem. She made me cry, because that's how I've felt so many times. Why do we humans hurt each other so much? We kill each other in wars, we imprison each other, and we break each other's hearts. Nature can never hurt us as much as we hurt each other."

Leandra sighs and gets up. "I'll visit her tomorrow when she's fully conscious. I can't be of much help to her tonight. I may be able to help her deal with the fallout from a broken heart. Mine's in the same tattered state as hers and it's already been eight months. I can come back and listen to her as a friend would and let Dr. White take over next week. Perhaps she needs a friend more than a doctor. And perhaps, if Dr. White agrees, you could offer to help Emma the same way you've been helping me."

"Leandra, if I could mend broken hearts with hypnotherapy, I'd probably be nominated for the Nobel prize."

She laughs and we both start to giggle. Feelings of friendship swell up in me and again, I want to be the one who helps her come out of the prison her illicit affair has built around her.

"Goodnight, David."
"Rest well, Leandra."

CHAPTER TEN

Leandra

After a good night's sleep, I get up at seven feeling emotionally restored and decide to go to the hospital to check up on Emma. Spending a couple of hours with her shouldn't delay me much with my dinner preparations.

When I have guests for dinner, I like to make many different dishes. I always want it to be not just a dinner, but a feast and a true culinary experience. I've always wanted Weylin to rent a house or an apartment with me somewhere, and for us to cook for each other, because he seems to be an accomplished chef. There are so many things he and I had no chance to experience together, but I have to remind myself to be grateful for having had so many unforgettable moments with him.

Adrian is still in bed when I leave. I plant a light kiss on his forehead and whisper I'll be back in a couple of hours. He nods almost imperceptibly without opening his eyes. The cat also doesn't bother getting up for breakfast and just stretches lazily across the bed.

I find Emma sitting in a chair and looking catatonic, her eyes staring through the window. Her affect is vacant, as if she has no soul.

"Emma?"

She doesn't register either my voice or presence. I pull up a chair close to her and sit down. I touch her arm gently and she stirs. She looks at me and her eyes reflect recognition.

"Why are you here? You're not my doctor."

"I've decided to check up on you. At this hospital, the policy is to discuss cases in meetings and brainstorm possible avenues of treatment. We believe that together we make more prudent decisions and are able to help patients more effectively."

"So you've heard I tried to kill myself."

"Yes, and I'm here to talk to you if you wish."

"As a doctor, you understand depression, anxiety, paranoia and other pathological conditions, but do you understand how it feels to be ditched with no warning? He'd told me we'd

99

always be together and we would weather my depression together. I lost both parents within a year and I couldn't cope with the magnitude of that loss."

"Emma, I understand the pain of a broken heart, the devastation people feel when they are dumped."

"Did it happen to you?"

"Yes. Someone I loved broke up with me and left me in shambles, in disbelief. I felt as if I was pushed off a cloud only to crash to the earth below. I was shell-shocked, shocked there could be so much love one day and nothing a few weeks after. I wept and lost weight."

"Did you consider killing yourself?"

"No, such a thought never crossed my mind because I love myself too much, and I forgive myself for having loved someone I shouldn't have loved. I forgive him, too, for hurting me beyond measure. I love life, I love my work and my family, and my patients, and I want to be able to continue to give love and joy to others. A lost lover certainly warrants weeping and sobbing, but not dying."

"But I'll never find another him."

"If you're lucky, you won't. You'll find someone who's different, who will love you no matter what, and be by your side when you need him."

"I don't want to trust anyone again. I made myself so vulnerable. I gave him the weapon with which to kill me."

"That's what we do when we give our hearts away, because at the same time we give someone the power to shred our hearts. But hearts should be given away, they are not ours to keep and protect, but instead to offer. We need to keep giving them away until we find the right recipient for that most precious of all gifts. If we allow ourselves to be vulnerable, we expand emotionally and spiritually, and if you guard your heart, you constrict. I also chastised myself for showing so much vulnerability, so much trust—and for allowing myself to be so weakened by love. But Emma, that's how we grow. We grow spiritually, we learn lessons in our deepest pain, and we heal and become stronger, deeper, kinder, and more emphatic. You don't want to grow in embitterment, coldness; you don't want to shut down."

"But how can I heal when I feel I've died, my soul has bled to death?"

"You are a poet. Your poetry will be a vehicle through which you will process the pain, and you will do it for as long as you need, until you release that despair. And through that act of creativity you'll be giving the beauty of art to the world; you'll show the universality of the suffering caused by lost or unrequited love. The best way to transmute pain is to sublimate it through art. Freud talked about the act of sublimating unrealized sexual urges through art. We can do that with *any* negative emotion. Then we become the alchemists who turn base metal into gold."

"How long did it take you to get over your lost love?"

"I'm still not over him."

"What do you mean? Aren't you married? Is it someone from your youth, a boyfriend from the time before your marriage?"

"No, Emma, it's not a long-lost boyfriend. It's complicated." I feel my cheeks turn red, and I don't know what to say because I don't like the direction of this conversation. I'm revealing too much. Emma is looking at me with compassion and tenderness. There's intelligence in her gaze as well as comprehension of the situation.

She takes my hand and says, "I understand, such things happen to the best people."

"What things…?" Now I'm sounding like a patient and she like a psychiatrist.

"You're implying you fell in love while you were still married. And since you're still healing, I assume it happened not so long ago. I'm sorry you got hurt as badly as I did."

And then the woman who had tried to kill herself two days ago hugs me, and as I'm feeling her bandaged wrists on my neck, I'm so connected to her, to all humans whose life situations have caused them suffering. Emma puts her head on my shoulder and starts crying. Her sadness suffuses the air in the room. I can't hold back my own tears, witnessing the enormity of her suffering. And I hope no one comes into the room and finds us crying, and discovers me in an utterly unprofessional situation. Instead of soothing and calming a patient, I'm weeping.

"I want you to be my psychiatrist."

"Aren't you happy with Dr. White?"

"I want you because you *feel* what you're saying to me. You understand what I'm going through. You're not afraid to show your own frailty and the harm love has done to you. It's like having a child and going to a childless pediatrician, or like getting married and going to a Catholic priest for marital advice." A wry half-smile. "I want a psychiatrist who's experienced a lost love. I want a heart-broken psychiatrist."

And then we both laugh. I tell her I'll continue to see her until Dr. White comes back. She seems satisfied, and says she's happy to have talked to me. I leave with a sense of accomplishment. Emma will recover.

As soon as I return home, I begin putting together an extravagant dinner for Adrian, my sister and David. Cooking helps me forget Weylin for a while. During those few hours it feels liberating not to be tormented by the loss. Adrian comes into the kitchen a few times and samples some of the many dishes I've made. We joke, laugh, share a glass of wine, and I feel gratitude for having him in my life and for feeling emotionally safe and sheltered with him.

How could I have betrayed him so unforgivably and why was he not enough? Questions to which I might never find satisfactory answers! Why do I feel no desire to work on rekindling the romance between us? I was always so ready to give advice to my patients on how they could reignite the romance and eroticism with their spouses, and yet I'm unwilling to even try. I feel so lost these days. Even though I find his company pleasant, I also fear I may have left my marriage for good, both emotionally and spiritually.

Wrapped in these reveries, I don't hear the doorbell at first. When I open the door, after a couple of additional chimes, I almost don't recognize David. He looks very dapper in black jeans and a black polo shirt, and I tell him so. My compliment pleases him. We kiss and hug like the best of friends and I hope my sister Cassandra likes him. After so many love fiascos and poor choices in men, I hope she falls for someone as nice as David, even though I shouldn't be making such wishes because, technically, she's still married. I also hope my elder daughter whose name is also Cassandra doesn't inherit her aunt's bad luck in love. My sister has made a fortune for herself and has always seemed to attract money to her life; however, the men she attracts deeply disappoint her.

David hands me a gorgeous bouquet of fragrant pale pink roses and a box of Belgian chocolates. I adore flowers and buy them often for myself. And chocolate is another of my sinful pleasures. A feeling of warmth for having had the luck to find a friend in him sweeps over me. I kiss him again, thanking him profusely for such lovely gifts.

Adrian comes out of his study and welcomes David with a big smile. They shake hands affably and David bends down to pat our cat who rubs himself against his leg. Very untypical of the cat! He is usually wary of strangers. I take it as a reliable sign that David is, indeed, a fantastic chap.

Cassandra arrives twenty minutes late. She's in a great mood and I wonder at the source of that.

"This is my sister, Cassandra, and this is David, my friend and colleague." I watch them looking for sparks between them, but I don't notice anything except for an exchange of polite smiles tinged with mild curiosity.

"I won't be able to stay long as I'm meeting some people later for drinks. It's the couple from Toronto I told you about who're considering investing with me in a big piece of land in Florida."

Cassandra's passion is real estate, and she has recently purchased a large lot on which she wants to build luxury bungalows.

We move to the table after a drink and the atmosphere is relaxed, warm and intellectually stimulating. We jump from topic to topic touching on world politics, the rise in mental illnesses, genetically modified foods and cars. Time flies and wine flows and I catch myself laughing heartily as if my heart has never ruptured. David pays me countless compliments for my cooking and says most of all he loves the spinach pie. I tell him I learned how to make it from a Bosnian housekeeper I had when my children were young.

The phone rings and Adrian takes the call. It's his mother, Agatha, who lives alone two streets down from us in an enormous house. She refuses to move to a condo, saying she's afraid that once she leaves the house, the ghost of her late husband will stop visiting her. She has never healed from his death, and claims he visits her every day. Her health is fragile as she suffers from ventricular fibrillation, and we're afraid we may lose her any day.

A nurse visits her daily, and a neighbor keeps her company most of the day. She often spends the night at Agatha's but yesterday she went for a week-long visit with her daughter, and Agatha is obviously feeling insecure being completely alone.

When Adrian hangs up I suggest he bring her over, but he says he'll spend the night at her house. He apologizes for having to leave, but I assure him it's not a problem, and David and I have a case to discuss. Suddenly, it occurs to me I could undergo another regression and find out what happened to me after I escaped death by drowning.

Cassandra stays for another half hour and we enjoy light banter over another bottle of wine. I feel a bit concerned, wondering if she can drive after four glasses of wine, but she assures me she is just slightly tipsy, thanks to stuffing herself with the delicacies I made. Once she leaves, I tell David I would like another session with him, even though we'd agreed we would wait a few days. He says he doesn't mind as long as I feel ready to embark on another journey to a past life. I fetch a digital recorder so nothing I say is lost.

We go into Adrian's study, furnished with comfortable armchairs. I put on Celtic music composed by Adrian von Ziegler and turn the volume down so the music is playing softly in the background.

"What did you think of Weylin's dream; that is, his erotic story spun around that dream?"

"Leandra, I'm not an expert in the matters of love, as you might have noticed, but what I can say is, his writing is erotic, sensual and it reveals most of all a sexual infatuation with you. And everyone knows how easy it is to equate sexual attraction to love. But so far, even though he mentions the word love, I don't see love in the sense that he wants a life with you, that he is making future plans to be with you, that he's committed to maintaining what you have now. But then again, under such circumstances, who can make any plans, and the only approach is to live in and for the moment. What I'm saying is, most of all I see his sexual fantasies couched in a thin plot. I'm not saying he wasn't fond of you, in love with you; but to know if it's really love, I believe you'd have to spend significant time together to get to know each other on a deeper and more intimate emotional level. And you would both have to be free of other commitments. But let's move on with our regression because it's getting late and we both need sleep."

Seeing Weylin and me through David's eyes, I realize how it can easily look like temporary sexual craze and not love. I decide not to give it another thought but to go instead into the regressed state as soon as possible.

I cannot discern whether I'm relaxed because of the wine I drank, or I am, in fact, feeling tired from having cooked all day. I just feel myself slipping into the state of regression in no time without even being aware of David's words inducing it. I just remember hearing him.

"Where has Faolán taken you?"

* * * *

Jilleen
I feel the warmth of the horse's body under me as my hands grip the rough texture of Faolán's coat. My face is pressed into his back and I want to sleep and forget the horrible ordeal of the last two days, but my mind is drenched with fear of what is to come. I now wish I could just go home and hide in my husband's arms and let him protect me from all evil. I'm also afraid of falling asleep, fearing I might slip off the horse and be trampled by its hoofs.

"Just a little longer, Jilleen. Fear not, I am taking you to safety."

For a while I seem to lose consciousness because the next time I am aware of my surroundings, I find myself in Faolán's arms. He's carrying me into a small house filled with the aroma of freshly baked bread. He gently places me on a stool, and I note the room is clean with white-washed walls; the fire in the hearth casts a glow all around. A black pot hanging over the fire wafts a most delicious scent of stew across the room, making me faint with hunger. The table with stools around it is sturdy and shiny and I cannot help thinking a very skilled carpenter must have made it with love. Two people besides Faolán are in the room, a short, fat woman with ginger-colored hair and a freckled face, and a huge man with a long black beard. In spite of his size, there is gentleness in his eyes which puts me at ease.

Their demeanor toward Faolán seems to be rather obsequious as they don't even dare look him in the eye. They pour steaming stew into plates and break the bread into four huge pieces, placing one piece beside each plate. They encourage me to eat, and with every bite I realize how ravenously hungry I am. I am also shivering in spite of the warm, dry clothes I'm wearing. As if reading my thoughts, the woman leaves the room and comes back with a thick woolen shawl and wraps it around my shoulders.

Faolán tells me I should go and rest and assures me he will be back in two days. I realize how weary I am as the woman leads me back to a little room.

I fall asleep immediately, but keep waking up shivering and trembling—a high fever racks my body. I feel cold compresses on my forehead and feet, and hear the woman tell her husband she fears I will die. I also hear her mention Faolán's name and I have a distinct feeling they are terrified of his wrath. *But if I die, it is not their fault!* They keep lifting my head and pouring some warm and vile-tasting liquid down my throat, and I swallow obediently. They place sheepskins over me to keep me warm, but the cold does not leave me.

The next time I wake, I am feeling better. The woman is sitting beside me and napping. When she hears me move, she wakes with a start and then grins widely in evident relief I have survived. She tells me she will prepare a bath for me and I will feel much better in no time.

The bathtub is made from artfully fashioned wood, and I am certain her husband is the carpenter who made all their furniture. The tub has a carving at each end representing fairies. I find the images beautiful and comment on them.

"My husband created them to make me happy. When I was a child I would always see fairies in our garden. It's a pity I can no longer see them anywhere. Maybe fairies show themselves only to children."

"Thank you for helping me through my illness. What is your name?" My voice sounds hoarse and cracked.

"Mary. My husband's name is Pádraig. We know who you are, and what awful fate befell you. God will help you, fear not."

Our conversation turns into a pleasant talk between two women. We talk about children, husbands, cooking, medicinal herbs, our likes and dislikes. Mary gives me cheese and bread and a cup of warm goat milk and I feel reborn after such nourishment. We go outside and sit in the sun until Mary tells me she has to work in the garden. I offer to help but she tells me I must rest and regain my strength. I reply I feel well enough to go home, and immediately notice a shadow cross her face.

"You need to rest, and it is very dangerous. If they see you, they will kill you; the people from your village, I mean."

"But my husband will protect me. He is the second most powerful man in the entire country. He has connections even with the King of England and he is surely looking for me."

"I'll tend to the garden now."

Hurriedly, Mary leaves and I sit in front of the house on a tree stump, facing the sun. The heat of the sun seeps into my body and I am feeling languorous and tired again. Just as slumber is weighing down my eyes, the sound of horse hoofs brings me back to wakefulness.

Faolán dismounts and his eyes are filled with light as he smiles at me. He pulls me toward himself and embraces me tightly.

'You are safe now, and you are with me."

"But I would like to go home."

"In a few days, when they are no longer looking for you."

"When I come back, they will see me, and will know I am alive. My husband will protect me, and they will not dare touch me again." My voice quivers with anger.

He is stroking my hair and planting soft kisses in it.

"Are you married? Do you have children?" My question takes him aback and he is silent for a few moments.

"Yes, I am married, but I do not love my wife. She is a good woman, a good mother, but we do not love each other. I want you."

There is a strange gleam in his eyes, and a steely countenance I had not noticed before. I realize I'm at his mercy, tucked away in the middle of a forest, in this solitary house, with no neighbors in sight. With trepidation, I realize he may wish to hold me here captive for a long time, if not forever, and I have nowhere to go, nowhere to hide. If I escape, I might get lost in the woods and die. My heart starts pounding violently while I try to appear undisturbed.

"I am so grateful you saved my life; I will always be grateful. Let's go for a walk." My throat is so constricted my voice is forced, but he does not seem to suspect any of the violent emotions raging inside me and takes my hand and leads me into the woods.

The trail we are on is barely visible. The air is thick with the buzzing and humming of insects, and the sounds and heat make my head spin. My clammy hand is in his and I follow him like a sleepwalker. We stop when I stumble over a fallen branch and all of a sudden his arms are around me and his breathing is heavy. I know what that means, but force myself not to shrink away in alarm and terror. When he kisses me I respond, and at the same time my lips touch his I dissociate myself from all feeling, as if my body and my soul split, and my body has decided to do what it has to do in order for me to survive. I will bide my time to devise a way to escape from this place.

He lowers me to the ground on a patch of moss and lifts my skirt. His hand is travelling up my thighs and I am barely breathing. I feel I'm about to leave my body and hover over it, witnessing its being penetrated by another body without its will and desire, when a scream jolts me back to my full senses and I hear Mary's voice calling for Faolán.

We run back to the house and find her bent over her husband who is sitting on the tree trunk in front of the house, holding his arm in obvious pain. Mary is crying and looking so lost and distraught, my only thought is to try and alleviate their pain, whatever its source.

"He was bitten by a snake, he can die. My own father died of snake bite."

She is sobbing and I can clearly see her fear is justified. His arm is red and swollen, his face as pale as death.

"Fetch a knife quickly!" I shout.

Faolán produces a knife as if by magic. I run into the house and thrust the blade into the fire under the pot in which vegetables are boiling. I keep it briefly in the flames and race out of the house, no time to lose. I cut a cross at the place of the bite and squeeze the blood out. I place my mouth over the wound and suck out the venom and spit it on the ground. I catch my breath and tell Mary what herbs to find and how to make a poultice. For a moment she looks like a stone statue, but then hurries into the house. I ask Faolán to squeeze out more blood while I help Mary make the poultice. Before I leave, I place my hand over Pádraig's wound without touching it. The warmth from my hand penetrates his flesh as I whisper a prayer of healing. I have always healed my son this way, and other family members.

I find Mary boiling water and putting sage and other herbs in it. Her collection of herbs is large, and I smile at her reassuringly, saying her husband will be fine. We find pieces of clean cloth and soak them in the poultice. I tell Mary we have to change the dressings on Pádraig's wound often, so we'll need more cloth. She opens a large chest and pulls out a beautiful white dress which she rips to pieces.

"This is my wedding dress. I was saving it for a daughter, which I still hope to have. She will understand her father needed it more."

We spend the next few hours tending to Pádraig, who came into the house and now lies in his bed. He never even whimpers, but endures all the pain with great fortitude. I tell Mary we will sleep in shifts and watch over him all night. Faolán has left us in the meantime, saying he will be back in two days.

All night long we change the dressings on Pádraig's wound. By dawn, we are both exhausted, and fall asleep with hope he will survive.

I wake first and immediately go to his side. He is still asleep, and even though he looks paler than ever, the swelling has subsided. He will live. I saved his life and hope they will feel enough gratitude to help me go back to the life where I belong, but I do not know if I dare ask for their help. I don't wish to bring these good people trouble with Faolán. I might just have to escape, and rely on providence to lead me back home.

As my hosts, or captors, are still asleep, I go out for a walk to clear my head and try to rid myself of the pounding in my head. I see a trail behind Mary's garden leading into the woods and I let it take me deeper into the forest. Very soon the trail widens into a clearing in the middle of which stands an old oak. Its beauty takes my breath away. I approach it and caress its bark reverently. I have always sought solace in nature and have always felt a soul-like connection with it. Suddenly, I have an idea—climb to its top and try to orient myself. Perhaps I will recognize a landmark from which I can find my way home.

I roll a stump to the bottom of the oak tree, step on it and reach for the lowest branch. As a child, I used to climb trees all the time, and had no fear of heights. As my skirt is in the way, I take it off and leave it on the ground.

I climb quickly, not wanting to risk being found by Mary. I don't look down or pay attention to the scratches I endure. The foliage is so thick it's almost impossible to see anything but the green hues of the leaves dusted with sunrays. I'm careful not to step on a branch which cannot withstand my weight. Soon I'm out of breath, and realize my strength has eroded significantly due to the horror of the late events.

Suddenly, I feel I have broken the surface of water and emerged into sunlight. I'm at the very top of the tree. The view is breathtaking and dizzying. I see a valley on the other side of the woods and a few scattered houses. By looking at the treetops, I estimate it would take me only a couple of hours to reach the houses if I go north. But anyone searching for me would search those houses first, so going in that direction no longer seems a good idea. Besides, I don't know if it might take me even farther from my home. I have to rethink this. I'll ask Mary if she has ever visited the village close to the estate I live on and will try to pry out from her which direction she takes, ready for when I decide to flee. Discouraged, I come down, put my skirt on and on the way back, pick blackberries to show Mary and her husband I'd gone berry picking when I disappeared.

On my way back to the house, a heap of spotted gray feathers under an oak catches my attention. As I come closer, I hear rasping sounds. I'm surprised by the sight of a large owl. When it sees me, it blinks and tries to flap its wings feebly. For some strange reason, animals have never been afraid of me, and I have nursed quite a few back to health, and later released them into the wild. Some come back and seek me out, and others I never see again.

I bend down and pick up the owl as gently as I can. The blackberries drop from my apron onto the ground, and I position the owl in their place.

I find Mary cooking something over the hearth. She looks both weary and relieved, and it's clear her husband is out of danger.

"Have some porridge, my dear. I will never forget how you saved my husband's life. I…I cannot imagine life without him. What kind of critter is that in your apron?"

"An owl, Mary. It is hurt. I hope you do not mind my efforts to heal it."

"You're a healer, that's for sure, and a good soul." She grins at me widely, as I pass her on my way to the small room— my temporary home.

I carefully examine the owl and find an injury with dried blood on its wing. It looks like an arrow hit its wing. I clean the wound and place the bird on a remaining piece of cloth we did not use last night when we were changing the poultice on Pádraig's wound. I find a small wooden spoon, put some water in it and open the owl's beak gently. I give it water a few times and then feed it a few morsels of chicken leftover from two nights ago. I leave the bird in peace after running my hands over it a few times and focusing on releasing sufficient healing power.

I clearly see the iridescent green color of energy emanating from my hands. This ability of mine is something I've always tried to hide, as hardly anyone would not attribute its origin to the Devil.

I check on Pádraig and am happy to see his fever hasn't returned. I have a meal of porridge with Mary sitting in front of the house.

"Mary," I start. "I cannot imagine life without my family. I want to go back home."

As soon as I have spoken, a shadow of fear darkens her expression and she turns her head away from me. I realize I should not have said anything. She goes into the house wordlessly.

When she comes out, she looks somber.

"Tell me about your family, Mary. Do you have parents, brothers and sisters?"

She sighs, sits on one of the logs and looks at the sun, squinting.

"I have no one but my husband, and I almost lost him. I can never repay you for saving his life. My mother died when I was sixteen. She was once the most beautiful girl in the village and had many suitors, both rich and poor. She fell in love with a blacksmith and married him and lived happily with him for a few months only…because he joined the other villagers who supported a nobleman in a fight against another nobleman—all over a number of pastures. The nobleman had promised everyone two acres of land if he won the battle, but he lost. Many men were killed, including my mother's husband.

"She carried his child, but she lost the baby because of her grief. She cried and cried until she cried the baby out of her womb with blood and tears. People expected her to die from grief. She owes her life to the care of her husband's parents who loved her like their own flesh and blood.

"Two years later when her beauty came back to adorn her, she married my father, who was a rich merchant. I had everything, nice clothes, toys, private tutors who schooled me. I can read and write. My mother laughed and smiled again, but from time to time I would see her crying. And then, death visited our home a second time.

"I was nine when my father died. One day, he just dropped in front of our house. He was bitten by a snake and when my mother found him, he was already dead. My mother would not leave her room for days; she did not even go to his funeral. It was her first husband's parents who took care of her again. My mother started saying she was cursed, and it was her curse that killed both of her husbands. No one could convince her it was God's will and not a curse.

"She started roaming the fields alone and would come back with torn clothes and fever in her eyes. Her beauty was leaving her rapidly and she turned into a ghost of the woman she had once been. She seemed not to notice me; I felt invisible. My only comfort was my books, especially the Bible, and prayer. It went on like this for a few years until one day some men brought my mother's body home.

"They had found her under a cliff. I believe she jumped to her death because life became unbearable. I went to live with my grandparents, who were not my real grandparents. They were the parents of my mother's first husband. In their house I met my husband, who was their grandson. Their widowed daughter also lived with them. He and I fell in love and married. Now I only have him, as our grandparents died and his mother disappeared in a storm. I want so much to have children, and I pray to God every day and night to bless us with a child."

She wipes her eyes and goes back into the house.

The day stretches on endlessly. Pádraig continues to sleep, Mary returns to the garden, and I start cleaning the house, having nothing else to do. I give the owl more water and some bread and when it opens its eyes, I see life returning to it. A jolt of joy lights up my heart.

The next few days pass quickly. Mary allows me to help her in the garden, and she and I laugh and joke while working. The owl is now perched on one of the many stakes marking the garden boundaries and seems to be on the way to full recovery. At dusk, it flaps its wings, but still cannot fly.

One evening Faolán appears. When he dismounts, his hands are full of presents for all of us and he seems to be in a very happy mood. Besides food and clothing for my hosts, he has a present for me. A pair of sturdy but comfortable boots, and two new dresses in which I can move around easily, as well as a dress so fancy and so pretty I dare not touch it. Where in this wilderness would I wear a blue muslin dress embroidered with gem stones?

I thank him and kiss him and have no doubt in my mind as to what I have to do. A plan is hatching. I will pretend I love him, I will bed him. Mary and her husband also will be convinced of my love, and in a few days, I will sneak out as soon as it is bedtime and escape.

But first, I will wait for the owl to get well and go back into the wilderness. I have become very attached to it. I have named him Waldis, because it is a male owl. At night, I let it perch on the chair in my room. I kiss it on the head and whisper to it all my secrets and plans. It looks at me unblinkingly with its yellow eyes and I sometimes think it understands me.

I take Faolán by the hand and with a coquettish smile I lead him into the woods. At the same moment, I am detached from my body and viewing us from somewhere above. He is impatient, and he lowers me to the ground on which he has placed his cape. His hands roam my body as if in fever; his kisses are burning my face and lips, so I dissociate myself even further from the physical experience while at the same time returning his kisses. I want it to be over quickly, so I wrap my legs around him and as soon as he enters me I start squeezing him and gyrating in order to heighten his pleasure and cut my torment short. Panting and gasping, he spurts his seed in me and I gently push him away. He is lying on his back, spent and satisfied, while I hide behind a tree and wipe myself clean with my dress, trying to expel his seed from my womb.

I lie next to him and tell him I want him to take me away to a place where we can live together. I know that will never be possible, but I want him to think I am his forever. He says that presently such a dream is not possible; we must live like this for some time. I say I understand and will patiently wait.

He spends the night with me, and I'm forced to go through the lovemaking ordeal once again. Fortunately, again he does not last long. Once he falls asleep I leave the house and sit outside. Suddenly, I remember I left Waldis in the garden. I find my way there in the dark, but he is nowhere to be seen. My heart pounds wildly and I cry out in pain. Have I lost everything dear to my heart? I call him softly, not wanting to awaken anyone in the house. All of a sudden I hear a swooshing sound as he lands on a tree branch near me. Relief washes over me, but it does not stop my tears from running down my cheeks.

"Don't ever leave me again," I sob, knowing Waldis is not the cause of my distress. I make up my mind. Tomorrow evening, as soon as Faolán leaves, I will make preparations to escape.

Waldis lands on the ground and I see he has just caught a mouse and is clawing at it. After his meal, he walks toward me and I whisper my plans to him and ask him to be with me until I find my way back home. I now clearly remember the direction in which Faolán and I came from the river on that fateful night. Our horse ride did not last long; I was just disoriented and tired. I will also innocently ask him tomorrow how far and in which direction the river runs. I just need to get to the river and walk upstream, go around the village to reach my house. I realize I need to travel in disguise.

The next day, after our lovemaking in the woods, I tell Faolán how I go for a walk every day, but am afraid of getting lost, and want him to explain to me where the river lies, and what the nearest village is—so I have some orientation points. In the dirt he draws me a map of the woods, the river, and the village beyond, called Grimwood, and even marks the position of Doverly, the village from which I was thrown in the river. I marvel at his faith in me is such that he even tells me how many miles away we are from each of these locations. Perhaps he mentions distance as a possible deterrent.

I also ask him about his home, and he adds it to the map. I kiss him fervently and tell him I wish he did not have to leave. He promises to come back in a few days. He will be in shock when he discovers I'm no longer here, and he will not dare look for me. In comparison to my husband he has very little power, and if I arrive safely home, and if my husband has not found out about Kieran, no one will be able to touch me but the king himself, who has no interest in me.

The next day, I tell Mary I want to make trousers of my old shift, because it will be easier to work in the garden dressed like that. Her look is quizzical, but she does not question me. Without her seeing, I also make a cap under which I plan to hide my hair because I want to look like a young lad during my escape. I sew in haste and my fingers are pricked by the big, roughly fashioned needle.

When my outfit is finished, I find myself trembling with the indecision of when to leave this new home. A part of me feels sorry to leave Mary for good, and I also fear Faolán might hold her responsible for my flight. As she and I had made many loaves of bread the day before, I am sure she will not notice a big chunk missing.

When the sun sets and she and her husband go to bed, I tell her I'm not feeling well, and would like to stay in bed the next morning. She says she will look in on me around lunch time when she returns from the garden. I give her a warm hug and tell her I love her.

As soon as they retire I change quickly, put on my new boots and step out through the window. My heart is beating wildly as I enter the forest heading in the direction of the river, hoping I can stay on the course. The night sky is lit with starlight and moonlight which assuages my fears. As if by magic, Waldis appears and flies ahead of me, landing frequently on the branches ahead, waiting for me to catch up.

"Take me to the river, Waldis, river, river," I start chanting. I feel a strange power imbue me to the bone; my fear leaves me and I forge ahead in the night adventure with a great hope of succeeding. After about two hours of walking, I hear the river—it calls me; it will aid me in my design. Maybe I *am* a witch, maybe the universe *is* moving through me and helping me…or maybe there is a God or Goddess who protects me.

Waldis does not go straight to the river, but turns left on a trail. I sit down to rest for a moment. After I catch my breath, I get up and continue on. I am grateful to Faolán gave me these boots, because without them I would not be able to go far. I don't see the river, but can hear it on my right side. As long as we continue on this trail, I know I am heading in the right direction, toward home.

After about two hours, I'm exhausted and about to give up. I have overestimated my strength and my ability to find my way. Waldis hoots with impatience, spurring me on. I take a few more steps, and find myself on a dirt road leading to Doverly. I was so close to home all this time, and my husband never even looked for me! I find that troublesome to believe. If Faolán had wanted to keep me away from everyone, why did he not spirit me away to a place much farther away? Perhaps it was convenient for him to keep me in Mary's house because his own home is near enough for him to visit me. The sound of wheels shatters my reverie, and I see an approaching cart pulled by a dark horse. I wait on the road hoping I won't be recognized by whoever is in the cart.

As it approaches, I put my hands in the air and call, "Help me, good man!"

The cart stops, and to my delight I recognize one of our stablemen, old George. When he had reached the age when he could no longer work, I ordered the other servants to take care of him and let him spend his days doing whatever gave him pleasure. Once a week he takes the cart and visits his son, who owns a piece of land given to him by a powerful man for his allegiance.

His son married Jane, a girl I helped by healing a hideous scar on her left cheek. The scar had made her disfigured. I could never understand why instead of feeling her gratitude, I could only feel her hostility toward me. In spite of that, I was kind to her, knowing how much she had suffered at the hands of the same nobleman who awarded her husband with land. She was a toy to use for his pleasure for a long time, until he grew tired of her.

When I recognize George, I almost scream with delight, "George, it is I, Jilleen!" I take off my cap and let my hair tumble down my back.

He is silent for a few moments and then yelps in joy. "Jilleen, lass, where you been? When your husband heard what happened, he had villagers hanged—them as stood on the bridge watching you thrown off. He had the gaoler killed as well, and is looking for the inquisitor."

"Take me home quickly. I will put my cap on in case someone comes along at this late hour. Why are you coming back home so late at night?"

"I can no longer be in the sunlight. My skin has some kind of sickness. Maybe you will find herbs that can help me."

"I shall certainly try to make ointments for your skin." I am so excited I can hardly breathe. We continue along slowly and just at the break of dawn we reach our land. Light rain wets my face and blends with my tears of joy. At the thought (one I had suppressed for so long) that I will see my son, my heart leaps in my throat and I am almost suffocating on happiness and disbelief, I am safe again.

It is still so early no one has risen yet. I bang on the door, and our cook Maureen opens the heavy door with its loud creak. She rubs her eyes and then screams when she sees me. "Master, master, the mistress is home!"

I run upstairs and burst into my son's room and then stop, not wanting to frighten him. I softly climb into bed with him and wrap my arms around him. He stirs in his sleep and a muffled "mama" escapes his lips. I kiss him again and again, then pick him up and carry him to my marital chamber. He does not waken when I place him in the middle of the bed.

My husband sits up in bed, confused. He seems to have aged since I last saw him, and it was only a month ago, unless I've completely lost all track of time. Without speaking, we embrace. Aiden wants to talk, but I point to our son so he gets up and takes me onto the balcony.

I had forgotten how beautiful the view was. The sky seems to be touching the line of the forest. I can see the lake in the distance and imagine the ripples the rain is making on its surface. I admire the meadows surrounding our castle and the farm houses and the gardens. It all looks like heaven even on this blustery, rainy day.

I tell Aidan how Faolán saved me and kept me safe until the time I could return. I explained how he tricked the villagers into thinking I would drown. I told him to forget all of that, and not take further revenge on the innocent and ignorant people. All should be forgiven, but he should exert his influence to prevent this crime of burning or drowning women as witches from ever happening again, at least in this region over which he rules. He tells me he knows who was behind it.

It seems it was his arch enemy Duogan who wanted me killed so he could punish my husband. Duogan had never expected Aidan would find out his treachery, and is now hiding in fear of reprisal. Duogan begrudges my husband his ties with the King of England and believes my husband is a traitor to his people. I know he is not. It is just—men fight each other over power. And that I do not understand.

"I shall find him, and his death will be slow and painful."

"Please, do not respond to violence with violence, it will just breed more violence and cause more bloodshed. You have no proof it was him. It's just a supposition. Let us forget what happened, and let him live in fear thinking you are looking for him."

"You must be exhausted and hungry."

"Yes, but I want to sleep first, and I want you near me to feel safe again." And then I remember Waldis and go out on the balcony looking for him. I tell my husband how I nursed Waldis back to health and how he may have followed me back home.

As soon as my head touches the pillow I fall asleep and have a vivid dream of Kieran, which I remember to the last detail upon waking.

* * * *

We are lying in a field surrounded by honeysuckle shrubs, and the heavenly scent of the blooms intoxicates us. Kieran knows I always keep honeysuckle flowers close by because I believe they help me to invite him into my dreams. To me, they symbolize love and devotion. I had said the plant meant a hidden secret, what our love has had to be. The twisting and coiling plant also represents entwinement of our bodies and souls. He knows I ascribe magical properties to the plant and its scent, that I believe it enhances my intuitive awareness and potency to see future events.

In my dream, I pick a whorl and move it across his face, neck and chest. His chest heaves as the sweet honeysuckle scent fills his nostrils. Crushing the whorl between our chests, he turns me over and is on top of me. A sudden mist descends upon us as he kisses me passionately, feeling my arms and legs coil around him like ivy, in a tight grip. As his tongue and his fingertips travel along my neck, my small breasts and nipples harden, and taste like sweet strawberries in his mouth, he tells me. Feeling his wet tongue on my stomach and in between my thighs, I shudder with the sweetness of pleasure. I can no longer tell if I am feeling his tongue or his fingertips on my love button as I twist my hips in a circular motion thinking the pleasure itself will become too much to bear. When I climax, I sit up, pulling him toward my face and begging him with my body language to enter me swiftly and deeply.

Instead, he takes my hand and helps me get up. He leads me to a small lake under a waterfall. We dive in and emerge at the other end, right under the waterfall. We climb onto rocks and venture behind the cascading water. The rock wall is wet and slippery as the rushing water sprays it; however, the space between the waterfall and the rock is sufficiently wide to accommodate us. He presses me against the rock, and our lips blend in a kiss of rapturous love. From time to time, he stops kissing me, takes my face in his hands and looks at me as if he were seeing me for the first time. He whispers words of love to me, barely discernible against the sound of water tumbling, rumbling and murmuring. I think I hear, "Don't you ever forget about me," but I cannot be sure.

As rays of sunlight penetrate and gild the mist, he and I fuse again into one body and soul. I raise my arms and grip a ledge at the moment he enters me; I let out a soft cry of pleasure and gyrate my hips in movement with his thrusting and gaining in intensity. The rock is cool and slick and I revel in the luxury of this summer day; our bodies are moving in unison of love and rapture, and our cries of pleasure blend with the awakening of nature around us, because it is early morning. At the moment of our climax, the mist suddenly dissolves and sunlight plays over the water like specks of molten gold. Nature awakens with summer glimmerings of flitting dragonflies, whispering boughs and trilling and blithe birdsong.

We slowly disengage and hand in hand immerse ourselves in the lake, swim across it and lie down under a weeping willow. I put my head on his arm, and he gently whispers my name and tells me he loves me. I whisper back, "I love you, K," calling him by the first letter of his name, as we both do when addressing each other.

His breathing deepens as he slips into a dreamless sleep. He sleeps so deeply and silently I have to place my hand over his heart to ensure he is still breathing. Unlike him, I am fully awake and alert in my dream because that is how I often dream. I embrace him and kiss his shoulders and his back. He does not stir. Sleep has painted his face with a youthful and vulnerable innocence.

My kiss on his lips is almost imperceptible, but he stirs and opens his eyes. The look in his eyes immediately reflects happiness over seeing me. We get up and go for a swim. When we come out, the heat is so intense our bodies are dry almost momentarily.

He embraces me as if he will never let me go, and I know it is time for another farewell. I can feel the color drain from my face as my heart is wrenched with renewed and singeing pain. At those moments when pain reigns and life and magic seem to seep out from my body, I recoil inside at the thought of the days and nights which are about to stretch ahead of me like an ocean of infinite sorrow. I cannot follow him into his life, and he has to stay outside the gates of mine.

In my dream, we came on horses to our secret meeting place. He now mounts his horse and slowly trots away. I walk away leading my horse by the bridle. I turn around and cast one last glance on the grass where we have lain. The spot now looks desolate and empty, and I see no traces of our love. Everything looks undisturbed as if a mortal had never treaded there. The waterfall splashes with insouciance, birds warble mirthfully, and insects buzz monotonously. There is no sign of us; it is as if this summer day had only dreamt of two people deeply in love, a dream that quickly evaporated under the blazing heat of the sun.
* * * *

When I awake, I feel drenched in sweat, and start sobbing. Events have frayed my nerves to the point of insanity. I look around in fear I'm only dreaming I am back home. I no longer trust my senses. I quickly leap from the bed and race downstairs to the dining room.

"Mama," my son cries as he runs to me, and I fall on my knees hugging and kissing him. Aidan is sitting at the table. I realize it must be past noon as they are having lunch. I forget Kieran and join my family at the table. I am so hungry I stuff myself with everything. My husband smiles at me and passes me cheese, eggs, meat and bread, and offers me a goblet of wine. While I am eating my son is sitting in my lap, and our servants are peeking into the chamber every few minutes. My husband invites them all in, tells them I am safe and sound, and offers wine to everyone to celebrate this moment, then gives the whole staff the afternoon and evening off.

The next few days, I don't leave my son for a moment. We play together, walk together, go fishing and tree climbing. I introduce him to Waldis, who has reappeared and found his new home on our land.

On the sixth day I think of Kieran and want to see him so badly I tremble. My husband forbade my going into the village, but he didn't mention going to the lake. I want to see Kieran so much I send a servant by horse to his home to deliver my message. The message, even if intercepted, will not be understood by anyone but him. He will know I will be waiting for him on the hill leading down to the lake.

Tomorrow at noon, I tell everyone I'm going for a ride to the hill, and will spend a few hours there resting and reading. They're all accustomed to my romping on the meadows and going to the lake, and probably feel relieved that normalcy has been restored.

Once on the horse, I enjoy the breeze playing in my hair and the intoxicating sense of freedom. I can barely breathe from excitement over seeing Kieran. I am gulping air as I try to get to the hill as fast as I can. Once I arrive, I leave the horse at the foot of the hill in a shady grove and climb up breathlessly to a large pine tree under which Kieran and I always meet. After about twenty minutes, I become nervous and afraid he will not be able to come. Just as I am about to fall into desperation, I hear footsteps. It is he, my secret love and my possible demise.

I cannot describe his expression when he sees me. He drops to his knees and wraps his arms around my legs as he cries, begging me to forgive him for not having been able to protect me from evil. I ask him to get up and we kiss like mad people while we laugh and cry. Holding hands we walk along a narrow path bordered with blackberry bushes. I am picking the ripe berries and feeding Kieran. Feeding quickly turns playful, and every time I put a blackberry into his mouth, he tries to mouth my fingers, and laughing, I pull them back before he bites.

My long white dress has embroidered daisies running down it. He has a long white shirt over his brown trousers. In my laughter, I hear seductive notes and every time his mouth closes around my fingers, I feel a shock reverberate through me, making my heart skip a few beats, and my nipples tingle and harden. The soft fabric of my dress suddenly appears diaphanous as my breasts become well delineated. Kieran notices the change and lowers his head to gently and sensually bite on them, causing me to let out a muffled cry of desire. Our lovemaking always makes me think of violent starbursts and velvety night skies illuminated by millions of firefly lights.

I take his hand and lead him downhill. The hill is very rocky and besides blackberry bushes, it is sprinkled with blooming shrubs. We start our descent gingerly as the slope is quite precipitous and it would be easy to lose our footing on rocks and pebbles that give way under each footstep. The view is breathtaking as the emerald-colored lake lazily stretches and shimmers under the midday sun.

We stop so I can admire a large, white, jagged rock. Kieran knows I am drawn to stones and rocks, and I can feel the mystical energy they emanate. The rock offers a bit of shade and I lean against it. He leans into me, kissing my eyelids, face and lips, while unbuttoning my dress. I sigh and tremble under his touch. The heat of the day makes the air hazy and saturated with the scent of wild flowers and herbs. Bees and other insects buzz incessantly, and the combined effect of fragrance and cacophonic buzz creates an atmosphere of dreaminess and torpor. He bends down and tears away a few florets from a shrub, crumples them with his fingers, releasing a powerful and intoxicating scent, and he rubs them around my nipples. Time and space dissipate in the vaporous heat of the day.

I rotate myself and push him against the rock. I rub myself against him and start to slide down his body to untie his leather breeches. I look up at his face and see it tense up and his eyes close in expectation of the thrilling touch of my mouth. At that moment, the sound of stones rolling down the hill jerks us back to reality, and we quickly move farther down toward the lake. Looking back up, we realize we are still alone.

The rest of our descent is quicker as we are no longer afraid of stepping on the treacherous stones. We are certain we are the only people on the small, white-pebbled beach. The lake is a mirror of green, with speckles of gold. We undress and plunge into the cool water, feeling light and free in our nakedness.

We kiss greedily, licking lake water off each other's lips. The beach is covered in sun-bleached rocks and we find one flat enough to lie on. I lie on my back, and close my eyes in complete surrender to the sun's warm caress. Water drops sparkle like stardust sprinkled carelessly over my body.

Through my closed eyes, I feel Kieran's gaze on my naked body. At that moment it is as if I have stepped out of my own body to look at myself through his eyes. Enraptured by his gaze infused with lust and also tenderness, I feel so beautiful. Sensuously and slowly, his tongue trails down my body licking off water droplets, searing my skin with unbridled flames of passion, and eliciting my moans and shivers of pleasure.

His fingers penetrate my wetness causing me to arch my back towards him in impatient anticipation. I slide toward the slanted edge of the rock, and wrap my legs around him as he enters my softness and warmth. I gently squeeze him inviting him deeper. Every cell in my body echoes his excitement and I no longer know where I end and he begins, or if the colors above me are those of the sky, or the lake, or both blended into one. Our lovemaking crescendo reaches its erotic peak and at the moment we let out a cry of ecstasy and our wanting is temporarily appeased, we hear a bird intoxicated with love call out to its mate. Lying satiated in each other's embrace it seems a whole new universe is born, not in pain but in joy!

Lying spent on the rock, my body still tingles with the marks of his lovemaking; with eyes closed I imagine his tongue and lips tattooing verses of erotic poetry on my skin. With arms and legs entangled we fall asleep, oblivious of the time of the day, our nakedness and the hard surface underneath us. I don't even think about what would happen to us if we are caught. It would mean certain death. Love is stronger than fear.

With a suddenness that shatters our shallow slumber, the first lightning tears into the sky and sunlight turns into darkness, and the darkness into dense and sticky black as menacing clouds shroud the sun. Large drops of warm rain shower us and the wind starts growing stronger, tugging at our clothes we are hastily trying to pull on. We scramble toward the hill. Disoriented, we realize the weather has changed from sunny to stormy in a very short time.

Surrounded by the rumbling noise of thunder and drenched to the skin, we begin our ascent of the hill grabbing at shrubs and branches in order to maintain our balance. Kieran staggers and scrapes his shoulder against a sharp outcrop of rock but continues to climb, holding me firmly by the hand. Any attempt to talk is unsuccessful as howling wind drowns out our voices and reduces our shouts to the softest of whispers. Trying to steady myself, I grab at some brambles and let out a stifled cry as I feel thorns pierce my palm. The pain subsides after a few moments and I forget it.

Reaching the top of the hill, we run toward a small abandoned house which once belonged to my husband's ancestors. We still keep some furniture in it, and use it sometimes to house visitors when we have our annual ball.

We never lock the door—it creaks open when Kieran leans into it. It is pitch-dark inside and I grope my way to the dining room table on which I find candles, a flint and firestone my husband leaves here. I call out softly to Kieran and ask him to light the candles.

Getting a spark of light seems to take forever. I hold the candle-wick close to the flint and just when we both want to give up, a spark flies and a tiny flame appears. With our hands we cradle it tenderly until it burns more steadily. The storm is raging and I fear the window panes might break into smithereens.

Exhausted, I lean against a wall, my heart palpitating wildly. I am mesmerized by the sight of the violent weather outside the windows. I begin to shiver from cold under the dripping wet dress, so I take it off. Carrying a candle, I walk into one of the bedrooms where I'm sure I'll find dry clothing. I rummage in a large chest until I find a white nightgown forgotten by either a female visitor or left by me during the first year of my marriage when Aidan and I would spend nights in this house wishing to be alone without servants. I grab the nightgown and use it to dry myself. Suddenly, Kieran is in the room; he also removes his clothes, then pushes me against the wall gently and leans into me.

Under weak candlelight, I notice tiny rivulets of blood trickle down from the scratch on his shoulder. At the same time, he takes my right hand and looks at my palm, which is injured from the brambles. Gently, I lick the blood off his wound, tasting its metallic saltiness and feeling that by tasting his blood, I have now captured a part of him for eternity. I shudder as I feel his tongue remove the blood from my palm. He raises his eyes and I see soft candlelight playing in them. His gaze is becoming more and more intense, its heat boring into my soul. Searching for each other's souls, we are finding hidden paths behind each other's thoughts, treading into the uncharted territory of each other's pure being and consciousness. Just as portals to our souls open and our energies touch and fuse into one, a bolt of lightning illuminates the room and colors it with a supernaturally blinding white, and the sky seems to split in two and tumble down to earth in thunderous fury.

At that epiphany of feeling no fear, but perfect tranquility, we are flooded by sudden and wordless knowledge. We read the same message in each other's eyes:

"Only now do I know, I have always known you. Only now do I know, I have loved you before. I just know not when...."

As quickly as it began, the storm dies down with what sounds like a loud sigh of exhaustion. We open windows to let the fresh scent of rain permeate the room. There is firewood in the fireplace in the corner of the room, and because we feel a slight chill on our skin, Kieran starts a fire using the candle flame. He is still naked, but I have put on the nightgown even though it is a bit damp. As the fire crackles and warms the room, we can see its reflection in the mirror on the opposite wall.

I have always been bewitched by the mirror's beauty. My husband told me it was his mother who received it as a gift from a suitor. No one knows where he bought it. My mother-in-law fell in love with the mirror, but not with the suitor. When they found his dead body in a meadow, and could see no marks of any harm done to him, people concluded he had died from a broken heart. Some visitors to this house have said that in this mirror a man's reflection appeared, a reflection of deepest sorrow.

The mirror is not hanging but leaning against the wall, and its height almost reaches the ceiling. It has a huge, ornate gilded frame and a crest on the top featuring leaves and flowers about which tiny fairies and dragonflies flutter, or sleep between the petals. An oversized, blue velvet armchair stands in front of the mirror. As the room is rather small, the fireplace light illuminates the mirror with an intensely warm glow. Flames dance seductively in the mirror, creating an illusion of another world behind it.

Kieran and I exchange glances and we both let out a soft moan. Our love is still in that early stage when one look is sufficient to ignite an instantaneous flaming desire. His eyes are dark crystals infused with love and wanting. I quiver with desire as he clasps me in his embrace. He takes me to the armchair and once he is seated, I straddle him, kissing him wildly. I turn around for a moment to look in the mirror and see the flames dance and lick my back. I look at Kieran and catch him looking in the mirror, enraptured by the sight. I can feel his excitement growing close to an avalanche of fiery culmination, so I move away from him and with a smile, I gaze at his image in the mirror, allowing him to admire his own beauty and allure.

He reaches for me and pulls me toward him. I straddle him again and let out a muffled cry of intense pleasure as he enters my moistness. I start undulating slowly and at the same time our nimble tongues, still burning with the taste of our blood, play in an embrace of their own across our hungry lips. The taste of blood seems to have released a fierce and voracious thirst for each other, a thirst that has been steadily growing since our eyes first met across the bonfire.

As I feel he is getting close to releasing his warm rapture inside me, I disengage myself from him again, and after a few moments, during which he is making whimpering sounds, I sit on him again, this time facing the mirror. He embraces me tightly from behind. My head falls back on his shoulder and his kisses are on my neck. The movement of our bodies reminds me of two verses in perfect rhyme. Our pleasure is depthless, timeless and nameless. I use the armrests as support against which I rise and fall like the ocean tides. The effects of chiaroscuro in the mirror and the reflection of our feverish union creates a mystical atmosphere, and I feel we have been transported back to that moment in time, perhaps centuries ago, when we first knew each other.

After a few moments only, our bodies go into rapturous spasms of climax. He is still hugging me tightly and kissing the back of my head. When I turn around to kiss him, he sees my face is streaked with tears. The frightful experience of the tempest, the unexpected and awe-inspiring moment of spiritual recognition and the passionate lovemaking have overfilled my emotional cup. His embrace is full of tender understanding, and he kisses away my tears until I smile.

As the fire starts to die down, I get up quickly and tell him I must go back home, and will let him know when we can see each other again. Then I remember that next week my husband and I have been invited to a masked ball at the castle of the most powerful man in the land, Lord Tyrone, a friend and ally of the

King of England. I ask Kieran if he and his wife have been invited and he confirms it.

We kiss and part and I run all the way home with my heart in my throat.

CHAPTER ELEVEN

Jilleen

The week is dragging on slowly and I cannot wait for the masked ball because I now know Kieran and his wife will be among the guests. The ball is the biggest event of the year, and because this year the guests have been asked to wear masks, there is frenzy among the noble women to have new gowns made to bedazzle everyone with their creativity. This year also, Lord Tyrone is marking his fifteenth wedding anniversary on the same day, and I sneer at the hypocrisy of the celebration as everyone knows he has had a lover for at least two years now. I would not be surprised if his mistress has been invited and if she wishes the lord's wife many more happy anniversaries. But who am I to pronounce such judgments?

Lately I have not been going out much, and have not been back in the village since I barely escaped death. My husband's knights, as revenge for the way I had been treated, have been terrorizing the villagers. I do not want to know or hear what evil deeds they have committed following my husband's orders. Violence breeds more violence and ignorance cannot be fought with brutality, but I have no say in my husband's decisions.

From time to time, cold fear grips my heart and I dare not think of the consequences of my betrayal should I be discovered. I am risking my life by loving Kieran and know I should stop before it is too late. But weak with love and desire, my thoughts return to him ceaselessly.

The ball cannot come too soon. I am also curious to see Kieran's wife. I feel compassion for her, and pray she may forgive me for hurting her even though she has no knowledge of what I have been stealing from her. I should not be doing this to another woman, to my 'sister'; because we are all sisters, and we should love and help each other. Lord knows the lives of most women are very trying. I want to meet her and squeeze her hand warmly and hug her.

The night of the ball comes and my hands are trembling as I dress. When we climb into our coach, I lean against my husband feeling the need for support. The ride seems endless and finally we alight at Lord Tyrone's castle. Thousands of candles seem to be lit on this starry night, with lights flickering both from the earth and the heavens, and I am lightheaded as if I were floating and not walking toward the entrance.

The Lord and his Lady welcome us. They are dressed as a king and queen, which is befitting. Their masks are golden like the color of their attire. They cannot recognize their guests, and they have to trust no one not invited will infiltrate their sumptuous event. Ever since Lord Tyrone visited Italy, his house has displayed Italian ornaments, music, furnishings. I have heard evil-tongued people reproach him for such ostentatious behavior and betrayal of local customs. Some have called him a sold-out soul.

I am dizzy looking at the lavish costumes. Ladies' jewels sparkle, as do some of the bejeweled daggers the men carry. I try to spot Kieran, but I don't see him among the crowd which undulates in colors of the rainbow, making my eyes almost hurt with so many impressions.

When servants announce dinner, we move toward the table, and my heart almost stops when I realize I am to be seated next to Kieran. Longing tugs at my heart and I feel like running away with him, but I calm as the realization of the havoc of devastation we could create flashes across my consciousness. Our longings can only be appeased temporarily, and we will probably spend the rest of our lives aching for each other. The searing pain I feel every time we say farewell is what I must accept as part of my penance for tasting the forbidden fruit of adultery.

Tonight our affair should be less perceptible, because attention will be on the Lord and the Lady of this magnificent palace. I have always found Lord Tyrone intimidating. He looks at me as if I am a juicy piece of meat and I am sure it is only due to his need for my husband's allegiance that he has not openly let me know he wants to bed me. I find him vulgar with his roaring laugh that reveals his rotting teeth and I shudder when I see the lecherous glint in his eyes. His black hair is always matted and greasy and his belly hangs over his breeches, bearing witness to endless nights of excessive drinking and eating. I feel sorry for both his wife and mistress, and probably more for his mistress because she is the one who has to tend to the needs of his passion. His wife should be thanking her for the sacrifice, because it cannot be anything else but a sacrifice of flesh for gold.

In preparation for this ball, Lord Tyrone insisted every invitee keep his costume in utmost secrecy so, at least at first sight, no one would be able to discern with any certainty the identity of the guests. I suspect the ulterior motive behind this plan was he could also invite his mistress to his celebration and he wanted to ensure she would remain incognito.

Even though Kieran and I never discussed the costumes we would wear, we easily recognize each other. He wears a floor-length black cape embroidered with opalescent dragonflies. On his head is a wide-brimmed black hat, and his mask is a masterfully crafted black dragonfly with sinfully crimson-red wings. Dragonflies are one of the symbols of our love and passion for each other.

Why dragonflies? I cannot explain. Perhaps our love will be as short-lived as a dragonfly's life.

The mask covers his eyes and nose, but his sensual lips are free. My costume is a long, shimmering, and intricate corset-style, lace-up backed dress. It is of an aqua-blue hue and very form fitting, sequined with hundreds of tiny emerald-colored beads and crystals. My husband purchased the fabric from a Venetian merchant and paid an exorbitant sum of gold for it. My mask represents a damselfly with luminescent cyan-blue wings, a perfect match to the color of the dress. My hair is hidden under a curly, blonde wig my husband, again, acquired from Italy. I wear chandelier-style, expensive large pearl drop earrings.

As I brush against Kieran, my heart lurching and fluttering in my throat, he whispers to me, "Jilleen, you are the soul of my soul," and adds, "I love you." Fiery passion and desire start coursing through my veins and I feel a tempest of silent sighs rise in my soul.

"My love has no boundaries...our souls are one," I whisper back.

The dining room table can seat eighteen people; however, with six extra chairs twenty-four persons are squeezed around the massive, excessively ornate mahogany table, which looks overwrought with the infinite number of inlaid details. An imposing chandelier hangs low, casting candlelight over the snow-white expensive sateen-weave tablecloth that must have come from Italy, like all other finery seen in our part of the world.

Unexpectedly, a gust of wind rushes into the room extinguishing many candles. The servants immediately start lighting the candles anew, and they close the door to the gardens from which the breeze came. The servants also light multitudes of red candles held by heavy frosted glass candleholders. Silverware and elegant glass stemware sparkle in soft candlelight, coloring the ambiance with warmth and mystery. In one corner, under a large painting of Lord Tyrone's portrait illuminated with light from a large gold wall sconce, a quartet of travelling musicians from Italy are playing madrigals.

I cannot help comparing the riches on display with the misery and hunger in many of the surrounding villages, where death is a daily visitor and often the only savior from their hell on earth. Trying to help the sick with my healing ability I have entered huts made from sticks and mud, and found sickly children and babies sleeping on earth floors. I would try not to cry and show my powerlessness before so much misery. In those moments I did not believe any God would wish to punish people with so much destitution that death would open a portal to salvation. I bring food and clean water, clothes and medicine, but I later cry from helplessness that I can do so little.

I often hide from my husband how much I try to help our fellow men. He would certainly flare up in rage when hearing I was visiting the sick, for fear I might get ill and die. Funerals are a daily event in our region. A few months ago I witnessed a young woman bleed to death in childbirth. She was writhing and screaming on a mud floor of her hut, and around her was the indescribable squalor which the most abject poverty creates. She left behind four small children. Without my husband's knowledge, I took the children to this woman's sister and gave her gold to raise them. I promised to continue helping her. Luckily, she was a good soul who loved these poor orphans and replaced their mother. Their father would visit every now and then, but he soon remarried and bestowed a life of misery on another wretched woman. I try to stop thinking of the suffering which is part of most people's fates, and return my attention to this evening of utter debauchery.

It is time to seat ourselves. I do not dare look at Kieran, but feel his proximity with every cell of my trembling body. He holds my chair and I sit down feeling my face burn under the mask. As soon as he is seated, he rubs his leg against mine sending electric tremors through me. Oh, how much in love I am!

On his right side I can see his wife. Even though her face is hidden under a white and gold mask, I know it has to be her. I do not like her costume. There are white feathers on the white dress, and white feathers in her hair making her look like an unsightly bird. If she only knew how much I love her husband! But, maybe there is a woman among the revelers who is in love with my husband...is anyone still in love with his own wife or her own husband? Servants begin serving a seven-course dinner and pouring expensive wine aged to perfection. Again, I think about how few people wide and far ever eat like this. Many people have never seen such finery. It looks like utter sinfulness. Having travelled through Europe, Lord Tyrone has, indeed, adopted some very fancy customs when it comes to hospitality. And his guests outdid themselves in order to appear worthy of his invitation. I wonder how much gold they spent on these ridiculous costumes, to participate in this soulless revelry and engage in these vapid conversations.

My head starts spinning and I think I am having an out-of-body experience watching the guests eat, drink and laugh, looking grotesque in exaggerated and almost fear-inspiring, multi-colored and elaborate costumes and masks. Where did they find such fabrics? Who sewed their gowns and costumes when few local seamstresses have the skill to produce such strange designs?

I am almost unable to touch the food on my plate or swallow a sip of wine as my throat constricts in excitement, and trepidation of someone noticing the body language and inappropriate touching between Kieran and me. His leg is now pressing hard into mine and his hand goes under the table travelling along my right thigh, caressing my dress and then squeezing me lightly. The table is high enough to hide this erotic but dangerous play from curious eyes. My excitement starts to grow and my breath quickens. The laughter around us is becoming rowdier with each additional glass of heavy red wine. I feel his hand lift up my dress and sneak under it. I slide lower down the chair and pull my dress high and let its fabric rest in gentle, silken waves. That evening I had decided to wear no undergarments. The fabric of my dress is diaphanous and I did not want the contours of undergarments to be discernible. I could just imagine the shock I would provoke if I revealed to others that I was naked underneath the dress.

His hand is now between my legs, and when I feel his fingers on my naked skin I cannot hold back a soft cry, attracting the attention of the man wearing a black mask of a malevolent-looking cat, sitting across from me. He asks me if anything is wrong. I say I have just felt a piercing stab of back pain that has been plaguing me for the past couple of weeks. He raises his glass to me and asks me which of the madrigals we have just heard is my favorite. I say I am a stranger to Italian music and love our local music. I am hoping he'll abandon this dialogue with me. He then asks me if I enjoy dancing and I say I do. At the same time I can see my husband talking with great interest to a woman dressed in yellow. A yellow veil is hiding her face, but I can tell by the way she is leaning into my husband she is enjoying his company immensely.

The man across from me tries to engage me in conversation again and asks me if my husband will be joining Lord Tyrone in the boar hunt next week. I reply I have no knowledge of such plans. In the meantime, the quartet of players is replaced by a harpist. The melody is so sad there is a lull in conversation at the table, and then the din of laughter drowns out the music.

A few minutes later the man across from me shifts his attention to the woman on his right who wears a mask representing a gold leaf. On her head, she wears a wig made of red feathers. The cleavage on her gold dress is deep enough to take his interest from me to her. I again wonder at her costume, and those of the other women. It seems every lady here was able to get the most extravagant outfit from Italy. Again, I cannot help but think about the decadence of such a small number of people living such rich and lavish lives while ignoring the abject poverty outside the walls of their estates.

Dancing has already begun and I find myself standing up when a man with the mask of a satyr invites me to dance. As I dance, my eyes are searching for Kieran. He is standing under a huge gilded mirror with a glass of wine in his hand, talking to a woman dressed as a fairy. She looks magnificent in her white silky robe and silvery translucent wings. He is talking to her animatedly, and even though I cannot see his face below the mask, I sense his fascination with her. I feel jealousy stab my heart and I almost laugh at the absurdity of the situation. He and I are already perpetrators of adultery, and now to be worried about infidelity committed by him is more than senseless.

I try to dismiss such feelings and continue to dance, trying to appear happy and carefree, but the thought he might soon replace me with another lover is seeping into my soul like poison. I try again to dismiss it, not wishing to believe his feelings for me were so shallow, and that infatuation wore the mask of love, but I cannot. The woman leaves the room, and a few minutes after he also leaves and I overhear him say to someone, "It is getting very warm in here."

Did he leave in search of her? I try to continue dancing, but when I feel my dance partner squeeze my waist in an untoward way, I abruptly stop dancing and tell him I am feeling unwell and must leave. I exit the dining room through the doors leading to a huge stone patio. Beyond it, a magnificent moonlight- and starlight-washed garden sprawls before my eyes. Stone-paved pathways crisscross the impeccably manicured lawn; exotic shrubs and antique urns that serve as flower pots are scattered in a way that reveals careful planning. As I walk, I pass several arbors and pergolas with climbing roses entwined around them. The ambiance is that of a paradise and I feel light and free for a moment. In front of me emerges an ethereal-looking white marble gazebo surrounded by white rose bushes in full bloom. The air is perfumed with their intoxicating scent, and I pluck a blossom to inhale its sweetness.

All of a sudden, I feel as if I have inhaled pure venom; my chest constricts with pain that feels like barbed wire in my heart and for a couple of seconds I cannot breathe. It is not the first time I've been flooded with pain over my affair with Kieran. At such moments, I feel the burden of adultery; my own self-image becomes tarnished and blurry; I no longer know who I am, if I am still a good person or an evil intruder in his marriage and a destroyer of two families as well as my own life. I deserved drowning. I was not accused of witchery for no reason.

Despite all rationalizations I invented to justify this love between two people who disobeyed the laws of nature and God, I know God cannot possibly forgive me and that we are, in fact, disobeying his rules. I know I have no right to love this man and be in his life, but I want him so much. I want to run away with him. What would happen to his wife and children if he ran away with me? Perhaps, they would be alright, as his wife is rich and she would find a new husband.

As tears stream down my face under my mask and blind me, a cold foreboding fills my heart. Something is about to happen, something painful, something bad. I am losing him and I feel it in my soul. I no longer know what I want and have a sudden feeling my world has fallen out of joint forever. I never wanted a lover; I just wanted one man to be my true love. And now, the sweetness of love I felt moments ago feels permanently dipped in poison and pain.

Distraught, I step into the gazebo and sit on a stone bench trying to make sense of my feelings. The white gazebo columns are also entwined with white climbing roses and a Grecian statue, representing a woman with a jug of water, stands at its center.

Voices out of nowhere startle me. I look around and see no one. I look up at the gazebo columns and notice tiny lights flicker around the whiteness of roses. The lights multiply and form two circles, and the circles turn into animal and then human heads. My head is spinning and I think it must be the wine making me see these visions and hear these voices. The lights start to circle around my head and I hear whispers but can barely make out the words.

A voice laced with malice is saying it is almost time to pay the price, while another voice, soft and tender, is asking the first voice not to impose its will and not to inflict pain. Now I am certain both the voices and the lights are produced by the effects brought on by the wine. I lean my head back against a column, close my eyes and try to ignore the voices, now speaking faster and even less comprehensibly. Fragments of phrases reach me and they all sound like arrows directed at my heart with their aim to kill me. The soft voice is accusing the malevolent one of malicious mischief and cruelty, but the response is laughter which sounds evil and makes my blood curdle in horror. Something terrible is about to happen to me or someone close to me! Are these the voices of demons that manipulate and dictate our fate, all for their sheer amusement? Does human suffering exist as the gods' entertainment? A feeling of helplessness and resignation washes over me.

When I feel a soft touch brush against my cheek, I open my eyes, but see nothing. The voices and the lights have disappeared and are replaced by laughter reverberating through the garden. It is the guests, and most of them have lanterns in their hands and look as if they are searching for something. A couple, laughing almost hysterically, is passing by the gazebo and I ask them what the chatter is about. The man says the host has just announced he has hidden a gift of precious gems in the garden and whoever finds it can keep it as a souvenir of this special night. The gems are rubies, his wife's favorite stones. Earlier that evening, before the ball started, he had given his wife a three-string necklace of rubies as his anniversary present.

How duplicitous! His mistress is probably among the guests sneering at his wife under her mask. The longer his illicit relationship lasts, the more expensive are the gifts he gives to his wife. And his poor wife may even know, but she cannot protest because she has no power. Most of us wives must obey our husbands, and carry the burden of the fate of being born a woman.

Again I feel fortunate for marrying Aidan, who is kind to me and allows me such freedom. Even tonight, if he has noticed I am no longer inside the castle with the other guests, he will assume I am admiring the gardens in my fervent need to feel close to nature. I never cease being astonished at how he has accepted all my peculiarities. And instead of feeling grateful to the point of kissing his feet, I have given my heart and soul to another man. Regardless of whether the voices I have just heard were wine induced or not, this cannot end well. I should never see Kieran again and I should change my strange ways.

The guests have dispersed all over the garden and I hear them from a distance. I am alone again feeling numb and empty. Just as I plan to look for my husband and ask him to leave this festivity, I see Kieran approach the gazebo. When he sees me, he takes off his hat and mask and hurries toward me. He drops to his knees and hugs me around the waist.

"I was afraid you left, but then I saw your husband and knew you could not have gone. I recognized him easily. A man of that size stands out. I had a feeling something was amiss."

"Something is amiss. Everything is amiss. I have a bad foreboding. I have heard voices predicting terrible things, and my own premonition is telling me something unfortunate is about to happen. I feel we are losing each other. I saw you with that woman…I saw you follow her out."

"Don't start inventing imaginings, Jilleen. Things cannot change between us, from one day to another, from one week to the next."

For a long time we have been so connected we would feel each other's pain even if we were thousands of miles away. But now, my premonition is telling me again I am losing him, something is changing and I cannot stop it. But I allow his touch to assuage my fear, my sorrow, and my doubts, and I take his beloved face in my hands and my eyes drink in his image. He takes off my mask and starts to kiss away my tears. Then he whispers love to me and I feel warmth and joy fill my heart and I am aflame again with deepest love. He takes my hand and whispers, "Let's leave the garden."

We head toward a brook—the boundary between our host's estate and a forest that belongs to no one. Across the brook large stepping stones lead to the other side. I step on the first one not noticing it is covered with wet and slippery moss, and I skid and fall into the water with a big splash. The water is cool and refreshing as the evening is exceptionally warm. I immediately feel Kieran's strong arms pull me up onto the stone. Trying to find my balance I hug him, fearing we both might fall. And then both of us break into a roaring laughter that threatens to throw us into the water. After a few minutes, still heaving from the unexpected amusement, he takes my hand and leads me to the other side. My dress is dripping wet and feels very heavy. Once we cross the brook I stop to take a look at my ruined gown.

Under the starlit sky, there is enough light to see the water has made my dress completely transparent. I stand as if naked, for I look enveloped in an aqua-blue skin. Kieran's gaze is transfixed upon me, igniting me anew with wild desire. He helps me out of my wet dress by carefully and adroitly unlacing its back. Once the dress is on the ground, he takes off his cape and enfolds me in it. The cape smells of him, and I wrap it tightly around me.

In front of us is a huge tree, thousands of years old; its branches are gnarly and its foliage lush and green. The trunk is hollowed out and its opening is large enough for us to squeeze into. The bottom of the cavity is filled with dry leaves which create a soft, rustling cushion. I remove the cape and spread it over the leaves. We lie down and embrace. Kieran glides his fingers through my hair and whispers endearments to me, breaking down all my defenses and enslaving me with his love. As always in such moments, the world around us disappears and we become two primordial humans fused in emotions that make us feel like one body and soul that would bleed to death if separated.

Our kissing becomes vociferous; I start licking and biting him at the same time like an animal in heat. With my tongue, I trace the line of his neck, across his chest, and down toward his navel and abdomen. My bites are probably leaving tiny red marks and welts on his body and I only hope they'll not be detected by his wife. Silvery slivers of moonlight are trickling into the cavity from above, and I wonder how the tree could still be alive with so many lacerations in its trunk. I gaze into Kieran's eyes and read love, devotion, and trust—as well as a desire to keep me in his embrace and his life forever. I kiss his eyes and drink the moonlight off his eyelashes, feeling my consciousness expand and blend with his and with that of the entire world around us.

We raise ourselves to our knees and embrace, never averting our eyes from each other. Our kisses become long, soft and exploratory and our passion that had been like an unstoppable wildfire moments ago is temporarily tamed. I start licking his ears with long sweeps of my tongue and feel him quiver with excitement. We try to relax our breathing and take time making love, postponing our inevitable parting. We make love and after we reach a rapturous culmination we remain in our embrace for what seems like an eternity. And then, as our passion exhales its last breath, he whispers love to me again....

After a few minutes, we get up and clean ourselves as best we can. My dress is drenched and I start shivering. I tell him I shall run into the house and find Lady Tyrone, explain to her I accidentally fell into the brook and ask her to lend me a dress. We kiss and promise to see each other next week once my husband goes hunting. I did know about the hunt when asked at dinner, but wanted to avoid further conversation with that unlikeable man.

I also despise hunting and avoid looking at the dead animals my husband brings home. All that lives has a soul, but I do not dare say that before too many people. I somehow feel I do not belong where I am; I should have been born in a different, perhaps some future time where men are kinder to each other and to animals.

When I approach the house, I see Aidan looking for me. He looks concerned at seeing my appearance, but I explain I walked too far and fell into the brook, and I will ask Lady Tyrone to lend me her clothing.

I go into the house and see Lady Tyrone in a corner looking pensively at the portrait of a beautiful woman. I approach her and when I address her, she looks startled when she hears my voice. I remove my mask and apologize for taking her by surprise. She takes off her mask and the look in her eyes now startles me. Her eyes look dead and dark as if there is not a speck of light and life left in them.

"What is wrong, my lady? It is your anniversary and you should be smiling and laughing and dancing."

"How can I smile and laugh and dance when my husband's slut has soiled my home with her presence? People must be deriding me and laughing behind my back. Now, I hear she is with child, that slut of his. I have endured this for too long. I thought he would get tired of her as he had of his other sluts...and there have been many of them, both servants and ladies. My feelings never mattered; he always told me the other women meant nothing but satisfaction for his rut. But to bring her to our home! That I will not endure!"

I am speechless. I am not able to lie to her and tell her it is not true, that it is only the product of evil and envious tongues spreading poisonous rumors, or that her husband loves her and has gone to great lengths to prepare this fairy tale-like celebration in her honor. I just look at her in silence.

All of a sudden her eyes become alive and an inner fire lights them. What I see in her eyes frightens me with its intensity. There is a gleam of resolution mixed with madness.

"I shall not be humiliated like this in my own home." She leaves me, running from the room, while I stand shivering from shock and cold.

I hurry after her, not knowing why I am following her into the gardens.

Laughter and sounds of reveling are heard from all over the gardens. A group of people is standing by a rosebush with glasses and goblets of wine in their hands. Some seem to be very drunk. I can see them swaying from side to side. Among them is Morgana, Lord Tyrone's lover, laughing and shaking her golden tresses. She has taken her mask off and looks lovely in her crimson dress with deep cleavage.

Lady Tyrone reaches the group. Before anyone can react or even acknowledge her presence fully, she produces a long dagger from her bosom, and stabs Morgana in the chest with a scream like sounds coming from the depths of hell!

There are more screams everywhere as Morgana falls to the ground. Blood spurts from her, but Lady Tyrone is still not done. In raging fury, madness and jealousy she is lying over Morgana, continuing to stab her.

Someone finally pulls her away and she screams and stabs him. Two more men try to restrain her and one of them manages to pry the dagger from her hand. She shouts, and kicks, and her screams reverberate in the night.

I feel so sick, I suddenly vomit. More screams erupt around me and I'm dizzy. A hand grabs me and arms lift me up and carry me away. I do not even recognize my husband until we reach our coach. Once Aidan puts me on the back seat, he wraps me in the woolen shawl I had left on the seat. He also removes his coat and wraps it around me. I tremble and shiver and start crying, utterly distraught.

The next few days I spend in bed delirious with fever. The fever breaks on the fifth day and I leave the bedroom disoriented. I believe God has forsaken me because I have broken his every law. I see sinfulness everywhere...my own sin...Lord Tyrone's sin...his wife's sin.

I ask the servants to tell me what had happened while I lay sick in bed and they tell me Morgana was buried two days ago, and Lady Tyrone has disappeared. My assumption is her husband has hidden her away so she may go unpunished for murder. Everyone else would be executed in public, but he is powerful enough to protect his wife. I should have expected him to go mad with pain over losing Morgana, but perhaps he did not love her that much, after all. I ask about my own husband and am told he will be back the next day.

I decide to spend the next few weeks with my son because I have been neglecting him.

When I wake next morning, I feel sick again. And then I understand...I am with child, but whose is it? My husband wants another son, but he may get my lover's son or—oh my God; I shudder in horror remembering that Faolán could also be this baby's father. I am frightened, but I am also excited and wish the child to be Kieran's because I want a child with him. Until I see the baby, I will not know who the father is, maybe not even then. How can I tell Kieran? Will he still want me? I cannot reveal what I did with Faolán because he would think I betrayed him.

The next few days I vomit almost every hour. My servants are attentive, and happy at the same time, because they have been wondering why for the past seven years there has only been one child. My husband is pleased and already talking about having another son to take hunting with him. I would like a daughter who will be my friend and confidante.

I do not dare tell Kieran the child may be his. I see him rarely now the weather has turned cold. We have met a few times but did not stay long together for fear of being discovered. He seems to be especially afraid of his wife finding out about us. She has inherited a very large estate from her grandparents and seems to be the one governing it, and making decisions which in most households are reserved for men. Even through the mist of my infatuation, I recognize a weakness in Kieran. He is not the type of man who would risk his pleasant life for love. But why am I saying that about him when I also would not leave the comfort of my life and risk rejection from the society I move in.

Everyone has apologized to me for my being arrested as a witch. They all have been saying it was a case of mistaken identity and the real witch has been captured and executed. I have not heard from Faolán, and have had fears he was the one behind my capture so he could save me and use me for his pleasure.

My days stretch out before me endlessly. As a pastime I get a tutor to teach me how to play the harp. The simple melodies I try to play have a soothing effect on me. I also read and embroider and make little clothes for my baby. My son keeps me company often and we read and write together. My husband and I want to send him to schools so he can become a learned man. I always fear another war will break out and I could lose my family.

I also fear the horrible disease that, a few years ago decimated the whole region, might return. At that time, everything turned into blood and rotting bodies in a matter of days. My husband took me to a faraway village where he has some relatives living in a house on the top of a hill. He did not allow me to leave for three months until the red death had run its course. I never thought life could go back to what it had been, but slowly it returned to our province and little by little the dead were grieved and some were forgotten. I lost my best friend, Fiona, and I still cry thinking about her. She was like a sister to me, my confidante; a young woman with a laugh that bubbled like a spring well. I touch my cheeks and feel the wet trail tears have left. How could God have taken away such a sweet soul? I hear myself sigh.

Over the next few months my belly grows very big, much bigger than with my first child. Kieran sends me a message that he needs to see me and I have no choice but to show myself and reveal my state. I am afraid he will never want to see me again; I am afraid of his fear when he realizes the child might be his and people might recognize him in the child's features. All of a sudden I am angry. What did I expect? That he would abduct me and run away with me and love me until the end of our days?

I meet him on a cool and sunny day on the hill leading down to the lake where we have met many times before. At first, he does not notice my belly hidden under a thick cape, but once he does his eyes widen in surprise and a shadow of unease crosses his face.

"Yes, I am with child and no, I have no way of knowing whose child it is. If it is yours, my husband will not know and will love it as his own."

Kieran blushes and is speechless. I can see how ill at ease he is, and anger chokes my throat again.

"I want nothing from you." Rage cracks my voice and adds a chilling tone to it.

"Please, do not be angry. I am just...I am just...I did not think." Strong emotion reveals a slight stutter in his voice that under ordinary conditions is not perceptible.

"People who make love make babies."

"I know, I just did not think it would happen." He sighs and adds, "This is such unfortunate timing because I wanted to...I wanted us to talk and perhaps...we should, I think agree we should stop seeing each other. I am finding it hard to cope with a parallel life. When I am with you I reach such heights of ecstasy and then must go back home to my dismal and empty life with my wife. I cannot live like that anymore. I know I may sound like a coward, but we are both risking too much. The circumstances are impossible, you must see that."

His eyes are welling up with tears, and my heart with fury, disappointment, pain...the cocktail of violent emotions is making me feel sick, and I look at him incredulously and no longer see a tender and passionate lover, but a cheat, a coward, a fractured soul incapable of true love.

He puts his arms around me, but I am stiff and tense and angry at myself, him, God, the world, life, my position that does not allow me to live the life I want, but instead one of enslavement within the confines of the existence I was somehow forced to choose. I can no longer make sense of this. How do other women tolerate their lives when they are not even spoiled like I am, when they have to fight to survive? How can I be unhappy in a home filled with wealth and abundance, in a home where I sleep in a soft, warm bed and am waited on hand and foot?

A part of me also recognizes this is the first time when Kieran and I meet and I do not feel his desire for me. A knowing fills me suddenly; a knowing not based on any fact, but still the truth of that knowing is irrefutable, because it is the voice coming from the depths of my soul. The woman from the ball is replacing me in his heart. Again, I wonder if I must be inventing all of it.

"Kieran, are you now leaving me for another lover?"

"How can you even think something like that? Of course I am not." His voice has a shiver in it, which awakens waves of frosty frisson in me, because I sense a lie from his lips for the first time.

Impulsively, I turn around and run back to my home never looking back, never wanting to see him again. The man I loved with the fieriest of all ardors and passions, with every fiber in my body, looks like a stranger whose heart is shackled in frost. My own heart feels pierced and lacerated by a thousand daggers.

I think I hear him call my name, but I do not stop running. When I reach the gate of my house, I am panting with exhaustion. At the moment I reach the staircase leading to my room, a sharp pain shoots through me like a bolt of lightning and I scream. At the same time I feel warmth trail down my legs and I realize it is blood, and I have lost not only my lover, but am also losing my baby. My own life may flow out of me with my blood and my child and only God can save me, if he is so disposed to save sinners.

My servant, Aibrean, also screams when she finds me on the floor. Soon, there are bustling hands around me, and someone carries me up to my bedroom. I hear someone exclaim, "Go fetch Caoilainn."

Caoilainn is the best midwife in the whole region, and I know I will be safe again once she comes. Many a woman has lost her baby like this and I know of no one who has bled and brought a healthy infant to the world. My thoughts are a web of confusion laced with fear, and a premonition the time has come for me to leave this world. Perhaps this is the final punishment for the sin I committed, for being unfaithful to a good, loving man. I should have drowned in the river and let the water wash away my sins.

My pains are agonizing and my screams reverberate against the house walls. I feel as if I am being ripped apart, as if the baby or the pieces of it are trying to come out, but cannot. I am mad with pain and hardly notice Caoilainn is with me massaging my stomach and inserting her hand in my womb trying to pry out its contents. She is rubbing herbs on me and inside me, but I feel I am rupturing and bleeding more and more heavily. I lose consciousness and when I come around again, through a thick veil I see and hear people crying.

From above I am watching my own body, drained of all life, lying on a bed painted with the crimson color of blood. My servants are kneeling and praying for my deliverance. I hear myself whisper my son's name with infinite sadness and the guilt of having to leave him, of having to abandon him due to the wrong choices I have made. I am enveloped in sudden blackness, and then in that blackness I see an opening, inviting me. I am moving toward it, and it becomes wider and wider, and filled with the most soothing white light, infused with love so warm and comforting that the feeling translates into one last thought: How can there be so much love in one place? I am drawn toward this light irresistibly, but a wild moan makes me look back.

My husband has just entered the room and is kneeling beside the bed weeping, sobbing and shaking and kissing my cold hand. Through Aidan's sobs, I hear the words, "My love, my only love, my wife, the soul of my soul, the heart of my heart."

I cannot leave the world in which I am loved so much, loved with so much honesty, with so much devotion. I look toward the light again and a see a woman smile at me. I know it is my grandmother, even though as an abandoned child I had never met her. I ask her if she will take me with her into the love and light, and she replies without speaking. My time has not come yet, the closeness of death is to show me the truth. I ask what truth, and she disappears before I have an answer.

"God has heard my prayers; God has given you back to me." I hear my husband's voice and feel his hot tears fall on my dress and mingle with the blood stains.

"The baby?" I whisper in the weakest of voices. My husband kisses me and his hot tears fall on my chest.

"There will be more babies. You will get well and there will be more babies."

I am too weak to cry. My chest heaves in pain and then darkness envelops me.

* * * *

Leandra

"Leandra, are you all right?"

I open my eyes not knowing where I am or who I am.

"Who am I?"

"Have a glass of water. This was a very long session; you must be exhausted."

I become aware of my body and identity. It feels as if my spirit left my body and is just returning, disoriented and without knowledge where its home is.

"David, I remember…he betrayed me. I know it." And I break down in tears and feel a disappointment the depth of which cannot be measured. When I come to myself, I realize David has not spoken at all. I now hear his soft voice.

"You were under hypnosis for two hours, and you revealed your disappointment and your near-death experience."

"What else did I say?"

He tells me the story of my own brush with death at an unspecified time in the past. And I remember most of it.

"David, what language do I speak when I am under hypnosis, and can you recognize from its inflection where exactly I could have lived?"

"Rarely do people speak in the language of their past life; they usually use their present-day language to describe events; however, some of the words you used you probably wouldn't say in this life going about your daily business. Under hypnosis, your accent and intonation do sound different from your normal accent."

I feel exhausted, but most of all I feel a nagging pain of disappointment in my heart. Kieran was not the man I believed he was. He left me, let me down, and betrayed me. Perhaps, Weylin is also not the person I think he is. The feelings of disappointment are replaced by deep resignation and emptiness. I feel like a leaf carried by the current of life, and I cannot fight or reverse the direction in which it takes me. Through these hypnosis sessions I have somehow experienced a catharsis and the fog in my head has cleared.

"David, I am recovering from the affair—it was just an affair anyway, regardless of the past lives and the fact we may have had a soul-to-soul connection at some point. Right now, I am ready to go to bed. Thank you for your time."

"It is almost midnight, and high time for me to take my leave. Thank you for the most scrumptious dinner. Your cooking skills quite possibly exceed your medical competence." David smiles warmly and hugs me, and again I feel the comfort of friendship swell up in me and I kiss him on the cheek.

After he leaves, I go to bed expecting to have vivid dreams of perhaps another past life, but I sink into a dark well of unconsciousness brought on by mental and physical exhaustion.

A lick on my face wakes me up and it's the cat wanting to be fed. I look at the clock and see it's seven in the morning. I get up, feed the cat and make coffee. I plan to spend the morning with my mother-in-law and relieve Adrian. My in-laws had a long and happy marriage, but I never asked Agatha, my mother-in-law, too many details on their life together. Ever since Adrian's dad Gregory died, I have been worried about Agatha's mental health as she has claimed Gregory's ghost appears in her bedroom at night, he strokes her hair and tells her not to grieve and to be happy because she is surrounded by love. Because she strongly believes he visits her regularly, she dismisses any suggestion to sell their seven-bedroom mansion and move into a smaller house or a large apartment. She fears he would not know how to find her again, and she wants to be sure that when it is her time to go, he leads her to wherever he is so they can be joined in eternity. I told Adrian at one point his mother might be having hallucinations and grief may have affected her mental health. Now, in light of my regression experiences, I realize I can no longer find a rational and scientific explanation for every phenomenon in the world. There is mystery and magic in the world.

I pull on a pair of jeans and a white long-sleeved T-shirt before I leave the house. Agatha lives two streets down from us, so it's convenient for us to keep an eye on her and visit her regularly. I have a key to the house so I let myself in. Adrian is in the kitchen drinking coffee. He looks pale and disheveled because he never sleeps well when here. I believe the thought of his dad roaming the rooms unsettles him.

"I needn't even ask you how you slept. You look tired."

Adrian sighs and doesn't reply immediately. I approach him and hug him and we embrace for a minute or so as if drawing energy from each other.

"She and I stayed up and talked about Dad. She told me she'd seen him the night before and he said he would soon come for her. That upset me even though I know there's no truth in it. She's still healthy enough."

We disengage and sit at the table.

"How did she react to what your dad told her?"

"Oh, she took it like someone would take good news. She actually looked flushed and sounded a bit excited, like a girl anticipating her first date. Morbid, if you ask me." He gets up and refills his coffee cup. He fills one for me, too, and we sip the morning brew in silence.

"Is she still in bed?"

"I heard her get up and I believe she's in the shower. I'm gonna head home and catch a few hours of sleep. I'm beat and can't stand the thought of listening to more of her ramblings. And she used to be so sane and down to earth, a no-nonsense woman."

Adrian shakes his head as he rinses his mug, wipes it dry with a paper towel and puts it back in the cupboard. The cupboard filled with beautiful and expensive mugs Agatha and Greg collected during their numerous travels together. Adrian leaves and I go upstairs and knock on Agatha's door.

When I open the door, I find her sitting at her writing desk. It's an expensive antique, a Louis XV piece shipped from Europe. Agatha is wearing a pale pink bathrobe that makes her seem even more fragile than she is. Her hair, which still has some streaks of black, is tied in a low ponytail. She turns around and the gaze of her blue eyes is piercing. A warm smile lights up her face.

"So glad to see you, Lea! Make yourself comfortable, dear. Have you had coffee and breakfast?"

"Yes, Aggie, I have. How are you feeling?"

"Very well. Much better than last week. Did Adrian tell you Greg was here last night?" There is a strange glint in her eyes.

"Yes, he did. So he still shows up regularly?"

"Almost daily. I told him I wanted to see him every day. It is because of me he's stayed earthbound. I haven't been able to let go of him after all these years. If I am to release him from this dimension, I have to go with him, and he knows that. Very soon he'll come to take me." She is looking at me with great intensity and I recognize a pleading in her expression. "You have to promise me, once I'm gone, you'll explain to Adrian he needs not grieve, as his parents are reunited in eternal love. You probably think I'm a crazy old bat, but Lea, never doubt the mysterious in life."

"I've changed in that respect and I'm no longer as close-minded as I used to be. A colleague who uses hypnotherapy in his treatment has convinced me there certainly is much more in this world than meets the eye; we just need to be willing to pull back the veil, as they say. What's that book you're reading?"

She's holding in her hands a leather-bound book that looks a bit frayed. I notice a little golden lock on its side.

"It's my diary. I started to write in it when I met Greg. Before you came into the room, I planned to destroy it, but now I've changed my mind. I'm giving it to you, but you have to promise me never to let Adrian read it. Children never see their parents as lovers or as sexual beings, and it should stay that way. But I want you to read the story of Greg and me, and keep the memory of us alive. At one point I wanted to write a book about us, but never trusted my talent for written expression. You'll probably be astonished, perhaps even shocked by my explicitness, but Greg awoke in me a volcanic passion I couldn't have imagined before then. You know, the type of passion you think is so exaggerated you only find it in fiction and sappy movies. But believe me, Lea, a passion of such magnitude is quite real."

"I've no problem believing that, Aggie."

She looks at me quizzically, but says nothing for a few minutes. If only she knew. But perhaps she'd understand if I told her my secret even though it was her son I betrayed.

When she speaks again, her voice grows feeble as the memories of the love she lost are flooding her mind. Now, I'm curious to hear their story. It seems to be one of unwavering lifelong love. I wonder why I never asked her to tell me how she met Greg. I also question why my daughters have never asked me and Adrian about our love story.

"How did the two of you meet?"

"We met on a dig in Greece. You already know Greg inherited a lot of money from his parents so he was able to pursue a career in archaeology; never lucrative, by any stretch of the imagination. Archaeology was his passion, and you should have seen his face when I first met him; you should have seen the glow in his eyes as he was explaining to a group of us post-grads the origin of a gold coin we'd dug up. At that time, he was an associate professor and he was only twenty-nine years old. What you don't know is, he was engaged to be married to a young doctor; that's something I always felt bad about, being the cause of their breakup."

She stops and takes a sip of tea from a dainty floral-patterned porcelain cup. Just as she loved archaeology, she has always loved everything ancient and her house is furnished with the elegance and opulence of an era gone by. For my taste, it is too cluttered with the countless artifacts she and Greg collected over the years. I often wonder what Adrian and I will do with all of it after she passes away. To auction off their memories seems sacrilegious, but I can't imagine myself living surrounded by so many objects, regardless of their monetary or sentimental value.

"Before I met Greg, I'd had a few relationships, but nothing serious. The last one was a year-long relationship—very bumpy because we had lots of fights and disagreements, mostly due to his jealousy. Our breakups and make-ups alike were tumultuous, but fortunately, after about a year, we both lost the desire to continue trying. Our split up was not dramatic, even though I can't say it was very amicable either. Very soon he had a new girlfriend. Seeing them together meant nothing to me, except relief he'd moved on."

"Did you feel attracted to Greg the first time you met him?"

"I never knew you could feel not only instantaneous physical attraction, but also a soul connection, like two souls set ablaze the moment their gazes lock. It's hard to explain. I hope you experienced something similar when you met my son." Again, she gives me a quizzical look as if she's sensing something.

I say nothing. How can I tell her that what she's describing I experienced with her son, but also with a man who seems to have followed me through several incarnations in order to awaken in me a passion of an intensity words cannot capture. I just smile and remain silent, nodding to show her I want her to continue.

"For the first few days, I was avoiding Greg because his presence made me feel insecure and highly vulnerable. He didn't pursue me, but whenever he would look at me, I would detect curiosity and probing in his look. One day, as I was working in extreme heat, a shadow made me lift my eyes, and I saw Greg lower himself beside me with a trowel in his hand. He smiled and said hello and started to dig. Feeling his presence so near me was disconcerting. It was like an electric field forming between us—I could almost see the sparks flying. We both stopped working and looked at each other. And he simply said it was high time we spent some time together and got to know each other, because pretending nothing was happening between us was not working; denying the magnetic pull between us served neither of us.

"My first instinct was to tell him that was totally preposterous and presumptuous, and he was misreading me, but instead I agreed, and suggested we go alone that evening to the tavern in the village, where we were accommodated, and could talk. And it was always like that between us. Honesty and openness and a complete sharing of thoughts and feelings with no holds barred. After we spent hours talking that evening, I decided to do something I also had never dreamed of doing. I spent that night with him, lost in the bliss of indescribable passion.

"What put a damper on my feelings of a newly discovered ecstasy was his revelation he'd just cheated on his fiancée with me. He said he was engaged to be married in six months. Caroline was smart and sweet and he loved her, but more like you would love a friend than a lover. They were compatible, but there was never any great passion between them. In the depths of his soul he'd always felt a tug, a yearning for something more, something powerful, but he never knew what was missing in his life until he met me."

"How did you feel, falling in love with someone who was cheating on someone else?"

"I felt so much in love, I thought I'd never recover if I lost him. My spirit was screaming I'd met my twin. I felt as if I'd known him forever. Everything about him was new and familiar at the same time. It's difficult to explain…"

Again I thought how easily I could relate to what she was telling me and felt tempted to confide in her, but knew I wouldn't. Were there really so many similar love stories, stories of soul recognition and passionate ignition?

"What happened next?" I ask, and she continues.

"He was scheduled to go back home the next day, but he changed his flight in order for us to spend a weekend together. He couldn't stay longer, because he had to attend a meeting during which he'd present our findings in Greece and based on that, he expected to receive a grant to support the project for at least another year. So we decided to go to a small island, and not tell the rest of the crew we'd be together. We didn't want anyone to know about our relationship. He promised he'd break off his engagement once he got back home, but would still like to keep this under wraps. He decided to keep me a secret in order not to hurt Caroline even more by telling her he was replacing her with someone else.

"I was just horrified at the thought of what his Caroline would have to endure, what painful truth she was about to discover, what I was doing to another woman. I was shattering someone's wedding dreams. Luckily, she hadn't bought a gown, they weren't living together because he travelled a lot, and she was busy building her clientele. There was just no turning back for either of us. The moment we met was the moment our life course changed."

Aggie sighs and takes another sip of her tea that by now must have gone cold. I am in awe of the power of her memory. It seems she hasn't forgotten even one detail of the time she first met Greg. I'm also so glad I decided to ask her to tell me about their life. She could have died and this beautiful love story would have been buried with her. Now I want her to tell me all about her life with Greg and especially how they managed to sustain a lifelong love for each other. She picks up the story again.

"At first, I told Greg to take his time breaking the news to Caroline, but I realized I didn't mean what I said, and asked him to do it as soon as he arrived back home. I wanted him to do it as soon as possible because I was afraid if he prolonged it for too long, he might forget about me. He may even discover he mistook sexual attraction for love and I wasn't worth his losing a life which held so much promise, for one still full of so many unknowns."

"What did he plan to tell her?"

"He said he'd tell her the half-truth; he wasn't ready to settle down and he wanted to work on the dig in Greece for another year, which would mean being separated from her for too long."

"How did you spend those three days?"

Aggie turns around and takes her diary from the table. She flips through the pages back and forth until she finds what she's looking for, and hands me the open book. "I'm going to take a shower now and dress, and I want us to go out for coffee and cake. He may come to get me any day now, but before I leave, I want to indulge in a few more earthly pleasures, such as the chestnut cream torte at 'Star-eyed Lucienne.'

"Isn't that a strange name for a pastry shop? But once you meet Lucienne, you understand. Anyway, on these pages I captured those three unforgettable days spent with Greg in Greece." She laughs wryly before continuing. "I started keeping a diary after I returned from Greece. I was afraid to lose those memories of me and Greg, and I recorded everything until Adrian was born. That was my way of freezing so many important frames of my life. But, I warn you again. Some of it is very explicit. I never thought anyone would read it, and intended destroying it before I died."

"Don't worry, Aggie. I can handle explicit, and explicit." We both laugh and exchange conspiratorial looks of two women of two different generations sharing so much, so unexpectedly.

She gets up from the chair with some difficulty and goes into the bathroom.

I look at the first page and admire her neat handwriting. It is almost calligraphic in its perfection. Mine's so awful I can't decipher my own notes, so I always type them. I'm eager to read her account of the three days they spent in Greece alone, and I'm even more eager to learn about the chapter of their life following the Greek episode. I start reading with a pounding heart that feels connected to all the hearts that have loved with a mad passion.

* * * *

154

Aggie's story

We reached our destination by ferry. When we arrived, it was already evening, but in spite of having travelled for nine hours neither of us felt tired. As soon as we found the first house that displayed a sign, in German and English, that they had available rooms, we rented one, showered and changed and went out to find a restaurant where we could have dinner and celebrate our little escapade. We were as excited as children stealing apples from an orchard; we walked holding hands and stopping every minute to kiss. I was puzzled at how easy it was to say 'I love you' to a man who was a complete stranger to me a few days ago.

...

A waiter led us to a small table with two chairs and we immediately ordered wine. I wanted to drink wine, drink in moonlight, revel in the heat of that night. I wanted to drink in Greg's gaze that was constantly seducing me, undressing me, making love to me, taking my breath away and making me gasp with wild desire.

Warmed by the wine and the heat of the summer night we began to move to the music. The sea beyond the white stone terrace was shimmering under the silvery moon glow. The air was saturated with the chirping of crickets, the scent of sea brine, Mediterranean grasses, and pine tree sap. A live band was playing instrumental music

...

My arms were wrapped around Greg's neck and his arms were clasping my waist. Our bodies were enmeshed, and in our white clothes, we might have looked like one body swaying in the light summer breeze.

I felt lightheaded, more from the love than inebriation; He was so close and I inhaled his scent; he felt like an extension of me, or like a missing piece in the puzzle called life that at that moment was complete, and which I hoped would stay complete for the rest of our lives.

I decided to allow myself the joy of believing nothing would plow us asunder, and we would never say goodbye, not even for a short while. I was already planning to join him on upcoming digging expeditions, to follow him around the world.

I lifted my head so my gaze could meet his and saw starlight glittering in his grey-blue eyes. We kissed, swaying slowly to the music. His hands were moving up and down my back

He pressed his body harder into mine and I clearly felt his arousal. The sexual attraction between us was as powerful as a hurricane, and as irresistible as the pull of a black hole. I had to ask myself if I was certain that what glued us together was love and not just a dizzying physical infatuation which would fade after a couple of years.

As I let out a stifled gasp of sexual desire, he whispered words of lust in my ear, making my blood froth and churn, and my breath raspy. During such moments over the last couple of days, I would start to feel faint and I was afraid I might pass out from this extreme excitement.

Suddenly, I knew what I wanted to do, even though it made little sense at … almost nine o'clock. "Let's pay and leave! Let's go to the lighthouse and climb up to the lantern room," I suggested. In the travel guide I'd read there was a legend surrounding the lighthouse, that this now-abandoned building was haunted by the ghosts of two secret lovers whose ill-fated love affair ended tragically. All the keepers and tourists who had stayed in it after it had been converted into an inn, abandoned it after many of them claimed to have seen ghosts.

"I thought you wanted to see it in the daylight when it wouldn't be spooky," Greg said.

"I want to see it in the moonlight, and I want to climb with you all the way up to the gallery, and to kiss moon rays off your lips." He smiled at the exuberance of my words.

We found ourselves on the boardwalk and walked slowly toward the lighthouse, which we still could not see as a grove of trees hid it from view. In the daylight it looked quite imposing, perched on a towering bluff into which steps had been chiseled to allow access to it.

"Have you had a chance to read about the mysterious history of the lighthouse?" he asked me, wrapping his arm around my shoulders, pulling me towards him. I wrapped my arm around his waist, leaned into him and kissed his cheek.

"I read all about it last night after you fell asleep. Isn't it interesting how lovemaking drains you, yet seems to reenergize me?" I giggled. "Anyway, this is what I read:

'Years ago, a young man came from the mainland looking for work. The town and the island had just lost its previous light-keeper. An old man, he'd lived in the lighthouse for at least sixty-five years. His health had been good until he caught a terrible cold which developed into pneumonia. The town folk tended to him; women brought him food and kept his fire going, but nothing helped. His condition deteriorated until he died one night in his sleep.

Five days after his burial, a young man showed up and was offered the job. His name was Florian, and he kept to himself. All the girls were casting glances at him hoping he would invite them to dance, but he only had eyes for Karessa, the vineyard owner's wife. She was beautiful, with curly brown hair and azure-blue eyes. She was vivacious and gregarious with an ever-present smile on her lips.

Unlike most other women in that small town, Karessa loved to roam the beaches, climb the cliffs, pick wildflowers, and most of all paint the seascape. A small souvenir shop exhibited her paintings, and tourists, who at that time did not come in droves, bought them readily even though they were not inexpensive. After a few years, she was making enough money to become financially independent.

People say Florian met Karessa on a cliff or at the beach while she was painting or aimlessly roaming. Allegedly, Florian is depicted in one of her paintings, sitting on a rock, his hair flowing in the wind, his gaze cast somewhere beyond the horizon.

A group of children discovered them one day, naked on the stone floor of the lighthouse gallery, enraptured in lovemaking and oblivious to the world around them. Word spread like fire, and the scandal rocked the town. People feared Dominic, known for his volatile temper, would kill both of them.

But he did worse; he locked her up in the house and wouldn't allow her to receive visitors or go outside the house. He destroyed her canvasses, her easel and brushes, and threw out her paints. His servants kept the town folk informed of her condition, which deteriorated by the day. According to servant gossip, she was losing her mind and becoming a mad woman, exhibiting fits of uncontrollable rage as if possessed by demons. One night, she broke a window and escaped.

The next morning, her broken body, and that of her lover, was found in the shoals beneath the bluff. They had jumped together to their death.

Over the next few years, several light-keepers were hired, but soon left, swearing they'd seen the lovers' ghosts roaming the lighthouse in search of each other. When their spirits would meet, happy laughter resonated within the walls. On other occasions, her inconsolable wails would send the light-keepers fleeing into the night, not returning to their quarters before dawn the next day.'"

"What a terrible story, but most probably some legend this town invented to attract more tourists. Haunted places never cease to intrigue people," he told me.

We reached the steps and I looked up. The climb was steep, and the sea waves, frothing at their crests, were crashing against the bluff. For a moment, I was gripped with fear of slipping and falling, or worse, of Greg falling and disappearing in the sea. The thought sent shivers down my spine and I tried to chase it away. He held my hand and asked me to step carefully as the stone staircase was partially wet with the rising tide sprinkling it incessantly. The moonlight was so intense that night every step was sharply delineated, and the lighthouse shone as a towering pillar of brightness against the dark backdrop of cypresses and pine trees. We finally reached the entrance, and for a moment I dreaded the door might be locked and we'd have to turn back. Climbing back down those wet steps filled terrified me.

The door creaked open, and a warm and musty darkness enveloped us. Through a window on the right, pale moonlight was shining over a narrow cast-iron staircase. We negotiated the steps, holding the rickety railing tightly, never looking down. After what seemed longer than twenty minutes, we emerged, out of breath, onto the gallery.

We moved close to the edge of the platform and leaned against the stone wall encircling it. I put my arms around Greg's neck. We kissed gently at first, and then I licked and bit on his lower lip rapaciously, and our tongues rushed toward each other and our breaths mingled their warmth. My desire for him was instantaneously reignited and my breaths started sounding feverish. His kisses were drugging me, transporting me to an unearthly place where dreams were born in their full splendor; they seemed to have a hallucinogenic effect because I felt I was floating toward the stars. He unzipped my white linen trousers, and I stepped out of them. He spread them over the wall, and I lay on my back across them, now feeling no fear of heights, and unaware the drop was staggering, with me lying two hundred feet above the ground on a wall which could crumble at any moment, hurtling me to death.

Greg raised my legs and wrapped them around his waist. He lowered himself and kissed me again. Then he removed his white shirt while I watched him, hypnotized, in disbelief of what we were doing in such a place. But, how I loved him! His gaze was boring into me; I felt weak from wanting him, and I wanted him inside me, and at the same time I wanted to prolong our lovemaking into eternity, lamenting silently these precious moments would fly by all too swiftly on the wings of implacable time. I knew I could get pregnant and perhaps, I might have even desired it. We never discussed protection and made love with utter abandon.

In the position I was, feeling the hard surface under my back, I could not do much, I could not move freely. Greg unbuckled his belt, pulled it out of its loops and passed the belt tip slowly across my lips, and then across my nipples making them swell and lengthen under the white, braless top, and finally down my stomach before he dropped it by his feet. I could not wait for his touch. I was feeling hot and feverish, embracing and caressing him lovingly, with my gaze on his naked, slim and sinewy body.

"I want you inside me," I sighed, but I knew he would take his time and subject me to sweet torment before he plunged into me. When he lay on top of me, I felt his tongue in my mouth, and that erotic taste made my head swim even more; once again I was plunged into disbelief of how deeply connected we had become.

My back was now chafing from the hard stone surface and I stood and pressed my body into his. He pulled me down onto his jeans on the concrete floor and we made breathless love. After our lovemaking subsided, we remained in our embrace for a long time. When I looked at him, we burst into laughter, incredulous of what we'd just done.

I felt tired and ready for bed, yet at the same time I wasn't looking forward to climbing down that treacherous staircase then the wet outer steps. We sat up naked on his pants. The starry night was warm and bedazzling in its magical beauty. I felt we were alone on a different planet and wished we could stay there much longer than a few days. Perhaps we should stay here all night and watch the sunrise, I thought. It must be a spectacular sight to behold from this vantage point. I kissed his temple and whispered into his ear I loved him with all I had in me. He whispered back how much he also loved me.

I must have fallen asleep and dreamed, for somehow I saw two figures dancing on the very wall on which I had lain. I wanted to call and warn them of the danger, but one of them turned toward me. I saw a beautiful face with sparkling blue eyes and rose-colored lips, looking at me. I tried to interpret the look: curiosity tinted with pity? Compassion? Or was it derision, disdain?

I wasn't sure until I felt her hand touch my cheek lovingly, and saw her eyes and lips smile knowingly. I knew who she was and heard myself say, internally, "Karessa, what is to become of us?" I was filled with sudden worry and dread of the future thinking Greg might decide to go back to his fiancée. Sparkles suddenly lit her eyes and in a voice full of love, she whispered, "Always treasure the moment, as that is all we are ever given, all we can ever hope for." She was looking at me intently as if reading my thoughts.

"Do not worry. You are a fortunate woman, because his heart is deep and his love is not the fast-burning lust which shatters dreams, poisons trust, and beguiles only to destroy. You have found your true love and…." The apparition disappeared before she finished, and I woke in the middle of the night disoriented, but filled with hopes of gold.

* * * *

I close Aggie's diary feeling connected to her more than ever. Her diary entry is my story and the story of every woman who has ever loved. We all lose in the end. I lost Weylin to circumstances that seemed to be insurmountable, Aggie lost Greg to death. Whatever we gain, we inevitably lose. I also feel privileged she would share something as intimate as this with me. My mother-in-law trusts me enough to leave her diary with me. I'm moved to tears. At that moment she comes out of the bathroom and enters her huge walk-in closet to dress. Just as I plan to read more of her diary confessions, she emerges from her closet wearing a pale pink two-piece pant suit. She has always worn the same size since she turned twenty. All her life she's walked and swum, and never overindulged in food. I've always admired such discipline and remember her telling me once jokingly she always wanted Greg to find her attractive.

I put the diary in my purse and she and I leave the house. When we are in the car, she asks me if I read her diary entry and if her explicit description of their lovemaking in the lighthouse shocked me.

"Aggie, nothing shocks me anymore. Your description was beautifully erotic and not explicit. Only a woman who is deeply in love can give herself with so much trust and abandon to a man. You obviously gave him your body and soul. Lovemaking that is erotic and soulful at the same time is the pinnacle of earthly and heavenly bliss. Thank you for sharing that with me."

She smiles and does not speak until we come to the pastry shop. Once we are seated, I ask her to tell me how long it took Greg to break the news to Caroline and how Caroline reacted.

"It took him two months and those two months were the worst time of my life because I could not stop fearing that in the end he would leave me and recommit to her. I was living in Montreal at the time, and he was in Toronto. We spoke on the phone every day. Our love was burning bright, but at the same time he was going through hell. He could not bring himself to tell Caroline the truth, so he'd started the process of detaching himself from her by telling her he'd been given a new grant which would support his archeological exploration in Greece for another year."

"She must have been disappointed to hear that."

"She told him she couldn't possibly leave her new practice to join him in Greece, but she'd be able to make a couple of trips that year. He told her he wouldn't want her to sacrifice her work and leave her patients. And then he started to find excuses to see her less and less, claiming he was overwhelmed with paperwork linked to the grant and putting together a team. He was not really lying about the amount of work, but he started to avoid her. When he was with her he would say he was tired, and then he'd start to mope and gradually a man who was witty and charming turned into a bore and someone who seemed depressed. He told me he despised himself for being a coward and not telling her the truth, but instead behaving like the biggest jerk, just so she'd get fed up with him and break off the engagement."

"Isn't it despicable when men do that when they want to leave a woman? They change their behavior so women have no choice but to break up. And they think women feel better when it's them who pull the plug."

"That's precisely what he was doing," replies Aggie. "He refused to go out, to see her family, would not talk about the wedding, would not make love to her. Caroline was a nice girl, but she was also proud and temperamental and at times short-fused. So one evening when she found him as usual moping, she blew a fuse and threw the engagement ring in his face and just stormed out of his apartment cursing him forever. And that was it. He was relieved, but also disappointed in himself. His self-loathing stemmed from the knowledge he could stoop so low and act so reprehensibly. He was hoping that one day she would find the right man and he would have a chance to apologize to her."

"Their break-up must have created a scandal among their friends and family?"

"It did, and he told everyone he was buckling under the stress from work, and not ready to settle down, and she was right to ditch him. He then went into overdrive painting himself black and telling everyone it was best for Caroline to get out of the relationship before it was too late. A few friends severed all ties with him. Caroline's mother cried but said she forgave him and assured him her daughter would find happiness eventually. Greg's parents were devastated; his dad screamed at him and told him he was losing an extraordinary girl to pursue a worthless career. Greg felt so guilty he just kept silent and withdrew from everyone.

"He was so distressed he avoided our phone conversations. All of that caused me a great deal of suffering, but most of all I was terrified I would lose him because in my heart, it had to be him or no one."

Aggie stops to take a few sips of coffee and to finish her cake.

"Luckily, all ended well. Four months later as Greg and I were getting ready to leave for Greece, because he selected me as a team member, he ran into Caroline in a book-store. She was not alone. She blushed when she introduced him to her partner. She said she'd sold half of her practice to this doctor, I forget his name, but Greg could tell it was more than a partnership between them. He felt so relieved; he hugged Caroline and gave her a big kiss on the cheek, which must have surprised this guy, and he wished them both all the best. He even joked, asking if she could be his family doctor when he came back from Greece. That encounter was the turning point in how he felt about himself. He could clearly see she was happy and it was the right decision for both of them to call off the wedding."

"Did you and Greg always have a happy life?"

"No one ever has a happy life always, but most of the time we were very happy. Over the years, we just became more and more connected, more and more intimate until it was unimaginable for us to be apart even for a few days. We were not only lovers, but the best of friends. We enjoyed each other's company and always had something to discuss. For that reason, I can no longer live without him. And, it is *my* time to go."

Her breathing becomes raspy and her eyes dim. I detect a strain in her voice as she says, "Promise me, Leandra, to help Adrian get over my death."

"What in the world are you saying, Aggie? You're still in good health. Didn't you just recently have a complete check-up? And the doctor said your heart condition was stable and you were good for another ten years at least?"

She smiles and starts to get up. I go to the counter to pay, and buy French onion soup and goat cheese quiche for her lunch and dinner. Adrian said he'd spend the night with her again, and she is happy about that, but makes me promise to come and visit her in the morning as soon as I get up. Her voice reflects the persistence in her demeanor, and I cannot understand why she'd want me to return so soon when Adrian will be with her. I readily promise to be there by eight in the morning. I'm no longer able to sleep in on weekends. All those endless nights of being on call have ruined my ability to sleep long and sound.

I spend the afternoon grocery shopping and doing laundry. In the evening, I read a few articles and then make dinner. After dinner, Adrian leaves for Aggie's house and I cuddle up with the cat and watch a movie. I feel exceptionally calm, as if everything were in order. Again, hope arises that I may be getting over Weylin. I sleep dreamlessly and wake up at six refreshed and in a good mood. I take my time showering and sipping coffee while watching the news.

I arrive at Aggie's house shortly before eight and find Adrian again in the kitchen. He seems to have slept better. He offers me coffee but I decline as I've already had more than my daily dose. I tell him I'll go up and see if Aggie is awake so we can take her out for breakfast.

I knock gently on her door and enter. She is still in bed sleeping. She does not seem to be breathing. My heart starts pumping wildly and I suppress a scream because the knowledge she has died washes over me. I take her hand and it's limp. I touch her carotid artery and there is no beat. As a medical student I'd seen enough dead bodies to recognize when there is no spark of life left in a body.

I lift the cover gently and gasp—she had put on her wedding dress. It was not a traditional wedding dress, but for her wedding she'd worn a beautiful white silk halter top dress. Her face exudes the serenity of someone whose life is in order. And death is now her proper place, her repose and new home. I have no doubt Greg has taken his bride with him. At that moment of realization, I start sobbing—not because of the horror of death, but because of its moving beauty and its power to reunite lovers, and because it tells me there is love beyond death. This is a sacred moment, and I stand motionless in mute awe and reverence.

Now I have to tell Adrian his mother has passed away, and I don't know how to. I cannot bear to think of his devastation—he was always attached to her. I'm also thinking of the funeral, and the need to call his brother and our daughters, and my head starts to spin.

When I come downstairs, it takes only one look between us and he understands. He reads the painful truth in my eyes and his chin starts to shake.

He drops the mug he's holding and coffee spills under the table, creating a brown puddle. He sits down and puts his face in his hands. I see his shoulders start to shake as sobs rack his body. I pull up a chair next to him and pry his hands away from his face and hold them in mine.

"She loved you very much, but she wanted to join your dad. He came for her."

He jumps up so suddenly I think he'll break the chair. A look of fury is in his eyes.

"Are you freaking nuts? You of all freaking people, to dare say something so asinine, so totally idiotic... Are you telling me ghosts exist and you...you, a respected doctor, now believe in ghosts and the afterlife crap?"

He's screaming at me and anger is coloring his face crimson red. But then anger gives way to a look of utter despair and sorrow, and he looks like an abandoned boy, his eyes spilling tears, disbelief and heartache.

"I was hoping that with my dad's death, I would finally have my mom all to myself, but he won again." His voice is tremulous and his eyes reflect his pain.

"What do you mean? You always had both parents, whereas I lost mine too early. They weren't even sixty-five when cancer took them away from me."

"But they were always your parents. They doted on you. You told me yourself you were the center of their universe, even when you were a grown woman. My parents were always focused on each other...they would always travel together. I could never understand why the hell she had to accompany Dad on each and every dig. I cried when they'd go away, and my brother and I would have to stay with live-in nannies. The presents they brought back were meaningless...I needed a mother."

"But she loved you very much—"

"She loved Dad more. Once people become parents, their kids should become their focus. Remember when my mother said children were just the fruit of the primary relationship? What she meant was, staying lovers was more important than being parents. That's why I wanted to be the best dad ever."

I've never seen Adrian so emotional and so shattered.

"You've always been the best dad possible. Parenthood is not easy, striking the right balance between being a good parent and at the same time, not neglecting your primary relationship. Tending to your spouse's needs can be tricky."

"I remember walking into my dad's study and finding them giggling, bent over some old piece of ceramic and telling me to wait until they finished with whatever they were doing. I always had to wait to be heard, and they were always each other's first priority." He is crying like an inconsolable little boy whose wound was just torn open again.

I want to cradle him, I want to kiss away his wounds, and realize no one else in the world has wounded him more than I, he just doesn't know it.

"How could she have died if she was all right yesterday? Didn't you tell me the two of you had a good time and she was well? She didn't suffer from any life-threatening disease, did she? Ventricular fibrillation didn't kill her, because the doctor said she was stable, right?" His eyes are wide and dark with sorrow, disbelief and shock.

"Adrian, your mother did not suffer from anything that would physically kill her so abruptly; I mean, overnight. Ventricular fibrillation can be serious, but the meds made her stable as did the *cardioverter-defibrillator*, so I don't believe her heart condition killed her. She suffered from… how can I say it best? She suffered from a dolorous heart, from love sickness of unimaginable magnitude. She loved you and your brother, but she just could not endure a life without your father any longer. She did try. Remember, she joined a bridge club, and even travelled with her widow friends, and went to the theatre and art exhibitions, did everything that would indicate she was living a full life. But that life was soulless and vapid. She's happy now."

"How the hell can you know that? Isn't it normal to grieve and then to move on? She had money, friends, her kids and grandkids. She should have found joy in us."

"People can suffer horrendous losses, they grieve and get better and can even be happy again. However, she could never let go of your dad, and that's why he appeared so often; that's why she saw his ghost. Not all couples are as connected as they were. Some people's souls simply merge to the point at which they cannot live without one another. For some, children are just not enough. I'm sorry to tell you that and add to your feelings that Aggie was never a mother to you."

"That sounds like typical female romantic bullshit. She never believed in ghosts." Again his voice is laced with anger, denial and resentment; I have difficulty explaining to him his mother had just decided to die.

"Listen, honey; she and I talked a lot yesterday and I understood she wanted to die. Whether or not your dad kept appearing is irrelevant. What matters is, she believed she saw him, she believed she was communicating with him, and she believed he was coming back to take her with him. Adrian, she died happy, and she asked me to try to explain that to you. She did not abandon you...she just felt she had to join your dad."

He sits down again and cries, "What are we going to do now?"

"I'll take a few days off and organize the funeral. I'll call the girls and see if they can come. They will be distraught because they were planning to spend time with Aggie over Christmas."

I try to hug him but he feels as stiff as a corpse under my touch. He doesn't speak; he is still obviously unable to process the magnitude of the news. I go to the other room to call his brother, but no one is home so I leave a message. I call my sister and two of my best friends, Claudia and Vanessa, and they promise to help me through this.

Next, I call a doctor friend who works for the medical examiner's office, and report Aggie's death. Word spreads quickly and the day becomes a beehive of activity. In the afternoon, Aggie's body is taken to the morgue, and funeral arrangements are made according to the instructions she left for her burial. In fact, the instructions could not have been simpler as she was to be buried next to Greg. I phone a florist's shop to order flowers and wreaths, all white because she adored white flowers, especially calla lilies.

That evening, our home is full of friends who've come to express their condolences. We go to bed after midnight, exhausted and sad beyond measure. In the meantime, Adrian has spoken with his brother who has already booked flights for him and his wife. They're lucky to have wonderful neighbors to gladly watch their two dogs and cats.

The next few days are surreal. The joy over seeing our daughters is mixed with sadness and tears. The funeral is a somber, but elegant affair, if one can talk about elegance in conjunction with death. After the funeral, we go to Aggie's house because Adrian's brother wants to take with him a few memorabilia. We urge him to take anything he wants because the house is brimming with artifacts and collectibles, but he only chooses three paintings.

His wife, Sarah, is not interested in anything. In the past few years she has embarked on the road to spirituality and has little interest in material possessions. Aggie left the house to her two sons and a considerable amount of money for each of our daughters. Before they leave, Adrian's brother and his wife tell us they plan to give their half of the inheritance to Adrian. They will never have children and already have more than enough money. We are astonished, knowing how many other families feud over property division. We hug and cry, and I feel so blessed to be part of such a loving and generous family.

Adrian says he can't imagine selling the house; I tell him he can take his time. Our daughters leave after three days because they cannot afford to miss more school. I cry because I feel I did not spend enough time with them, and I barely saw them, but they comfort me saying we'll make it up over Christmas. Adrian returns to work, and has to leave on a business trip the day after. I'm all alone at home, feeling empty and disoriented. During the last two weeks I was so overwhelmed with Aggie's death I rarely thought of Weylin. Once alone, I go into my secret email account from which I used to write to him, and review some of his pictures. The first picture is of him leaning against a large pine tree. As soon as I see his smiling face, I am filled with unbearable longing, and love, and wish I could take his face in my hands and kiss him.

And then I weep, as I've never wept before.

CHAPTER TWELVE

David

I'm with a patient when I hear my phone vibrate. I have a session with Leandra in the afternoon, and wonder if she may wish to cancel, having been under an inordinate amount of stress lately. Her husband has been having an exceptionally tough time grieving his mother's death and she's told me she's been overcome by trying to comfort him. Moreover, I have a feeling hypnotherapy has not had a healing effect on her, but rather aggravated the rawness of her emotional state.

I'm tempted to glance at my phone, but don't, out of respect for my patient whom I have been treating for the past twelve years. She's one of my cases which fill me with a great sense of pride, accomplishment and faith that psychotherapy can, indeed, heal a fractured soul. With a history of sexual abuse and multiple suicidal attempts, Karen is now as normal as anyone can ever be. She no longer needs therapy; however, she still comes twice a month for short appointments. I have a sense she does not dare sever ties with me completely for fear she might experience a relapse into her previous state of darkness and semi madness.

After five minutes, Karen gets up and gives me a hug of gratitude. She leaves on my desk a box of cupcakes. After she closes the door, I look at the text message Leandra sent me.

'I've registered for the conference in Barcelona. Weylin's also on the list. Expecting resolution from the encounter.'

She and I had never discussed the upcoming conference in Barcelona. I may have mentioned to her I had no plans to go because during that week I'll be visiting my mother. Somehow, I didn't expect she would want to go back to the city holding so many memories for her.

I hope the encounter with Weylin will give her a sense of closure, without reopening the wounds still bleeding under a thin bandage of time, space and the silence between them. As a clear-headed observer, I'm tempted to tell her she's fallen in love with a romantic fantasy and illusion, and Weylin's love for her was

169

probably just a transient sexual infatuation, but I hope she will come to the same conclusion on her own, and let go of the past.

Just as I'm about to glance at my watch, Leandra storms into the office, blushed and excited. I don't have to ask her why she's excited.

"I broke the silence after ten months. I sent Weylin an e-mail saying I was looking forward to seeing him again. He replied immediately, saying 'Likewise.' He also wrote a few lines about his work and life. However his e-mail contained no allusions to us and the past we shared." She spurts it all out in one breath and is looking at me wide-eyed waiting for my reply, as if for an important prophesy.

"I'd like to warn you; if you can, curb your expectations, please. You need to avoid allowing yourself that same degree of vulnerability. Be prudent, and don't expose yourself to more potential hurt. Perhaps you shouldn't even go. Or, go with no expectations. Remember, expectations break hearts all over again. And your heart has not healed yet. There's only a thin bandage of time over it. You could undo all the progress we've made."

"I'm sure that won't happen. I have no expectations. Perhaps we can be…just friends. There's no reason why we couldn't stay in touch."

"You may be deluding yourself. I believe you're still in love with him. Your feelings are raw, and you haven't healed much, even though ample time has passed. He may be over you, which may be sufficient to shatter your dream of rekindling the affair. After break-ups, many people try to play the friendship game. Friendship in your case would be a mask behind which you'd be hiding hopes of reconnecting with him as your lover."

She blushes, but shakes her head in denial. "I'm not trying to rekindle the affair. Can we now start the session?" She's sounding both impatient and excited. Her anticipation of their meeting obviously has had a very deep effect on her.

I nod and refrain from further discussion of her new state of mind. This development may easily undo any progress we've made in therapy. If we have even made any…I'm not so sure. The excitement I see in her face cannot stem from anything else but hope that seeing him again in the city in which she broke her wedding vows would reunite them. She's ready to forget the pain he caused her by withdrawing from the relationship. Has anyone ever figured out human nature, especially the mental disorder called love? I sound so cynical, even to myself. And I also feel powerless to help her, and annoyed she's reverting to delusional thinking, not admitting to herself she's still hopeful she and Weylin will reconcile. I hear myself sigh with exasperation.

She seems to relax quickly into a state of receptivity, and I regress her. For a while there is silence. She seems to be in a state of hypnosis, but does not respond to my questions as to her whereabouts. I wait patiently and ask her again if she knows where she is and what year it is. She is still quiet.

Just as I am about to ask again, she replies—in a voice that's not hers; it's the voice of a young girl. I have never been able to explain why during some regressions patients speak in their own voice, even though they are much younger or older in the lives of which they are speaking, and some speak in the voice of the person they were in the respective past life.

Sometimes, I let doubt gnaw at me that it's all hocus pocus, and I may actually be doing them more harm than if I just prescribed anxiolytics and anti-depressants or did traditional cognitive therapy. And why did I agree to hypnotize a woman whose only problem in her otherwise highly privileged life is her difficulty to get over a lover?

I cannot fathom why she's still clinging to this illusion of love, albeit a vibrant and exciting illusion she has created. Why can't she accept that she invented this person based on one facet of his personality of which he allowed her a glimpse, under the restricted circumstances of illicit love? How could such a brilliant psychiatrist lose her emotional compass to infatuation? How could it have been anything else but infatuation if they spent only twenty days together over the span of a year and a half? And most of that time was spent in the secrecy and confinement of hotel rooms. Not enough time to get to know a dog let alone a man.

I hear myself sigh and brace myself to remain professional and to let go of judgmental thinking in order to allow her to undergo as many more hypnotherapy sessions as she may need. I also catch myself thinking she should feel lucky life has placed before her an obstacle so much less devastating than a real tragedy. I should tell her also plainly that if her lover had truly loved her, he would not have allowed her to be the one to break up because he started behaving so pitifully. He should have told her openly he wanted to end the love affair. But men tend to do that. Or, maybe everyone does. They start behaving in such a way the other person has no choice but to terminate the relationship. True love should not recognize barriers of timing, space and circumstance, but infatuation does.

She interrupts my judgmental rumination and I'm grateful, as I could feel an unwelcome wave of impatience creeping up on me.

"It's eighteen-fifty-four…perhaps eighteen-fifty-six, I'm not sure," she says.

"Who are you and where are you?"

"I'm in Rome, but I'm not Italian. I'm English, I'm twenty…a young lady. I'm very spoiled by my mother. She's not my biological mother. My real mother died in childbirth with my brother, but my step-mother, she's a mother to me. She has no children of her own, so both she and my father lavish me and my brother with affection.

My brother's stayed in England; he wouldn't come with us. He dislikes travel even within England and is apprehensive of new places. In fact, he tends to be anxious about all sorts of things. He's afraid he might fall off a horse, so he doesn't ride; he's afraid he might get stung by a bee or get lost so he doesn't roam the fields with me. I'm so different from him; I crave novelty and excitement and there's little that fills me with fright."

"Where are you exactly?"

"In the villa we've rented for a few weeks. It's a magnificent house, large, and filled with light because it has huge windows. I admire its garden most. It's big, and currently in colorful bloom. There are roses, and wisteria, and honeysuckle, and the air is filled with their heavenly scent.

"I'm standing appraising myself in a mirror. I'm tall and willowy, with long black curly hair. I have a few freckles on my nose I try to hide with a powder my step-mother purchased in Paris. My dress is sky-blue with sloping shoulders, and a rounded bust. My waist is small, accentuated with a wide belt embroidered with tiny dragonflies. A dragonfly brooch is attached to my bust; I love dragonflies. I don't know why these delicate insects which live one short summer have made me fall in love with them all over again. In French, they are called 'libellule', and 'libellula' in Italian. They sound much nicer than 'dragonfly'."

With that, she enters into her past life fully.

"I'm extremely excited being in Rome, because it's my first travel abroad. My parents have indulged all my wishes and whims, and this was one of them. I've also had many tutors because I'm interested in so many subjects. I play the piano, and know some Latin and Greek, and I'm fluent in French and Italian. I'm also learning how to paint, and I write poetry. I love Elizabeth Barrett, Samuel Taylor Coleridge, and Alfred Tennyson—I could read poetry day and night. To indulge me, my father has invited Coleridge and Tennyson to our home in England on two separate occasions. I asked them to sign their books of poetry for me. Tennyson was kind enough to ask me to show him poems I've written. I did it blushingly and hesitantly, but when he praised me, I thought I had touched the sky, the stars and the clouds.

"I also daydream a lot, and my dreams are about love…about that perfect love that will happen when I fall in love forever, and when someone loves me fervently and ardently with a love so unfaltering he never even notices other girls. I don't know why I believe in such love when around me I see so many lusterless marriages between people who have married for status, or to rid themselves of debt, or to merge two large estates into an even larger one. It is inconceivable in our circle to even think of marrying below one's social status, and I'm quite aware ours is a high one, with an ancestor line trailing back all the way to the early kings of England."

I interrupt, asking, "Can you read to me some of your poetry?"

She lets out a small scream of delight. "I love poetry recitals. Let me recite to you two poems…not the full ones, but one stanza each, and you tell me which one you fancy more."

She sounds like a child at play now. I'm astonished how Leandra has completely vanished, and this new persona has emerged out of the recesses of her subconscious.

" 'Tears, idle tears, I know not what they mean,
Tears from the depth of some divine despair

Rise in the heart, and gather in the eyes,
When looking on the happy autumn-fields,
And thinking of the days that are no more.'"

There is a pause during which a smile continues to light up her face. "Now, listen to this one:
'The dawn of my sorrow turned into day,
And the day glided into a night of pain.
I could not discern light from shade,
Nor song from a piercing wail!'
Which do you fancy better?"

I don't know much about poetry, and, in fact, I've never enjoyed reading poetry or fiction, but even a poetry ignoramus like me can easily recognize the dilettantish character of the second poem or what seemed to be the beginning of one. Yet, I want to indulge this young girl, so I say "I find something very appealing about the second one."

She claps her hands in delight.

"What is your name, young lady?"

"Juliet Leicester."

"Tell me about your stay in Rome." And again, she is immersed in this life.

"We arrived here two days ago after touring Italy. I'm weary of travel and happy we shall be staying in Rome for six weeks before we leave for France. My parents have already found me a tutor to help me perfect my Italian. I have not met him yet, but I have been told he is a poet and a painter who gives lessons in Italian because he is a man of small means, and needs the extra income to support himself. My parents have not been introduced to him. He was recommended by Count Madruzzo, a friend of the Earl of Shrewsbury who is a close friend of my father's. The Earl visits Rome once a year and stays for four months. The climate has a salubrious effect on his tuberculosis, but I have heard rumors that the salubrious effect stems more from his affair with an opera singer, and that's the reason his wife never accompanies him to Italy.

"Both Count Madruzzo and my new tutor, whose name is Carlo, I believe are coming to supper tonight. The Count is also a patron of Carlo's art and has even offered him board in his huge palazzo. He must be a very generous man.

"I am so excited to meet new people, and I'm even more excited to wear my new Italian gown, one of many my parents have bought me. It's made from pink silk, and has a pink lace trim around a wide skirt."

Silence envelops her again, but the smile does not leave her face. I am looking at so much innocence my heart constricts, because I sense this innocence will be shattered soon and the purity of her heart and mind will be contaminated forever. I don't know from where my foreboding comes. Perhaps in my practice I've seen too much pain, disappointment, mental illness, despair...

Her eyelids flutter suddenly, and I ask her to tell me what's happening around her.

* * * *

Juliet

My new tutor has just walked in with Count Madruzzo. When my eyes meet Carlo's, my heart skips a few beats. I've never felt anything like this before. It's a recognition, as if we have met before, but I know such a thing is not possible. How is that possible? How is it possible to feel some sort of current run between him and me, like lightning. Is that how it is when people are attracted to one another?

Carlo is very tall and slim and has a narrow face. His eyes are pale blue and grey and his hair is raven black and falls on his shoulders in soft, large curls. At first I think it must be a wig, but it is not. He is dressed in a long black, striped jacket and a snow-white frilled shirt. His clothes look well-made and expensive, and I also notice a large gold ring on his forefinger. I cannot but wonder, if he is an artist of limited means, how can he be dressed in such finery?

Without any modesty, I look into his eyes and again feel familiarity and connection. My own feelings perplex me and especially the warmth spreading through my entire body. I extend my hand and he plants a kiss on it, which sends shivers through me like bursts of sparks and bolts of lightning. Could this be the beginning of love? Is this how it starts, with a spark between two souls threatening to turn into a wildfire?

All of a sudden I'm terrified of the unknown sensations and wish to retreat to my room. At the same time I feel Count Madruzzo's gaze on me and when my eyes meet his I see suspicion, mistrust and disquiet in their gaze. My confusion and insecurity grow tenfold.

My parents invite our guests to take seats in huge blue brocade and gold upholstered chairs, and soon we are sipping tea. The count is drinking wine; he says he only has tea when he is feeling unwell. My father looks at him with a hint of disapproval, then turns to Carlo and asks him to tell us about himself. In a soft voice he tells us his father abandoned him and his mother when he was five. His mother remarried soon after, and has been living in the countryside on a large estate. His step-father is a rich nobleman, and his mother and he have three children. He adds he does not see them often, that Count Madruzzo has been kind enough to let him live in his palazzo, and there he paints, writes poetry and gives Italian lessons to foreigners.

I'm surprised by such openness and honesty before total strangers. Such sincerity is considered distasteful and vulgar in the world we come from. My parents steer the conversation away from Carlo and start chatting about the Italian weather, which is unusually hot for the month of June.

Every now and then Carlo and I lock gazes, and every time he looks at me, Count Madruzzo's glance, filled with cold scrutiny, flails against me and it feels as if he is erecting a shield between Carlo and me. Perhaps he is being protective of this man like a father."

"Juliet, why don't you show the garden to Mr. Di Francesco?" My mother now turns to Carlo and adds, "Our Juliet adores gardens and would like to have her lessons in the gazebo. It is large and beautiful, and I have no doubt you will find it a comfortable, quiet and suitable place for teaching her Italian."

The count starts to get up, too, but then relaxes into his chair. Carlo follows me outside into the garden, drenched in sunshine. Everywhere you look, flowers are in full bloom, and bees and dragonflies flit about making the air shimmer and buzz. My heart starts beating violently once I feel Carlo's nearness. He's not close enough to touch me, but I feel his presence so intensely it creates discomfort in me, and stirs feelings of imminent danger. I feel as if I should be taking flight, but from what I do not know.

I find it difficult to converse with him and all our exchanges sound contrived and artificial, yet at the same time I feel a force of great magnitude pull me towards him. We reach the gazebo and sit on a large chair with yellow cushions.

"Mr. Di Francesco—"

"Carlo, please. May I address you as Juliet?"

His blue eyes bore into mine, penetrating to the depths of my soul; I feel so vulnerable and so afraid that this stranger will have a power over me and will use it to wound me mortally. If this is the beginning of love, I find it a bit frightening because it feels as if I am about to lose control over my emotions.

"Yes, you may, but not in front of others. I would like to begin our lessons as soon as possible." I sound like a stranger to myself, incoherent and a bit disoriented. The young men in England in whose company I often find myself do not unnerve me in this way. I even suspect that James, who visits us often, has more profound feelings for me than he is willing to confess, but in his presence I feel composed and confident. Now, my self-assuredness seems to be deserting me.

"I am at your disposal, Juliet, day and night. What I wish to say is, please feel free to choose the days and the time that suit you best."

"Tomorrow at eleven would suit me. I would like lessons every day." As I was uttering those words I could feel myself freeze with fright of what is to come. I had not even planned to have lessons every day, but only twice a week. It is as if someone else was speaking on my behalf and directing my life in a new direction. A dark premonition fills my heart with dread, and I do not recognize myself. I have always been a cheerful and happy girl who never expected anything bad would happen to her. Why this dread all of a sudden?

The next half hour we spend in what to an outside observer would seem like light banter, but it is not. Something is clearly developing between us, something viscous and irresistible, and foreboding. We talk about his English, and he explains that through Count Madruzzo he met an English lady who taught him English in exchange for Italian lessons.

I get up suddenly and my abrupt move seems to startle him.

"I am looking forward to our lessons, Juliet." He takes my hand and kisses it and my skin burns as if branded. I feel myself turn crimson and I want to flee and hide in my room never to come out again.

Once back in the parlor, I summon all my strength to appear composed. I feel this burning urge to talk to someone, to gain understanding about these strange sensations, but I do not know in whom I could confide or if I shall even be able to find the words to describe these sudden and previously unknown feelings. As an avid reader, I have read a lot about love, but having never felt it, I was not certain I would be able to recognize it.

I excuse myself with a headache and go to my room. I close the door and throw myself on the bed feeling drained of all energy. Emma, my maid, knocks gently and comes into the room.

"Are you feeling all right, my lady?"

"I have a slight headache and need to rest." I wish I could talk to Emma and ask her if she has ever experienced the sort of feelings which have shaken me like an earthquake, but that would be improper. All of a sudden I begin to feel a sense of confinement. I wish to speak openly about my feelings, and shudder at the thought I must bury them because my family would certainly be shocked by them. I wonder how one knows what love is, how one recognizes an attraction that would mean suitability for marriage and a life together.

Even if I dared mention something of the sort to my parents, they would never consider Carlo as a possible suitor for me because girls like me do not marry their tutors. They marry lords' and earls' sons who can build them mansions and provide them with a comfortable life. At this time, quite a few English noblemen are in Rome and I know my parents are planning a ball for the purpose of introducing me to fine, young gentlemen who are acceptable as my suitors both here and back home.

Emma leaves the room and I'm left alone to my tormenting thoughts. How will I be able to tolerate Carlo's presence in light of the feelings he has awakened in me? Should I tell my parents he is not to my liking, and I find him odd, or not polite enough? I already know I shall not do that. I already know I shall face this trepidation overflowing in my heart; I know I shall not shrink away from whatever experience life has set before me. Life is a torrent, and I shall surrender to its flow without resistance.

* * * *

"Where are you now, Juliet?" She is silent, but her eyelids are fluttering, indicating something important might be happening. After a deep sigh, she begins again.

* * * *

Juliet
I'm in the garden with Carlo. Our lessons are frequent because I have convinced my parents I am so in love with Italian I want lessons every day. I have become very fluent, but more importantly, I have fallen in love so madly and know now what love feels like. It puts tremors in my soul; it brings wild and crazed butterflies in my stomach swarming madly in an attempt to fly free; it lights sparkles in my eyes I know I must hide from others. It is loss of appetite; it is disrupted sleep and, most of all, it has brought obsessive thoughts about him. I am consumed by this fire that's coursing through my veins. I feel I have fallen victim to insanity and I fear what I might do. When he takes my hand, I become so weak and feeble, my speech becomes incoherent, I am no longer me, and I do not recognize myself. When I look into his eyes, my own reflection stuns me like a blazing sun; I see my love in his gaze, I see my adoration.

I'm also terrified of our discovery. I fear Count Madruzzo because he comes often to our house and looks at me searchingly, and I believe he is searching for evidence of feelings Carlo and I may have for each other. But I also don't understand. He should be happy in the knowledge, if indeed he knows, or suspects his protégé loves me; after all, not only am I wealthy, but also considered beautiful and cultured and intelligent and sharp-witted and very confident and self-possessed for someone still so young.

The air in the garden is infused with moisture because it has just stopped raining. My feet are wet from the short walk from the parlor to the gazebo. We are sitting across from each other and I am reading aloud from Dante's Divine Comedy and translating the text into English. I have just translated the verse, 'There is no greater sorrow than to recall happiness in times of misery,' when I decide to stop the lesson for a while.

"Carlo, tell me about your mother. Why do you never talk about her, and why do you see her so rarely?"

He looks pensive and is stroking one of the two cats we adopted when we arrived in Rome. The cat is lying on his lap and sleeping. It's a magnificent white male, extremely friendly, and I let him sneak into my bedroom at night and sleep on my bed.

"I don't have a close relationship with my mother. My mother is a beautiful woman who was always more concerned with her beauty and male admirers—even while my father was still with us—than with being a good mother. She remarried only one month after my father left us, and I believe he left us because he would not tolerate her flirting, her spending on pretty dresses, her disappearances from time to time. I have no need to see her, because she has never been a true mother to me."

"It must be painful to feel abandoned by both parents. You must have felt deserted."

"Yes, I have felt deserted many times, and now I fear you will desert me, too, because you will have to go back to England, and also, a girl like you cannot possibly love a man like me."

"A girl like me does love a man like you." As soon as I utter these words, I blush in disbelief of what I have just said. I do not recognize my own voice and my own lack of decency to declare love to a man I have known for a couple of weeks. My senses have left me and I feel as if demons have taken possession of me. And I wish the demons could be exorcised, but I know they cannot because they have taken complete possession of my mind and heart. Love is not a pleasant feeling; love is a delirium and torture and bodes self-destruction.

"Juliet, my love, I am in heaven and your words are celestial music. I...I love you with my entire soul. I want to elope with you."

We are gazing at each other and the desire to touch is so hard to resist, but we do not dare because we could easily be spotted. I get up, leave the gazebo and go to the farthest corner of the garden and squeeze behind a large lilac shrub and the garden wall. Carlo is behind me and as soon as I turn toward him, he showers my face and my neck and my hands with kisses. I feel faint and dizzy, and think I will swoon. His hands trail my body and only when he tries to lift my skirt, do I regain my senses and stop him.

"I must go back into the house now. I will see you tomorrow." I try to walk slowly and leisurely toward the house, hoping no one has noticed our interlude.

The house is quiet, and no one sees me go up to my room. I'm so excited I have difficulty breathing. My chest is heaving and constricting and I am in pain so deep I wish to jump out of my own skin. I want to be with him, and the yearning is tearing me apart. I never knew one could feel like this about another person. It feels like a lethal and fatal illness, or even a mental malady, something from which one can never recover.

I think about having to go back to England in a few weeks; my heart stops at the thought. I cannot possibly part from him. I should marry him and stay in Italy. I am well aware, even to mention something like this before my parents would be considered utterly scandalous. They are polite and generous people, but they view Carlo as someone inferior to us, someone who could never be allowed entry into our class.

There is a knock on the door and Emma enters.

"I have a letter for you, my lady."

I take the small envelope and thank her. She asks if I need anything and after I shake my head because I cannot find my voice to speak, she leaves me with a look of puzzlement and fear in her eyes.

My hands are trembling as I open the letter.

"Amore mio, la mia mente e il mio cuore sono incandescenti; ho un solo pensiero ed è per te, ho un solo desiderio ed è quello di stare con te. Ora che ci siamo trovati, dobbiamo fare di tutto per stare insieme per sempre. Tuo per l'eternità, Carlo."

I am reading his words in Italian and translating them into English almost simultaneously: 'My love, my mind and heart are on fire; I have only one thought and it is you; I have only one wish, to be with you. Now we have found each other, we must do everything to stay together forever. Yours in eternity, Carlo!'

I continue to shiver, and call for Emma and ask her to draw me a hot bath. She has a worried look on her face and I wonder if she suspects us. She has certainly noticed how eagerly I await my Italian lessons, and how I've insisted Carlo come every day instead of twice a week as we had originally arranged. My parents, fortunately, see nothing suspicious in my newfound interest in Italian.

"My lady, your mother has asked me to let you know invitations for supper at Count Madruzzo's palace arrived today."

"When is the supper?" I am so excited to hear I will be visiting Carlo's home, I almost leap from the soapy water.

"In two weeks."

"Emma, do you think Count Madruzzo is an exceptionally kind and generous man to have taken in a young artist abandoned by his parents?"

A shadow of revulsion distorts Emma's pretty features for a heartbeat.

"I suppose that must be the case." Her tone is strained and artificial.

"Emma, you do not fancy the Count much, do you?"

"My lady, I try not to form opinions of anyone, but to do my job and serve this household as best as I can."

"Emma, what is happening with you? You and I have always spoken freely. You are my, my...confidante. I prefer talking to you than to my friends, you know that."

"My lady, I do not like the look in the Count's eyes when he observes you with Carlo. I see an evil gleam in them, mixed with...mixed with... I cannot be certain, but sometimes it looks to me as if he fears you. I am disquieted in his presence. It is as if a negative energy emanates from him. It is hard to explain."

"You usually have no difficulties expressing yourself. Perhaps he is very protective of Carlo—"

"My lady, I hope...I hope Carlo does not fall in love with you, because that would only cause him pain to love someone he could never have." She blushes and I know that, in fact, she wanted to say she hoped I would not fall in love with Carlo.

"Have you ever been in love, Emma?"

She is helping me out of the tub and wraps me in a great white towel. She is quiet for a few moments and her eyes mist over with some distant and still painful memory.

"Before I came to work for you, I was in love with someone. He was a member of the family for which I worked, and that is why I had to leave before anyone became aware of my feelings."

"Did he show feelings for you, too?"

"I believe he had feelings for me, but his family expected his engagement to their friend's daughter, a rich heiress. She was also very lovely, I must say. He never gave voice to it, but I could feel something between us, some magnetism, and every time I would feel it I would move away, leave the room as soon as I could finish serving. I still think about him…often." She sighs and sorrow fills my heart for all the lovers who cannot be together, those that are torn asunder by social convention, the expectations of others.

At that moment, I have an epiphany of how little freedom we all have. I can choose what I want to study, I can travel, I can eat what I like. But it all unfolds within carefully defined boundaries, within a strict set of unspoken rules which few would dare break.

I dress and we go downstairs. My parents are in the parlor waiting for supper to be served. I am surprised to see Count Madruzzo with them and an older lady dressed in black.

"Our daughter, Juliet," my father introduces me to Countess Abelli. She is very tall, and very unsightly. Her hair looks lifeless and its color reminds me of the Tiber in heavy rain, brown and muddy; her skin is sallow and sagging and her black eyes are deep set and filled with the blackest of melancholies.

"My sister is in mourning, and this is the first time she has left her house in six months. Her husband died unexpectedly."

"My deepest condolences," I murmur and take a seat opposite the Countess and watch her sip tea. The atmosphere is tense and I become very uncomfortable and wish to leave, but to do so would be impolite.

"How did your husband die, if you do not mind my asking?" My father is trying to make polite conversation, but by the look on my mother's face, it seems he did not choose the best question to break the silence. The countess leans toward him, not understanding his question.

"My sister has a hearing problem and you need to speak more loudly."

My father repeats his question in a louder voice, which sounds very strange as he is a soft-spoken man. The countess replies in correct English, but with such a heavy Italian accent we all strain to understand her.

"He drowned. He was found in the Tiber one morning. We do not know what happened, if he was pushed, if he had fallen in…" She chokes and hides her face in a lace handkerchief.

"May I show you our garden, Countess?" I am surprised by my own words, but I feel compassion toward this grief-stricken woman.

She looks up and for a moment I think she does not understand my question because her face is full of puzzlement, but she gets up and follows me out of the room.

I start chatting about our white cat, and the new black one which we adopted because I insisted. I ask her if she has children, but she says she does not, she only has her brother. She asks me about my life in England, and I tell her about our beautiful stone house covered with climbing roses and ivy, and as I describe my life in England, I become nostalgic and wish I could go back home and take Carlo with me. I also feel a longing for James, a truly good friend and a very amusing lad. I ask her about Carlo and she says he is a pleasant and hard-working young man, who makes a good companion for her brother.

"Juliet, my brother is an eccentric man and does not like many people, but he seems to adore Carlo. But I must tell you— my late husband never got along well with my brother, and I could never understand why. I was distressed—my husband considered my brother a most depraved and evil man, but my brother has never hurt anyone, so I do not understand.

"I should not be telling you these awful confidences. You are a delightful girl and I hope you visit me soon." Her mood has lightened and she seems to be enjoying our stroll through the garden. Just as she is about to say something, we hear the gong and return to the house.

I am feeling ravenous as I have not been eating sufficiently for days. At the table I sit next to Count Madruzzo. He appears extremely curious about my lessons with Carlo and wants to know all the details of our conversations. I feel mistrustful of his intentions and scrutiny, but I pretend to be in a very gregarious mood and outline for him the books we read and discuss. I want him to believe we do not discuss anything personal. He asks me if I am looking forward to going back home and I reply, "As a matter of fact, I was feeling nostalgic tonight, but I am sure it is a transient emotion. I must admit I am looking forward to the supper at your home in two weeks. I understand your palace is magnificent and your collection of art unsurpassed in this city."

He seems to be flattered and now relaxed.

"It will be my pleasure to show you my art collection. But, talking about England, I have no doubt there are many young gentlemen who are pining for your return?"

I laugh and do not reply. My mother who heard his comment says with a smile, "We hope Juliet will start noticing all those young gentlemen who have been flocking to our home for the pleasure of her company. We are all especially fond of James Wickleton, and I would not be surprised if he proposes to Juliet in the next few months. In fact, I would not even be surprised if he shows up in Rome."

My mother gives a smile of conspiracy and exchanges looks with my father. It would make them happy if James proposed to me. He and I have known each other since we were children, and are able to carry on endless conversations on myriad subjects. He is good-looking and wealthy, the latter quality making him irresistible in my parents' eyes. He is also unusual because he despises hunting, which makes him the butt of jokes of many other noblemen in our circle of friends and acquaintances. I admire him for his self-confidence, and courage to stand up and not conform to customs and social expectations. Even though I am aware of the bond that has developed between us over the years, I can presently only think of Carlo. James is like a ghost to me and I can hardly picture his countenance before my spiritual eyes.

Count Madruzzo seems to be very pleased to hear my mother speak so glowingly about James, and suddenly I am overcome by the feeling, I am sitting next to a large snake. How that thought crept into my mind, I know not, but I trust my intuition.

After supper, I talk for a while longer with the countess. She and I are sitting alone in the garden again. The night is warm, and moths swarm the lantern under which she and I are sitting on a bench.

"Countess—"

"Call me Laura, please."

"I am sorry to see so much sadness in your eyes. I hope time diminishes your pain, and fills your heart only with beautiful memories of your husband."

"Thank you, dear. At this moment, I cannot imagine I will ever be rid of this suffocating grief, and again feel joy. I feel such need to somehow connect with my husband. I will confide something in you. I have decided to see a medium in Nettuno. Some people have told me she channels spirits, and I wish to learn if that is true. If I could only talk once again with him!"

"Are you not afraid she is a fraud preying on people's despair and loss?"

"I am aware there are many frauds who only rob people of their money. But she apparently does not even have a set fee and allows people to leave her as much money or other gifts as they believe she deserves, based on the service they have received. Would you like to accompany me? Perhaps you will find what your future holds. Young girls always want to know what dashing young gentleman they are going to marry."

Her teasing invitation surprises and delights me, as I would love to experience something new. I have never had a reading by a fortune teller, and have never believed anyone had possession of supernatural powers.

"I would be delighted to accompany you, if my parents agree. When do you leave?"

"In three days. I plan to stay for five. I have a small house there, and relatives who live just outside the city. I plan to visit them during the day and come back to sleep in my house. You will be most welcome and I am certain you will enjoy the company of my family. They are known to be hospitable and have the best wine in the region. I hope your parents allow you a glass of wine here and there?"

Her mood has lightened at the prospect of us going together to Nettuno and a warm smile spreads on her face to erase some of the previous gloominess and melancholy.

"I shall ask your parents' permission tonight to take you with me." She sounds resolute and almost happy, and her eyes have a renewed sparkle. "Your companionship will cheer me and dispel my gloom, at least for a short while."

"Laura, where did you learn English so well?"

"I had a British governess for many years and visited England on a few occasions." She abruptly changes the subject of our conversation and says, "My brother thinks a special bond might be developing between you and Carlo and he is concerned you might break Carlo's heart."

I am so taken aback I feel my face burn with mortification. "I shall certainly not break Carlo's heart because I do not break my tutors' hearts and they don't break mine. He is teaching me Italian and that is the only bond between us. What in the world would make your brother say something as preposterous as that?"

"Please, do not be offended! I meant no harm or insult. My brother is just…he is just so protective of him. I believe it is time for me to go home."

Her brother is already at the door bidding my parents good night. When we join them, Laura asks my parents if they would allow me to accompany her for a few days on a trip to Nettuno. They immediately agree, seeing a valuable opportunity for me to stay with her relatives and practice my Italian. They discuss travel arrangements and a few minutes later, we have the itinerary, and I feel very excited about having my fortune read.

As soon as they leave I go to my room, and the excitement over the trip with Laura is suddenly overshadowed by the revelation of her brother's insinuations. Why is he observing Carlo and me so intensely? He makes me feel uneasy, and I wish to avoid finding myself in his presence ever again.

That night I dream of being chased by a demon down a dark alley. My heart is pounding in terror, and in an attempt to escape I throw myself into a dark, cold river. I wake up in a sweat, panting for air. I am too afraid to go back to sleep, so I read until seven in the morning and then call Emma to help me wash and dress.

I am restless the entire morning and cannot wait for Carlo to come so we can hide behind our Italian lesson and spend time together. I tell my parents I will be waiting for him in the gazebo. Just as I sit down and open my book, Emma comes with a letter. My heart leaps up in my throat fearing Carlo cannot come. Disappointment washes over me.

When I open the letter, I do not recognize the handwriting so I turn the page to find the signature. I am surprised to see it is from James. He has never before written me a letter, so I am curious to learn why he decided to write to me now.

* * * *

Dear Juliet,

After a sleepless night during which I was tormenting myself with the question of whether to write or not to you, the decision to write prevailed. Please do not reply to this letter. I want to hope that what I am about to say will resonate in your heart, and my feelings for you will find their echo in yours. As a highly intelligent girl, who is wiser than her age, you must be already intuiting what I am about to reveal. Juliet, I am laying my heart bare before you, to lacerate it if you must, or to cradle it gently in your hands like a piece of most fragile bone china.

I have loved you for many years. I have mustered the courage to admit what you must have seen in my eyes all along. I do not wish to sound conceited when I say that, as the most eligible bachelor in our shire, I am aware of how many girls are dreaming of becoming the object of my attention; but my heart is closed, and it has been closed for years to anyone but you. I may be one of the last romantics who believe in eternal love, in finding that one and only person to love for all my life.

Juliet, yes, this letter is my declaration of love, my promise to love you forever, and my promise to be loyal and faithful, to be yours alone. My love will not be fickle; I shall never inundate you with a love so great you find it almost excessive to bear, only to leave you thirsting after a love no longer there. We have all witnessed such cases of love which erupt like a volcano only to burn out like a straw fire a short while later. You will never crave love because an inexhaustible source of it resides in my heart.

Human words are fickle, I am aware of that, but my love for you has already passed the test of time and of distance.

Juliet, I shall wait patiently for your return to England, and I shall pray you reciprocate my feelings. I shall dream of asking for your hand in marriage, and of building you the home of your dreams, and making you and keeping you happy until the end of our days.

All my love belongs to you, sweet Juliet.

James

* * * *

My mind is blank. His declaration of love did not astound me because there were always feelings of warmth between us, and I have always enjoyed his company. He is also a handsome man, and I can easily recognize the reaction in girls when they see him. However, I thought we would continue only as friends because we know each other so well, we have so much to talk about, we have so much to laugh about together. Perhaps I should have considered the possibility of falling in love with him, but that I did not can only mean…we should remain just friends.

Before I have time to process any further what I have read, Carlo enters the garden. His eyes are alight with love and I tremble with the sweetness of anticipation of his secret kisses. He sits across from me and we drown in each other's eyes, setting my body on fire and igniting my mind as if stars are exploding in it, in the most vibrant and brilliant colors. He takes my hands in his and the fire in me burns even stronger and brighter, and I gasp for air.

"Juliet, we need to spend some time together…alone. Let us go to the coast for a weekend. Could you get away from your family, could you find a reason to travel alone?"

"No, Carlo, that is quite impossible. I could not possibly invent a reason compelling enough to allow me to travel alone anywhere. I do not even go out alone in Rome without Emma or my parents."

Then I remember Laura's invitation to Nettuno, which presents the opportunity for me to see Carlo alone. I still do not know what I would tell Laura, but I could say I would like to stay in

Nettuno alone while she is visiting her relatives. I could feign feeling unwell. Her family does not live in the town itself, but some ten kilometers away on a beautiful estate. I could say I would be writing or drawing in her house; Carlo could come to Nettuno, but not reveal his plans to either the Count or the Countess. I cannot believe I am hatching a plan that could bring such shame and infamy to my family, but I am helpless before these feelings of insanity. I hear myself lay out this plan to Carlo, still in disbelief of what I am saying and planning to do.

Carlo can hardly breathe with excitement.

"Juliet, you would really do that for me? My love, this is the happiest day of my life. Just the thought we will spend two days together makes my blood boil. I have been to the countess's house twice. Her bedroom is on the first floor, and there is a guest room on the ground floor. There are also other bedrooms on the first floor but you can insist on sleeping on the ground floor. You can leave the window open, and I can easily climb in. She falls asleep early and with her poor hearing, she could not possibly hear us. The room is in the back of the house. In the morning, I will hide there or in the garden, until she leaves to visit her relatives. The garden is unkempt and there are many places to conceal me. The house is also rather isolated, so no one is likely to detect us."

His face is bright red and there is fire in his eyes. I am starting to feel faint and am afraid I might pass out from so much emotion and the idea of following through on this plan which could ruin me. I tell him we must be extremely careful to not reveal anything. I also tell him the Count makes my skin crawl and I always feel I'm being watched by him.

Carlo agrees we must be discreet in the next couple of days, and starts talking about Nettuno again.

"My darling Juliet, if our plan comes to fruition it will be a paradise on earth, with you and me together. I wish those days could turn into eternity and we would never have to part even for one day."

* * * *

Leandra falls silent again, and I wait for her to continue. This is the longest session I've had with her, but she seems relaxed and happy, so I don't wish to bring her out of her state of regression. I also hope in this session she may find the answers she's been seeking, and Barcelona will bring her final closure to this torment that someone like me finds self-inflicted and fortuitous. Much ado about nothing! But then again, I've never been in love to that depth, or that level of insanity. I still think her inclinations of romanticizing love in every lifetime have caused her to build a fantastical world centered on Weylin, Kieran and Carlo.

Leandra now starts talking excitedly.

* * * *

Juliet

Oh, what a beautiful place Nettuno is! The air smells sweet of a perfumed summer. The whole city is washed in bright sunlight. Laura's house is so lovely, perched on a hill overlooking the town. She sometimes rents it to tourists, and the next renters are arriving in several days, a French family of four. Laura has known them for a couple of years, and is happy they love her house so much they keep coming back. She also pays a local girl to clean the house regularly. The girl, Maria, will come every day and cook and clean for us, but will go back home in the evening.

Today, the Countess and I decide to walk into the town and in the early morning she will visit her relatives. I have already told her I will sleep in tomorrow morning, and draw alone, and she has nothing to worry about as I will not be leaving the house. She says she is reluctant to leave me alone with Maria and asks why I changed my mind about seeing her family, but I explain I'm tired of the bustle of Rome and feel the need for solitude. I confide in her that James has written, and I need time to consider his revelations and impending proposal. I also say I plan to write to him, and she seems to be satisfied with my explanation.

For the next couple of hours she is silent, and I assume she is absorbed with her own pain and the anticipation of meeting her husband through the medium. I know how high her expectations are for the séance.

191

She and I follow the town wall and admire the view. My heart is beating wildly at the thought of Carlo's sneaking into my room tonight. What if she hears him? I am also frightened of what is about to happen between us. I know this will be the night I lose my virginity, but I have so hopelessly lost my heart, virginity no longer matters. I am astonished at having this reasoning and am convinced love does something strange to the human brain, incapacitates our power of thinking. I want to stay with him, marry him and never return to England. I feel so intoxicated and so not myself. I cannot even begin to comprehend how such feelings get awakened in us humans; the force is of such magnitude it renders me completely enfeebled with desire. I am terrified of my own frailty and vulnerability. I am terrified of my future, of the scandal once we are discovered or once we announce our intention of staying together.

After Laura and I have walked the fort, we stroll down quaint winding streets inhaling the smell of fresh cooked fish and baked goods. I am feeling a lump in my throat knowing if I am discovered, a revelation like this could both destroy my parents and disappoint them, beyond any possibility of repair or forgiveness, or my own redemption.

People look at me in curiosity and men smile at me invitingly even though I am in Laura's company. I feel I am floating on air. My mind is so foggy I have difficulty discerning my own thoughts or feelings; everything is a blur. I still do not want us go back to the house because the hill is steep and the climb is long; besides, it is only four o'clock and Carlo will not come to the house before eleven, to ensure Laura is fast asleep.

We find a café and order coffee. We talk about her relatives and she tells me one of her cousins has recently given birth to a stillborn boy, and is feeling such profound sadness over her loss, hardly anything can make her smile. Laura wishes to lend comfort to her by spending a full day in her company. Perhaps her cousin might also be interested in seeing the medium and hearing some hopeful news about future babies.

I still feel the glances of passersby on me, but I do not give them my attention. Laura tells me I draw their interest not only because I am pretty, but because I look like a foreigner. I find it hard to concentrate on our conversation and even hard to swallow coffee or the pastry I ordered. My heart is aflutter and I am starting to hyperventilate. I doubt my own sanity and powers of judgment. I feel as if someone has put me under a spell and I have become a complete stranger to myself. After about an hour we get up and search for a place to eat. I dare not tell Laura I am not hungry, and once we find a restaurant and sit down I force myself to eat half a plate of pasta.

After dinner, we head back to the house. I try to be agreeable company, but swirling thoughts of love and Carlo distract me from the topics of our conversation. I am in love, so deeply and so hopelessly that I feel doomed.

The walk is not easy because the hill is rather steep, and my shoes are not meant for climbing hills. Laura and I give each other a hand for support and, completely out of breath, we come to the house. I turn around to admire the sunset and the shimmering sea.

We decide to sit in the garden for a glass of wine. She says it helps her fall asleep. She asks me again to sleep on the first floor, but I assure her I will be all right alone on the ground floor, and I am absolutely enchanted by the room. I also remind her I plan to sleep in late so I shall say goodbye to her tonight and see her tomorrow evening. I pour her one more glass of wine in spite of her protests, hoping it will make her feel sleepy. Our trip has been exhausting as well as the climb, so I expect her to bid me goodnight at any moment. And after she takes a few more sips, she sighs deeply and stands up, faltering and woozy.

I get up and she hugs me and tells me not to leave the house until she returns in the evening. She adds that Maria will come in the morning and prepare breakfast. I assure her again I will be fine, and I will spend the day writing to James, reading and drawing. She says she will be home for dinner and mentions her family will most certainly pack a few delicacies for her to take home. The garden has several fruit trees and I tell her I will also have a plate of figs for breakfast, and I will not need Maria all day.

Once in my room, I unpack and take a bath using lavender-scented soap. The water is not as warm as I would like it, so I shiver. I miss Emma's help.

I open the window. It is only about one meter above the ground and anyone could climb in with ease. Normally, I would never dare sleep so close to the ground for fear of someone breaking into my room, but tonight the intruder will embody my destiny itself, in the form of Carlo. The night is warm and cricket song fills the air. The music they make mingles with the scent of pine and lavender and the combination has a drugging effect on me as I drift toward a deep slumber.

I want to scream, but feel his lips on mine and realize he has come and is in my bed. I do not know how long I was asleep, but in this moment I feel alive as I have never felt, with my all senses alert. Even the cricket song sounds louder than before, and the scent of lavender is more intense than I remember. Carlo's hands caress me and my arms instinctively wrap around his neck. I hear myself moaning with desire of an intensity I cannot fully understand, and had been unknown to me until this moment.

Silver moonlight is dripping on us and the bedroom furniture, tingeing the room with a strange whiteness. Liquid fire is coursing through my veins and my breath is coming out in gasps as if I were suffocating. Through the thick haze in my brain I notice my dress is on the floor and Carlo is lying on top of my naked body. When did my sense of shame and propriety vanish? Who am I?

His tongue is everywhere, in my mouth, alongside my legs, my stomach, and my thighs and in between my legs. So this is lovemaking. So this is how it feels when you wish to devour another person, explore every crevice of his body.

A sharp pain between my legs elicits a scream from me, but he stifles it with his deep kisses. He is moving inside me and a sense of pleasure is mixed with the discomfort. We are both giving muffled cries like two animals in the throes of agony or ecstasy. All of a sudden Carlo is lying limp on me. He lifts his head, and his eyes are glazed with love and adoration.

I feel wet between my legs and when I look down I see it is blood. I am well aware of blood accompanying the loss of virginity and am not alarmed. We embrace and he whispers in my ear, "Don't you ever forget about me."

"Are you casting a spell on me?"

"No, it is not a spell or a curse; I just want to be in your life forever. I dread a future without you."

I am exhausted. He puts his arm around me and kisses my hair and I drift into a peaceful sleep.

A soft ray of sun frolicking over my eyelids awakens me from the sweetest of slumbers. With my eyes closed, I try to remember where I am. The scent of wisteria reminds me of my new surroundings. A jolt of exhilaration shoots through me as I open my eyes and absorb the beauty around me. It is as if I now see the room for the first time. It is large and bright and sparsely furnished. The walls are painted a pale shade of yellow, making the room look permanently sunlit. In one corner is an elegant armchair upholstered in blue and yellow brocade. The frame is made from blond wood that displays delicate and elaborate floral carvings.

The one huge window would be flooded by sunlight if it were not so close to the ground and wisteria blossoms weren't filling half its frame with pendulous clusters of lilac flowers. The drone of a lonely bumble bee comes through the window screen. The bed I am in, with its down-filled pillows and mattress, is as soft and as comfortable as a white fluffy cloud. Because the room is on the ground floor, and the house is made from thick stone, the temperature in the room is very pleasant, almost cool in spite of the hot summer.

I silently get out of bed not wishing to wake Carlo, my love with whom I am stealing three days and spending them in this enchanting town. Once Laura comes back, I do not know how I can hide Carlo from her. What if some of her relatives come back with her? He cannot possibly stay in my room unnoticed. Could he hide in the garden? My head is spinning from worry. It seems daylight has brought with it all the impossibilities of this situation.

I cast a glance at him. In his sleep, he looks so youthful and innocent, his features relaxed and serene, and his breathing almost imperceptible. My heart lurches with tenderness. He is sleeping naked and is completely uncovered. I blush looking at a man's naked body for the first time and fear grips my heart at the thought of what we have done. I should tell him to leave immediately, but I know I shall not. I am tempted to kiss him, but instead, I tiptoe to the bathroom. I can still smell him on my skin. The traces of last night's lovemaking have left me reeling with incredulity that I dared to do what I did, and that lovemaking could transport one to a new dimension, to a place where one feels as if standing in the presence of God. Could there ever be a more mystical experience than that? From the bits of stories I used to overhear, it seems many women found lovemaking an unpleasant marital duty. Perhaps they are not in love with their husbands.

After I wash, I put on a long, white dress, exit the room and step barefooted onto a stone terrace overhung with grape vines creating a cool shade. The terrace is enclosed by a low stone wall under which more terraces are covered with citrus, fig, olive and other fruit trees that cascade down to the seashore. A medley of intoxicating scents permeates the air and I inhale greedily the luscious morning. The view from the hill on which the house is erected is breathtakingly splendid. The sea is shimmering in its early summer glory bedazzling the admiring eye.

An old wooden table and chairs sit on the terrace, and I see the table is already set for one. At that moment, I hear sounds in the kitchen and find Maria there. She is short and pudgy, with long black braided hair. I introduce myself to her in Italian and she blushes. I tell her once she makes breakfast she is free to go home and come back in the evening to make supper. I also stress she need not come into my room to clean.

I hurry back into the room and whisper to Carlo he must not come out until I call him. I go into the garden and pick a handful of figs. Maria comes out from the kitchen carrying cheese, bread and fried eggs. I reassure her she can now go home. Once she leaves, I bring from the kitchen another plate, slice the bread and place a piece of cheese on each plate, as well as a slice of ham. I pick a few wild flowers and put them in a glass in the middle of the table. The smell of breakfast fills the air, attracting a cat. I put small pieces of ham on a plate, and fill a bowl with water, serving the cat under the table. I am grateful to Maria for bringing this food.

Just as I am ready to call Carlo, I feel his arms around my waist. I turn around and kiss his smiling lips. "I love you, K," I whisper. "I love you, J," he whispers back. We have started to call each other by our initials, and I call him 'K' and not 'C.' It just sounds right; it is as if I've called him that before, in some distant time and place no longer accessible to me.

As we eat, we gaze into each other's eyes wordlessly. He told me many times during our Italian lessons he hoped nothing but joy and happiness would arise from our love; nevertheless, for me, pain has often been the main ingredient in this secret liaison. My secrecy is laced with the guilt of having to hide our relationship from my parents and his protector, the impatience of waiting for him to appear at my house, and the loss I feel with his leaving our house after our short lessons, not to come back sometimes for a couple of days. Even though I wanted daily lessons, he told me the Count would not allow it. He could never give me a satisfactory explanation as to why it would distress the Count if he was giving lessons every day.

After breakfast, we decide to spend the day at the beach and pack a lunch of fruit and sandwiches. We also fill a bottle with water flavored with lemon and take two large towels. Carlo tells me if we want to avoid being seen, we should take a path which leads to the other side of the hill, and not toward the town. The last time he stayed at the house he explored the surroundings and discovered a secluded beach. I am certain the descent will completely ruin my shoes, but that is the least of my worries swarming in my head.

I tell him Laura will return that evening, and he cannot be seen at the house. He promises he will go into town and come back late to my room. I worry Laura might not go back again to see her family and it will be impossible for him to hide in the house. He asks me not to ruin the day by panicking, so I try to calm myself.

It is a long and steep descent to the sea, but it feels like walking through a wild paradise. This side of the hill does not have terraces planted with fruit trees because the soil does not seem to be of the same richness; however, there are oleander shrubs, agaves, lavender, sage and many other verdurous varieties, the names of which I do not know. Every few minutes we linger to kiss and revel in the wonderment of being together and enjoying love in its fullest unrestrained luster. For a brief moment I feel he and I have already walked down this hill, but know it must be a false memory.

When we reach the beach, we search for the most remote spot where we can be alone. We come to a small inlet that makes us gasp at the beauty it has kept hidden. It is a perfectly oval cove surrounded by tall, craggy cliffs. Deep nooks and recesses are cut into the face of the bluffs, allowing shelter from the scorching sun. Pine trees and cypresses tower over the pristine pebbled beach. The monotonous dithyramb of crickets is mixed with the soft murmuring of the ever-so-slightly rippled sea. Scents of Mediterranean herbs and grasses blend with the smell of brine and pine tree sap, besotting our senses. Close to the shore, reefs and rocks protrude from the aquarelle blue sea, and on these tiny islands sea birds perch, preening their feathers and crying intermittently in their shrill clarions.

We find a spot under a pine tree and roll out the towels. Certain it is unlikely for anyone to stumble upon us (there are few tourists around at this time of year) Carlo strips naked and lies on his stomach on one towel, exposing most of his body to the sun. I pull up my towel close to the pine tree, still dressed, because I did not bring any clothing for swimming and would not dare undress even on a secluded beach. Carlo's nakedness is making me feel uncomfortable and I fear someone may pass by and see us. I lean back against the tree trunk and start leafing through a book, knowing I will not be able to read. After about half an hour, I cast a glance at Carlo and think he has fallen asleep. I become concerned he might get sunburn if he does not move deeper into the shade.

And then unexpectedly, I start feeling delicious tremors and a reawakening of desire for him. I open the bottle of lemon water, lie on top of Carlo and start kissing his ears. He moves and moans softly. I spill droplets of water on the nape of his neck and quickly lick them off along with the beads of his perspiration while he quivers at the cool touch and lets out a stifled yelp. I continue to sprinkle water across his shoulders, lapping up the juice and eating the occasional lemon pulp. I continue this erotic play of sprinkling and licking, not recognizing myself and my boldness, marveling at my utter insanity. His moans are turning into deeper groans and he begins to writhe, stimulated by this erotic play. At the same time, I feel the liquid fire of increased wanting course through my veins.

I shed my clothes off in great haste, and sprinkle lemon water over my nipples and he sits up, his mouth enclosing my nipples, sucking on them greedily and causing me sweet agony. I dip my fingers in the liquid and brush his lips with my fingers and he sucks on them. I kiss him and his tongue curls around mine and our joining takes on a note of frenzied hunger. He whispers he wants our tongues to dance together. We are welded again in infinite love and I can feel my heart and blood throb, and feel myself fall into the deepest well of ecstasy. How I wish I could eternalize these glimpses of heaven!

The caress of his hands and fingertips over my naked body is feather-like, igniting my passion and opening a thousand raw nerve endings. The azure sea and sky are mirrored in the blueness of his eyes glazed over with lust for me, and I feel myself dissolve in his arms. I touch his hair, cheekbones, and lips wondering if we are truly together or if I am dreaming a vaporous dream of love. I want a lifetime with him, and I want to fight for that lifetime, rebelling against all convention and expectation. Like a beam of a distant lighthouse on a stormy night, a faint hope flickers that we may not encounter much opposition once we announce to the world our intention to stay together.

I find myself lying under him, and watch his beloved face tense up as desire takes a firm hold over him. He whispers how much he loves me and I feel myself melt into him. His lips slide down my body and his tongue stamps every pore and every cell of mine with his image, his scent, his taste and his love—I believe nothing could ever obliterate even if in the near or more distant future life forces us to say a final goodbye.

I let out a squeal as his tongue slithers between my legs and I convulse with a pleasure that inundates all my senses with longing. At the same time, I hear the flapping of wings and wonder if my scream was loud enough to shatter the peace the gulls had been enjoying. Once we fuse, time seems to stop and the world around us disappears as we immerse ourselves in a universe in which we are two entities woven from love and entwined in the everlasting and yet fleeting moment we share. Soaring through the delirium of erotic delights, I suddenly look up toward the sun and silently call I never want us to part, and hurl a wish to the universe and to all pagan or man-invented gods to allow us to stay together.

POISONOUS WHISPERS

When we come back to the house, my nervousness renders me unable to relax and I ask him to leave before Laura comes back. I am terrified he might cross paths with her or Maria on his descent into the town. Fear fills me at the thought of our discovery. What if my parents find us out? I break down in tears. His embrace is warm, his eyes are full of empathy, but nothing helps. I have lost all my courage and want him to go back to Rome. He promises he will spend the night in town and leave for Rome in the early morning. I tell him our lessons will resume as soon as I come back, and I plan to also ask Laura to return to Rome as soon as she has had her fortune told.

Once Carlo leaves, I feel so desolate and lovelorn I believe my heart will shatter. This day spent with him has gone by as quickly as the flicker of light produced by a firefly in a dark night. The hours we spent together were like a beautiful dream intermingled with our sober reality. Our lovemaking was an erotic journey which filled me with an immeasurable sense of wonder. How is it possible to desire someone to the point of madness? How does one know how to make love? Is that what other couples experience as well? I wish I could ask someone. I wonder if I could ask Laura.

When I look up, I see the sky has darkened as if a storm were gathering. My fear increases manifold, imagining a violent storm might prevent Laura from coming home. I miss Carlo painfully. When he embraces me, the universe around us vanishes and I so easily forget the languid sun and the argent moon, the smiling stars, and the raging storms, and most of all, I forget who I am as defined by society and family and heritage. With him, I simply float suspended in love and want to stay forever in that state. When people lose that kind of love, how can they continue living?

Laura must have loved her husband the same way, because she seems to be perpetually sad and very few joys can penetrate her veil of sadness. Perhaps the fortune teller will tell me Carlo and I are meant to stay together. Now, I am also becoming impatient to learn what lies in store for me.

Maria's voice interrupts my reverie. She smiles shyly and goes into the kitchen. I wonder if she saw Carlo on her way up to the house. Suddenly, my thoughts of Carlo make me cry in despair. My weeping is interrupted by the sound of stones being crunched under someone's feet and I hear Laura call my name. I stop the sobs and run into the house to wash my eyes with cold water in the hope she will not notice my state.

"I'm here, Laura." I try to sound cheerful.

Laura looks at me quizzically.

"What has happened to you? Did I wake you? You look distraught, and you have a sunburn. Did you spend time in the sun?"

"In fact, I did. But how was your visit? Tell me about it."

"I spent a splendid day with my relatives. And look what they have packed for us. Wine and cheese and bread, and even cherry cake. I could barely climb the hill! My cousin Ricardo wanted to walk up with me, but I would not allow him. He has a weak heart and I would be afraid his heart could not take the strain. And I decided not to go back unless you accompany me."

I feel relieved Carlo is gone. He must be exhausted. He travelled for so long only to go back immediately. I wonder what kind of lie he will tell the Count as to his whereabouts and his abrupt return. I wonder if he will pay a visit to his mother before going home.

"Certainly, Laura! I should be most pleased to meet your relatives. I must also tell you I am also very interested not only in what the fortune teller will reveal to you, but also in what she may say to me about my own future. Thank you for taking me with you."

Maria comes out of the kitchen and tells us dinner is ready. We enter the dining room, which is rather small but very cozy.

"Have something to eat, my child. I shall go straight to bed. Ricardo will wait for us tomorrow morning at the foot of the hill and take us to his estate. His coach is very comfortable and you will enjoy the short ride. But you do look unwell. Is everything all right?"

To dispel her worries, I clap my hands and smile innocently. I also have a couple of spoonsful of pasta.

"Oh, I am quite well. The fresh sea air has a strange effect on me."

I hug her and ask her to tell me about her husband before she goes to bed.

"Were you very much in love with him before you married?"

She looks pensive and a shadow of sorrow clouds her eyes.

"I was madly in love, so much I was willing to elope with him. My parents, god bless their souls, did not look favorably upon the prospect of my marrying the only son of the wealthiest wine merchant in Rome. His parents had come from Sardinia and made their fortune in Rome. After his death, they moved back to their home village."

"How old are his parents?"

"His father is sixty-two and his mother fifty-three. My husband was thirty years old when he died."

She sighs and a lonely tear rolls down her cheek to disappear among the beads of sweat on her neck. For the first time I realize Laura looks older than her actual age. Grief has aged her.

She unbuttons three buttons on her black dress, obviously suffering in the heat of this summer day in her widow's garb.

"Upon their realizing I was about to throw myself into the Tiber if I could not marry the man I loved, my parents relented. Later, I discovered that even though we were nobility, we did not have money, and ultimately they decided to allow me to marry on the condition no dowry would be expected. So we all won.

"The only dark spot on my happiness was the mutual loathing my husband and my brother felt for each other. I could never understand the source of their enmity. Before he died, my husband promised to reveal a secret concerning my brother, but I never learned what it was…I am sorry, my child, but I am tired, and wish to retire."

"Before you go, Laura, can you tell me if what happens between a man and a woman…I mean, can you tell me if lovemaking was pleasant for you or did you simply endure it as some women do? Forgive me for asking such intimate details, but my curiosity has always been, how shall I say, it has been untamed." I feel myself blush and avert my gaze.

"Those are the moments when you feel closest to God. Those are the moments when not only bodies, but souls merge in the holiest of unions. One day you will know such bliss."

Laura's eyes fill with mist and she gets up, plants a kiss on my head and trudges up the stairs with a heaviness in her tread as if carrying the universe on her shoulders. A deep sense of tenderness for this new friend in my life overwhelms me and sobs rack my body again, sobs of empathy for everyone who has loved and lost. A bleak premonition gnaws at my insides signaling I will soon be counted among them.

The next three days we spend with Laura's relatives on a beautiful estate covered with fig, olive and citrus trees. Laura will not hear of leaving me alone again, and the relatives insist we not return to Nettuno in the evening. There is so much food served at every time of day I think I will burst. Both Laura and I are happy and carefree surrounded with so much gaiety and true affection. I speak Italian with complete ease and fluency and learn many new expressions. The weather is hot and sunny, and I miss going to the beach and swimming. Even though I am preoccupied with these many new impressions, I still think about Carlo day and night and am eager to return to Rome. Tomorrow, Laura and I are visiting the fortune teller, and Laura is excited at the prospect of reconnecting with her husband. It would be so wonderful if such a connection were possible.

Ricardo drives us back to Nettuno in his coach and we arrive one hour before our meeting with Lucrezia, the fortune teller and medium. We spend the time with Ricardo in a small tavern enjoying a lunch of fresh-baked crusty bread and minestrone soup. We laugh and joke, and Ricardo teases Laura about her wasting money on crooks and cheats like Lucrezia. He says he has heard people swear she connected with their dead ones, and her predictions of the future were accurate, but he does not believe in such stories. After our meal, he walks us to Lucrezia's house, and says he will wait for us in the same tavern where we earlier dined.

As we are walking, my legs become weak, but I try not to show my discomfort. I am still feeling bruised and chafed between my legs from the lovemaking with Carlo. This is another fact of life I've learned through experience, as no one has ever mentioned it in my presence, and I had not read about anything like it in any of the multitudes of books I have devoured. My intimate parts feel like a wound. In spite of the pain, shivers of pleasure run through me from time to time in anticipation of more encounters with Carlo.

The sun feels so hot on my skin when we leave the tavern I fear my nose will burn badly. I forgot my bonnet in the room and Laura seems now too distracted to notice my hatless state. With her fingers, she is twisting the gold cross pendant hanging from a thick gold chain.

"Are you afraid of hearing something terrible from the fortune teller?"

"No, Juliet, I so wish to talk to my husband once again, to know he is in a place where there is no pain. I just need to hear he is with the angels."

As we continue walking, a terrible thought befalls me. What if I get pregnant or what if I am already pregnant? The thought sends shivers down my spine. I am so distracted I do not notice when we reach a small stone house at the end of a narrow street. Ricardo bids us goodbye and Laura knocks on a green door using an ornate, lion-faced brass knocker. After a few moments, a short, fat woman with a warm smile on her face opens the door and welcomes us in. She takes us to a small parlor and asks us to make ourselves comfortable while we wait for Lucrezia.

The room is dark, as sunlight cannot get through the windows obstructed by the lush vegetation growing wild all around the house. The furniture is elegant, but shabby. I look around and the only color I see is blue, all shades of blue. I wonder if it is symbolic for the psychic.

The door opens and Lucrezia walks in. I am astonished by her beauty. Lustrous black hair falls in soft curls around her face and reaches to her lower back. Her eyes are emerald-green and her lips are full and red. Her complexion is porcelain-like, and I wonder how such a beautiful woman has not been snatched by some rich nobleman.

Her smile is warm and genuine when she greets us. She asks us to sit across from her at a table, then takes from her pocket a deck of cards. She asks who will go first and Laura says she wants me to have a reading first, and she will help and interpret in case there is something I do not understand.

She shuffles the cards, closes her eyes and her lips move in a silent prayer. When she opens her eyes, she says her spirit guide has appeared and will answer my questions. She adds, she is just a vessel through which he speaks. She spreads the cards on the small tabletop and her gaze bores into my soul as I feel fear well up in me. I cast my eyes on the cards and notice they are large and old and have tattered edges. Their color is faded and it is evident she has used them many times. Lucrezia starts to talk to me in Italian, but my comprehension is blocked and I turn helplessly to Laura, who starts to interpret. At the same time, Lucrezia is not looking at the cards, but seems to be listening intently to someone invisible to us, speaking to her.

"My spirit guide has summoned your mother. Your mother is standing right behind you—a lady full of beauty and grace, dressed in green, with a string of white pearls around her neck."

At the mention of green I almost jump, because green was Mother's favorite color, and most of her dresses and gowns were green. That color accentuated the green of her eyes. And she was buried with a string of pearls around her neck because she always wore it, a gift from my father.

"Your mother wants you to know her love has always enveloped you, and she has always watched over you. She is happy you found a mother in a woman with a heart of gold, the woman who has made your father happy and who has loved you as if you were her own child."

Her warmth, love and light embrace me, and at the same time tears run down my cheeks. I do not know if I can trust anything this stranger says, and I am trying to think how she could have learned all this information about me, but have no answers.

"You have entered a tumultuous time of your life, a time in which love is mixed with pain and the poison of disappointment, a time of discovery and change, a time in which a great storm will scathe you, but will not destroy you. You trust too easily, and you place trust in the wrong people."

As I am listening to her, I'm trying to relate her words to the current events of my life. Should I not have trusted Carlo?

A brief silence ensues while Lucrezia is consulting the cards and at the same time she seems to be listening to my mother or whoever it is who has appeared.

"Someone you love deeply has whispered poison in your ear; that poison will find its way to your heart. It will lead you on a path of self-destruction. But you are strong and your strength will help you overcome disappointment, and your disappointment will open up a source of empathy in you, and enable you to provide spiritual healing to others. Your pain will lessen the pain of others; your spiritual path will lead you to growth. You have entered a karmic phase of a past life in which you are connected to a man you have loved in many lifetimes and whom you will love in future lifetimes until the lesson has been learned."

She touches a card and continues.

"This is a sorrow card. The sorrow is deep, the deepest. It is the sorrow of lost love and lost innocence, and it spans many lifetimes. It is the sorrow of lost trust and shattered dreams; the sorrow that lacerates the soul and flings it into the depths of agony. You will go through it again now, as you have already done in previous lifetimes. But again, you are fortunate because in this lifetime, like in the previous ones, there is a man by your side—"

She stops and looks at the card depicting a warrior.

"There is a man who loves you with everything he has in him. This love is not fickle. It will not change its essence with time, once the fires of passion are reduced to a small flame. His love will pull you out of the throes of insanity. But you need to learn to appreciate that kind of love if you wish to exit the karmic cycle; otherwise, the lesson of pain and loss will continue to repeat."

What is she talking about? What insanity? She must be talking about Carlo. But how can she know? My thoughts run wild, creating a headache.

"Children will be born out of that marriage and you will live long enough to enjoy their childhood. You will outlive your husband, but you will remarry. Your second marriage will not rest on passionate love, but on friendship."

"Is my mother still here?" My voice is hoarse and my throat aches.

"She is still here. Do you have a question for her?"

I want to ask my mother about Carlo, but have to phrase it in such a way that Laura will not understand what I am talking about. I try to ask a question, but my throat is constricted and I realize I am crying silently. A soft caress on my cheek startles me and Lucrezia says, "Your mother loves you very much and she understands your sorrow. He is not the man you believe him to be."

"What man?" I realize my voice is laced with impatience and its tone is almost confrontational, but Lucrezia does not seem to notice.

I cannot find my voice anymore, but I want to ask about Carlo. I want to hear we will be together, and it is not him I shall lose. Warm compassion exudes from Lucrezia's eyes. Her voice is soft and soothing when she says, "I understand and know, as I have not been spared the sting of love. You love a man and your love is genuine, and it will not permute easily; he loves you, but his love is shifty, shallow, and sways toward the place where he feels the safest and most protected."

She closes her eyes again and whispers, "Spirit guides, what message have you for this young lady?"

My stomach is knotted and I feel nauseated. I do not know what to make of this, for I am in utter shock. I tell myself it is all a show put on by a masterful director. It cannot be anything but nebulous rambling, with bits of what sounds like truth, but what could easily be lucky guesses. I want the session to end and I want to go back to Rome as soon as possible.

"You have free will, and can still take a different route to avoid immense sorrow by embracing the weaker sorrow."

I get up impatiently and say, "Grazie, signora Lucrezia."

The look in her eyes is still one of deep compassion and I feel ashamed of my mistrust, but I do not understand what she has said to me—or is it that I refuse to understand? I am also aware I am not really present in the moment or focused on her words as I cannot stop thinking about Carlo.

Laura takes my seat and I sit in an armchair under a window. I am facing Lucrezia, but even though Laura's back is turned to me I can sense her hope to contact her dead husband. Poor, desperate woman! Despair brings out gullibility in some people, and others prey on it.

A deep voice breaks the silence and gives me such a jolt of fear I jump in my seat. I look around expecting to see a new visitor in the room, but then I realize it is Lucrezia, now speaking in a different voice.

"Fabrizio, is that you, my love?" Laura manages, choked by sobs. I strain to understand what Lucrezia is saying because her Italian accent is now unknown to me, and then I remember Laura had told me her husband was from Sardinia.

"Laura, my angel, I am sorry to have left you. I did not leave you of my own volition, but I was pushed into the Tiber."

"Who pushed you, Fabrizio? I will have them hanged."

"Laura, I wish for you to find peace and happiness. Do not seek revenge, but beware your brother, for he is a snake, a depraved and dark soul. I wish you would leave Rome and go live with my family in Sardinia. They love you and you will find happiness there."

Laura is weeping now, and Lucrezia is bent over as if in pain.

"My dying was horrible, but I am at peace now and surrounded with love. You, my darling, have many years to live before we are reunited. Rejoice in every moment life brings you. Sardinia will give you a new life, and there will be much happiness coming into your life. Never doubt that!"

Laura is trembling and weeping, and just as she is about to speak, Lucrezia comes out of her trance and resumes the session in her normal voice.

"Your husband's spirit is no longer with us. I hope his brief presence has given you some comfort."

"How did you know he was from Sardinia?" Laura asks with a tortured voice.

"I knew nothing of his background. I only channeled his spirit. I do not even know what it was he said to you. I hope you have received the answers you were seeking."

Laura gets up and starts fumbling in her purse to find money to pay. She asks how much she owes and Lucrezia replies there is no set fee, and she can leave whatever she feels is appropriate for the service she received. I do not see how much money Laura is giving her because she places a velvet pouch in front of Lucrezia. Lucrezia does not touch it, but turns toward me and says, "I hope you love yourself enough to allow yourself to heal fully and never look back."

I want to ask her what she means, but I am too shocked by what I have just witnessed. I do not know if I even believe Laura's husband has appeared, or if Lucrezia has just put on another great show after she collected information about Laura. How difficult would it be to find out who Laura was and what her family situation was? But why make such accusatory remarks about Laura's brother?

Laura and I squint when we come out of Lucrezia's dark house into the sunshine. We walk silently to the tavern and sit in the shade of a grapevine canopy.

"Juliet, you look so pale and unwell. The reading must have shaken you terribly. And I cannot even start to comprehend I may have actually spoken with Fabrizio. Am I being naïve and gullible? Is it only my desperate need to believe that he appeared?"

"I have no answers to your questions, Laura. I just wish to go home as soon as possible. I am not feeling well; it is the monthly curse." I hear myself laugh nervously and at the same time I wonder why I felt compelled to lie.

With a trembling hand, Laura takes a sip of the water the waiter has just brought and nods in agreement; she also wants to go back home. She looks around in search of Ricardo, but he is not where he said he would wait for us. She reminds me we cannot leave without him.

I feel tired and uneasy as my thoughts return to the reading. Lucrezia's words do not bode well. If I understood correctly, what awaits me is some terrible disappointment, but I should be able to heal from whatever befalls me. A great longing for Carlo stirs within me. Oh, how I want to be with him again and how I wish we would never part. We have to talk. I want him to propose to me and I want him to talk to my parents about our marriage. A feeling of nausea hits me suddenly and I am afraid I will have to vomit, but the feeling passes.

We spend an hour at the tavern waiting for Ricardo. Laura cannot stop talking about Lucrezia and again expresses a suspicion Lucrezia must have somehow found this information about her and her husband in advance; she then remembers it was one of her nieces who made the appointment with Lucrezia and who told Laura she had referred to her only as her 'aunt Laura from Rome' without providing any further details. Lucrezia only knew aunt Laura wanted to contact her deceased husband.

Lucrezia could not have had knowledge of how he had died or where he was from.

"Juliet, this may be utter lunacy, but I shall write to my in-laws in Sardinia and tell them about the message their son had for me. After that, if they agree, I shall move there and surrender to my fate. Rome now holds no appeal for me. I shall sell my house and buy one near my husband's family. I need to close this chapter of my life and open a new one."

The prospect of starting a new life colors her cheeks with a blushing rose tint and puts diamonds in her eyes. Even if the séance had been a hoax it does not matter, because it has brought fresh energy to Laura, and it makes me happy to see so much optimism in her. This is also the first time I have seen her laugh heartily, and I feel gratitude to Lucrezia for effecting such a profound change in Laura.

We order wine and after a couple of glasses we are both semi-inebriated when Ricardo appears. Looking at him I realize for the first time how huge a man he is. I also notice, for the first time, not only is he a large man, but also a rather unsightly one, with a mane of black hair, a short, wide nose, and small, black, beady eyes. He hugs Laura warmly as if he had not seen her for a long while and apologizes for not having waited for us. He had met an old acquaintance who insisted he join him for a glass of wine at his house. He gives his typical roaring laugh and it is easy to see why everyone in the family loves this benevolent giant. I wish he were always around as someone into whose arms I can run when I need shelter from the punishing world around me.

He orders more wine and some cakes and we spend the next hour in a most pleasant, laughter-imbued conversation with him. He is sorry we are going back to Rome and hopes we come back soon. I tell him my family plans to leave Italy in two weeks, and I am certain I shall feel nostalgic for all the wonderful people I have met and places I have visited.

The train ride back to Rome is long and I sleep most of the way. I slip into a stupor-like lethargy and have no wish to talk. Fortunately, Laura is also pensive and quiet, probably stunned by the fortune-teller's revelations and probably contemplating her move to Sardinia. I have only one desire—to find a way to marry Carlo and bring him back with me to England. He speaks English well, he is educated, and my father could find him employment. A part of me knows I am being irrational and inebriated with love. My parents would think I have completely lost my mind if I dared even mention such a possibility. But shouldn't one fight for love and shouldn't love conquer all obstacles?

I lose track of time. By the time we reach Rome I am so exhausted even the thought of Carlo cannot revive me. My parents are surprised to see me so soon and their expressions show their concern for my health, but I assure them I am well, and retire to my room immediately.

The next morning I send a message to Carlo that our Italian lessons may resume. I receive an answer from him two days later apologizing he cannot come before next Monday. I am so disappointed I feel a physical ache. I cannot understand what would prevent him from coming to see me. I tremble at the thought he may no longer love me after having had me. I feel fear tangle my stomach into a tight knot and my eyes well up with tears. I find it hard to breathe, and my body threatens to shut down, and I fear I will die. I always thought love awakened only the most beautiful and pleasant feelings and not these stabs of piercing and lacerating agony. Perhaps there is another girl in his life…

The next few days are pure torture and I cannot recognize my countenance in the mirror. My mother wants to call a doctor but I refuse. I look and feel like a ghost and wish I could expunge this maddening love from my heart and regain my lost insouciance and happiness.

On Monday, Carlo appears fifteen minutes before our usual time. He seems to be happy and in a good mood. It is raining and we cannot go to the garden, but instead seek the privacy of the library. My parents are having lunch with some friends and we are alone with Emma and two other servants. I ask Emma not to disturb us. She gives me a strange look, but says nothing and only nods.

In no time we are on the floor making love and I forget the unhappiness of not having heard from him for a few days. When we are lying spent from the frenzy of lovemaking I ask him why he could not come last week, and if he knew how his absence had created storms of sorrow in me. He explains he and the count went on a trip to Aquila to visit friends. He says he missed me, and his love for me grows by the day. I believe him, as all my insecurities are put to rest.

Carlo stays for two hours; I chatter away about Lucrezia, and Laura and her plans to move to Sardinia, and in my happiness I mention how I would like him to leave Italy and come to England with me. I look at him with the expectation he will say something indicating we will never part. Perhaps I am even expecting him to propose to me because I say I have found the love of my life, and there can never be anyone else. In the exuberance of my hopeful imaginings, I hardly notice a shadow cross his eyes. He looks at the floor and tells me he cannot leave Italy.

"What would I do in England? How would I make a living? My art sells here only when the count invites his friends to his home and exhibits my paintings. Those who buy them, I suspect, buy them to please him because he is powerful and very influential even within the highest of circles."

"But I would find it hard to stay in Italy. I do not believe my parents would continue to support me if I told them I would leave my life in England to stay with you."

A thought shoots from somewhere in the back of my mind telling me I am behaving unlike a lady, but I dismiss it.

"Let's practice Italian," Carlo interrupts me and bemuses me completely by changing topics. I tell him in Italian I love him and he replies, 'Anch'io,' meaning 'likewise'. I yearn for him to whisper words of passion to me, but he opens a book of poetry and asks me to read aloud so we can have a discussion in Italian. I oblige reluctantly and time flies by, until he must leave.

The next few days he comes regularly and my parents wonder why I want so many lessons in a row. My mother looks at me suspiciously and I do not know how much longer I can keep this secret. Whenever I try to talk with Carlo about our future together, he becomes evasive. I am nervous because we are going back to England so soon and not coming back until the next year. I cannot imagine life without Carlo, and waiting for his letters would be a torture. I plan to initiate a conversation about our future together when I see him Saturday night at dinner at the count's house. I need to have time with him alone.

This all-consuming love I feel imbues me with courage to sever ties with my old life, and start a new one in Italy. I could give English lessons here and could find employment in a school. I also have a large inheritance from my grandparents, which is kept in trust for me; I will have full access to it in a year when I turn twenty-one. That alone would be enough to live comfortably for many years to come. That money is also the means to my independence and I should perhaps wait until I have it and then announce to my parents my plans to move to Italy. I am excited and can hardly wait to see him tonight and tell him I have a solution, with the only requirement that we wait for a year. That should not be too difficult.

* * * *

Leandra is quiet again. I also notice her face is red and her knuckles white, indicating emotional turmoil. I'm eager to hear the rest of the story but the feeling in the pit of my stomach presages an unraveling that will probably follow the pattern of her previously remembered past life. My palms are wet from nervousness and it is more than obvious I am reacting as a friend would and not as a disinterested psychiatrist.

Her voice startles me because it has a shrill overtone.

* * * *

My hands tremble as I try to dress for tonight's dinner. My azure-blue silk dress is resplendent. . The neckline is embroidered with tiny multi-colored, gem-studded dragonflies. My fascination with dragonflies and fairies has never left me, and I ordered the seamstress add them as ornaments. A very skilled goldsmith made them and my father paid a large sum of money to please me. Oh, if he knew what I had done, he would certainly disown me and banish me from his home.

Emma puts my hair up and fixes it in place with beautiful diamond pins, and I fear I might lose them if they fall out. The mirror reflects my glowing appearance and dancing eyes. I am deeply in love, and I have the means of overcoming the obstacles to our life together, never to be parted from my lover again. I keep repeating these words and turn them into a mantra in hope they will bring me what I want. I have broken so many rules, but I am the creator of my own happiness and destiny. I feel as powerful as a goddess in control of her own and other peoples' fates.

The palazzo in which the count and Carlo live takes my breath away. It is completely white, and has three large balconies overlooking perfectly manicured grounds in the middle of which a pond graced with a couple of snow-white swans glitters, lit by moonlight and the light of torches. The flowering bushes everywhere seem to make the air itself tingle in delicious colors and scents. The gardens are illuminated by numerous oil lamps and torches so one can almost see into every little corner. Everything reflects wealth and sophistication.

There are statues and two gazebos, and all of a sudden I feel I have been here before. I get a sense I've known a garden like this and someone once loved me in a place like this. I shake off that irrational thought and walk into a wide, white marble foyer.

Servants, impeccably dressed in black and white uniforms, greet us with glasses of wine. I take one because lately my parents have agreed it is appropriate for me to have an occasional glass. I know I have to sip it slowly because it quickly goes to my head, and tonight I need all my wits about me.

The count has about twenty guests this evening, and many of them are arriving at the same time we are. Their dress is a display of the utmost finery, and again I have an uncanny feeling of déjà vu. Expensive jewels glisten around the lovely, as well as the shriveled necks, while the conversation soon turns into din as guests begin to debate the value of the comic element in Rossini's operas, a subject of no interest to me. But I realize nothing is of any interest to me anymore, except Carlo, who still has not appeared.

I smile vacuously at everyone who starts a conversation with me and respond automatically; drawing from my cache of polite phrases, platitudes and other general statements devoid of meaning. At the same time, my eyes dart in all directions as I wait for Carlo to appear.

The sound of a bell invites us to the dining room and the servants show us to our designated seats. At that moment Carlo appears and the frenzied swirl of butterflies in my stomach threatens me with nausea.

The seating plan is such that I find myself beside a short and bald man, with white pudgy hands, who keeps wiping beads of sweat off his forehead. He introduces himself to me, but I immediately forget what he's said. Again, a sense of déjà vu washes over me and my nerves are so frayed I am fearful of losing my grip on reality.

Carlo sits on the same side of the table I am sitting; however, he is one seat away from the table head where the count takes a position. I am very disappointed—I'd hoped we would sit next to each other and his close vicinity would, as always, electrify every cell of my body. I crane my neck to see him, but it is hopeless.

I look around and find the dining room so gilded and ornate it is hard to isolate any singular piece of art. Whoever decorated this interior obviously had limitless funds but limited taste. I would find it suffocating if I had to live among so many artifacts. I have always preferred the soothing ambience of natural settings.

Food starts arriving and from every course I eat a little. I force myself to appear in a festive mood and I join in light conversation with the people around me. I am aware they are paying me compliments, but it feels as if they are pouring water into a sieve as nothing touches me or stays with me long. My only hope is that after dinner when we mingle again, I will have a few minutes with Carlo alone. Perhaps we could steal away into the garden; perhaps I can ask him to show me the greenhouse. Again, a feeling I have somehow been here before or in a similar setting, but in a different country, fills me and I dismiss it, ascribing it to my overheated emotional state.

After dinner, guests spread out into the two parlors, and some exit into the garden because the night is warm and balmy. I manage to catch Carlo's glance and I move toward him.

"Is it possible for us to be alone for a few moments and talk?" My voice trembles with anticipation. Again, Carlo looks ill at ease and I try to penetrate his veil of discomfort.

"Is something wrong, Carlo?"

"No, it is just…the count expects me to mingle with the guests and entertain them."

"Aren't I a guest and aren't I the youngest guest and would it not be expected you entertain me?" I recognize the displeasure in my voice and at the same time a premonition of something bad about to happen overtakes me. "Can't you show me the garden? Wouldn't that be appropriate and hospitable?"

"Yes, of course," Carlo says, casting a glance across the room as if seeking someone's approval.

In the garden, he walks alongside me but with sufficient distance that we do not touch even accidentally. I feel tension within him, and I cannot interpret the meaning of this strange behavior. At the same time, I realize the timing is wrong to tell him about the plans I have hatched. My enthusiasm over the possibility of us sharing a future together will not be echoed by him, at least not tonight. The moment is very strange, and I want to know why.

"Carlo, I sense something is very wrong, I sense you are hiding something from me. I do not understand why you cannot…why you are hiding your feelings for me. I am sure I could convince my parents to accept we are in love and we wish to stay together. But there is something about you these days I cannot define. Can you tell me what is wrong?"

"It is complicated. I depend on the count's financial support. He would not be pleased if he found out about us. I am his only heir…."

"But what is wrong with me that he would mind your being in love with me?" My voice becomes a screeching pitch. "Aren't I beautiful, rich, educated, well-spoken? Does he mind that I am English and not Italian?" I am almost crying. I feel humiliation because I am so open with my feelings, which somehow no longer seem to be reciprocated. The night is ruined for me and anger fills me. I fight the urge to hit Carlo, to slap him, but I just turn and walk briskly back to the house.

I almost fall as I bump into Count Madruzzo. I apologize for my clumsiness and look into his eyes, and with utter astonishment I see pure hatred there. I recoil in horror of such unexpected recognition.

"Why do you hate me?" I blurt out, unaware I even want to confront him like that.

The look of hatred disappears and is quickly cloaked in false concern.

"Hate you? My dear, I noticed you looked distressed and I was compelled to learn what was vexing you." The tone in his voice is so feigned and cold I shudder as if facing a snake.

I am tempted to tell him Carlo and I are in love, but just as I open my mouth to say something an inner voice stops me. I cannot help casting a look of revulsion at him before I flounce back into the house.

I look for my parents and discreetly whisper in my mother's ear I would like to go home because of a stomach-ache. She asks me to be patient for a while longer because my father is engrossed in a discussion about politics with a few male guests and, knowing how much pleasure he derives from this, she does not wish to interrupt him. Some of the guests are British and American and they quickly form a circle in which an animated discussion continues, along with the brandy served after dinner.

I decide to walk around the villa and look at the paintings. There is hardly a speck of wall space left uncovered with a painting. There are portraits, landscapes, battle scenes, religious scenes, most done in heavy shades of scarlet and blue. I leave the parlor and walk into a large, empty room and realize the paintings here seem very different. I come closer to one and see it is signed by Carlo. My heart flutters and with great interest I study them.

There are no people in the first of his works I study, but only nature in its beautiful and untamed wildness. One painting depicts a ship ravaged by a storm; another displays a field of flowers swaying in strong wind. I go from one painting to another and I cannot find even one showing peaceful, friendly and serene scenes of nature because storm, hail, rain, or snow is the leitmotif in each. But it is the last painting which makes me gasp in horror.

It depicts two hands flailing wildly, killing dragonflies. On the black ground a dozen or so dragonflies in all colors are lying dead. In the top right corner of the painting a dragon is spewing fire and extending its claws toward the flailing hands. What could this mean? Is Carlo the dragonfly slayer in the painting? Is he killing dragonflies because they are fragile and defenseless and he cannot kill the real dragon in his life? Is he sacrificing dragonflies?

I am trying to comprehend the symbolism in this disquieting scene, but reason fails me. However, I can understand why his paintings do not sell well. There is such a disturbing menace in them, so much frustration, attempted but failed rebellion that would most surely provoke disquiet in the eye of the observer. Instinctively, I touch the canvas and withdraw my hand in shock when I realize my finger is wet. The paint has still not dried, which means he has just finished it. I wonder when he started the painting because it seems he completed it upon his return from Nettuno. He knew I was coming to dinner tonight, so he could have assumed I would see the painting and find the depiction shocking. After all, he knew of my fascination with dragonflies.

Still shaken, I come to the end of the room and notice a half-open door leading to another room. Wondering if more of Carlo's paintings are to be found behind the door, I push it gently, but stop when I hear voices. A voice, laced with fury, is hissing in Italian, "I forbid you to ever go there again. I shall tell them myself, I shall find a reason, or else you will find yourself on the street. You betrayed me…you betrayed my magnanimity, and worst of all, my love. I do not know if I can ever forgive you."

In shock, I recognize the voice that replies is Carlo's.

"There is nothing between us but friendship. How can you even think I was in love! You are just jealous and possessive and you do not allow me freedom to have friends other than yourself."

In his voice, I hear defensiveness and accusation. My mind is a dark sky for a few moments until a bolt of lightning illuminates it with knowing the conversation is about me. I feel frozen in time and space, like an ice statue. Their voices reverberate through my senses, but I cannot grasp the meaning behind the words, and can only feel passion, pain, venom. There comes a silence, and it startles me out of my frozenness. As if in a dream, I peek through the opening and mutely witness a scene that becomes the first step of my descent into insanity.

Carlo and Count Madruzzo are kissing passionately, and I cannot process this vision of two men kissing with such ardor. I have heard of an unnatural love, but thought it rare and depraved and as something dissociated from love, but associated with sin and bestiality. How can my Carlo be in such a sordid relationship, in the clutches of an evil he can never escape? And for him to choose the love of a reprehensible man over the love and life I was willing to offer him for eternity! Now I understand what Laura never understood: Fabrizio was trying to tell her about the depravity of her brother.

I turn away from the most repugnant scene imaginable and run outside. I do not stop running until I reach the farthest end of the garden and then start retching and vomiting into a rose bush. At that moment the fortune teller's words resonate in my head and I finally understand her warning. My shock is so huge I think the pressure building in my head will make me disintegrate into pieces, each drenched in pain.

I know I have to go back into the house, find my parents and leave this horrid place and this horrid country never to come back. I want to go back to England tomorrow, back to normalcy, back to safety, back to the world of order where every part of my life has its proper place.

My mother's eyes are filled with alarm when she sees me. I must look like a ghost, drained of life. She puts her shawl around me and whispers, "My poor child, you look ghastly."

She and my father take me outside and I walk in a state of utter shock, and disbelief that for a moment causes me to think I am merely dreaming and will soon wake up from the most abominable nightmare. Back home in my room, I sob and weep and shake and go into convulsions and my mother kisses me and strokes my hair, and cries with me not knowing how to help me.

"Tell me, my child, tell me. Share your burden with me. I shall not judge you; I shall be there for you as I have always been. What is tormenting you, my sweet child?"

Through sobs and the heaving of my chest I confide in her. I expect shock and condemnation over losing my virginity before marriage, but in a soothing voice she tells me all will be well. She adds we shall never see these abominable men again, and I will forget this disappointment with time. She promises not to tell my father a word of this and to keep this as our secret. She will tell him I have food poisoning, probably from shellfish, and she will persuade him to leave Italy immediately. She also has an additional argument because her aunt wrote informing her of a grave illness she has succumbed to, and my mother, as her sole inheritor as well as caretaker, feels it her obligation to return to England promptly.

And we do return to England after two days. I have no recollection of the trip or my arrival as I am running a high fever and become semi-comatose. I drift in and out of consciousness and during the moments I am lucid and alert, I see nurses and doctors around me and I feel cold compresses on my forehead. Many times during these brief periods of consciousness I am aware of James's presence in the room.

Floating between life and death, I find his presence always seems to pull me towards life, especially when I feel his hand hold mine. Time has stopped. I feel like a human pendulum swinging back and forth between complete madness and death, and at times decide death is preferable.

When I finally come around, I am too weak to talk, but wanly smile at my mother and James. My mother looks haggard and tormented and James infinitely serious and older than his real age. I ask for a mirror because I want to see my reflection to convince myself I am truly alive because I feel dead. My mother tells me it is not a good idea. She adds my illness was eight weeks long and the family was afraid I might die. I am too weak to tell her something in me did die and I was afraid part of me would never feel alive again. I wonder how many people go on living when carrying within them shattered souls. I want to ask the doctor who checks on me several times a day if souls can heal fully or are they always crisscrossed with deep and ugly scars.

The doctor's name is David and he sometimes stays with me. His eyes are full of compassion and I confide in him, breaking down anew before him. He listens attentively and tells me the worst is over, I am physically out of danger, but emotionally I still need to heal. He tells me people rarely die of broken hearts, but the effects can linger for many years. He takes me outside for short walks and soon his visits turn into something I start looking forward to because I see him as a guardian angel. His gentleness is disarming and his calmness has a soothing effect on me. What I find strange is, I feel as if I have known him forever. I make him promise that once I leave the hospital he will visit me and we shall nurture this newfound friendship.

My recovery is slow in spite of David's help and daily presence. It is clearly not my body which is not healing fast, but my mind. From time to time it still feels suspended in a well filled with darkness. Few things give me joy or stir within me pleasure or delight but also nothing stirs a reaction of pain either, because my heart is shackled in frost. The remnants of my soul are surrounded by armor, not allowing anything to penetrate. At times, I believe death has not completely let me loose of its clutches and may yet return to reclaim me.

Gradually, I begin to eat and sleep better, but in spite of my daily activities and conversations with David, I am living only a breath away from death. I can hardly remember ever having felt the vitality which photos of me seem to exude. When I look at myself in the mirror, I do not recognize the girl with hollow and dead eyes. My eyes are not the only hollow part of me; I feel hollowed out both physically and spiritually, even on the day I am discharged from the hospital.

James visits me every few days and takes me out for walks in the fields around our estate. We sit under my favorite willow tree even though the weather has turned cold. One day, just before he comes to take me for a walk, I actually feel happiness in the anticipation of seeing him. The change in my mood, however slight, gives me hope I am finally on the mend. As days go by, the moments spent with him start filling me with flickers of contentment followed by genuine joy. James brings me books, chocolates, and flowers; he tells me jokes to pry laughter from me. He does not speak of love but the look in his eyes reveals not only love, but adoration, respect, and friendship. I cringe at the thought of how he might feel about me once he has learned the ugly truth. Would he see me as licentious, lascivious, and utterly immoral? And after a few months, I decide to put him to the test.

One day in early May, as we are enjoying an unseasonably warm day rowing on the river which flows through the farthest end of our estate, I tell him the whole story. While recounting it, I look at him defiantly and start feeling anger when his face pales and his rowing becomes erratic. At the same time, I am glad to finally express deep emotion, albeit negative. There is hope I shall surface into the light once again.

"I loved him madly, and I would have done everything and anything to stay with him, but he was a coward tied to a life that made him financially comfortable and secure; he was a coward who never would have changed anything in his life to be with me; he was a man who did not love me, who was only infatuated with me for a short while, who cruelly awakened my love and trampled on it in the most depraved way!" I am almost shouting and my voice frightens the nearby ducks, which flap their wings and vanish from our sight quacking in disapproval.

The sun is pouring gold on the emerald-colored river as a soft breeze rustles the tender springtime foliage of the trees. There is so much beauty around us yet so much darkness, poison and dirt in me I wish I could just vomit it all out or cut myself open and bleed it all out into the river until my wounds close and scar over it all once for good.

James is still silent as he rows the boat to the bank under our willow tree and extends his hand to help me out. His grip on my hand is firm.

We sit under the willow tree and I find myself trembling with an emotion I cannot define. We look at each other and he puts my face between his hands and looks at me with the intensity that bores and burns into my soul. His voice is hoarse when he talks to me.

"Juliet, what you experienced in Rome, and what you have just recounted, shows you trusted a snake disguised as a man; you saw love where lust was cloaked as love; you abandoned your principles, your upbringing, you bared your soul and gave your heart to someone undeserving. I do feel slighted because you did not respond...or rather, you did not reciprocate my feelings, which have always been pure and constant and unfaltering. But I shall never say I love you one day, and six months later discover my heart has emptied of that love. And I wish I could kill that worm of a man, that depraved bastard. No wonder his own parents rejected him. They must have known what a beast they created. And to think his betrayal almost killed you, as you allowed yourself to descend into a state of such despair, you reached the brink of death. How could you have done that to yourself? Why was I not good enough? Why did we have to come to this?"

His voice cracks as anguish and shock seep out.

"James, you need to leave and never see me again. I do not deserve you, but I did deserve the despair and the illness, and perhaps I even deserved to die. What I did was unforgivable. It was a bout of insanity. Now, when I think back, I cannot fathom what it was that made me fall in love with him. I had not understood the nature of love before it happened. What I want to say is…it is one thing to read about love and imagine it, and another to experience it in its full tumultuousness. I still do not understand the force that connects two people. But I can now discern the different kinds of love. I do not know what else I can say. I cannot reverse or obliterate the past. But you must leave me; I am so completely adulterated."

"No, you are not adulterated! You simply made a mistake, a horrible mistake, it was pure misjudgment, misjudgment of character, situation. You were too innocent to know, too naïve. We shall overcome this…this horror together and emerge stronger, and our bond will become fortified. I shall never leave you because that would mean abandoning all my dreams."

"Aren't you repulsed by me, as I am no longer what I once was? I am spoiled goods and should not even hope to marry."

His answer is a kiss, a passionate kiss that surprises me and stirs feelings of affection I thought I had lost forever. I see my hand touch his face and I feel a faint smile frolic on my lips.

"James, I need time. I cannot be rushed as I am still healing, and that road is long and arduous with many setbacks."

"I shall give you time, I shall be your healer, and I shall always be by your side."

"I know you are honorable, James. Someone in Nettuno told me you would be my true love." I smile a smile of joy, the smile of a bright future. But in my heart, there is still an oozing wound.

CHAPTER THIRTEEN

David
I look at my watch and realize Leandra has been under hypnosis for over two hours. Her body language indicates exhaustion, so I bring her out of it. When she opens her eyes, I can clearly see fatigue, but after a few moments it seems to disappear and she says brightly,

"I have a feeling I might have uncovered a lot this time. Some of it I remember, and what I remember is a happy ending with Kieran…I mean Kieran with a different name. I cannot recall the name."

"The name was Carlo in that lifetime. Sorry to disappoint you, but the happy ending was not with him, but someone else."

"Oh, so this was another past life in which we did not end up together. After you give me the recording I can listen to another one of my life stories when someone I love abandons me. I have certainly found the story of my life. The pattern certainly doesn't change much, does it?" There is an undertone of irony and self-deprecation in her voice.

"As far as I am concerned, we have plenty of evidence stemming from these regression sessions to point out that Kieran, or whatever his name happens to be, disappointed you and betrayed you again and again. I'm certain if I regress you again, the findings would be identical, as a clear pattern has emerged. You have noticed it yourself—"

"I have to go now." She interrupts and I realize she didn't hear what I said.

A feeling of vexation catches me by surprise and I feel like shaking her, hitting her over the head with a hammer to knock some sense into her and leech this toxic addiction out of her. Because she's going to Barcelona in a week and because she has re-established contact with Weylin, albeit only on a supposed professional basis, she's obviously hoping their love affair will be rekindled. I feel sorry for her and impatient with her at the same time. My expectation is someone as educated, intelligent and usually level-headed as she is would finally understand the lesson, and realize she has formed an unhealthy attachment to a dream, a fantasy, and in her reality she is fortunate enough to have everything she needs, everything most people lack in their lives.

It also occurs to me we have never really discussed her relationship with Adrian. It's quite possible there is a serious fault line in her marriage, which the illicit affair has just accentuated. I plan to ask her about that, but she is already at the door.

"I have to make up the lost hours, and I don't think I will have time to see you before I go to Barcelona, but I will be in touch. Do you want me to email you or send you messages through Facebook?"

"Leandra, do I look like somebody who uses Facebook?" I'm starting to sound exasperated, even to myself. "I need to warn you, you're exposing yourself to rejection by going to Barcelona. You're being foolish and are clearly in denial when it comes to your motives. I'm sure you are still attracted to him and harbor hopes of reviving the affair. You should be feeling resentful and embittered and angry. He betrayed you in every…incarnation." The tone of my voice has an angry overtone.

"I expect support from a fellow therapist and not harsh judgment."

"I am more than your therapist. As a friend it's my duty to tell you what you need and not what you want to hear. He betrayed you over and over again. How hard is that to understand, goddammit? You're ready to forgive him at the cost of another wounding. It's so obvious. You...you are behaving like a masochist running back to the person who shattered you." My voice is getting louder and I don't like it.

"If you had forgiven your parents for betraying you, you would not have built an ice wall around your heart preventing love from entering. Your parents were lost in the maze of their own pain and they hurt you not because of ill intentions, but because of their ineptitude in dealing with their own trauma. I think your vicarious witness of the betrayal in my past lives has triggered the trauma of your feeling betrayed by your parents. Your stuttering and anger have little to do with me. Don't you see that? It's a case of projecting your unresolved issues onto the events of my life, or my past lives. And you are shouting at me, and your knuckles are turning white. I won't tolerate that, not from a friend and certainly not from my psychoanalyst."

"You are ready to forgive him and...and that is a weakness."

"You are wrong, there is strength in forgiveness. Not forgiving makes your heart grow thorns. I think I'm done here."

"Fine! I also think this concludes our sessions. We may have wasted each other's time." The slight stutter in my voice and the seething anger that cannot be stemming from my disapproval of Leandra's plans to go to Barcelona create in me a sense of becoming undone. And I am afraid to face the person under the slipped mask.

"Anyway, thanks for trying to help." Her voice sounds feigned and strained.

"I haven't helped you. You have to help yourself—" She's already gone.

I do not hear from her over the next few days. I am tempted to send her an email of apology but cannot bring myself to write to her. Tomorrow, she flies for Barcelona for a chance to see Weylin again. My premonition for their encounter is dark. And I shake my head over all of this because it is starting to look like much ado about nothing. Half of the world is starving, dying, the planet has been so ravaged our very existence may be in peril, and yet Leandra and I are spending valuable time and energy analyzing why her lover has disappointed her in every lifetime. Maybe she should take a year of leave and go to Africa and volunteer as a doctor. Giving to others should help her adjust her compass and shift her focus of attention to a pursuit of more meaningful endeavors.

Two days later, I receive an email from her.

Hey, David,

I am enjoying Barcelona again and roaming the city with Sabine Klein, a psychiatrist from Berlin I've met a few times at other lectures. We were the first ones to arrive. Weylin is supposed to arrive tomorrow evening and I'll see him at the reception organized at the hotel by our host. David, I feel calm and composed and ready to meet him and start a new chapter in our relationship, and that is one of friendship. I also want to tell you I listened to the recording of my last hypnotherapy with you and am starting to think I somehow invented all those past lives, and it cannot really be true that what I said under hypnosis had actually taken place.

The weather here's warm and sunny and I already have a bit of a tan. The food is delectable, and the wine so delicious, Sabine and I drank a full bottle over dinner. I plan to take a sleeping pill tonight to diminish the effects of jet lag.

Hope you are well. Don't work too hard and try to go out and have some fun.

Hugs and kisses.

Leandra

P.S. We both displayed inappropriate emotions during our last session. Forgive me. Your friendship means a lot.

I'm glad she sounds upbeat, but the same foreboding doesn't leave me. I still believe she's in denial about the situation, and she doesn't want to face the evidence exhumed by her past life experiences. She's saying she wants friendship with Weylin, but it's clearly a poorly cloaked desire for reconciliation with him. I see elements of addiction and obsession in her behavior, and the time that's elapsed since their break-up has not made any positive difference in her case. She's a tough nut to crack. But that doesn't excuse my outburst and I plan to apologize.

She is also right about my suppressed feelings. Leandra will be pleased to hear I confronted my mother during my weekend visit and our conversation left us both in tears. I was finally able to articulate what I never could as a boy. I apologized for breaking her figurines and shared my painful feelings of abandonment and betrayal. She was speechless for a few moments. Then she hugged me and cried and cried; her hot tears soaked not only my shirt but also my heart, melting its frost. Hearing my mother apologize for failing me emotionally, when I needed her most because she felt so entangled in the web of her own pain, broke the wall of resentment I had built. And I felt hopeful that, just perhaps, I've seen the last of my demons. I left her house with a huge sense of relief, promising to visit soon and take her out to dinner.

A knock on my door interrupts my reverie. I hear myself sigh and turn my attention to my next patient who comes in. It is a young woman suffering from claustrophobia and a fear of flying. She cannot advance in her career because she only accepts business trips to destinations she can reach by car. I have been seeing her for six months, but we have not made much progress. Today, however, she tells me she's just come back from a trip to Paris and not only was she not frightened of the flight, she also enjoyed the experience and has never felt so liberated, happy and light. So after all, I was able to help her. This realization seems to diffuse some of my frustration with Leandra.

The afternoon flies by and it is already five in the afternoon when I finish with my last patient. Just as I am getting ready to go home, the phone rings and to my surprise it is Adrian inviting me to dinner. He says that since he is feeling a little lonely without Leandra, and since he assumes I may also miss her after all the time we've been spending together, he thought we might enjoy an evening of good food and wine and conversation. I'm suspicious of his motives and only hope he's not jealous of my time and involvement with his wife. God forbid he thinks there might be something more than friendship or a collegial relationship between me and her.

I meet him at a little Italian restaurant called, 'Ambrosia,' so popular one needs to make reservations three weeks in advance. When I mention I'm meeting Adrian, and I'm shown to a nice table in a bay window, I can't resist asking the waitress to explain my luck of getting the best table without a reservation. She laughs and says Adrian is a frequent quest and a good friend of Mr. Bianchi, the owner, and there's always a table available for him. I sit down and a minute later a man with a thick beard and moustache appears and proffers his hand to me.

"I am Mario Bianchi. May I offer you an aperitif while you are waiting for my savior Adrian?"

"Savior…?"

"He put away behind bars an entire racketeering ring which had victimized me and my business for years. I can never repay him for liberating me of that evil and enabling me to run my business in peace. You didn't hear of the trial two years ago?"

228

"No, I'm afraid not, even though I've been aware of restaurants being hit by the racket."

"A very positive side effect came from the trial. I was one of the witnesses, and because the name of my restaurant was mentioned so many times, the trial became the best advertisement I've ever had, and business boomed so much I had to hire several more people. Now I'm thinking of buying this whole building and adding a storey. But then again, I'm getting on in years and my only son has no interest in being a restaurant owner."

At that moment Adrian appears and they hug and kiss like the best of friends. Mario leaves but reappears with a bottle of wine, telling us it came from his vineyard in Italy. He stays to drink a glass with us and leaves after persuading us not to order from the menu, but to allow him to surprise us with a selection of his specialties.

"Have you heard from Leandra?" I ask Adrian and he nods, looking pensive. I notice he's wearing a suit and I assume he did not go home after work to change into something more casual. He also appears tense and nervous.

"David, I know you'll say you cannot disclose much, but I need to ask you if Leandra seems alright to you. She told me she's been seeing you professionally because she's been suffering from insomnia and menopause symptoms, but I'm certain there's more to it. She's been acting strangely, she often looks distracted, as if she'd been crying—and I've no idea what's bothering her."

"Has the relationship been going well between you two? I mean, is it sound and strong?"

"After so many years of marriage—and I understand you've never been married yourself—most people, I guess, do everything they can to make their relationships function. It's like running a ship; the roles get divided, sometimes through explicit and sometimes through silent consent. You have babies, change diapers, attend your children's school plays, cook dinner, do laundry, go to work to make enough money for a bigger house, take vacations, buy new cars, and suddenly you realize everything in your life functions like the parts in a well-oiled machine.

"But with time, you also realize the passion that once burned like a volcano has burned out. You and your wife have developed so many other interests and built such separate worlds for yourselves, the cords which connected you so tightly at one point have become loose. What I'm really trying to say is, I feel Leandra and I have drifted apart and I'm now panicking because I'm afraid I'm losing her. I don't know what to do to rebuild the intimacy in our marriage. When I see that distant look in her eyes, I fear she's fallen in love with someone else and is planning to break the news to me any day. I don't know what else could have affected such a change in her.

"And there's something else I see in her eyes that scares me. When she looks at me, I sometimes see the worst possible reflection of myself, and wonder what attributes she gives me. I shudder at the thought her look means she no longer loves me or admires me as she once did. She used to be so fascinated by me."

"It could just be menopause, stress at work, her missing the children..." As I am saying this without much conviction in my voice I hear in the background Alessandro Safina's rendition of the aria "I Believe I Still Hear," from the *Pearl Fishers*. The music distracts me and I'm no longer listening to Adrian attentively. When the piece is followed by "Dido's Lament," as if he read my thoughts, Adrian says, "Mario is an opera buff. He's the type of man who cries in opera. His wife was also an opera lover, but died from cancer a few years ago. He says when he's listening to opera he feels his wife's spirit envelop him in love. David, to return to Leandra, do you think something serious is wrong with her?"

"I don't think it's anything serious. I believe she's been under a lot of stress at work, and this conference will do her good and help her relax. Why don't you talk to her? Why don't you go away on an exotic vacation and re-examine your relationship to see if there are any issues between you which need to be resolved, habits that need to be changed, improved; talk about expectations that have not been met, disappointments that have not been expressed. I've never been married, and as it stands now I may always remain a bachelor, but I understand quite well how complicated human relationships can be, and I also know unions can be harmonious and happy if the people are compatible with each other and if their bonds are based on love, trust and respect.

"I think you need to start showing more interest in Leandra. You may need to find time for her, to woo her again, court her again. Underneath the psychiatric professional is a very romantic woman, a woman who's still in love with the idea of love. You need to find a way to shift her energy and attention back to you."

"That implies her attention has shifted elsewhere or toward someone else. Are you saying there is another man in her life, that she has a lover?"

"Even if I knew, I would not be able to disclose that information…." As soon as I say that I realize, even though she is no longer in a relationship with Weylin, she's still as unfaithful as she had ever been. I also wonder if Adrian has had affairs.

Our dinner starts arriving, one delectable dish after another, and the topics of our conversation become lighter as we discuss politics and books. The evening turns into a pleasant and entertaining engagement, especially when Mario rejoins us. After a couple of bottles of wine I start feeling drunk, and am grateful and scared at the same time when Adrian offers to give me a ride home. He must be just as drunk as I am even though he doesn't show it. I'm glad tomorrow is Sunday and I can sleep in.

Sunday is quiet. I spend the day reading and writing an article on phobias and their treatment. I stop work only to make a sandwich. After last night's feast of Italian delicacies which included fish and meat, my stomach is not ready for any elaborate or rich food, and I cannot even imagine having anything alcoholic. In the afternoon I take a nap, and then continue working on the article. At some point I stop and contemplate my life.

All of a sudden a feeling of emptiness creeps in and I realize how lonely I've become. It would not be too late still for me to have a family, if I met the right woman. I wonder whether I may not be the right man for anyone. I have become too set in my ways, as I love my freedom and am not sure if I could merge my lifestyle with someone else's.

But this evening, the feeling of loneliness sits heavy on my heart. Adrian also seemed to be lonely last night. Perhaps his loneliness scared him, and perhaps he realized that even with Leandra his loneliness still hangs like a dark cloud above him. I remember him shaking his head as if trying to decipher or pinpoint the exact moment when Leandra and he started to become alienated from each other.

Perhaps most couples only recognize the rift between them once it becomes too wide to close again. And then, it's not a big leap to jump into infidelity under the right circumstances. Infatuation quickly turns into the illusion of love, and if those people leave their respective marriages and start a new life together, it probably doesn't take long for another rift to appear again and for solitude in the two to emerge. Perhaps it is impossible for two people to love each other forever; perhaps it is only possible to tolerate one another forever because there is no easy way out. Perhaps those who stay together are very good at rationalizing why they should stay together; they may be in perpetual denial of their emptiness and unhappiness, because few people can find happiness within themselves, and thus continue to seek it outside themselves.

When I look at the clock, I see it's midnight. I decide to take a sleeping pill because it's clear I won't be able to fall asleep for a long time due to the nap I took.

When I arrive at the office the next morning, I check my email first, and as expected, find Leandra's email in my inbox.

Good morning, David,

Adrian wrote to say the two of you spent a wonderful evening together at Mario's. You must have noticed the lovely background music in the restaurant. Sometimes I think I go there for the music more than the food. Anyway, I'm pleased to see Adrian and you get along fine. He's not an easy man to like, as you may have noticed.

I saw Weylin last night at the reception. We chatted pleasantly for a while, but later I noticed he was with the woman from Norway, the same woman I saw flirting with him at the earlier conference. She is quite flirtatious, bubbly and she never left his side. It was clear there was a connection between them. I also noticed whenever she would leave the reception to go outside to smoke, he would follow her. His arm was wrapped around her shoulders protectively, as they were climbing down the staircase to leave. At some point, we all found ourselves in the same circle of people, and when she got up to leave and go to her room, she cast a meaningful glance at Weylin as if letting him know he should follow her in a few minutes. He and I talked a bit longer about his kids and work, and then everyone left for their rooms. When I arrived in mine, I received a text message from him saying, 'Nice to talk to you again, W.' I replied saying I was happy to have talked to him and to have diffused any awkwardness, and I would always cherish the beautiful memories.

I hope you're not working too hard. Perhaps you and Adrian can get together again before I come home.

I will write tomorrow.
Warm regards from hot Barcelona,
Leandra

After work, I get together with a colleague to play tennis. I've neglected exercise lately and feel sluggish. He easily beats me in two sets and after the game we go for a couple of beers. Over drinks he tells me he and his wife are divorcing. She met a man at a conference, fell in love and is leaving him. I almost choke on my beer thinking infidelity is becoming a fad.

"What the fuck is wrong with humans?" I exclaim.

Michael looks at me in surprise. "I've never heard you swear before!"

"Mike, I've been dealing with human nature for so many years, and as a species, we are a disappointment in spite of the technological and scientific progress we've made, the symphonies we've composed and the inexpressible beauty we've created. I think I'm in the wrong profession; maybe I should have pursued my dream of becoming a marine biologist. But go ahead and tell me what happened."

"How can someone tell you she loves you a few weeks ago and then currently tell you she's leaving you because she loves someone else? How can people be so fickle?"

"Michael, she doesn't love him, she's sexually infatuated. She'll only know if she loves him a few years down the road. She's not thinking rationally now; she's acting under the influence of chemicals in her brain. It's like drinking and driving, a case of impaired reasoning. People become bored or dissatisfied for different reasons with their marriages, and they fall in love with a stranger who uses all his charm and wit to woo them. It's an exciting and thrilling game because it's all new, and you're discovering and conquering unknown territory. You love your own reflection in the eyes of that stranger, and after a few years, the effects of the drug called infatuation wear off and you find yourself in the same old despair of dissatisfaction. No wonder second or third marriages stemming from infidelity break down more quickly than first marriages."

"I'm devastated by her betrayal and her lies, but I still love her. How can I love someone so dishonest?"

"You love her because you are still attached to her and the life you had with her. We form attachments to people, situations, our past, and letting go is one of the hardest things we have to do. Forgiving is another. You are hurt and the sense of betrayal you feel cannot be measured, but you still love her. Sometimes we feel the most love at the moment when we realize we've lost someone. Your wife may realize after a certain time, once the sexual infatuation fizzles out, she's made a mistake and she may want to come back to you.

"Or she may discover she's hit the bull's eye by meeting this man. Or he may grow tired of her and find a new lover. You know all of this already. No relationship comes with a warranty. You have to wait it out. Time can tell you how this will further unfold. One day she may want you back and will find out you have moved on. In your case, if it comes to divorce, it won't be as difficult as it is for people who have children."

"There are two dogs and a cat, and I cannot imagine giving up even one of them." Mike lowers his head and his shoulders start to shake in silent weeping. His voice is a whisper when he says, "How can anything hurt so much? I want to die."

"A broken heart is one of the most painful of human conditions. It should be added to the list of psychiatric conditions; unfortunately, there is no quick cure for it, and everyone must suffer through its course. I wish I could give you a painkiller for that."

"How can there be so much love at one point and none a few weeks later? We spent a fantastic weekend hiking just last month. I don't understand. How can I no longer matter, or did I ever matter to her...." He's sobbing now inconsolably and attracting curious glances.

"Mike, all in life comes and goes and very few things offer us any lasting value. The only non-fickle and consistent love is that between parents and children, and humans and dogs perhaps. Romantic love is the most volatile, fluid, and inconsistent love. Unless it transforms into a deeper form of connectedness, it evaporates. There are, however, many couples whose love grows over the years, whose attachment for each other deepens, and once they reach old age, it often happens that one dies right after the other dies, because the bond is so deep and strong they pull each other into death. I believe there are people who are each other's soul-mates through multiple lives. That's why I use past life regression as a form of therapy."

"What should I do?"

"Just like everyone else you have to overcome adversity, rebuild your life, rise like the Phoenix from the ashes. It's a platitude to say 'time heals', but it does make the pain fade as it, so to say, covers memories with the patina of oblivion."

"I wish I could go there now. I wish I could fast-forward time and be my happy self again." He stops crying, but sadness and sorrow are etched on his face. Again, I contemplate on how I have never experienced such a loss, as I've never fallen in love with anyone so deeply. Witnessing the lacerating power of love, I feel content its blade has somehow spared me. But at the same time it makes me feel almost less human, and I wonder if I really want to leave earth without having felt such a powerful attraction. Perhaps it's still not too late for love to find me. Especially now; after the conversation with my mother I feel as if a Sisyphean burden has been lifted off my heart.

After two more beers we part, but agree to meet regularly on weekends to play tennis. I watch him as he leaves, a defeated man, and for a heartbeat, I feel an aching compassion for all betrayed lovers.

I'm surprised not to hear from Leandra for the next three days and my assumption is she and Weylin have probably reconnected and are enjoying illicit bliss again. However, what she has revealed under hypnotherapy strengthens my belief she has exposed herself to another disappointment. I wish I were wrong.

POISONOUS WHISPERS

The day flies by again and after my last patient leaves, I
phone Mike to see how he's doing. As expected, he sounds
depressed and tells me he's taken a few days of sick leave, but is
now having second thoughts, about going back to work to gain
some distraction from the debilitating hurt he's feeling. I tell him to
be gentle with himself, to give himself time to heal and not to rush
forward with any major decisions such as divorce. I also tell him
that since his wife has left him, perhaps her lover who's also
married will come to his senses at hearing her expectations, and
he now should do the same. She may experience some very
sobering moments and realize she has believed in a fantasy, and
the reality is her lover might suddenly get cold feet.

He replies he doesn't know if he could ever trust her again
if she asks for their reconciliation. His trust has been irreparably
broken and he feels his heart has been laced with a poison he'll
never be able to expunge.

Because I lack personal experience in the matters of heart,
I feel I'm not the best person to offer advice. I am like a Catholic
priest counseling marital couples on how to make their marriages
more successful. Again, I wish I'd been exposed to genuine
suffering of the type found in Goethe's, *The Sorrows of Young
Werther*. I would be able to generate empathy for such losses,
empathy from my own heart and not from my mind. The way I
view such situations is rather simple. If she no longer wants you,
forget her, and you move the fuck on and find someone else who'll
appreciate you and love you unfalteringly. Chapter closed,
discussion ended!

It seems to me it's easier to treat depression or anxiety
than a broken heart. Everything I say sounds a meaningless
platitude, but he seems to appreciate my interest in his story. As a
psychiatry colleague, I'm sure he has, like Leandra, helped
countless numbers of people, and yet, when it comes to self, he's
as helpless as the rest of us. No amount of knowledge or
understanding can assist you in alleviating your own anguish.

Before I go home, I stop by Mario's and order a take-out
dinner of lasagna. He adds a small carton to the larger one as a
complimentary serving of breaded zucchini. He hugs me warmly
as if I were his closest friend of many years. Even though this is
the second time I've seen him, he looks to me like one of the

happiest and most optimistic people I've ever met. I wonder if it is the mask he shows his patrons, or if he's genuinely joyful. Next time I come to his restaurant I'll ask him. Perhaps he can share some wisdom and advice I can pass on to my patients.

After dinner, I put on *The Pearl Fishers* DVD with Renee Fleming in the main soprano role and pour myself a white wine. Even though I'm thoroughly enjoying the opera I've seen so many times before, once again I experience a sense of loneliness. Lately I've been feeling alone more and more often. I also realize I miss my talks with Leandra. Perhaps I should get a cat or a dog, or even a wife. I laugh at the sequence of the items heralded as able to diminish human loneliness.

I realize the wine bottle is empty and I've consumed a full liter of wine. The state of drunkenness only amplifies the loneliness, and I go to bed with feelings of Weltschmerz constricting my throat and chest. Perhaps I should ask Leandra for quid pro quo treatments, because I may also be in need of psychiatric help. I certainly don't believe all my childhood and other issues have ever been successfully resolved, in spite of the mandatory psychoanalysis I underwent as a psychiatric resident.

I fall into a fitful sleep, full of nightmares. The sound of the telephone ringing is a welcome, albeit abrupt wake-up lifting the dark fog of a nightmare, the content of which I can't remember, but the weight of which I still feel sitting heavy on my chest. Before I pick up I look at the clock. It is two a.m. and my first thought is someone must have dialed the wrong number. Very few people have my home phone number.

I answer and hear an almost inaudible, "David," followed by breathing that sounds like someone hyperventilating.

"Who is this?" I ask groggily.

"Leandra." All of a sudden a bad presentiment fills my stomach with a feeling of nausea.

"Is it you, Leandra? When did you get back from the conference?"

"I'm still in Barcelona…flying back home tomorrow."

I wait to hear her continue, and I don't even care she's calling at such an ungodly hour. I'm wide awake now, and I want to know how her encounter with Weylin has gone, but I already know it did not unfold as she was hoping. Kieran, Carlo,

Weylin...all of them trampled upon her heart, one lifetime after another. I hope she's finally learned from these lessons, so she doesn't have to repeat them again.

"David..." She's hyperventilating at the other end so I ask her to sit down and have a sip of water before we continue our conversation, which, in fact hasn't even begun. After a minute or so she comes back, sounding calmer.

"You were so right. I should have listened to you. I've had a huge setback. I've allowed him again to break my heart. I'm back at square one when it comes to healing and getting over him. It was much worse than I ever expected...it was horrible, just awful."She's crying and sobbing and talking at the same time

I cannot make out what she is saying. "How did he break your heart again? And please, calm down, I cannot understand you. Leandra, where are you calling from? You'll be paying a fortune for this call."

"I don't care what it costs. I have to talk to you." There is silence again and then she speaks, sounding more composed.

"The first night when we met at the reception, as I've already told you in my email, we had a pleasant conversation as colleagues, but we were never alone. I also couldn't detect any signs he was still attracted to me. I told you he spent most of the evening with a beautiful woman from Norway, the one who had flirted with him in Berlin the first time I met her. But she was flirting with everyone else, too, so I wasn't paying much attention to her. So, she was again by his side and casting glances at him, showing some kind of secret bond they shared. And I told you he and I exchanged text messages that same evening, and I thought the feelings were friendly between us.

"The shock came the next day, and continued throughout the week. In the same city, in Barcelona, which had symbolized so much to me, he was inseparable from this woman. David, they were together at breakfast, lunch, dinner, after dinner, every coffee break, when sightseeing...it was so obvious he had another lover and completely forgotten me. It was like watching a replay of a movie in which I'd played the main leading role the first time, and now I was replaced by another woman. What kind of man is he? Did I meet Dr Jekyll and Mr. Hyde on two different occasions in Barcelona? How could he have fallen in love again so soon?"

She's sobbing again and is obviously in deep distress. I cannot help thinking if this doesn't sober her up and pull her out of this obsession and addiction, nothing else will.

"I am not jealous of her because I like her immensely. Jorunn is charming, engaging and irresistible, and she likes me. And David, a colleague who was sitting next to me in the conference hall kept telling me I was making strange sounds as if hyperventilating. Imagine how embarrassing that I would be hyperventilating from stress and shock so openly! But you cannot imagine how much strength it took to look and sound in a good mood, when I was literally falling apart, dying on the inside, watching the man I was in love with enthralled by another woman."

"So did you tell him how you felt?"

"Yes, I asked him to talk to me one last time, explaining I was looking for closure, to end that chapter of my life. We met yesterday after she left. I told him I was shocked that in the city in which I was hoping for closure, closure hit me like a ton of bricks when I realized he had another lover."

"What did he say?"

"He denied it, and said she was just a friend. He said I was accusing him and making him feel uncomfortable. He also asked why would he need to justify himself, and insisted he was just having a good time. I asked him to tell me why we'd broken up and he said it was because he could no longer cope with the stress of living in two parallel worlds, and also because of the circumstances. Throughout the conversation, I felt I was extracting answers from him he didn't want to give.

"I asked him if he had a difficult time after our break-up, and if he had felt tempted to write to me. He replied 'yes', but it all sounded forced, as if he could hardly wait for an unpleasant conversation to be over so he could get away from me."

She stops talking and I hear her breathing heavily. When she continues, it is clear she's still crying.

"He told me he had no good answers to my questions. He said, 'Leandra, remember I'm an introvert, and I go inward to bury negative feelings, and have stuffed away a lifetime of bad energy. I hope it doesn't come back to haunt me, to punish me."

"I realized he had buried me nine feet deep in a coffin stamped, 'Closed files, do not reopen!' and I was forcing him to exhume that long-ago buried file which no longer meant anything to him. He then added, 'I'm a mess and have unpleasant thoughts about my life.' My first instinct was to rummage in his closed files, in his pain, to help him heal. I asked him if he wanted to talk about it, but he said he didn't because he had so much self-pity. Oh David, I felt like such an idiot, rambling on and on."

She stopped talking again and her hyperventilation returned. I thought she might find an inhaler useful, but didn't say so, only waited for her to regain control.

"David, I sounded so disconnected, but perhaps the only clear thing I managed to convey was that I was still in love with him despite all the betrayals in the past and present and future lives. I asked him to forgive me for making him feel uncomfortable, and when we hugged to say goodbye, I told him I'd missed hugging him. But he was unresponsive. I lovingly trailed the side of his face with my hand, and I bared my heart again and gave him one more time an ice pick to hack it in a million places. And he did, by loving another woman and showing me I no longer meant to him what I once did. I felt I'd lost him all over again."

She is silent again and with her voice full of cracks she continues.

"I humiliated myself. He was in love with someone new, flaunting it openly, and all I wanted were crumbs of friendship from him, anything to keep him near. I feel like an idiot, a fool. David, look at me—I'm a betrayer, accusing another betrayer of betrayal. I'm disconnected. I'm confused and in despair, and that's making it hard for me think rationally. I'm in a shell-shocked state…once again."

"Leandra, I'm sorry the ending to your story had to be so stressful, but I didn't expect anything better. If I were to hypnotize you again, you would tell me another story from your past life in which Weylin broke your heart. Can't you see the pattern?"

"I don't know what I see. I can't think straight. I'm filled with anxiety. I'm in emotional overdrive; I want to forget him, but I doubt it can happen quickly even though he has ruptured my heart—again. Now, I can imagine him enjoying his reflection in the mirror of her eyes, until that mirror cracks, and he finds himself alone once again with his unlovable self. Oh, I'm sounding so spiteful. David, how can someone who betrays her husband expect her lover not to betray her? It's a karmic circle. What you sow is what you reap."

CHAPTER FOURTEEN

Leandra

On the flight home I feel stunned, dazed and frozen in a haze of disbelief of what I'd just witnessed in Barcelona. Is life really composed of a series of random moments, coincidences? He supposedly wasn't even scheduled to come to the conference, but replaced a colleague at the last moment. And that colleague, who couldn't come, has no idea how the circumstances which prevented her from coming affected my life!

How interconnected we all are, how often happenings in one person's life produce a ripple effect in another's. Who knows what decisions I've made in my life that may have hurt someone without my being aware? And, oh my God, the karmic punishment! How can you not believe in that? How can you not believe in the cosmic law of cause and effect? My heart is so ruptured I feel close to being dead. I wonder, will natural optimist in me weather this emotional devastation.

And what about Adrian? Is there still love between us? When was the last time he and I burst into spontaneous laughter? When did our marriage die without an announcement, without an abrupt change to make the dying noticeable, to alert us and alarm us in time to resuscitate it? I have no answers to any of these questions; all my training and knowledge cannot do anything but leave me stranded on the shores of doubt, confusion and renewed pain. I feel I'm bleeding anew from every pore, and every breath I take hurts.

What's the purpose of falling in love illicitly, and having all your illusions shattered in the worst possible way? What lessons does life want to teach me? Questions are swirling in my head until I start feeling dizzy and nauseated. I go to the toilet and vomit, not even feeling the sudden turbulence. Normally, turbulence reawakens my fear of flying, but I feel so numb fear cannot penetrate my thinking. I try to empty my mind of all thoughts and emotions, and sleep for a couple of hours. Ahead of me is a period during which I have to put my own life under the microscope of introspection, and try to make sense of it.

When I do arrive home I go straight to bed. I take a sleeping pill to ensure a few hours of uninterrupted sleep. Adrian wants to make love but I avoid it, claiming exhaustion. I no longer want his touch, and sex with him feels like an unwelcome chore, a ritual to which I subject myself. He doesn't even seem to notice I'm no longer there, I'm no longer present in our brief, albeit still frequent sexual encounters. Having known magic for a few months spent with Weylin, and remembering the magic from my previous lifetimes with Kieran and Carlo, in my present life there is only a void.

The next day is Sunday and I go through the motions of cooking, unpacking, doing laundry, floating through life like a ghost suspended between two worlds. Adrian and I go out for dinner at Mario's and as soon as the waiter serves the appetizer of *FrittoMisto* and leaves, Adrian says, "I'd like us to have a heart to heart talk."

I'm surprised—this is the first time I've heard him say something like that. He sounds serious, and I'm sure now he suspects something.

"I believe we've neglected talking to each other in any meaningful way…" He pauses, struggling to find the right words.

"Our life together has been like a well-run ship on which every crew member fulfills their responsibilities. The main crew members were the two of us, because we've always tried to spare the girls any chores, and let them have a perfect childhood and happy teenage years."

"I believe they're grateful for that. They always felt sheltered and privileged. In fact, they didn't even turn out spoilt, in spite of that life of privilege."

"Yes, I agree. I think as parents we were highly successful, but at the same time, we somehow… how can I put it? We've stopped interacting with each other on a meaningful level. I feel we are…disconnected from each other emotionally. I cannot pinpoint when it started. I was too busy to notice, expecting our relationship was strong, not susceptible to significant change."

I wonder why it's so hard for us to have such a conversation. We've obviously lost the intimacy of being able to share deep thoughts. I suddenly realize how shallow our communication has been for the past few years. And now, it feels we're talking like strangers, even if we think there's nothing new to learn from each other.

"Building a career and raising kids took a lot of energy from both of us, and I wish I'd been more observant of the danger of taking that energy and displacing it. Not that the children and our work didn't deserve focus, but somehow, too little energy was devoted to our relationship. Do you agree?"

Adrian's expression is so pained I feel sorry for him, but I don't know what to say.

"What I've noticed is…you've changed, and I'm not even sure in what ways. I find it difficult to define that change in you because…like I said…or did I say that…anyway, I'm not even sure how it's manifested. You seem to be detached, absent. I see sadness and sorrow in your eyes. I often wonder if it's because the girls have left home, but you've assured me you're content as long as they're happy and satisfied with the choices they've made."

He falls silent and I notice a hint of a tick on his face. He's obviously having a difficult time expressing his thoughts and feelings, and I understand. He's always been practical, composed; he's always known what he wanted and what he had to do to attain his goals. His life path did not meander along winding roads. While he sips his wine pensively I feel my level of stress rise, and think I'm going to burst at the seams. I'm nearing tipping point, when the dam will break and an ocean of tears will flow, drowning my marriage. He looks at me quizzically and I know he expects an answer, an explanation or a confession.

My instinct tells me to lie; to list a few excuses: mental exhaustion, work-related stress, tragic patient stories that have affected me. I rationalize it is better not to hurt someone than to cause them immense pain, but I realize it is betrayals, lies and deceit which have sapped my energy, destroyed my peace and joy; and if I'm ever to regain them, I should start by telling the truth. I never dreamed of revealing to Adrian what I'd done, because wounding him with the truth seems cruel, senseless and pointless. I would advise any patient of mine not to disclose the truth if they want to save their marriage, but I'm so hurt I feel an irresistible urge to hurt him, as if my pain could be diminished by that.

Tears start to spill out of my eyes and for a few minutes I sit in silence, mute. He looks at me with grave concern on his face, expecting perhaps to hear I've been diagnosed with terminal cancer, and that's why I've been acting strangely.

"Adrian, I cheated on you." My voice is hoarse and cracked. To my great surprise, a shadow of relief appears in his eyes.

"I was afraid it was something worse, like you were seriously sick and hiding it from me. So, I assume you had a one-night stand at one of your conferences, and it's now killing you for having tasted forbidden fruit."

Adrian's look is full of expectation and hope it is as simple as that. A little bit of fun on the side, a few forbidden moments that meant nothing the next morning, because no one in their right mind would risk a solid marriage because of a fling.

"It is more complicated in my case." I sigh deeply before I continue, because all of a sudden I'm at a loss for words. There are no right words, nor right tone to admit treason to someone who has trusted you.

"I didn't just cheat…I mean, I didn't just have sex. I had an affair for almost a year and a half. I fell in love, and traveled to Europe to meet him. Yes, it was partly business, but it was also for our illicit encounters. I loved him and did not want the relationship to end, but I was never considering leaving you, just as he never had any intentions of leaving his family for me. I betrayed you, Adrian. I loved him, and I found magic with him. I know it was just fantasy, it was just an illusion, but it felt so real.

"I've been seeing David and undergoing hypnotherapy. David's a believer in reincarnation and, during the sessions, I learned this man had let me down in every lifetime, and will let me down again in the next incarnation, unless I learn the lessons inherent in these relationships. The problem is, I'm not even sure what lessons I'm supposed to have learned in the past lives, nor this one. The only lesson I've learned is that it hurts like hell to be dumped after you believed it was love. Maybe the lesson is not everything that feels like love is love."

"Are you still in that relationship?"

Adrian is as pale as a ghost. He's having trouble swallowing and he blinks at me in disbelief and shock. What I've just told him has probably not even registered fully with him. It will take a few days for him to acknowledge the seriousness of my transgression.

"We broke up because he said he could no longer cope with the stress of living in two parallel worlds and he didn't want the ups and downs. But I don't believe him. The reason he no longer wanted to be with me is, he was attracted to someone else and is in a relationship with her. She took him away from me and he allowed himself to be easily caught, which tells you he never really loved me; for him it was only a fling. You cannot imagine how that hurt me beyond measure. Adrian, I'm devastated because my lover betrayed me. I betrayed you and he betrayed me and his wife."

"Did you ever think about me while you were screwing this other man?" His tone is now angry, menacing, laced with freezing cold.

"I felt guilty many times. I felt possessed by demons I couldn't exorcise. I was carried away on the wings of the passion you and I lost years ago. I won't say I couldn't have helped it. I plunged into that experience head first, and I played an active role in the seduction process. I couldn't resist the pull and I didn't want to resist it. All my integrity and all my principles dissolved almost overnight. It was madness, insanity and I felt so intoxicated. I lost my mind and my heart, and what's worse, what is so sick is—I'm not over him.

"I *want* to be over him, I want to expunge him from my heart, from my blood. But I'm powerless. He still resides in me and that's awful. It's horrific to have betrayed you once and to have to now betray you again by baring my grief before you, my grief over unrequited love. If you want to divorce me, I will completely understand, because what I've done is unforgivable."

Our main course arrives, but neither of us can eat. I pick at the salad and pour myself a third glass of wine. I feel drunk and desperate. Like a worm, sorrow burrows into my soul leaving holes of pain nothing can patch, at least not at this moment. Adrian's face is so white I become frightened. He's squeezing his wine glass so tightly I'm afraid he'll break it and cut himself.

"You are telling me you are grieving the loss of an *asshole* who has simply replaced you with another lover who, I suppose, is younger and prettier and sexier?"

He's trying now to hurt me in revenge, making me look at myself in an imaginary mirror to show me I'm no longer either young or desirable.

"And you can't get over him? What the fuck is wrong with you? You used to be a model of rational thinking even with your wild imagination. How many patients have you helped who were in the same situation? Where did your reason go? Surely you knew married men have mistresses, and they tell their mistresses their wives 'do not understand them', and their wives 'do not want sex with them'? That's certainly what I'd tell mine if I had one. And I wouldn't even be lying, would I?"

He is fuming now and I'm afraid the people around us might hear his raised voice.

"How could you have fallen for a cliché? So, did he tell you his wife avoided sex with him and no longer loved him?"

I don't reply. His tone is of a hissing snake and his eyes are flashing with hatred.

"Yes, he told me that—and I fell for it. I trusted him. Like I said, I believed it was love. And I'm sure you know it's much easier to see the mistakes others are making, in the way they act or feel or think, than to see your own. I can help others, but I haven't been able to help myself. I am not stupid. On the rational level I see things for what they are. He was infatuated with me for a while, and then his infatuation fizzled. It was shallow and it burned out like a straw fire.

"Perhaps he's not even capable of forming a deep bond with anyone because of his abandonment issues. He was abandoned by his parents and raised by his grandparents."

"Why are you telling me this? Why the fuck should *I* care about his life and his issues? Should I feel sorry for the guy who hit on my wife and then dumped her?"

"Adrian, what you and I have built is strong, solid, meaningful. According to David, I had that kind of love in all my previous lifetimes, but I always fell for the lover. I always chose fickle love over the more stable, deep and unfaltering kind. The easiest and most logical solution for you might be to leave me, because your trust has been broken. You'll always wonder if I'm thinking about him, if I'm day-dreaming about him. You'll never be certain if I'm truly over him, or if I'm fully present in our marriage.

"I know if I say I never meant to hurt you, it will not and cannot take away your pain, just as Weylin's words (his name's Weylin) that he never meant to hurt me did not alleviate what he inflicted upon me. He awakened my love, but he never meant to love me for a long time. He even said at the beginning, a long-term relationship between us was not sustainable given the geographical circumstances and our responsibilities. Adrian, I never thought I would have been capable of having a love affair; I never thought I was seeking one. I met him, and felt an instantaneous physical attraction without having even spoken to him or learned if he was charming, interesting, or smart. We started by exchanging emails and very soon I found myself in love.

"Now, I've confessed everything. It makes me both feel better and worse—I hate the fact I've wounded you so deeply. If you had betrayed me like that, I think it would have killed me. Few things can be as painful as that. I'm sorry to have done this to you, but if our marriage has any chance of survival, it can start now, from a clean slate."

All of a sudden Adrian stands and leaves without saying a word. Some people turn their heads and look at us with curiosity. I wanly smile back. I understand his shock, his anger and disbelief. I'll give him time, because I also need time to sort out my own feelings, to heal and to forget. I need a clear head. My heart has misled me, taken me so far astray the result is only pain.

I pay the bill and go home in a cab, as Adrian has taken the car and left me stranded. I don't blame him. My confession must have swept over him like a tsunami. If this doesn't destroy our marriage, nothing will. This must be the ultimate test of durability and resistance.

When I get home, I immediately note Adrian has moved into the guest room. We'll need counseling if we decide to mend things between us, but first we need to give each other time to let the roiling emotions simmer down a bit. I have no idea how much time I'll need to clear the fog in my head.

At work I learn another article of mine has been accepted for publication by a prestigious scientific journal. Weylin had contributed to my research by giving me data he'd collected in his clinical work, which confirmed my own conclusions. I write to let him know I will be acknowledging him. He replies immediately saying he's happy I'm including his name as one of the contributors, and asks me for the link to the article. He also mentions there have been cuts at his hospital and he's going through some challenging professional and personal difficulties. I write back attaching the article and saying I hope the current period of professional and personal uncertainty is soon behind him and his life takes the shape he wants. My email is light, witty and breezy.

A few days later, Weylin replies: he'll read my article after he has come back from his two-week trip to Asia. His reply is brief, and reads as if written in great haste, just to get me off his back. There's nothing personal in it, no sign of the friendship I was hoping for. I cancel all my patients, and tell my secretary I need to work. I lock the door and spend almost a whole day crying. I've allowed him to hurt me again, and I can't shake off this unhealthy attachment which has been a continuous source of suffering for me. I feel so utterly hopeless and helpless. My mind tells me to cherish the beautiful memories, to consider the time spent with him as a gift to my life, as enrichment and the opportunity to re-evaluate myself and my life and make changes for the better.

But my heart is intransigent in its clinging to memories I wish to relive by reconnecting with him. My heart refuses the truth—he no longer loves me. Because I've still not accepted it, because I'm still resisting it, I'm the one re-traumatizing myself. He is done with me and I can no longer blame him for what I'm feeling.

What a curse it is that love relationships of any kind are rarely over at the same time for the two people involved! I feel like a pseudo-psychiatrist, trying to help others get over painful break-ups by offering sound, rational advice without really understanding why anyone would want another who doesn't want them in return. It used to be so simple in my mind. You understand the situation, take concrete measures to overcome it, and extricate yourself from it. You eat and sleep well, you exercise and socialize, you find creative outlets, and you write a diary or letters to yourself that you gently give to a river or any running water so symbolically the river may take your pain away…

Fuck! I will never give such lists of activities to people again; I will never underestimate the devastation of a broken heart inflicted on the poor souls who feel eviscerated by the anguish of loss! I believed people should let go of the past quickly, easily— even though I never said so to my patients. Now, even after a year, I haven't begun to let go, although he's shown me unequivocally in so many ways I no longer play any role in his life, and he has no need to see me, write to me, talk to me or acknowledge my existence.

I'm aware the article I sent him was a ruse, a hook to try to reel him back into my life again. I'm also aware my thoughts of friendship were the means of deluding myself with noble motives, when I still wanted more than friendship. I'm humiliating myself, almost begging him to come back using whatever means I presently have at my disposal, but nothing can work because he no longer wants anything to do with me. How wrenching it is to want to disentangle oneself from this emotional trap, and yet to feel trapped in it, to be unable to free oneself from its stranglehold.

What is the difference between me and my patients who suffer from depression and anxiety? The chemical misbalance in their brains renders them helpless against feelings of fear when there is no cause or reason to be fearful. I can imagine the mess in my own brain, the mess which created this self-delusional behavior, the irrational behavior of wanting a married man who not only has a wife, but also a lover. I need to see David as soon as possible, because I can't get out of this quagmire on my own.

That evening when I arrive home I hear sobbing from the guest room. Adrian is crying. I knock lightly on the door before opening it; he's lying on the bed face down and weeping. My heart breaks. I lie beside him wishing nothing more than to efface his pain. Tears stream from my eyes. Again, I'm amazed at the tears I shed as if I have an inexhaustible source. I shouldn't have told Adrian about my betrayal. I shouldn't have hurt him this way. No one can forgive a marital transgression of such magnitude. I know I wouldn't be able to forgive. I can expect to be served divorce papers, which I would readily sign under any conditions he attaches.

We cry together. Our sadness, sorrow and dejection hang in the air and feel tangible. I have difficulty believing I will ever be whole and happy again, that the light in my soul will ever flood this cursed, dark malady out of its shadowy recesses.

"What do we do now? Where do we go from here?" Adrian's ruptured voice startles me and stops my tear flow.

"Adrian, I'm not able to ask for forgiveness, because what I did was unspeakable and inexcusable, and the pain I inflicted upon you is unforgettable. I *am* willing to do everything to make it better, I am willing to invest *every* effort into rebuilding and resuscitating our marriage, but I have no strength left in me. This experience lifted me to the skies, and then flung me down without warning. I'm not the same person. This has changed me and destroyed me."

"But I love you. Your betrayal makes me want to kill you, kick you out on the street—but it would be wrong to kill my love. But I wish you could just quash your love for that man who doesn't deserve it, who stole you from me only to jilt you. But that's what you deserved…that's what everyone deserves in such a situation. I can't throw away all these wonderful years we've spent together; I cannot allow that demon of a man to destroy us. I hope to God his wife finds out about his philandering ways and kicks his butt out and takes him to the cleaners and he finds himself all alone and unloved."

"Don't wish curses on anyone. Who knows what burdens he carries? I need to forgive him and let go, not wish him ill because he hurt me."

The rancid edge in Adrian's voice sounds like acid seeping out of his soul and it burns holes in mine. The air seems to be composed of toxic fumes, and breathing it in will poison both of us.

"Was he great in bed? I bet he was. I bet that's why you've been avoiding sex with me."

Poison is drenching me to the bone. I don't reply; my answer is implicit in my silence.

He sits up and extends his hand to help me do the same. He takes my face in his hands and says in an agonized voice "I am prepared to forgive you, if you promise to break off all contact with him, professional and personal, for good."

"Adrian, I'm in no position to make any promises, because I've lost trust in my own resolve, my willpower and my sanity. I'm more aware of my present frailty than I ever was of the strength I once possessed. You know me, and you know how strong and ordered my beliefs and my world were. What happened feels like a karmic relationship, like destiny, like a lesson from past lives. Like I said in the restaurant, I still don't know what the lesson is because I feel I've only learned lessons in the agony that follows falling in love at the most inauspicious of times.

"I have to heal, and thus far I've not done a good job of it. I'll continue seeing David for his professional help. I don't want to lose you, because you are the last beacon on an ocean of darkness. I'd made some progress, but I've had a huge setback and have to start all over again. I won't ask you to stand by me, but if you do, it will make my journey back easier."

"What if he asks you to meet him again? What if he wants you back?"

"Have no fear. I assure you he is over me. He has a new lover and he seems to be smitten by her. I can't believe we're having this conversation. Don't worry—he rejected me, he rejected me as a lover and as a friend, and if you now reject me as your wife, I will completely understand. But if you don't, if we survive this, then we might become invincible as a couple." I emit a nervous laugh and add, "It sounds almost deviant that a husband and a wife would be discussing her ex-lover. I can't find the words to express how sorry I am to have hurt you!"

"If you knew back then what you know now, would you have still done it?" He looks at me as if our future depends on the answer I give. I have no intention of lying anymore.

"Yes, I would have done it. I will never lie to you again and will tell you even the most brutal truth."

He jerks as if I had struck him physically.

In a shaking voice, I tell him, "If you did to me what I did to you, I would leave you in an instant. I would not tolerate such treason. I don't know why you don't hate me. I loved another man and I'm still aching and pining for him. Or it's also possible I may be just insulted, and my ego is bruised because he replaced me. I don't know. My feelings are one big knot of yarn that cannot be disentangled. I no longer know myself, and need to deconstruct and reconstruct myself. And I'm well aware that if you stay with me, you may never be able to trust me again."

"If after a few months you aren't out of this nightmare, and you're not fully reconnected with me, then we will talk divorce. I'll put aside my own bruised ego, because our marriage deserves a second chance. Perhaps…I could also see David." He is silent and crying again. "I must have left you unfulfilled in more than one way, for you to seek another man."

"There's one thing I know intuitively," I reply, "and that is, even if I'd met Weylin at the time we were both free, he'd have disappointed me and we wouldn't have been happy. I seem to remember him now from my past lives, because I feel not only the pain he inflicted on me in this lifetime, but also in all the previous ones."

"You really believe that nonsense?"

"I do believe it. You can listen to the recordings if you want. That is, if you can stomach my revelations without revulsion at what I have repeatedly done in several lifetimes! I warn you, it will be torture."

"I can't limit the amount of truth I'm willing to take. I want it all, even if it kills me. I may have asked you before…did you ever consider leaving me?" he asks.

"No, that was never an option. I would have never taken that risk, and neither would he. It would not have led to happiness, but to devastation and pain for innocent people. We would not have lasted long anyway. I know that now. It was a fantasy I needed; it was an illusion, still tearing me apart, but I will be whole again... I just need more time, and hopefully, one day we'll laugh at this obstacle we overcame on our marriage path. Now, would you like dinner? I can make us a potato frittata with salad."

"I'm not hungry. I think I'll go to a movie and spend the night at my mother's house."

"I can go to the movies with you, but I'm afraid I'd be terrible company."

"I'd rather be alone."

"Why aren't you furious with me, angrier than you are? Why don't you have hatred? Why don't you smash plates and glasses, slash my favorite paintings?"

"I feel dead. It's like...all the pain and torment have somehow anesthetized me, which makes me fear how I'll feel once the numbness wears off. I feel...somehow amputated," he says, sighs in deepest disappointment, and leaves.

I go into the kitchen to make myself something to eat, but instead I pour a glass of wine and sit at the kitchen table. The phone rings and startles me out of the torpor I'm feeling. When I hear my daughter Cassandra's voice I cheer up.

"Mom, we haven't spoken in a while. How was Barcelona?"

"It was a lot of work, but I also managed to have some fun. Why are you awake at one in the morning? Have you been partying?"

"No, I just had a long chat with Ariadna and now I'm calling you with some big news. Sorry, but I had to tell my sister first."

My two girls, who seemed to be arch-enemies when they were growing up, are now the best of friends. Nothing could please me more.

"Can I guess the big news?"

"Sure."

"You've been doing great at school, so I'll say it's not about school. I'll venture to say it must be about love, because there's nothing with more impact on us than love, right? So, I'd say Friedrich probably proposed, declaring undying love for you, and you've accepted. I just hope you finish your Master's first before jumping into marriage."

"Mom, you're unbelievable! You read minds; no wonder you're a great shrink. Yes, we got engaged last night and had a huge bash. Too bad Ari couldn't come; too much school work. I'm so-o-o happy, I could sing and dance on rooftops!"

We spend an hour on the phone talking about their wedding plans. I'm happy to hear both girls are coming home for Christmas and staying an extra week. I shudder, thinking of what they would think of me if they knew what I've been experiencing. I also fear they'll notice the strain between their dad and me. They'd be devastated if we divorced, because on so many occasions they've thanked us for giving them a home filled with love and harmony, when so many of their friends had to suffer through the pain of their parents' divorces. I wonder how many people stay married for their kids' sake.

After the conversation, I feel a bit better. I text David to ask him if he can see me tomorrow after his last patient and he texts back, agreeing. After that I try to read, but the words float before my eyes revealing no meaning. I decide to take a sleeping pill again and disappear in the oblivion sleep brings. I despise myself and feel renewed aversion toward Weylin.

CHAPTER FIFTEEN

David

I'm not sure how to deal with Leandra's problem. I'd expected her to heal by now and I don't understand why she's still thinking of this Weylin, or why she's still putting herself in a position which allows him to hurt her. I'm sure he has no intention of hurting her anymore; he's over her and has moved on with his life and his pursuit of happiness. Her behavior is showing addictive propensities.

I get called to the ER for a consult on a suicide attempt. It's a case of a seventy-year-old widow who tried to kill herself by gas. Her son found her unconscious and was able to open the windows after he heard a hissing sound from the stove. As a firefighter, he immediately understood the situation and called nine-eleven. I talked to him in the waiting room and calmed him, telling him his mother would survive because she'd not been exposed to the leakage for too long. She cannot talk now because she has an oxygen mask, but tomorrow he'll be able to see her. He tells me that after his dad died, she hasn't been able to come out of her depression and has been refusing to see a psychiatrist. Her financial situation has also significantly deteriorated, and as they never had many friends, she has found herself very lonely.

He's busy and still single, and realizes he hasn't offered much support to his mother. I assure him we'll take good care of her, and I personally would provide her with counseling and evaluation. He leaves the hospital looking relieved.

Before I go back to my office I do a couple of more consults in the ER, and by the time I'm back in the office it's time to see Leandra.

As soon as she comes in I notice a change in her. She looks calmer, or maybe more resigned and accepting of the circumstances.

"How are you doing?"

"Today I'm feeling more at peace with myself."

"What brought that about?"

"My decision to never write to Weylin again. Every email I've written to him under the pretenses of professional communication revealed to me I still had hopes and expectations. How else to explain when I received his last email, in which he's simply telling me he doesn't have time to read my article but will read it and comment on it when he comes back from his vacation, it threw me into a crying fit for hours? If another colleague had written the same, I would've thought nothing of it. I believe I've come to the end of this story; I believe I've exhausted the last glimmer of hope that things could go back to the way they'd been."

"Leandra, what have you learned from the hypnotherapy sessions?"

"It's obvious—in every lifetime, I experienced intense passion with the same man, and the same man betrayed me."

"What did you learn about the nature of that love and passion?"

"I know where your question is leading. The answer is addiction. It wasn't love, but addiction. I was addicted to the powerful feelings of passion, of the forbidden, of the magic and fantasy I created in my own mind, and of the qualities I attributed to this person I didn't even know. My bond with him was deep and his bond with me was shallow and easily dissolved, in this lifetime and in all the others."

"He could possibly be a hungry ghost."

"What are you saying?" she asks with a look of incomprehension.

"It's a concept from Chinese Buddhism. Hungry Ghosts are creatures who have a mouth the size of a pin hole, a huge empty belly, and are constantly on the prowl for nourishment. Whenever they try to drink, water turns into fire and ash in their constricted throats, making them even thirstier.

"When you apply the concept to addictions, a hungry ghost seeks fulfillment in love and cannot find it. Weylin temporarily found love in you, and is now finding it in Jorunn. The Hungry Ghost concept is applicable not only to love and relationships, but to careers, goals, aspirations and whatever else we latch onto with our hopes and strivings. You saw much meaning in your relationship with Weylin; you saw magic in sexual attraction; you saw and felt soul-mate energy, a fusing of two kindred souls on all levels. Because you found so much, and expected so much, and because you reached such highs with him, your lows were ruinous! You did not expect in any lifetime he would jilt you. And of course you cannot comprehend how so much love in one moment could become nonexistent in the next. That's why I believe he's a typical hungry ghost.

"I'd say his soul is so full of holes, any nourishment of love just seeps through and leaves him even more dissatisfied. He cannot find love because he does not love himself, and he does not love himself because subconsciously, his parents abandoning him made him feel not good enough. In his perception, his wife's refusal to have sex with him means rejection, abandonment and tells him he's not worthy of love. You couldn't have filled his need for love for long, because what you gave him turned to fire and ash; also because of the impossible circumstances. He seems to be a coward, an anxious and worrying soul, and his anxiety will probably destroy his relationship with Jorunn because he will not want to risk the safety net of his marriage for too long. Or he'll become attracted to someone else and start the exciting game of seduction all over."

Leandra looks pensive when she says, "I wish I knew for certain I will never allow myself to get hurt by him again. I wish I could love him in an unattached way, if such love is even possible."

"Once you let go of the attachment, once you have forgiven him fully for the hurt he inflicted upon you, once you stop being angry at yourself for feeling so attached and unable to let go, you might start feeling love for him in a non-judgmental way. You will be able to retrieve the beautiful memories without feeling the pain. You may start viewing the painful experience as a gift of transformation.

"It's a gift you will now be able to give to your patients, because you are more human and compassionate now, and you'll not be analyzing their love afflictions scientifically, but also emphatically. You'll be able to cry with them and truly feel their anguish. Until now, as a happily married woman who had chosen her mate wisely and married for love, you might have found it difficult to understand how addicted people become to others, and continue loving abusers, and continue hoping those who don't want them now may want them one day, so they continue pining after those who cold heartedly rejected them.

"Through you, I've also learned a lot; I've learned how love can ambush you unexpectedly and fling you completely out of your carefully constructed life. You'll never be the same, but you will be a better and a stronger person for the experience. You already are."

"I feel angry with myself for still obsessing over him. I want him out of my heart. How do I do that? Why can't I be like him and just bury it inside me 'six feet under', and never think about it again? Why did it have to matter to me so much, and so little to him?"

"Relationships are often imbalanced. When my last girlfriend broke up with me, I was all right, but she wasn't and she tried to win me back and told me she'd only broken up with me to shake me up. Weylin broke an implicit promise of love, not a promise he'd leave his family to be with you. He dissociated from his feelings when he had to, as he probably had to learn in his youth in order to avoid feeling abandonment and rejection. He hurt you because he'd been hurt, and you hurt Adrian because you'd been hurt. You are behaving destructively and self-destructively. I don't believe you revealed to Adrian what you did in order to wipe the slate clean and start your marriage again on a basis of honesty. In my opinion it's better to withhold the truth, if it means not hurting someone, than to spit it out and ruin a relationship forever."

"Based on all his writings to you, I must say I see mostly lust and erotic fantasies you fulfilled for a while. There were statements and proclamations of love, but they were like a thin golden thread interwoven into a dense fabric of sexuality. In his dreams and writings, he never mentions or implies an eventual life together. It is sexual infatuation with a veneer of love. And it's no wonder your imagination would go into full swing, reading words drenched with so much passion; you saw love where there was lust and shallow emotional attachment; you saw gold where there was glitter."

"How could I have been so blind?"

"You were fulfilling a deep-seated need for love, romance, and fantasy. You were writing your own fairy tale and you allowed him to play the hero in it. And he's a man dissatisfied and frustrated with his sexual life, but a man who still finds his family life sacred. You were always secondary to him. And you knew it. He risked a lot by meeting you and it's possible his fear of his wife discovering his betrayal prompted him to break up with you.

"Or, he fell in love with someone new and more exciting. Sorry to be so honest. Regardless of what happened during the regression session, be it real or unreal, you answered your own questions. The pattern was sexual infatuation on his part and a deeper attachment on yours because, as I said, as a healthy person you are capable of building deep bonds. I've never bonded with anyone deeply for a long period, and it's a deficiency I've recognized and accepted in myself. Perhaps all's not lost and maybe...just maybe, I will meet someone special and fall in love forever. In fact, I'd like to experience what you have, but not the torture and torment of it."

She looks crestfallen when she says, "I know I have all the answers in me, but I still cannot get out of this fixation mode. Why can't he be friends with me?"

"I have no good answers for your questions. Perhaps he's angry you ambushed him with your accusations in Barcelona and feels perfectly entitled to have another affair, and feels he owes you nothing; you're just an ex-lover. Ergo, not really important, because love affairs are not real relationships. Or perhaps you are an unwanted reminder he's a scumbag who's ready for cheating, but not for an honest dissolution of his marriage, and a fresh start which comes from integrity. Or he may still harbor some feelings for you, but doesn't want to acknowledge them.

"The bottom line is, you have more than enough reason to disengage yourself from thinking about him, from harboring any hope of reconnecting with him. The healthiest approach is to cherish both the memories and the lessons the experience has taught you. Leandra, there's nothing but embers left from your affair. Embers! Prudent people stoke small flames, but not dead embers—because if they do, the embers disintegrate into ash. By expecting him to reply to your email on the article, you were still stoking the remains of what was once a fire. He may reply, and it will be congenial and neutral and he won't leave any hint in his reply that he wants to hear from you again. Any further contact with him delays your healing and holds you captive in an unrealistic hope that one day a different kind of email will come from him. It won't, and in this case it's a stroke of luck for you, not to get what you want."

"I feel humiliated for trying to get him to be my friend, for feeling so disappointed when rejected, even as a friend."

"Feel what you have to, and allow your feelings to ebb and flow until they fade away, hopefully for good. Just as the anxious mind tortures itself with fears which don't exist, your mind has tortured itself with a love story that didn't really exist. You're still going through withdrawal, because it's hard to give up on all the highs you felt when you were with him. As cruel as it sounds, you were his sexual sidekick, a sidekick he would never have allowed to change his life in any significant way. But again, that's your luck.

"Again, acknowledge the feeling; cry, howl, and release both the feelings and him. Release him with love, compassion and forgiveness, because he also carries the aftermath of rejection and the reality his dreams might not come true. He gave you what he could, but could give no more. If he now gives more to someone else, well, that's a new love story. Maybe because he received so much love from you, he'll be able to love more deeply and genuinely not only another woman, but himself, because you showed him he was worthy not only of your love, but of self-love, too. And spiritual wellness begins at self-love, and from that circle, concentric circles of all-encompassing love spread like ripples on a lake."

She sighs, and two solitary tears roll down her cheeks. "I just hope I can cry one last time and know it's the last time I mourn him. I want this torment to end so I can see if I can work on my marriage. It's such a hollow feeling to feel so ruptured…it's like my soul has exploded and I need to put all the pieces back together, stitch them seamlessly back together."

"It does not need to be seamless. The seams may show, but they will be gilded with strength. Consider your suffering as a gift of growth and spiritual advancement. All these insights will not make you stop feeling lovelorn overnight. It will take as long as it takes. The more it mattered, the longer it takes to heal."

"I'm afraid of this fixation. I find it so unhealthy. I think about him every day, I wake up in the middle of the night and my thoughts go to him. Fighting my thoughts doesn't help, and accepting them is just as bad, resisting them doesn't change them. Being aware of them makes me realize—I'm just stuck in one place...in this fucking quicksand. Sorry!"

"Time and distance will get you where you should be. We've dissected everything we could and further analysis will not bring more insights. Looking at your situation, I have to compare it with mine, because something may be seriously wrong with me. When a girl would dump me for another guy, I wouldn't feel any long-term pain, but would tell myself she didn't deserve me. And when they would try to reconnect, I expected it because I guess that's how vain I am. I'm lucky I never let my self-esteem be affected by rejection...but then again, I've never been insanely in love or in lust. It's much easier to live with temperance than tempests in your heart."

"How will I know for sure it's over?" she asks with the naiveté of a teenager experiencing heartbreak for the first time.

"You already have the answers, to all your questions. You would know them even if you weren't the seasoned psychiatrist you are. It will be over the moment both your mind and heart tell you the same thing. It'll be over when you meet him the next time and are able to see him for who he is; when you no longer fall for his vulnerabilities that once disarmed you; when you notice his stutter and that doesn't make him more attractive, when you realize how broken he is but no longer wish to come even close to the shards of his soul. It's over when you see him through the prism of reality, and when you realize you've been in love with your own love story.

"Too bad your brain was still too hazy for you to see that in Barcelona, to truly see a man who never gave thought to mortally wounding you by showering another woman with his affection and attention so openly in front of you. Even I, who lack a lot in the romantic department, would have taken into consideration that an ex-lover whom I had left in a devastated state after a break-up she did not want, might feel slighted seeing me with another woman. But, obviously, you need to get beaten over the head a few times before the fog in your head clears."

She laughs and says, "This isn't the first time I've suffered heartbreak, but it's the first time in a very long time. I will be all right, of course. This is all a part of midlife crisis. All these explanations and analyses, just to convince ourselves what we desire is really not good for us. Sour grapes, that's what it is."

"You sound sarcastic, which is untypical of you. Be grateful the experience has changed you, making a better, deeper, more emphatic loving and lovable you. Perhaps that's why your life paths crossed, for him to hurt you most deeply, so that out of destruction a more beautiful person might emerge. Perhaps the darkness he gave you, you transmuted into love and light, and that was the reason he came into your life over and over again, through all the past lives. I've been hearing nurses say a few patients mentioned they'd never seen a psychiatrist as empathetic as you.

"You were always respected as a doctor, but the word empathy wasn't mentioned before. So why don't we cheer up, lift our chins and go out for some nibbles and a glass of wine? And let's toast to a new beginning, and close this chapter in your life never to reopen it. A deal?"

She smiles and shakes my hand firmly and says, "It's a deal!"

I'm not sure I believe her, because addicts of any kind relapse easily into their bad habits.

CHAPTER SIXTEEN

Leandra

I've been meeting with David regularly, but we've been talking less and less about Weylin. For the past few days I've been feeling detached from the whole experience, and I no longer feel in love with him. However I don't trust myself, and fear I might fall back into that awful state of longing. This morning I received an email from him. He commented on the article I'd sent him and wrote about his trip to Asia. It was a warm and friendly email, ending with a question, meaning he expected an answer. I'm aware I should no longer have any contact with him, but I'm surrendering to the river of life without struggling to swim upstream but rather, letting the water take me wherever I need to go. If there is still a lesson to be learned from this experience, if he will linger on in my life, if all has been said and done, he will vanish. I won't question the events, but instead let them unfold according to the plan of the universe. I'll reply to him without inserting any questions indicating I'm hoping for an answer, and we'll see if the correspondence finally dries up.

So, I write a long reply, commenting on one aspect of the article he disagreed with. I also decide to send my reply on his birthday. I compose the response over a few days, revising and editing it until I'm satisfied there are no questions. I wish him a happy birthday at the end, with no indications I expect further correspondence. He writes back a couple of hours later saying my birthday wishes were by far the most intellectual ones he's received. Again, his email is nice, but short. He ends it by saying he needs to go as his family is serving him birthday cake.

I nearly reply to say I'm laughing at myself for sending a text in the wrong genre for the right occasion or vice versa. I don't. I feel we've exhausted all reasons for any further email exchange, and our story has come to the end.

The next couple of months I immerse myself in work. I notice I listen to my patients' accounts of their problems with a presence, a focus and empathy I hadn't felt until now. I feel connected to all of them, as if the universality of pain and loss has woven visible threads between me and the rest of humanity. I'm so moved by some of the life stories I cry with my patients, unafraid they will start doubting my sanity, professionalism or knowledge.

My own story of loss seems more than trivial and paltry in comparison to a mother who has lost her son in a senseless war, and needs psychiatric help as her grief is depthless, even after two years have passed. Grief does not come with an expiration date, especially in the case when a parent loses a child. I try to help my patients with so much fervor and dedication I stop from time to time to ask myself why I'm putting so much effort into helping others all of a sudden. And the answer is clear. By helping others, I remove focus from myself, and give attention to real people with real problems.

I organize a small support group to which I invite spiritual teachers, energy healers and motivational speakers. I pay them out of my own pocket because the hospital does not have funds earmarked for such spending. I hold meetings in my house because I am all alone since Adrian moved out.

He came back a couple of times to collect more clothes and personal belongings, and we haven't spoken in over three weeks. We both need time and space apart before we decide if investing into the rebuilding of our marriage would be worth the necessary time and energy. I'm learning to live with the wounds Weylin inflicted on me, and how to caress them tenderly with my spiritual fingers as portals to the sacred.

On the day when a sense of emotional equilibrium returns, I get an email from one of Jorunn's colleagues in which he is asking for David's email address he's lost. Before signing off, he makes a casual remark that Weylin is visiting their hospital as he's initiated some joint research with Jorunn. Before I even process that, the wound in my heart reopens and emotional blood gushes out full force. They are illicitly together under an umbrella of legitimate reasons, and the pain of his betrayal accumulated through the lifetimes knocks the air from my lungs, undoing the progress I have made toward recovery.

If I could excise this weakness and powerlessness in me with a knife, I would do it without any hesitation. Just as I saw the light of liberation from his clutches, the pain of loss fills me to the brim. And I wonder how was I ever able to help anyone else deal with their loss, when I am spinning my wheels for what seems like an eternity. And nothing helps. My resolve to change the pattern of my thinking, my fury with my weakness, my acceptance of my unacceptable feelings, my maniacal immersion into work, have had little effect. I feel cursed and doomed and chained to the feelings of a most hopeless unrequited love. I pick up the phone to ask Fiona to cancel the group meeting at my home I'm holding with several patients, but instead I decide to muster all my strength to help those dealing with heavier burdens than I carry.

After work, I go to the cemetery and sit on Aggie's grave. I cry and talk to her and ask for her help, and ask the Universe for its help in regaining normalcy. My life before I met Weylin now seems a perfection of stability and contentment. Sitting so forlornly on her grave gives me no solace and no peace. A storm is raging in me, ripping apart the world I've been trying to rebuild. I go home and take a shower, then lie down with cold compresses over my eyes in hope of reducing the puffiness.

Then I pour juice into pitchers and lay on silver platters an assortment of cakes I bought at Aggie's favorite pastry shop. All is ready for my session.

My patients come almost simultaneously, creating a crowd at the door. There are three women and one man among them. Women always show more readiness to share their experiences which doesn't surprise me. As this is the third time the same group has met, there is no need for introductions. They already know each other's stories.

Marge is twenty-nine, but comes across as much more mature and older due to a constantly pinched expression and a defiant and almost belligerent look in her eyes. She has short, frizzy red hair and freckles. Her eyes are the most beautiful part of her face—emerald-green and very expressive of her swiftly shifting emotional states. Her source of distress and depression stems from her fiancé having left her abruptly without much explanation and vanishing into thin air. As someone who has always suffered from low self-esteem, she convinced herself her inadequacies were to blame and he had every right to leave someone as unworthy as she is.

Christina suffers from a generalized anxiety disorder. She's functional thanks to Zoloft, and doesn't need to attend these meetings, but she enjoys our conversations. Her husband is a sea captain and every time he has to leave home and go back on ship after a short vacation, she feels utterly devastated. She's still in love with her husband, and their every reunion is an ascendance to heaven and every parting a renewed plunge into the abyss of despair. He is her pillar of strength, and when he leaves, she feels abandoned, helpless and left to the mercy of life. Christina's manner exudes an arresting gentleness. She is a true lady, with a beatific face, gorgeous curly red hair and a statuesque figure.

Nimmi comes from a wealthy family from Malaysia. She married a man she never loved because of circumstances she could not control. One day when she was at the beach with a group of friends, a young man who had been showing interest in marrying her stopped his huge, luxury car on the road parallel to the beach. Nimmi doesn't know if her friends conspired to push her into his car, but finding herself in the car, she first felt alarmed and angry, then thought she could take advantage of the situation and ask him to allow her to practice driving.

As fate would have it, half an hour later when he sat again at the wheel and she took the passenger seat, her brother drove by on a motorcycle and stopped the car. Even though she had done nothing wrong, her parents felt she had shamed their family. Two days later, the young man's father called her father asking for her hand in marriage to his son, Aakash. Nimmi's father told her she did not have to marry Aakash, but she felt obliged to do so in order to save her family's honor.

After they had their first child, they left Malaysia in search of a better life. Her husband was a trader in silk rugs and his business boomed. They had two more children and their wealth grew exponentially and proportionally to her unhappiness. Gradually, her husband turned into a jealous and possessive tyrant who started to accuse her of flirting with other men and cheating on him. His accusations turned into verbal and physical abuse. One day she could stand it no more and left him, and took her children with her. They moved into a shelter first, and stayed there for a month until her parents sent her money to rent her own apartment.

The next ten years brought great financial struggle. She divorced her husband, but could not get support from him as he proved his company was doing poorly and he was facing bankruptcy. She knew he was hiding huge sums of money in offshore accounts. What has helped her through the difficult times and depression has been her faith and psychotherapy. In the meantime, she also completed a Master's degree in business administration and found very lucrative employment. She seems to be fully healed, and hopes to show others that trying times are transient, and obstacles we overcome teach us compassion and humility.

Dennis is a thirty-seven-year-old man who'd been extremely athletic and adventurous until he got lost in a snowstorm during an expedition in the Yukon, after which his right leg had to be amputated due to severe frostbite. His left leg was miraculously saved; however, he has little sensation in it. Realizing he could no longer lead the lifestyle he once did, he attempted to commit suicide one night by jumping off a bridge. But a passerby pulled him back and called the police, who then brought him to the ER when I was on call. Dennis is a strikingly good-looking man with curly brown hair and blue eyes, and I'm a bit surprised his looks haven't suffered due to his alcohol abuse after the accident.

I start the session by asking everyone to pick one person and comment on what they think that person has in their life for which they should be grateful. I also want them to come up with suggestions as to how that person could change the way they think in order to change the way they perceive their reality and circumstances.

Dennis begins by using Nimmi's example. "Nimmi has been able to emerge from hell and completely rebuild her life. I admire her strength and resolve, and the way she protected her children, and has been able to give them a pretty normal life. I'm in awe she finished her Master's degree, and found a good job so she could become completely independent. She literally turned her life around and can now be grateful for all she has in it...healthy children who're doing well in school, a great job, her house. And from what I see, she no longer needs therapy. What she now needs is a guy to love, someone decent and stable, not a creep like her husband had been. How the hell did you manage to come out of the woods so completely?" Dennis asks Nimmi directly.

"My faith helped me, because I always believed God loved me and whatever burdens he sent my way were for my spiritual evolution. I had to be strong for my children in order to protect them. I could not fail...I could not go to ruin, because of my children. No matter what, we are firstly parents. My faith filled me with resolve to succeed against all odds. Even under extremely dire circumstances, I could find something to be grateful for. For example, finding Dr. Springfield was a blessing, and hearing at school how well my children were doing made me feel blessed and grateful. At one point in my life, I made the wrong decision to marry the wrong man because I believed my cultural circumstances demanded that. For every wrong decision you make, you suffer the consequences, but life also gives you opportunities to make right decisions, and change those circumstances."

"I wish I could think like you, and not be wondering how to do myself in because life is so frigging unbearable. I'm really keen on hearing if anyone can see anything good in my life."

Christina looks at Dennis with kind eyes and says, "I see a very handsome young man, who has become extremely cynical and bitter because of an unfortunate accident. But, you're walking thanks to the prosthetics, and you still have a healthy body—even though with your alcohol abuse and your self-defeating way of thinking you're risking losing that health. You have a university degree, and could land a job and get off disability if you only changed the way you look at yourself. You could, for example, become a "Big Brother, and help troubled teenagers by showing them how the human spirit can prevail over terrible circumstances. Your self-pity is holding you back from finding a new purpose in life which would bring you joy and pleasure. I suggest you dress up one evening and come to my house, and I will introduce you to a few young women I know, and perhaps you'll be lucky to fall in love, and that love will be the torch leading you out of your darkness."

Christina smiles sweetly at him and Dennis laughingly says, "It's a deal. I'm willing to give it a try. Things can't get much worse than they are right now, because if this ain't rock bottom, then I don't know what is."

"And you, Christina," Nimmi starts, "it is so obvious you should be grateful for having shared such deep love with your husband. Whenever he leaves, you should see him off smiling, because you know you will be reunited after a couple of months. I wish I'd had such love in my life even for a month."

"At least no one dumped you out of the blue," Marge chimes in. She turns toward me with fire spewing from her eyes and venom from her mouth, which takes me and the others by complete surprise.

"And you, Dr. Springfield, with your house looking like a fucking museum and a BMW parked in the driveway, and your 'manicured' lawn, and these fancy cups and crystal glasses, what the hell can you know of loss and pain, when everything in your life seems like a fucking fairytale?"

I'm astounded by how caustic her voice sounds, almost laced with hatred. She has never lashed out like that at me. Before she started seeing me, she had been David's patient, but she showed deep mistrust of his ability to help her, and insisted she be assigned a new doctor. David told me of her belligerent attitude and how difficult it was to get through to her and establish a rapport of trust and respect.

"Marge, pain and loss connect all of us in this room and outside this room. If you had a BMW, the connection between us would be insignificant and trivial, and any talk about our cars would be meaningless conversation. I have *been* in pain for over a year. That pain stems from someone I loved leaving me, and I'm struggling and cursing myself for not being able to get over it. I am trying to help you overcome your sorrows and depression, while at the same time I feel imprisoned and emotionally exhausted from trying to forget someone who put my world out of joint. And I feel hexed for not being able to disentangle myself from this unhealthy web. I feel so happy when for a few days in a row I'm able to feel liberated and indifferent. However the feeling never lasts longer than a few days, and invariably there's always something that happens to fling me back into the pattern of aching for that person and going through hell, because I still hurt over the fact he replaced me with someone else.

"When looking at all of you I feel ashamed and humbled. I cannot shed something as insignificant as getting over someone who stopped loving me; he probably never even loved me, and fell in love with someone else. You are all dealing with much deeper issues. I feel like a hypocrite with all my psychiatric knowledge telling you what you should and should not be feeling or doing. I'll say no more, but please know—my personal life is in shambles."

"But you have so much going for you. You have both legs."

After Dennis says that, the room is silent for a moment and then laughter rings through it as if he said something really funny.

"Yes, Dennis, I'm grateful I'm healthy, I'm grateful I have wonderful children and a job I love and all of you in my life, but in spite of having both legs, as I've said, I'm no stranger to emotional pain. I lost my mother-in-law recently and miss her terribly. I may have lost my husband for good, but don't even know how to feel about it. I feel the loss of his presence in this home. I can see in your eyes you know what I'm talking about. Yes, I was unfaithful, and my lover betrayed me with someone else. He simply replaced me and erased me as he has always done throughout my past incarnations.

"I see puzzlement in your eyes. Yes, you heard me right…a colleague of mine does past life regressions in certain cases where conventional therapy doesn't seem to work. Not that I needed conventional therapy. I see I've shocked you. I also need compassion and understanding because I'm stuck in the quicksand of my own erroneous thinking and feel helpless. I should have already forgotten this man, but I haven't and I think it is almost pathological and it is certainly pathetic…this…my inability to forget him. I realize I am repeating myself.

"At this moment, I feel like a fake, like a quasi-doctor who's supposed to provide her patients with tools and mechanisms for dealing with depression and changing their thoughts about their situations, and yet, I'm a perfect example that knowledge and the will to change your thoughts about a situation and let go of the past don't always work, in spite of our best efforts. Or maybe the more effort we invest into fighting something, the more that condition persists. It should be easy enough to change thoughts about my situation, right? I fell in love with a married man who replaced me with someone else, and I should have just forgotten the whole thing, remembering the delicious fun I had. I should not have revealed this indiscretion to my husband, should have moved on merrily with my life. After all, it should've been a fling, a moment of misjudgment, a sign of temporary weakness, insanity, right?

"However, the more I'm trying to work on myself and move on, the more stuck and helpless I feel. I just don't know what the hell's wrong with me, or how I could have fucked up my own life so badly and needlessly. I will understand if you ask to change doctors. Oh my god, I feel so unprofessional and embarrassed and ashamed. But, I'm still in so much pain and it makes no sense. The loss just does not seem to be commensurate with the amount of pain I still feel."

There is shock, and silence, and I'm afraid I will lose all my patients by showing so much fallibility and weakness. They will no longer see me as a doctor who is proficient in treating her patients. What if they sue me for malpractice? What if they write to a newspaper complaining about my unprofessional behavior causing them more stress? But then again, I'm not charging either them or the medical insurance for these meetings. I'm doing this on my free time. I look at them with some apprehension, expecting them to get up and leave. Instead, one by one, they come to me and give me a hug.

"Welcome to the world of humanity," Marge says. "And thank you for allowing yourself to fall off the doctor-in-authority pedestal. I always thought you were so goddamn perfect, that you were always judging me and seeing me like shit, while just playing the professional doctor part. What I wanna say is...I mean, you're a great doctor, but now I see you're a good person, too, who opened your home and heart to us."

Upon hearing Marge say that I break down in tears, and then into the laughter of relief, which quickly spreads around the room like wildfire.

"Holy fuck...Dr Springfield had a lover," Dennis hoots with laughter.

"And you told your husband and he left you. What were you thinking?" Marge pipes up. "Are you out of your fucking mind? Your husband is some kinda hotshot lawyer, and now some young bimbo will pounce on him and give 'im the best blowjob ever and you'll be left with this huge house and in a financial shithole after he divorces you and your divorce lawyer bleeds you dry. And for what, because of some creep who probably told you his wife is frigid, doesn't love him or appreciate him. Hey, wake up and call your husband before it's too late. You're no longer so young you can think there's another love waiting round the corner."

The rest of the evening is filled with a sense of lightness, fun and camaraderie. The connection that's developed among us is almost palpable. The doctor/patient barrier has crumbled, and we're sitting like a group of friends on a mission to help each other. We sit on the floor in a circle and hold hands for a few minutes. I get up to make coffee and tea and while I'm in the kitchen I hear them chuckling. I find a stash of high quality Belgian cookies in a cupboard and put the box on the floor. The next hour turns into such a pleasant evening tea party I decide to hold these sessions regularly.

After tea and coffee, they leave one by one. After they've all gone I clear the table, leaving the plates and cups in the sink, and sit in the sunroom with a glass of wine. I'm still infused with the enthusiasm and satisfaction of having had an extremely successful evening, during which both pain and tears were shared, as well as hope and a shyly emerging joy.

The gratitude expressed at the end of the evening for my full participation in discussion by baring my own heart moves me deeply, and I feel warm all over knowing I can make a difference in the lives of many people. I don't plan to share my own life with my patients again; this was an uncalculated risk I took, but the result was so unexpectedly positive, as if everyone realized for the first time I was human, too. I laugh aloud and pour myself another glass of wine.

It's an unseasonably warm October night and probably one of the last Indian summer days. I wrap a light woolen shawl around my shoulders and drink another glass of wine. I'm thinking of Weylin and before I know it, the last drop of wine swirls in the glass like a solitary drop of blood. My head is spinning. Feeling drunk, I leave the sunroom and step into the backyard. Falteringly, I go to a small stone bench under a wild cherry tree. I prop a cushion I brought with me against the back of the bench; I don't want to feel the touch of cold stone.

I lean against the cushion and look up at the sky. The stars blink indifferently, their lights appearing in my field of vision as brightly lit torches one moment, and in the next, as almost invisible specks of glitter. Sadness and alcohol are coursing in my veins and my ears are buzzing with the murmur of distant oceans, which makes me think I am developing Tinnitus. I slide forwards on the bench enough to lay my head on its back, which I cover with the cushion. That position makes my head spin even more, and I fear sooner or later I'll have to vomit.

Just as I'm about to get up and go to bed I hear voices. For the first few moments, I believe the murmur in my ears has intensified, making me imagine voices, but then I hear a whooshing sound shoot through my head, and at the same time a soft breeze tosses my hair gently around my face.

It's then I hear quite distinctly a male voice say, "Playing with humans is an inexhaustible source of amusement. It surprises me how successfully she is rearranging the shattered pieces of her life. I created circumstances of extreme duality in order to grind her spirit to dust, and her spirit has remained strong and pure. I can make her perish forever, but I shall play with her a little more."

My bewilderment peaks, especially as I realize I actually do not hear voices, but strange sounds my mind translates into language.

"Why do you hate humans so much? Why did you feel compelled to prove human love is worthless and meaningless as you place so many obstacles before them? You splintered soul-mates asunder." The female voice is soft, but I detect an underlying hint of menace in it.

"True soul-mates find their way back to each other. Didn't you argue human love had the power to shine its way out of darkness? He failed each and every test throughout the centuries. In his core is cowardice and weakness. He will remain a tormented soul in search of love he cannot give or keep even when he finds it."

"You are spinning a web of curses. You cursed him and he cursed her with a whisper that poisoned her heart and soul. And the source of your malice is that I once loved a human and he died loving me. Is that not proof enough that undying love exists among humans?"

"Humans are soulless vermin."

His voice is hissing and my head is spinning so much I lie on the ground not daring to move. I close my eyes, hoping when I reopen them the voices will disappear. I'm drunk and it's the alcohol making me hallucinate. There cannot be any other explanation.

But when I open my eyes I see a glittering veil in front of me, and shapes moving behind it. I extend my hand wanting to pull down the veil so I can get a glimpse of another dimension, of some parallel world in which magic reigns and is inhabited by deities or supernatural creatures interfering with or shaping our fate. Just as I'm about to touch it, it shimmers more brightly and moves away from my hand. It's as if someone is toying with me, because the sounds behind it remind me of derisive laughter.

"It may be too late…there may be too much brokenness…her soul bears the scars of deep lacerations…trust cannot be easily recovered. When in that paradisiacal garden they made a wish to be together one day, I believed you would allow me to alter the circumstances in their favor. But you defeated me by altering his mind about her, by emptying his heart of love for her and filling it with shallow attraction for someone else.

"I no longer wish to continue this game of cruel manipulation, nor do I wish to predict its outcome when you control it. You have tested his love for her throughout the centuries, proving he always failed her. But he had no chance of success with your interference. You turned him into a dragonfly slayer. Unfairness and balefulness propel your actions. Leave them alone. Let her heal. Let her forget his whisper urging her never to forget him." Her voice sounds pleading.

"My interest in human love has waned. I've proved to you its fickleness. Humans kill and fail, and betray each other. They are worse than beasts to each other. You loved one and so you try to find goodness in this most reprehensible species. For Leandra, the karmic circle of betrayal has closed. For Weylin, I have something in store he shall not enjoy one bit."

"Stop bending their fate. Observe them, but do not manipulate them. Let them meet again without any obstacles, so we can see if the love that once bonded them has burned down to the coldest of embers. And if it has, let her heal completely. Have mercy on these humans who have paid with searing pain for the few moments of magic they shared…the magic you allowed. You were the one who set the trap for them to meet and fall in love." The female voice sounds feeble and resigned.

Through my drunken stupor, I believe I recognize the voices of the pagan gods I dreamed about immediately after my break-up with Weylin. If they experimented with me, and us, perhaps there is a chance they will leave me to my fate now. I hear them speak for a few moments longer, but their words no longer make sense even though they are loud enough to understand. It seems they are now speaking in a language that doesn't belong in this reality, one my mind can no longer translate into anything that would make the least of sense. Trying to process the experience, I'm gripped with fear I'm hallucinating, or falling into mental illness.

With my heart thumping and mind disoriented, I stumble back into the house, and fall on the bed fully dressed. The room around me is moving, the sounds in my head and ears are whistling, hissing, pounding, shouting, and I feel I am standing on the precipice of insanity.

When I do open my eyes, it is morning and sunlight is streaming into the room—I left the curtains open. I blink in confusion; I don't remember when I came to bed or what happened last night. My throat feels parched and my mouth tastes acidic. When I get up, I stumble and fall back, pressing the right side of my head in a futile attempt to diminish the throbbing ache. Meeko jumps on the bed and I realize he must have spent the night outside, because I don't remember letting him into the house last night. It also occurs to me I probably left the backyard door open so he could come back in. I must have been really drunk to leave the door unlocked.

I summon all my willpower to get up and take a cold shower. The touch of freezing water makes me squeal, but then I slowly adapt to the temperature. I shiver when I come out. A cup of hot coffee makes me feel better. I wish Adrian were here, having coffee with me, and a painful longing for an atmosphere of comfort and familiarity pierces my heart. Perhaps the source of marital demise for many people is this dichotomy between our concurrent craving for security and comfort, juxtaposed to the need for mystery and the thrill of the unknown and novel.

I take two Advil gels before I phone my daughters. I've recently neglected phoning them regularly, and feel guilty of being a failed wife and mother. Their cheerful voices, full of good news about their schoolwork and life in Europe cheer me up. Cassandra is still floating on clouds of happiness over her engagement to Friedrich, and says he'll probably come home with her for Christmas. Ari says she's started dating a young physicist who, believe it or not, is 'not nerdy one bit'. Chatting with my girls restores my mood completely and I go to work with a smile on my face.

Before reaching my office, I almost bump into Alex Birchmeier, our director.

"Good morning, Leandra. How are you?"

"Very well, Alex. A bit rushed this morning. Got up too late."

"I was just going to forward you an email I got from one of your patients. And it's really good news. She wants to donate quite a bit of money to our ward in gratitude to you. Congratulations! What stands out in her email is the word empathy. She says she's never had a more empathetic doctor. Again, well done!"

My work seems to become more and more successful as word spreads about the compassion I show toward my patients. One patient told me she'd never seen a doctor so genuinely interested in her patients' problems. I'm proud and flattered, and at the same time I realize work is not what matters most. What mattered most I've managed to lose, due to my belief in fantasy and my mislabeling of feelings that weren't love. I laugh at myself. How easily I could have dissected another person's misconceptions and delusions about affairs, but be totally blind to my own before they plunged me into a sea of unnecessary suffering.

I'm tempted to phone Adrian and invite him for brunch, but am not in the mood for getting the cold shoulder. He has completely withdrawn, and refuses to speak with me. I expect to be served express divorce papers through his legal connections, but nothing has arrived yet. Who could blame him? The magnitude of my treason cannot even be described.

When the phone rings I think it is him, and hope it's that case of synchronicity when you hear from the person you've just been thinking of. Instead it's my friend Andrea, a nurse who took an unpaid leave of absence to care for her sick husband.

"Hey, Andrea! What a lovely surprise to hear from you. How have you been and how's Bob?"

She tells me Bob's health has improved greatly and there are few signs of stroke left. She should be back at work in a couple of weeks. And then she drops the bomb and tells me she and Bob saw Adrian in a restaurant. He was having dinner with a red-haired woman, who looked much younger than he. As Adrian and I are of the same age, it means the woman in question is also much younger than I am. Andrea then asks me if things are all right in my marriage. I tell her we're considering divorce. She is speechless for a few seconds. I tell her I have to leave because I'm having lunch with a friend.

I hang up and sit on the floor in disbelief over the amount of harm I've inflicted upon myself. I couldn't keep Weylin, and I've lost a wonderful husband who'd been the love of my life until that fateful conference. How can we ever throw stones at fate when we ourselves engage in so much self-sabotage? I want to cry, but the well of tears has dried, and numbness weighs down on me more than pain ever did. I dread this feeling of carrying a dead soul around like a dead fetus.

CHAPTER SEVENTEEN

David

I'm meeting Leandra for lunch today. Over the last few weeks, we've spoken a couple of times on the phone and exchanged a few texts. I'm afraid the news of Weylin visiting Jorunn to initiate a joint research project was another setback for Leandra. And I certainly still disapprove of her telling Adrian about Weylin. A self-destructive, yet fortuitous act, if you ask me.

We meet at a place called 'Ambrosia.' She comes ten minutes late; unusual as she is extremely punctual. Out of breath and looking pale, she hugs me and says, "Sorry...had a bad morning. Too much wine last night."

"How did your group session go?"

"Interesting, with some unexpected turns. I broke down in front of the group, but luckily, it seemed to have had a positive effect—the doctor stepped down from her 'know-it-all-about-human-psychology' pedestal and joined the ranks of other wretched humans. Then I got drunk and had audible hallucinations—"

"What kind of hallucinations?"

"I heard again the same voices I've heard a few times in my dreams. You know, the voices of some supernatural beings I sometimes believe are playing with me; not only with me, but with Weylin, and who knows, maybe all of us. It's as if I hear sounds my brain is somehow able to translate into human language. It's difficult to explain, but it freaks me out and makes me think I may be losing it; like getting mentally ill."

"Perhaps the reason you had this experience is that the veil between this and other realities has thinned due to the past life regressions. Maybe you're able to access another reality or a parallel world most humans cannot access because they've disconnected from nature, from their intuition, or soul."

"Are you freaking serious? You sound like a quack."

Her laughter is contagious and I join her in it as all of a sudden I see how flaky we must sound. Good thing there are no patients around to overhear us.

After she stops laughing, she looks at me despondently and says, "I'm not any further along than I was when I sought your help over a year ago. No, that's an exaggeration. Sometimes I get these urges to portray myself as a victim, but the truth is, I am doing much better and detaching from the recent past. It no longer hurts. What hurts more is the anguish I inflicted on Adrian. What a *stupid* move. I could kick myself for telling him."

"I wish I could've helped more, but I must say I was mystified by the lack of progress. But then again, maybe I shouldn't have been, because if that's the energy from your past lives, it's expected it might still have a strong hold on you. Good to hear you are snapping out of it."

"Do you really believe it was past life energy keeping me tethered to fantasy? It probably has nothing to do with my past lives and supernatural beings playing with us humans, but with some deep flaw in my own character, a flaw I'd never been aware of. But enough about me! I'm tired of talking and thinking about me. Oh, I forgot to tell you, the colleague who told me about Jorunn and Weylin working together on a project didn't write specifically to tell me that, but to ask for your email address. Did you hear from him?"

"Yes, last night. I didn't have a chance to mention it before, but in two weeks, I'll be holding a workshop for psychiatrists interested in using past life regression therapy. I've already booked a small conference room at the Hilton."

"How did you advertise the event?"

"Through the hospital website. Five people have already expressed interest and Lars was one of them. He wrote since to cancel his participation. I didn't think you'd be interested."

"On the contrary, I want to attend, too. Maybe it's not quackery after all."

She emits a forced and nervous laugh, then adds "Imagine if Weylin and Jorunn want to attend. They can spend a week together, and not because they believe in your hocus-pocus treatments. In fact, he'd scoff at the very idea. Imagine they come and I'm subjected all over again to the ninth circle of hell witnessing how easily he's replaced me. Please promise me—if it happens, you'll turn their attendance down, saying the workshop is at capacity."

"I've already set the limit to ten participants. I certainly wouldn't want to see you traumatized again, but Leandra, hasn't this gone far too long already? Don't you think if you saw them together again, you'd finally find closure? You'd finally realize and absorb he has let you down always, and always will, and you've learned your lesson? You can then try to work on your relationship with— Speak of the devil!"

When Adrian walks into the restaurant with his arm draped around a woman's shoulders, I look at Leandra, expecting shock, but her face is inexpressive of any emotion. On their way to a table they cannot avoid stopping at ours.

"Ginny, let me introduce you to David Stone, the psychiatrist I told you about. And this is Leandra, my...." He blushes as he hesitates whether to label Leandra as his 'wife' or his 'ex-wife'.

After I shake hands with Ginny (who looks petite and pixie-like, as if she was arrested in her growth to full womanhood) Leandra stands up and with a genuinely warm smile shakes Ginny's hand and says, "Delighted to meet you, Ginny."

Ginny looks at Adrian questioningly and then at Leandra and says, "Delighted to meet you too..." and laughs as if the introductions contained some humorous element. Her laughter has a bell-like ring to it and she comes across as someone extremely likeable, open and gregarious.

"I hope you are Adrian's ex-wife...because I'd rather be on a date with someone's ex-husband, than a current one and be a part of someone's marriage. I don't think I'd be good at playing the other woman." She laughs again, but her laughter reveals discomfort. However, her openness is disarming and I see Leandra respond with deep affability in her voice.

"Don't worry, Ginny. Adrian and I are separated even though not officially divorced yet. Your presence or absence is in no way linked to our relationship. Enjoy your meal! Few places offer such gastronomical delights of the quality you'll find here."

"Thanks, and it was nice meeting you both." They move away from our table and I look at Leandra, still trying to read her reaction.

"I'm alright, David. It's a shock, but I'll survive. He has every right to date after what I did to him. And the answer to your question about why I'm not working on my relationship with Adrian is simple. I believe I've cut Weylin out of my heart, but I still don't trust myself. I'm like an alcoholic who has stopped drinking but lives in constant fear someone will offer a glass of brandy and the craving will return and will power will dissolve. In that sense, I still consider myself unfaithful. Marriage needs clarity, openness, commitment, lack of any ambiguity of feelings and clear intentions of fidelity in order to be set back on track. I cannot work on it half-heartedly. And quite possibly, Adrian has moved on and wouldn't even want to try to rebuild what I demolished singlehandedly."

"I wouldn't bet on it. His body language revealed all but indifference."

"Before I can even begin to think of saving my marriage, I must somehow exorcise fully the feeling of being enslaved in this mindset that still makes me obsess over Weylin from time to time. I cannot get him out of my mind completely; I often feel complete indifference toward him, but I still dream of him. And I also imagine writing to him, telling him about all my grand self-delusions, including my hope we could be friends. In my mind, I still talk to him, and I want all of that to stop.

"A couple of nights ago I dreamt I was getting married to him in Stonehenge and just as we were about to exchange rings made of flowers, he transformed into a wolf which attacked me, and as I screamed in horror, a huge white she-wolf came to my defense, growled at him and he retreated behind a stone with his tail between his legs. What a coward! I woke up feeling revulsion and aversion toward him...I despised him and his cowardice.

"Believe me, I *want* to let go of him with total indifference. Your regression techniques and therapy have been helpful in that sense. That's why I don't need any further sessions to again learn he's wounded me and betrayed me in even more past lives. The karmic circle of betrayals has closed. Again, enough about me. What else is new with you?"

"I've been rebuilding my relationship with my mother and feel great about it. Plus, I haven't felt angry since our fallout in my office before your Barcelona trip. And, I'm seeing someone."

"Hey, that's breaking news! Do tell."

Our meal arrives—grilled sea bass.

"Are you sure you don't want a glass of wine with this?"

"Are you kidding me? I'm still feeling queasy from last night's excesses. Now, who's the lucky lady?"

"Someone from the gym. She works there as a yoga teacher. She's into meditation, spiritual retreats, organic gardening, energy healing…she's someone who leads a healthy life and who seems totally balanced emotionally, physically and spiritually. What a change from our hospital world. Anyway, she's almost too good to be true. Oh, I forgot to mention, she's quite a cook, too."

"Have you fallen in love?"

"I like her a lot, and I'm attracted to her, but my feelings don't even compare with what you experienced with Weylin. I'm not inspired enough to write erotic tales or poetry or to sing her serenades under her bower. I'm afraid there's not much of a romantic in me." I hear my own wry laughter.

"I'd like to meet her."

"I'll invite a few friends over to my place and order food, maybe from here. I plan to invite you and Adrian…I guess, not Adrian. You might have to come without a date."

"It wouldn't bother me to see Adrian at your place, but I'm not sure how he'd feel about seeing me. Excuse me for a moment?"

As she leaves the table to head toward the ladies' room, I also notice Ginny moving in the same direction and wonder if they'll find themselves washing hands beside one another.

I pour myself a second glass of Chianti, enjoying the taste and watching its ruby color sparkle in the flickering candlelight. As I'm sipping wine I'm thinking of Mia and our last night's lovemaking, and my fear of being an inadequate lover. I must say I expected more passion from her, but perhaps it takes time for two people to become attuned to each other's minds and bodies. One thing is obvious though. This probably won't be the volcanic type of love and passion Leandra had with Weylin. But moderation preserves sanity.

Her fish is getting cold and I'm wondering what's keeping her so long. I look over at Adrian's table, and he's sitting alone and fidgeting in his chair. Our gazes lock and he smiles somewhat wistfully.

Leandra comes back striding purposely in her usual business style.

"I was wondering if you were feeling unwell."

"I chatted with Ginny in the ladies' room. David, this is all so surreal I'm thinking I might be lucid dreaming. My husband is on a date with a woman I just met and happen to like. I'm still healing from being dumped by a lover who fell in love with someone else. I'm realizing more and more there is an unseen interconnectedness in the world. Jorunn and Ginny and Weylin's wife and I are all interconnected, even though only I am fully aware of that. Who knows how many other threads are in that fabric."

"What did you talk about?"

"She wanted to know if Adrian and I were done, because she's very much interested in him. Her honesty is so...so disarming. She seems down to earth, she knows what she wants, and isn't afraid to ask questions. I told her he was a great guy, smart, funny, reliable, a fantastic dad, and she looked at me with eyes wide and asked why in the world we separated. She'd asked Adrian, but he only said we'd hit a big reef. I said I also couldn't tell her the reason at this time. She wanted to know if I'd try to win Adrian back, and if the kids knew of our separation, and she had lots of other questions. What's bizarre is, I find it so easy to talk to her; I mean I felt no jealousy or competition, just...as I've already told you, strange connectedness; this oneness of all I'd never been aware of before. She was a complete stranger to me an hour ago, and now we have discovered a thread between us, a tie of such great significance."

"Have you then totally given up on Adrian?"

"He and I will always be connected. I've known him for ages. We are soul-mates and will continue being soul-mates even after we divorce—if we divorce. He's not talking to me, but I feel unequivocally he doesn't hate me for what I did, even if he's not ready to forgive. Tonight, he and I locked gazes for the briefest of moments, and there was recognition in that gaze...recognition of the bond between us. That bond is not easily dissolved. David, do you believe we all have made soul contracts before our birth, and our life paths have been preordained? I may have already asked you once."

"I strongly believe in past lives, and I also tend to believe in our life paths being generally preordained for the purposes of our soul's evolution; but also, we are free to make choices. You could have chosen not to get involved with Weylin, but then again, maybe you selected to walk into that fire, so you could finally learn the lesson you hadn't learned in previous incarnations. Maybe I'm only now ready to have a real relationship which will last, because only now can I distinguish between my own relationship and the sad one my parents had. On another note, I think there's a woman three tables down casting a glance at us. Do you know her?"

"Where?"

"To the right, behind Adrian's table."

Leandra cranes her neck and then exclaims, "Christina…a patient! I'll go over to say hello and meet her husband. Excuse me again." As she walks past Adrian and Ginny, she stops briefly, places a hand on Adrian's shoulder and makes what seems to be a comment on their meal. Ginny laughs and with a smile on her face, Leandra continues to the table behind them and hugs the woman who stands up. The man also stands up and shakes hands with Leandra. I watch her talk animatedly to both of them and clap her hands at something the woman says. After a few minutes, she comes back very excited.

"You won't believe this. This woman is a patient from my support group. During our last gathering she offered a young man, who'd lost a leg in an accident, an introduction to some of her younger friends. Apparently, at a party at her home he did meet someone, and they're now dating. Not only that, it seems to have been a case of instantly falling in love."

She's so genuinely pleased when her patients are doing better, she reminds me of a child who has just got a toy long wished for. And then she sighs and looks in Adrian's direction.

"David, the last couple of years have been surreal… certainly including my experience with hypnotherapy and regression to past lives. As I mentioned earlier, there are moments when I believe everything's preordained, and even decisions we make, despite our believing they originate from our free will, are also manifestations of the fate we're living out. How did I find myself in this spot, at this table, close to the person who has been a part of me for so many years yet is now galaxies away even though he's sitting almost across from me? And all that has happened to me is so insignificant in comparison to what other people have suffered and are going through. And it's even more insignificant in the big picture. In the vastness and timelessness of the universe, our individual lives are briefer than the flash of a firefly's light."

"Yes, we are but a flicker of light and our lives pass and end quickly. And yet, I believe we come back, and even though I'm not religious, my intuition tells me there must be more to life than to be born, to experience growth, and then to fall into decrepitude and oblivion. There must be some higher meaning transcending the biology of birth and death."

"But with this awareness that our lives will end, and change is the only constant, why can't we just move on and leave behind our past experiences? Why is it so difficult to open new chapters in our lives without looking back? Why do we obsess over the most trivial things in our lives, like running late, being stuck in traffic, and coming back home and noticing dust all over the furniture? We're in constant search of meaning, and we assign meaning to meaningless things around us. Nature is indifferent to us, and if a god exists, he or she is also indifferent to us, our pain, struggles, suffering. The voices I sometimes hear in my dream, the same voices I heard during my regressions, tell me we are like leaves the wind plays with in idleness, or curiosity, boredom or pure spite. Ginny thinks I'm still important to Adrian who was and maybe still is very important to me, but we are all squirming in the quicksand of life, fighting the final dissolution of our form, yearning for immortality, eternal youth and love and passion and it is all slipping through our fingers and we cannot keep anything for long—"

"Whoa, you're really getting philosophical on me and you haven't even had a drink."

"David, I need to detach from all feelings in order to reattach to the right ones. I simply must close the Weylin chapter and focus on rebuilding sense and meaning in my life. As I'm saying this, I realize I'm not even making sense. And I shouldn't be talking about myself tonight and I've monopolized the evening precisely by doing that. Tell me more about this new love in your life." She sits back, watching me.

"As in most new relationships, everything's smooth and easy and fun and almost effortless. For now, it feels very promising. She hinted a couple of nights ago she'd love to have kids, which got me thinking about the possibility of becoming a father. That's a thought I haven't shared with anyone but you. I find it hard to share it even with myself because it frightens me."

"David, maybe procreation is the basic meaning of our lives, just like in the animal and plant world. Go for it, even if the relationship doesn't work out ultimately. You're over fifty years old and this is your last chance to be a dad. It will change your life dramatically, and bring you so much love you can't even comprehend it. And don't think about your parents and the demise of their marriage. This, here and now, is your time to expand your life experience through parenthood. Invest into this relationship. If it feels right, it probably is right."

Her speech is passionate and oozes genuine affection for me, making me in turn feel tender love and friendship for her. She's a truly wonderful woman, and I love watching her smile. At this moment her eyes are sparkling with enthusiasm for my new relationship. I don't often see people care so much about my happiness, and I feel moved. I watch this woman in admiration. She has turned her life upside down and has suffered so needlessly, and I haven't been able to help much. I take her hand and tell her I appreciate her friendship deeply, and I want her to regain her emotional balance and happiness. I even joke, saying I'd give her a referral form to see Dr. Gray for some electroshocks so her brain could revert to its original state of pre-Weylin sanity. Her laughter is filled with mirth when she tells me she feels as if she has started to recover from a long bout of illness.

"David, I've noticed one disturbing pattern. Oh, I'm talking about myself again. As soon as I feel I'm getting over Weylin, and I'm becoming indifferent because he's betrayed me, and also because I shouldn't be having an affair with married or single men…anyway, as soon as I have a few good days and am feeling as if I've recovered, something happens that invariably flings me back into a state of despair, longing for him with heartache, tears, and I don't understand that. It's like some higher force decides to pull my strings again, like a human marionette. Or, it makes me remember his whisper telling me never to forget him, and then I feel hexed again. Perhaps this time, it's truly over…I hope it is, because I'm so tired, and I want so much to reclaim my old life—"

"Really nice meeting you!" Ginny's voice interrupts our conversation and both Leandra and I reply with a warm "likewise." Adrian is the only one who seems to be in a sour mood and in a haste to leave.

After they distance themselves from our table, Leandra almost cries out, "It's our anniversary in two days! I just remembered. I wonder if Adrian will call to…but what can he call about? To wish me a happy separation? Of course, he won't call."

"Why don't you call him? You'll be the one offering the olive branch. Perhaps with Ginny in the picture now, he'll feel avenged and will agree to talk to you. There's nothing more civilized than two people parting on amicable terms and continuing to co-parent their kids from separate homes."

"There's nothing I'd wish more than to reconnect with him as a friend, but I have no right to expect anything more of him. I must have hurt him in an unimaginable way. His sense of rejection, his feeling of having been replaced in my heart by another man, must have diminished him in so many ways no amount of revenge on me can restore that sense of self-worth we all need. He was so certain of my love and loyalty, and the shock of discovery couldn't have possibly faded."

"Why in the hell *did* you have to tell him? I just can't get over that…"

"I felt so wounded I couldn't resist wounding him, as if he was to blame. But maybe he is to blame…"

"What do you mean?"

"I mean, maybe there are no innocents. I cheated because there were gaps in my emotional life I wasn't fully aware of. Being so busy with his professional life, Adrian stopped being the romantic lover of our early years, and neglected me in some way. He wasn't aware of my needs, because *I* wasn't aware of them— until I fulfilled them temporarily with Weylin."

"But no one can fulfill your needs unless you tell that person openly what it is you are lacking. Men are not mind readers. Weren't you also busy building your own career? If you'd been more aware of the state of affairs between the two of you, you'd probably have tried to reconnect with Adrian on all levels.

Instead, your family functioned as a well-oiled wheel that never stopped turning, but was still suffering from the corrosion of emotional disengagement. And no one even noticed. Then again it shouldn't come as a surprise, because it's easier to ignore the existence of something lacking in one's marriage than to give it one's full attention and try to resolve it. Men, and I recognize this in myself, in particular are known for sticking their heads in the sand."

She sighs and looks like someone who no longer has any answers to her questions. To arrive at clarity requires the passage of time.

"Thanks for this lovely meal, David. I should go now and do some house-cleaning. I'm overbooked tomorrow and the next few days. Our kids are coming home in six weeks and I'm starting to count the days. I've neglected the house and it needs thorough cleaning. My regular cleaning lady is away for two months so I'll find someone else, or end up doing it myself. I hope you keep your word about inviting me to meet your girlfriend."

I get up to hug her. She seems both fragile and strong at the same time.

"I'll text you with the time and date, and will probably organize it in a couple of weeks." I stay to wait for the bill and watch her leave. On her way out, she stops at the bar to say goodbye or hello to a man sitting alone.

Another patient? A friend? Another wounded soul seeking solace in alcohol and hoping to meet someone who will change his life? If all of us could walk around with our souls exposed and all our scars on full display, we would probably be tempted to walk up to each other and exchange hugs and words of comfort.

CHAPTER EIGHTEEN

Leandra
The next two days are insanely busy. Between my regular work hours and those spent on call at the ER I've no time to stop for a decent meal, a leisurely coffee, or think of Weylin, Adrian, kids, or anything else. When I finally return home from the last ER visit at eleven pm, I can barely walk. My thoughts are mangled from sheer physical exhaustion. The shoes I've always found comfortable have given me blisters. My feet are swollen from extended hours of sitting and I want to soak in a hot, honeysuckle-perfumed bubble bath. While the water is running and filling up the tub, a feeling of loneliness sets in and the house turns into a cave of aching emptiness, devoid of love and warmth only a family can infuse. I've lost my family and I've lost a lover, and I'm left alone with a cat that bolts out the backyard door as soon as I feed him.

How did I end up here, in this emotional desert? And like a flare launched from a sinking ship a memory of my wedding shoots across the darkness of my thoughts. Today is our wedding anniversary—a dull ache unfurls at the bottom of my soul and gains an intensity fed by my reflections on what I've lost. I expect a deluge of tears, but instead a dry ache produces painful heaving of my chest.

I step into the tub with my brain frothing with turmoil. I submerge myself in the foamy water and close my eyes, trying to relax. I open them again when I hear the chirping sound of my phone. I extend my dripping arm toward the towel shelf to grab a hand towel, dry my hands the best I can. I look at the time on the phone wondering if I could still be on call. As there's no message, I check my email and my heart skips a beat when I see one from Adrian. He remembered our anniversary as he always has. I was the one who forgot it one year and felt terrible for it. I open his note, lean my head against the inflatable bath cushion and read.

Lea,
I don't know why I'm writing…but somehow I couldn't
ignore this day which, under different circumstances, would be a

celebration of our wedding anniversary. Or, it's on this special day I want to write and explain how I feel about our separation, about your betrayal, about your shattering our family. And the shattering is not over yet, because we still have to tell our kids. And what do we tell them? Do we lie, and say we have grown apart but will always be friends, or do we tell the truth? Do we forever tarnish in their eyes the image of their perfect mother?

What the hell happened to the girl in the white polka-dot dress who told me with such conviction I was her true love, nothing would ever change that, and nothing could ever come between us? What happened to the woman who despised adultery in others as an immoral act and a serious, even fatal, flaw of character?

When did you stop loving me? When did you stop respecting our marriage? How could I have not suspected anything? How could I have not noticed sudden falsity in you? How did I not feel you weren't there with me, in my embrace, but with someone else in your mind, heart and thoughts?

Can you even begin to understand how much you diminished me by wanting someone else; how you shriveled me by showing me a total stranger could replace me in your heart at the flick of a switch? When I imagine you in bed with this repugnant and most odious stranger who's ruined my life, I want to jump out of my own skin. It's the most unbearable anguish I could ever have imagined. It's the kind of pain I've tried to lessen and erase by using other women, but—unsuccessfully. Relationships that start out as vindication against someone who's smashed your heart just cannot work.

Ginny is an incredible woman who's had the bad luck of falling in love with me. She looks at me as if I am at least a demigod…in her eyes I'm super handsome, smart and funny, and she sees in me all that you stopped seeing a long time ago. I am both highly flattered and unmoved at the same time, and the reason is simple. I feel poisoned by your betrayal, and I don't know if anything can dilute or neutralize such poison. Ginny's love is ineffective in that respect. The more she loves me, the more enraged I feel over what you did to me. There is no compensation for that.

POISONOUS WHISPERS

Lying in bed at night, I feel the poison of your treason course through my bloodstream and corrode me inside out. Last week, feeling uncontrollable fury I smashed two antique vases Aggie had paid a hefty sum to get restored. Remember, the white-and-blue ones from Greece that meant so much to her because my dad had given them to her? I smashed them, wishing I could hurt you as much as you had hurt me. I want to hurt you much more than your asshole lover ever could have by ditching you. I wanted you to be jealous of Ginny the other day, but you obviously didn't care I had someone in my life. Ginny even told me how much she liked you, and she felt it was mutual. The taste of Tiramisu turned bitter that day.

Before I started dating Ginny, I had sex with two different women I met in a bar. Making love felt like punishing them for your sin. I was fierce, but tried to give them so much pleasure they would want to see me again. And they did, but I couldn't put myself through it, and told them I was no longer interested. I sounded so callous to myself, and can only imagine what they thought of me. I want to betray you, but I haven't because my heart is like a jagged rock no other woman can penetrate in spite of all my efforts. There can be no real ecstasy, no real fulfillment in soulless sex, and therefore no betrayal of the heart.

I may be different from most men, but I can't tell if I am because I haven't confided in any one of my friends. They all wonder why we split up when our relationship looked so ideal to most of them. Maybe I'm just too old and embittered for the dating scene. I've never envied single men who went through women like disposable razors. I always wanted a great family filled with love and harmony, just like the family I was raised in.

All this dating and sleeping around has made me feel more despondent than ever. I like Ginny, and have a bond with her and like having her in my life, but I already know it is not, and never can be, what you and I had; and I will have to disappoint her because there's an expiration date imprinted on this relationship.

She told me last night she felt she was the 'other woman', even though you and I are separated, and technically I'm not cheating on you. She even started crying over the thought I might go back to you. And though I have never mentioned it to her, I do sometimes think I want to try to forgive you and attempt to rebuild our marriage.

Most often I hate you, but in that hate and fury I also love you and I want you back. And then I never want to see you again, and I think it is okay to stone adulteresses to death in some countries because it's a sin against God, even though I've always been an atheist and know there's no God. I feel powerless in my rage against you and my inability to let go and start life anew. I don't know if I can forgive you, if I could ever trust you again. And I hope that for years to come you reel from the wound inflicted on you by the sleazebag you fucked. I'm sorry…I realize I'm cursing you and I'm being uncharacteristically crude. But why the hell didn't you tell me you felt unhappy?

You should have told me when there was still time to repair the holes in our marriage. Are all men as clueless as I was? Every marriage has problems and yet, people do not jump into others' beds. If you'd just had sex with him, I think I'd be able to deal with that. But you loved him…oh my god, you loved someone who did not really love you! Because if he had, I'd have lost you for good. But because he didn't, he left me a small ray of hope. I should thank him for not loving such an extraordinary woman.

This is written in a moment of weakness, so don't write back. I need to think more, and I need to heal more. Good thing the girls won't be home for another few weeks.

His email is unsigned. My tears are falling into the tepid water. At this moment, he and I are fused in the energy of pain. I regret telling him about my infidelity. But some marriages crumble into ashes only to be reborn and rebuilt stronger. I have seen that. People forgive, pain fades and love is given a second chance. Perhaps it is impossible to restore the passionate kind of love that lives only at the beginnings of relationships. But strong, committed and meaningful love is possible. I just don't know if I'm emotionally restored enough to invest effort into resuscitating my life with Adrian. And yet, I cannot imagine losing him for good.

The water has gone cold, and I drag myself out of the tub. I barely touch the bed when I fall asleep and find myself in another lucid dream. For a moment I think I'm not even dreaming but have somehow stepped through the membrane David was talking about the other night and entered a parallel reality. David has told me he believed my regressions have opened the gates through which I can access more of the subconscious, where evidence of my past lives lies hidden and needs to be excavated. I know now my fear I might be descending into mental illness was unjustified. I am sane, in spite of these strange dreams and the voices I sometimes hear. It is as if my sixth sense or what the New Age philosophy calls the Pineal Gland or the Third Eye, has somehow been activated by the emotional pain I've suffered.

Aware I'm dreaming, I'm walking through tall grasses of a field. The moon is full on a warm summer night. The air is pierced with Cicada song, and the scent of herbs is trying to awaken some distant olfactory memories in me, memories I cannot yet recall. The surroundings seem serene, and yet I'm frightened. When I turn around, I see a forest casting shadows in the moonlight. One shadow seems to move and follow me, and I start to run toward a semi-circle of large white stones. I seem to know the place, and yet I cannot remember it. Perhaps I am visiting a past life location. I reach the rocks panting and hide behind one trying to calm my breathing. I am still aware this is a dream and no harm can come to me, but the fear is crippling and it makes my legs go weak.

Close to the rocks, a brook flows hidden by thick shrubbery. The night is still enough for me to discern the sound of running water and I move in its direction. It is a struggle to go through the thicket to get to the brook, and my dress snags and tears on the brambles. In the folds of my dress I find a silver dagger and try to make an opening in the dense growth by cutting away at the twigs. I am surprised at how adroitly I handle the dagger, as if I had done so many times before.

Before I wade into the water I cannot help noticing how rich the banks are with medicinal herbs and how easily I recognize them in spite of the darkness, and know how they need to be boiled so they can be used as cures. Was I a healer in a past life? Is that why studying medicine has held so much appeal?

I reach the water and want to wade across the brook, but keep losing my footing on the slippery stones and falling. The water is splashing around me so loudly, whoever is following me will have no trouble locating me. Just as I climb out of the water and step on the grass-covered bank, something pounces on my back and knocks me down. I kick wildly and manage to extricate myself from the grip of what felt like large paws. I run and hide behind a tree. My heart is thumping so wildly I cannot hear anything else. When I muster up enough courage to peek out, I find myself face to face with a snarling animal which looks like a huge hyena. I stare into its yellow gleaming eyes, and after a few moments realize I am staring into Kieran's face, which is contorted with viciousness. I pull out the dagger again and hear a voice whisper from the top of the tree.

"Let her kill him, let her kill him."

"She is a healer not a killer," another voice replies.

The beast retracts into a crouching position and then stands up on its hind legs transforming itself into Kieran…then Weylin…and then back to Kieran until it is one face with fused features of both men.

"Jilleen, it is I. You have been trying to forget me and I cannot allow that." He extends his arms toward me and a surge of sexual energy ripples through my body, setting every nerve on fire. My physical reaction to him must stem from an ancient imprint in my DNA because in his presence, my power seems to dissipate. Automatically, I fall into his arms. I touch his face and look into his eyes, and watch in wonder how their greenness gives way to a glittery yellow hue. As my face comes close to his shoulder my nostrils are filled with the odor of treachery and the sensation fills me with utter bewilderment. How can skin smell of betrayal? How can I know that?

He clasps me in a tight embrace and I feel claws puncture the skin on my back. At that moment inhuman power fills me and I push him away with such force, he falls. I pounce on him feeling the power and fierceness of a she-wolf fighting fiercely for her freedom. The next moment, I raise my hand aiming the dagger at his right carotid artery, and just as I am about to stab him his eyes turn green again and fill with so much fear and cowardice I only scratch his neck and draw a thin rivulet of blood.

"Let her kill him, let her kill him," the same voice chants again, poisoning the air with malice.

"You have loved me through eternity. You cannot kill what you love." His voice is a whimper.

"I will not kill you. I don't kill, I love, and I heal. But not you, not anymore." Emptied of all fear I start to get up, wanting to leave, but notice almost invisible cords run from my heart to his. *"So these are the emotional cords I read about,"* I think aloud in astonishment.

All I need do is to cut them and be free of him forever. I take out the knife again and look at the cord to decide where to cut. He is still lying on the ground, his eyes following my every move. The cord is translucent and at the same time reminds me of a leafless willow twig.

"If you cut it, I will vanish. I might even die." His voice is weak and strained.

"I want you to vanish from my mind. If we ever made a soul contract to incarnate together so you could teach me lessons in love, loss and betrayal, I want that contract to terminate now. You will teach me nothing more."

Blood is still running down his neck and chest from the cut I made. Before I cut the cord, I place my hand on the wound on his neck and hold it there. I do not want to heal the man who has wounded me so deeply, but the healer in me cannot deny wellness to anyone. When I remove my hand, his wound has closed and the bleeding has stopped. He takes my hand and puts it into his mouth. In the past, that would send electric currents throughout my whole being, but I exert a huge effort not to feel anything, and I succeed.

"We will meet again if you do not cut the cord," he manages in a stuttering voice.

I'm not listening to him, but am concentrating on the cord. I want to touch it, but my hand cannot grasp it. I lift the knife wishing to sever it with one blow, but whispers stop my hand in midair.

"She will kill him if she cuts the cord."

"But if she does not, she will never be free. She will never forget him. To remove the curse he cast on her, she must cut the cord. Otherwise, she will always hear his poisonous whispers."

My blood freezes in horror. His death would be my freedom. That cannot be. Cord-cutting removes attachments and does not harm anyone. Indecision paralyzes me. I look into his face and see a sly demonic smile.

"Jilleen, remember the wish we made together, the wish that one day we would be permanently together, and we would not harm anyone by our doing so?"

"I made that wish with Weylin, and you are Kieran. Or, are you both of them, or many more who have hurt me throughout time?"

He raises his hand to stroke my hair, but I retreat, mistrustful of his intentions. He suddenly sits up and grabs me by the hair, and with all my force I lower the knife and sever the cord. Blood splashes from it and soaks and blinds me. Once my vision clears, to my surprise, I see a new cord trail from my heart towards his. And I understand—I am the one attached to him, and he had detached himself from me a long time ago.

Furious with myself, I sever the new cord before it reaches him and attaches itself to his heart. He is still bleeding and may be dying, but I keep retreating and holding my hand over my heart, hoping to prevent another cord from forming. When I fall backwards into the brook, the shock of cold water over my face wakes me up.

The clock shows two am and I'm wide awake, trembling from the frightful dream. I quickly write it down because I want to tell David about it. Perhaps he can help me interpret it, even though it does not seem to carry much symbolism. It shows my struggle to forget the man who asked me in a whisper to never forget about him.

The urge to call Adrian is overwhelming. I want to ask him to come back home, to hold me all night and tell me we will clear the wreckage of our marriage and build a stronger one. I want to tell him to apologize to Ginny on my behalf, too, but mostly, to just come home and help me return to normalcy. Yet I know I cannot do it until I feel completely committed to being the main architect of a new and stronger relationship between us. I am no longer who I was, but I need to find a better version of myself who will work on healing us.

CHAPTER NINETEEN

David
The last few weeks have been hectic, and my appointment book is getting crowded. Mental illness seems to be spreading like the mediaeval plague in our part of the world. Two of my patients have recently told me they were considering going to the Amazon in search of a shaman who could give them Ayahuasca in hope they might find healing from depression in the resultant psychedelic experience. Some are in such despair they request electroshocks, and inquire about deep brain stimulation. With the advent of the Internet, patients have been enabled to research their own illness, making their own diagnoses. In the last couple of months, only one of the seven new patients responded well to hypnotherapy. He seemed to be a renewed man when he came out of the trance. My next patient is Chris Weber, a gay fashion designer who suffers from severe panic attacks, claustrophobia and anxiety. I keep the office door open when he is in session.

When he comes in, I cannot help but admire his taste in clothes. He is slim and tall, and has striking blue eyes. His black hair is cut short in the back, but falls in a long wave over his right eye. He keeps pushing it away with a coquettish move of his perfectly manicured hand. Today he is dressed in black jeans and a black turtleneck, and the only contrast to the simple elegance is a shiny, grey, snakeskin-patterned belt with a silver buckle. His shoes are made of black suede, and look soft and expensive.

"How are you feeling, Chris?" He's one of the patients who told me he was considering trying psychedelics because all medications he has tried have given him a number of side effects, the most bothersome being delayed ejaculation. His partner of five years has been avoiding sex with him for that reason, which has resulted in a strained relationship.

"Dr. D., I've done a lot of research on Ayahuasca and am planning a trip to the Amazon."

He has always addressed me as Dr. D. and I don't mind the moniker. "What have you found out, Chris, and what are your expectations?"

"I read up on the experience of many people who've tried it, so I expect to reach a mystical state. I want to explore my mind, feelings, and the source of my depression that conventional medicine cannot explain in any better terms other than 'a chemical imbalance in the brain'. I've read that studies prove the serotonin levels are increased in long time users. I expect and hope to be delivered of the hell I've been living in."

"But you've been stable on the medication I've prescribed, and able to go back to work. I don't know much about Ayahuasca, but I do know it could be lethal if mixed with antidepressants. I also know studies are being made in which doctors are trying to determine the benefits versus risks of concoctions derived from plants and mushrooms. I did read anxiety has been reduced in terminal cancer patients who were given Psilocybin mushrooms. I may research this further, because the time may come when psychedelics will be administered to patients by psychiatrists under controlled conditions. Anyway, as I said, a *mix* of medications can be fatal."

"Oh, I won't be on any medication by the time I arrive in Peru."

"Why did you choose Peru?"

"It's become a major center of Ayahuasca tourism."

"Aren't you wary the increased demand and popularity have set the stage for fake shamans and other shady characters to surface, taking advantage of gullible tourists?"

"I spoke with someone who's just come back, a client of mine, wealthy and a big-time buyer of my designs. He's given me the name of a well-respected shaman. Anyway, I feel I've nothing to lose."

"Is Mario going with you?"

"No…things are a bit tense between us. I'm getting tired of financing his expensive tastes and habits. He keeps saying he's looking for a job, but I see no evidence of it. I fear he's with me because of the lifestyle I've given him."

His voice becomes tremulous and his gaze drops to the floor. The movement of his Adam's apple indicates difficulty with swallowing. Chris is a very sensitive young man and, being gay, his life is anything but easy, in spite of having been raised in opulence and privilege. His parents were painfully disappointed when they learned he was homosexual and determined to pursue a career in fashion design, not in his father's steel factory.

"I'm also apprehensive of leaving him for two weeks. I don't trust him to respect my home, and not bring strangers in and party all night."

Chris is cracking his knuckles while speaking.

"I've invested so much into that relationship, emotionally, financially. I'm going on this trip in the hope of getting completely cured of depression. If I can do without meds, I'll no longer have delayed ejaculation as a side effect. That's really taken a toll on our sex life. I have to put so much effort into reaching an orgasm I break out in a sweat, and I can sense Mario's revulsion. He doesn't say anything, but I can feel how badly he wants it to be over so I can leave him in peace. Dr. D., you've helped me a lot, and I've come a long way, but I need to try this, too. I'm concerned about one aspect of the Ayahuasca experience. I dread its vomiting and diarrhea, but understand almost everyone has to puke before they have these life-altering experiences."

"Chris, you're an intelligent and educated man, and I'm sure you've gathered enough facts to make an informed decision. If all goes well, the experience shouldn't harm you. But, will it help you? I'm not so sure. I'm certainly not against alternative treatment methods. I've been a proponent of hypnotherapy for many years even though many colleagues have scoffed at it. Your depression is not as serious as you believe it is. Also, Zoloft has stabilized you significantly but, unfortunately, there are side effects. And there's a very direct correlation between your depression and your relationships. You try so hard to turn every relationship into perfection; when it falls short of your expectations your depression takes a turn for the worse. It's not unusual, as we all get bogged down by daily happenings, unmet needs, but how many relationships have you had in the last three years?"

"Three or four...four. They all took advantage of me and my generosity."

"They took what you allowed them to take. You were buying love, affection and loyalty from the very beginning of your relationships. We've already been over this, and how from the very beginning of every relationship you try to impress your boyfriends with your money and success. You hide the person you are behind the glitz of what money can buy. You never give them a chance to get to know the real you, the sensitive, warm-hearted, intelligent and erudite man who is a great conversationalist, a perfect listener, a giver."

"Animals are more grateful than people. I should just give up on love relationships and devote more time to animal rescue. I'm placing so much hope on this trip. I feel…how can I say it best…I feel rot and corrosion eating at my soul. I feel a malaise of spirit, as if I've not been whole for a long time, if ever. I always have this fear of loss; fear my collection will not be well received; fear I'm not lovable enough; fear every relationship I enter I'll have to abort after a short while because it won't develop into something healthy and viable. It's like a piece of me is always missing, as if I misplaced a part of myself and I just cannot find it.

"I've read how shamans can bend time and space and enable their spirits to mingle with the cosmic spirits, and they can do it for other people. I hope by drinking Ayahuasca my spirit is released; or rather, the content of my subconscious rises to the surface and I face what I have to, and I relive painful moments from the past, in order to release them completely. I want to locate that missing piece of myself—a gaping hole inside. Am I making sense?"

"Chris, of course you're making sense. You have an extraordinary ability for articulating your feelings. I wish you the best of luck in your search for answers. We all have unanswered questions, and there are few people who can say they feel truly whole and complete, in harmony with their internal and external worlds. Some may have everything, and yet feel an undefined longing for more, for something they cannot even define.

"To digress from the metaphysical and return to reality, I think you need to set boundaries with people. You jump into every relationship with too much enthusiasm and too much openness. You give away your heart too quickly without testing the waters first. You are highly excitable and almost naïve in your belief every new relationship you enter is finally the gate to heaven."

"Why can I not seem to find a kindred soul, a soul-mate?" He is twirling a strand of his hair and looking forlorn. "And these are also questions I plan to pose to the spirits of Ayahuasca. I trust my intuition on this. The decision to travel to Peru is the right one."

"Chris, you remind me of a child perplexed that Santa Clause has not appeared in person on Christmas morning. Even if you found a soul-mate, the relationship would be complicated from time to time because soul-mates also come with egos, insecurities, vulnerabilities, defenses and everything else that makes us flawed humans. And sometimes, soul-mates can wound you more deeply than those who are not your soul-mates."

We spend another half hour dissecting his issues. Through the door I see my secretary has left for the day as Chris was my last appointment and I've extended my session with him by twenty minutes. When he gets up, we shake hands warmly and he promises to come back and see me upon his return. Alone in my office, I sit at my desk and finish my notes on the session.

As I get up to leave I see a text from Mia asking me why she hasn't heard from me all day and if we can get together tonight for drinks. I'm often too tired to go out and prefer to see her at my place. I'm afraid she'll soon start showing disappointment over her unmet expectations and another chance at a meaningful and lasting relationship will go belly up. So far she's been very understanding and we're planning to invite a few friends over to my house for dinner on Saturday. I've not met any of her friends yet, and I want her to meet the very few I have. I plan to phone Mike and see how he's doing. I see him very rarely, and the last time we talked he and his wife were in therapy. He's so resentful and embittered over her betrayal I doubt therapy will be of any help. The reason she came back to him is because her lover broke up with her.

Before I leave for the evening, I check my mail and see that the sender is Jorunn Berg. I open it and read:

Dear David, I hope I'm not too late to register for your workshop on hypnotherapy. I have just seen it advertised and it would be fascinating to learn a new method for self-discovery. I'm always in search of innovative treatment techniques, even those which are somewhat unorthodox. I hope to hear from you soon and look forward to meeting you in person.
Best regards,

Jorunn

I wonder how Leandra will react when she again sees Weylin's new lover. I cannot turn her away, because there is enough space, with only six psychiatrists registered. I'd planned to accept ten participants in order to give everyone sufficient chance to practice the technique on the five volunteers I found among my patients, but now there will be eight participants, including Leandra. I write back immediately to confirm receipt of her email and her registration. Her response is instantaneous and she says she will book her flights and hotel promptly. She also mentions she'll arrive two days early to recover from jet lag and do some sightseeing. At least Weylin has not written expressing his interest in the event, because in loyalty to Leandra I'd have no choice but to turn him down with the lie I can't accept more people. Later, I could always say there were last minute cancellations.

I also realize Jorunn will be in town on Saturday, and I decide on the spot to invite her for dinner. As I press the send button, it occurs to me Leandra might not be happy about seeing Jorunn, but then again, it may give her a chance to get to know her better and perhaps even find out it was much ado about nothing, and Weylin did not jump from one love affair into another. I also seem to recall she told me she liked Jorunn immensely and found her irresistibly charming.

Mia's text comes as I'm unlocking the door. She'll be over in a few minutes with a hot dinner she made. She's also bringing cold beer. I feel a smile light up my face in anticipation of a pleasant evening filled with her optimism and giggles.

I quickly shower and change into jeans and a red Polo shirt. I set the table, put on an Allesandro Safina CD, and with the first notes of music, the bell rings and Mia walks in with sparkling eyes and hands full of bags.

The evening is perfect. We eat dinner after we've made love. The pleasure was intense, and yet, I cannot help but compare my sexual life with that which Leandra and Weylin shared. Perhaps illicitness is the secret ingredient of ecstasy. But, what I now have is woven of calm, comfort and warmth, and I'm happy with it. I don't think I would want a love raising me to heaven one moment and ripping my soul apart the next.

"So how many people do you plan to invite for Saturday?" she asks me.

"No more than ten. We can have a catered dinner. I don't want you to slave away in the kitchen—"

"No way! I enjoy cooking, and besides I want to show off my skills to your hot-shot doctor friends. I also have lots of frozen cakes I made weeks earlier, so I plan to bring them all. I want a feast."

"We can do the shopping tomorrow after work."

"I don't have classes in the morning, so I can buy most of the food. I know what I want to make, so don't give it a second thought."

We cuddle on the couch and turn the TV on. After a few minutes, I start feeling drowsy and go to bed. She joins me and we fall asleep with arms around each other. I don't think I've ever felt happier—or more fearful I might lose this piece of newfound heaven.

Over the next two days Mia and I exchange a number of texts but don't see each other. She tells me she's got everything under control for the Saturday dinner and her best friend, another yoga teacher, is helping her make the appetizers. She tells me she's bought a new tablecloth, silver placemats, napkin rings and candles. As a bachelor my kitchen supplies apparently do not include such finery. I insist on paying for everything she's bought, and she accepts. After all, yoga teachers don't make nearly as much money as psychiatrists and it is my dinner party. And without her help, I'd feel quite helpless. For the first time in years I feel my home will be filled with love and warmth when I open the door to welcome my guests. I'm in such a heightened mood, thoughts of engagement and marriage start swimming in my mind. I need to consult with Leandra on how to proceed, because fear taints the coin's other side of excitement.

CHAPTER TWENTY

Leandra

My hands are trembling as I rummage through my closet to pick the dress for tonight. David told me Jorunn would be there as well as Adrian, but Ginny is unable to come because she had to attend an out-of-town funeral. I'm nervous about seeing Adrian, and also curious about Jorunn. Thank God, Weylin did not sign up for the workshop. I couldn't bear seeing him and Jorunn together again. I feel grateful to David for promising me he would turn Weylin down. Weylin's only interest in the workshop would be the opportunity to see Jorunn. He always showed contempt for hypnotherapy, just as I had at one point.

I'm looking forward to seeing Jorunn. There always seemed to be a mutual attraction between the two of us, but I never had a chance to get to know her better. She came across as someone extremely flirtatious, both with men and women; but also as an amiable, likable, sparkling and simply irresistible person. I probably could have never been able to compete with her over Weylin, even if I had wanted to fight for him. But there's also some logical fallacy in that, because when people are truly in love with one person, they are immune to the advances of others, so there can be no competition.

I always felt that security with Adrian, and Aggie always jokingly quoted Agatha Christie who'd said 'archaeologists make the best husbands because the older their wives get the more interested in them they become'. Aggie also felt she could never lose her husband to another woman since the bond between them was too strong. I remind myself—I was the one to break that bond with Adrian.

I find a form-fitting dress with an asymmetric cut, and a shimmering, sequined shoulder. The length is mid-calf, which I always find elegant. The dress is colored two shades of green which blend at the line of asymmetric separation. I take off the tag as I've never worn the dress and go into the bathroom to look for a green eye shadow and green eyeliner. All of a sudden it means so much to me to look my best, to be dressed to impress. Vanity, thy name is Leandra!

My heart flutters when I knock on David's door. He opens it with a face lit up with a wide, warm grin. Mia is right behind him. She hugs me and says, "So-o glad to meet you, Leandra. David keeps talking about your friendship and superb professional relationship. Now I see how beautiful you are, I think I should be jealous." Her laughter is genuinely warm and tinkling.

Hugging her back, I reply, "Happy to see my friend David has finally struck gold. And thanks for the compliment. I need it tonight more than ever."

"I think I know why." She winks disarmingly and I wonder if David has spilled my secrets to her. I discard that thought immediately as unfounded. She obviously knows Adrian and I are separated, and may be wondering how he and I will interact tonight.

When I walk in I see Adrian standing with a glass of wine talking to Jorunn and a man I don't know. Jorunn is wearing tight, black pants and a white, flowing shirt cinched with a gold belt. Her shiny, black hair looks styled and her face is beaming with smiles as she listens to Adrian attentively. A pang of jealousy shoots through my heart as I expect Adrian may fall prey to her charms, too. When he turns around and sees me my heart stops. I lock gazes with the man I have loved for so many years. There is recognition in our non-verbal exchange, as well as awkwardness and a shade of embarrassment. My instinct is to go to the other side of the room and join two women who seem to be engaged in an animated conversation involving a lot of gesticulation. Instead I bravely walk toward Adrian, hug him and ask him how he has been. He plants a superficial kiss on my cheek and murmurs he's alright. Somewhat flustered, he tells me I look great.

Jorunn seems delighted to see me, and after I'm introduced to Mike, she and I enter a lively conversation about hypnotherapy, her life, work and family, and touch on the developments in my life since we last saw each other in Barcelona. She tells me she's been married three times and believes she has found the right man in her third husband. She has two sons from her previous marriages and a girl from her current marriage. She tells me the last time she saw me she felt there was a connection between us, but we've never had the chance to talk. She radiates light and love; she is like a lamp-post in the dark velvet of the night attracting winged creatures into her halo without burning them. I find it impossible not to like her and even more impossible to feel jealous or threatened by her. I cannot resist telling her how lovely, warm and approachable she is and her response surprises me.

"That's the reason I'm often misunderstood, and both men and women hit on me, misreading my intentions."

"It is also because you are very flirtatious, I would say."

"I am. I even flirt with my own husband every day and he loves it."

"Isn't he jealous of your flirting with others?"

"He does ask questions, but he knows me well and understands that, unlike him who is very introverted, I need people. I thrive on people's energies. I need human interaction, whereas Anders' world is complete with me and our daughter."

I'm tempted to mention Weylin, but I curb the impulse and say, "Do you plan to introduce hypnotherapy into your practice?"

"I don't know. I must admit I may have deceived David into believing I'm here strictly for the course when, in fact, I want to undergo the treatment myself in search of answers."

"He may need more guinea pigs to illustrate his procedure, so I'm sure he won't mind regressing you, too."

"Have you tried it?"

The question catches me off guard, but I have no problem in being partially truthful.

"Yes, I have. We have all been psychoanalyzed during our training, just like you must have been, but I wanted to try something unorthodox. I was also in search of answers, and have found most of them…at least, I hope so."

Just as she's about to ask me for more details about my experience, the sound of a bell interrupts us and Mia's cheerful voice invites us to the table. I find myself sitting opposite Adrian and Jorunn. Mike takes a seat on the right of Adrian, and a colleague psychiatrist with whom David and I work sits on Jorunn's left. He's a new addition to our staff, Allan, and I cannot recall his last name because it is long and complicated as he's Finnish. He's short and pudgy and always in a suit. I heard some nurses poke fun at his formality, not only in the way he dresses but also in the way he speaks. David and Mia take seats at the head of the table, while Rolf, another colleague psychiatrist and friend of David's, is on my right, and the two women I still haven't been introduced to sit on my left. Mia introduces them as her two best friends and fellow yoga teachers. Their names are Ingrid and Annie and they look sleek and fit. David says three more people unfortunately couldn't make it.

Dinner is delicious. There are at least six appetizers consisting of smoked meats, a variety of cheeses, white asparagus with sauce Hollandaise, crostini with different toppings, shrimp with avocado salad, and mini corn muffins. After a few bites of each I'm already starting to feel full. Wine flows, and with every new bottle, laughter becomes more and more insouciant. David mentions his hypnotherapy workshop, and I can tell Adrian is all ears.

"David, if you need volunteers for the workshop, I'll gladly participate," Adrian says, much to my astonishment.

"You'd be the last person I'd imagine volunteering for this." I look Adrian straight in the eyes. "You never believed in anything outside mainstream science. Where does this change come from?" I ask.

He looks at me, smiles and says, "Maybe I don't have all the answers to my questions. Maybe I'm becoming more, how would you say, spiritually adventurous."

Jorunn turns to Adrian and engages him in a conversation on hypnosis. She's laughing, flirting, shaking her rich mane of black hair, touching Adrian, but he seems to be listening to her only perfunctorily. After three glasses of wine, I'm amused listening to the people on my left and right and across from me. I look at Jorunn and smile at her. There will always be women smarter, younger, more beautiful, interesting and captivating than I am and comparisons are useless, unproductive, and self-defeating. Everyone is unique and everyone has a different reason to be in this incarnation. I smile at catching myself thinking of reincarnation as a fact of life.

After dessert, we get up and disperse, to mingle in the rooms of the apartment. It's the first time I realize how large David's place is. The terrace itself is at least 600 square feet in size, and as this is another unseasonably warm night even though it is November, we put our coats on and flock outside with wine glasses in our hand. I find myself talking to Adrian.

"Any news about the kids?" he asks.

"I talked to Cassie this morning. They're coming in four weeks, as planned. She told me she's been shopping for gifts and asked me what to buy for you. She was looking for a cashmere sweater, but I think you already have enough of them." I feel tremulous talking to him. I betrayed him so terribly and am now chatting with him, smiling at him, and feeling attracted to him. I also notice Jorunn casting glances at us, and the idea she may also find him attractive renews a feeling of possessiveness in me. Adrian looks very handsome tonight in blue jeans and a black V-cut long-sleeved T-shirt. He is dressed casually but chic. Short, coarse stubble flatters him and gives him a masculine look. His hair has grown and he's lost a few pounds.

I ask him about his work and he tells me about a new prosecutor, who tripped on entering the courtroom, fell and ripped his pants. We laugh at the silly story, which is not really funny, and I'm soon astonished at catching myself flirting with my own husband. All of a sudden, there is so much to tell, about our work, our kids, the now leaking roof on Aggie's house, the old books he found in the attic and wants to show me, the huge offer he got on the house but refused to sell because he wants to renovate it and stay there.

I want to tell him I miss him and don't enjoy living alone. I want to tell him the bed's too big and empty, that we should try again, and that at this moment I feel like moving into Aggie's house with him. I want to ask him to phone Ginny and tell her he has to break up because he still loves me; I want to say so much, but I can't. Like a huge lump, my own betrayal is stuck in my throat.

Mike and David join us and David refills our glasses from a newly opened bottle of wine.

"Mia is a fantastic cook," I tell him. "The fish was out of this world."

"Yes, she's good at everything she does. She's a keeper, that's for sure." David turns to Adrian and asks, "Were you serious about being hypnotized and regressed?"

"Yes, just tell me when you want me to come."

"I plan to spend Monday explaining the background of the method and my experience with it," David says. He continues, "On Tuesday, I will start with volunteer sessions mixed with more theory, so I suggest you come on Thursday, after lunch."

"Who's your first subject?" Adrian asks.

"Jorunn wants to go first. She's very eager to experience it firsthand. I assume you're okay with Leandra observing your regression?" David adds, looking somewhat flustered. He doesn't know if Adrian will want me to witness his experience, but Adrian says he would insist I be there, and looks at me. In his eyes I see some tenderness and a flicker of forgiveness.

The rest of the evening is spent in a light, breezy and even happy atmosphere. Jorunn is the first one to leave feeling jet-lagged, and Mike offers to give her a ride to the hotel. He's obviously sparked by her charm and seems to be in a great mood.

Adrian and I leave at the same time and he walks me to my car.

"How are things with Ginny?" I ask, but don't want to hear the answer.

"Good, considering the circumstances. I shouldn't have written that email."

"I'm glad you did. You had every right to share how you felt. It was a kind email considering what I did…how I betrayed you. I can never apologize enough and I can never expect your forgiveness. But, I dare hope we can be friends."

I'm saying something I don't fully mean, because I'd like him to give our marriage a second chance, but cannot say so, because I don't trust myself with being able to invest sufficient effort into rebuilding it.

His hand gently caresses my cheek, and an involuntary tear trickles down my face. He smears it with his thumb and his gaze penetrates my soul.

"You will never be able to grasp the enormity of the pain you inflicted…it's impossible to describe. A part of my soul has been burnt by it completely."

"I never should have told you. That was such a mistake. I never wanted to hurt you or anyone else. I was only ready to accept my own pain because I should have known a mistake like that had to end in suffering."

"Are you saying it was a mistake?"

"How could it have been anything else? I fell for my own delusional thinking. Yes, I had this need for romance, for the beginning of love when everything is fresh, beautiful, untainted, when people are still mystified by each other, when there's so much to learn and explore, and when there's youth to be recaptured. It was all too tempting, and I projected my own needs, needs I hadn't even been conscious of, onto a man who couldn't fulfill them. He could give me an illusion of love, but there was only passing infatuation. Adrian, I've suffered and ached but have deserved all that, if for anything, for wounding you so needlessly. I fell in love with a man who cheats on his wife, a man who needed from me affirmation of his worth because he felt unappreciated and unwanted by her. Then he met Jorunn, who gave him even more affirmation and boosted his self-esteem."

"What has Jorunn got to do with that?"

"He replaced me with her, but she doesn't know I've been his lover. So we're all interconnected in this, in this…this macabre circle of fate. I don't know what else to call it. A weird entanglement."

He's shaking his head in disbelief. "Are you in touch with him?"

"Not really. We've exchanged emails because I sent him information about a publication he'd requested. He has no interest in communicating with me and I don't hear from him for months on end. He ended his last email by saying he hoped to see me sometime, but it's a meaningless pleasantry."

"Do you still love him?"

"I don't know. I'm over him even though I still think about him. I'm happy I married you, even though we're no longer really married. I mean, we're separated. I know he would've been wrong for me, and what I'm saying is not just a case of sour grapes."

"You don't sound convinced."

"Adrian, I'll never lie to you again. Feelings change from day to day. Most days I feel I'm over him. It rarely hurts anymore, but what hurts is my inability to totally expunge him from mind, my blood, and my feelings. He feels at times like a jailer of my own choosing, the jailer of my thoughts. Maybe I'll always have feelings for him, and maybe I'll just have to live with that. I don't regret losing him. I regret losing *you*, because what we had was real, sound, true, and healthy, in spite of a lack of romance, which fades anyway from most marriages. I fell for an illusion and in the process I lost true love. I was so tempted to call you a few nights ago when I had a bad dream, but I cannot wreck your life twice. We can still be friends, I hope."

His eyes are misty and through that mist I can see infinite sadness. He tries to say something, but he chokes up with emotion, turns away and waves me goodbye.

CHAPTER TWENTY ONE

David

Two participants cancel at the last moment, so in the end, there are six of us in a conference room which can seat thirty people. I could have held the workshop in my own apartment, but it's too late now. Luckily, the hotel director is a former patient whom I managed to cure from depression, and he's charging me a token fee for this large, bright and comfortable space. In turn, I've also charged the participants a very low fee covering the costs of coffee, lunches and the room.

I open the workshop with introductions, giving a short background of my own interest in past life regression therapy and then I ask the participants to introduce themselves, and state what their expectations of this workshop are and what prompted them to register.

"My name is Akio Himura. I am from Tokyo where I have been practicing psychiatry for twenty years. My interest in hypnotherapy began last year when a young patient, who had attempted suicide, kept telling me about a recurring and terrifying dream, in which he was thrown into a well to die. In one of those dreams, he learned what his name was and the name of the village in which he lived, and even the year he lived there. I did not believe any of that could prove true, but I helped him do some research and we discovered that such a village, not with the exact, but a similar name, existed in the nineteenth century. I even travelled with him there and he took me to a place where the remnants of a well could be seen. He broke down near the well overwhelmed by emotion. But at the same time, getting to the bottom of his fears and nightmares helped him embark on the road to recovery. Everything was genuine about this young man and so I became intrigued. So I am here to find out more about hypnotherapy and past life regression because, if I had been familiar with the method or believed in it, I might have helped this young man earlier, and others as well."Akio's English is grammatically perfect, but his accent causes me to strain to understand him.

"Akio, we can often find fragments of past lives in our dreams. Your patient recognized the source of his trauma and you helped him unravel the mystery and start healing. He helped you open your mind to new knowledge. You certainly did not ignore pointers to the sources of his problems and did not label him as delusional. Thanks for sharing this story."

I turn to Leandra and realize the energy flowing among all of us is full of hope, affection, friendship and genuine curiosity. The vibes in the room carry the promise of a successful workshop.

"My name is Leandra and I am David's colleague, friend and patient. I found myself in a period of great pain and seemingly unanswerable questions, and hypnotherapy, in my view, was something belonging in circuses and cabarets as cheap entertainment. Sorry, David, but you know how I felt about it. I didn't believe in reincarnation or anything not supported by scientific explanation. I have changed my beliefs now. I've become a believer in magic, past lives, synchronicities, and so on. I've experienced strange dreams and have heard voices that at times frightened me and made me doubt my sanity. I still can't explain some of my dreams and the voices I heard. Anyway, with David's help, I've been able to make sense of certain events that happened to me. I want to learn more about this technique by watching David regress other people, but I don't know if I'll ever wish to become a hypnotherapist, or if I have the ability or talent for hypnotizing patients. You're probably expecting to hear what trauma prompted me to seek David's help. I'm sorry, but I'm not willing to share that here because it's irrelevant. Suffice it to say, I've found answers to some painful questions and I'm much better. I'm very happy to spend the next few days with you."

The next person to speak is Dieter Becker from Hamburg. I've seen him at several conferences. I'm surprised he registered. He's a proponent of cognitive behavioral therapy and a world-renowned specialist on substance abuse. His clinic has become a celebrity haven and rumor has it that only celebrities can afford the exorbitant prices.

"Ich bin…sorry, wrong language. Must be the jet lag. My name is Dieter and I am here because I will vacation here for two weeks. My wife will join me and we plan to rent a car and tour the country. It was my wife who suggested I learn more about hypnotherapy because it interests her. She's a psychologist who works at our clinic and she believes we need to expand treatment options for our patients. Anyway, I am here to hear what you have to say." He laughs at his use of homophones, 'hear and here.' "And if you wonder why she is not here, I mean my wife, she was too busy to attend. One of us had to stay at the clinic."

His voice has a supercilious note in it and his reasons for coming sound unconvincing and somewhat disjointed. He gives us all a wide grin. I wonder if there's any condescension in his beaming expression, but cannot detect it.

In a singing voice, our Italian participant introduces himself. "I'm Giovanni Acone from Ancona. The reason I'm here is I recently had a patient I hypnotized, and who under hypnosis spoke a language I did not understand. It was my first attempt to hypnotize my own patient. I did not record the session so I never found out what language she spoke. She was also telling me of the déjà vu she experienced while travelling through Greece, so I think she may have spoken ancient Greek when under the trance. She's severely depressed, and nothing I've tried has helped much. I'm the only person at the clinic who wants to try new methods of treatment. My uncle, who died last year, often told me he'd lived before and he knew it for a certainty. His stories always fascinated me. But, I'm taking up too much time. Sorry."

"No, Giovanni, you're not. Please, finish what you wanted to say."

He appears flustered. He is also the youngest participant and looks no older than twenty-five. He seems to be unsure of himself and is hiding that behind his large eyeglasses. "No, I have nothing else to add…for now."

The atmosphere of amicability, curiosity and relaxed acceptance is thickening. Jorunn is the last participant to introduce herself.

"I am a Norwegian psychiatrist. I didn't come here to learn a new technique. Sorry, David, if I've given you the wrong impression. I might have misled you. I'm here to undergo a past life regression because I believe, I know, I've lived before. Something bad happened to me in this life when I was fourteen years old, and I'm sure something bad happened to me in a past life. I've been dealing with claustrophobia and anxiety since I was a teenager. You have no idea what it took to fly for nine hours straight to get here. I had to sedate myself to a catatonic state in order to prevent panic attacks. I strongly feel I can find some answers in my past lives for the suffering I've had to endure in this life and I am volunteering as your study subject. Please, David, let me help you demonstrate the technique as a volunteer, and please help me explore my past so that I can tame my demons."

For the first time Jorunn does not look like a femme fatale, but rather like a frightened yet hopeful child. Her face reveals deep vulnerability and I feel tenderness toward her. Maybe her flirtatiousness is just a defense. I also notice for the first time how she keeps touching her left cheek and running her fingers over some imaginary fault line in her skin.

I assure Jorunn I will gladly regress her so everyone can see how the technique works. I continue the session by giving examples from my practice of patients who found healing after their past life regressions, who were able to free themselves from debilitating phobias, depressions, drug abuse and more. I discuss fragments of past lives experienced in dreams and how we as psychiatrists can connect them to the sources of present illnesses. I recount my first case of past life regression when I hypnotized a man in order to help him get rid of a debilitating obsessive compulsive disorder of washing his hands countless times a day and still feeling dirty. He showered at least five times a day, and his skin was inflamed and cracked from the abuse. The hypnosis regressed him to his childhood, and he remembered his mother kissing him and telling him gently to wash his hands after he had played outside or cuddled with their family dog. Those were very happy times. The next time I hypnotized him, I suggested he go back to an even younger age hoping to find a source of trauma to explain his obsessive need for cleanliness, for scraping his hands raw with coarse soaps.

"He surprised me. He said he was nine years old, and working in a hot and sweltering coal mine with many other children in Victorian-era England. Coming back home after a hard day's work, he would try to wash the grime off his face and arms, but the water in the tub was as dirty as he was after his five brothers had washed in it before him. When the weather was warmer he would go to the river and swim, but the grime would stick to his skin stubbornly and he could not scrape the filth off even with river stones. He would watch in awe as town children walked by him looking so white and clean. He felt like a scrawny, dirty, half-plucked raven no one noticed or wanted to touch. His last memory was one of an explosion in the mine when dust and fire swallowed him. After that session he spontaneously stopped excessive showering, soon his hands healed, and his life improved dramatically. All it took was for him to realize the source of his behavior was something that happened a long time ago, and his present life circumstances did not warrant such obsessive compulsive behaviors."

I show them a video of a session during which a woman was recounting her experience as an Italian nun living in a convent in the seventeenth century. She was speaking Italian and based on what she'd told me about her life, she'd never been to Italy or Europe before, had only a high school education, and didn't speak any language other than English. I asked Giovanni to listen to the recording and translate it for me, and he told me some of the words were unknown to him because they were no longer in use. He confirmed the woman sounded like a native Italian, who spoke a dialect different from his.

"Could she have prepared that speech, could she have rehearsed it to fool you?" Dieter asks.

"Theoretically, she could have researched that dialect, and she could have found someone who spoke it, and she could have dictated in English to that person what she wanted to say to me. That person could have translated it into that dialect so she could describe to me in detail her life at the convent, the garden she was responsible for, the prohibition of singing and her singing in secret, her pain and suffering thinking of her life outside the convent walls when she was a young girl as the youngest of four sisters, and so on and so on. She told me her family wanted to avoid paying a dowry for her marriage, so instead they sent her to the convent. Yes, she could have found all of this on the Internet, but I would be hard pressed to find the motive behind such a scam. What would she be gaining by making a fool out of me?"

The rest of the day I spend sharing with them a few more cases and then discussing the technique of putting patients in a deeper state through which they can access past lives, reliving the emotions and experiences linked to traumatic events that happened to them in those incarnations, and discovering if their past life traumas have been transferred into their current incarnation. I also mention that not everyone can be regressed, and not every successful regression results in healing. This method is just another tool to use as a supplement to more traditional techniques or medication therapy.

We finish the session at seven that evening and go out together for dinner. I notice a pensive look on Jorunn's face. While waiting in the restaurant, to get a table outside on the terrace, she says to me, "You are my last hope." Noticing puzzlement in my expression she adds in a low voice, "My marriage is on its last leg. I've tried every kind of therapy, but nothing has helped. I hate myself, and I've always despised myself."

Leandra and Dieter are looking at us and she stops speaking for a moment. Once in the restaurant, Jorunn's mood changes completely and she laughs and giggles and shakes her dark mane, bats her eyelashes and is charm incarnate. From time to time she traces the invisible line on her face. She hugs and kisses Leandra as if they were best friends. I am mystified, and curious to find out more about her.

"I'm the first to get regressed tomorrow," Jorunn says loudly. "I want you all to be there and learn the technique by my example. Then, we can all dissect together what we learn about me and if I have lived before. David, does everyone have a past life?"

"No, some are new souls, so to speak, and some have had many past lives." I still find Jorunn intriguing. With all her charm and coquettish behavior, there seems to be a strong narcissistic facet to her as well.

After a couple of more glasses of wine and conversation on many different topics, Dieter blurts out of the blue, "This trip is the last chance my wife and I are giving our marriage. For the past few years we have grown detached from each other, both busy with the clinic and other people's lives, but not our own. We kept piling up money, our fame spreading of our work and success, renovating our house, buying more real estate, without even noticing we had become strangers to each other, until one day over breakfast she said she wanted a divorce. To say I felt hit by a

Taser would be a huge understatement. I looked at her and noticed she was no longer blonde but a redhead. All I could say was, 'When did you change your hair color?' She said she'd had a new hair color and cut for the last four months.

"I burst into tears. She'd never looked more beautiful than at the moment she told me she wanted a divorce. Then I asked, 'Who is he?' She said there was no one, and she would never cheat on me, and she wasn't even interested in other men. To cut a long story short, I felt like I had awoken from a dream, or come out of a thick fog. What I managed to do is convince her to join me after this workshop, and go on vacation with me. I did not want to cancel this workshop. So, wish me luck!"

Leandra says vacations can sometimes bring about miraculous recoveries in marriages and she's seen many relationships bounce back. Dieter laughs nervously and turns to Giovanni to say, "Your turn now. What's your real story? What black hole is hidden in your soul? Hey, it even rhymes." His laugh is uproarious.

Giovanni turns crimson red and in a stuttering voice mumbles, "How could you tell?"

"Tell what? Everyone carries some kind of pain, darkness, distress, and I figure this is a perfect occasion to unload some of that burden. As professionals, we might be able to help each other shed light on where we, personally, were unable to see that dark place in us that needs illumination," Dieter replies.

Giovanni is still looking unnerved and is shifting his gaze from one object to another in the room. Dieter seemed to have found a chink in his armor and deep discomfiture is oozing through that aperture.

"I'm gay, and recently revealed that to my parents. They are very religious and feel shamed and guilty that they failed as parents and did not bring me up properly. I haven't been able to explain to them it has nothing to do with them. Now, they pretend I never told them and refuse to discuss it, mention it or otherwise acknowledge it. I don't dare mention I have a long-term partner. It's killing me what I did to my parents."

And then he perks up, turns to Jorunn and says, "Someone as beautiful, lively and enchanting as you cannot possibly have any dark spots on her soul."

She looks around and her irises are wide, dark islands surrounded by a sea of blue. She seems to be contemplating what or how much to say and then sighs, takes a sip of wine and begins:

"Oh, what the hell! I didn't come all this way, half dead from fear of a major panic attack on the plane, to pretend and wear the same old mask. I know what you all think and what you all probably see. A beautiful, sexy, seductive vixen set on charming the pants off everyone. And you're right. I have a compelling need to be liked, admired. I need to see a beautiful reflection of myself in the eyes of men and women I meet because, like a drug, it temporarily fills the void in me, the void in which I feel ugly, unlovable and unwanted.

"I'm a victim of sexual abuse. When I was fourteen years old, my stepfather started abusing me. It started one day with me running into his arms for protection because a seagull overflew my head really low, and I was always irrationally terrified of birds. A bird had never pecked me or chased me or done anything that would instill fear in me, but that day Ĥe hugged me and then his hand ended up on my left breast. My breasts had suddenly developed with my first period. Little by little he started fondling me more intimately and one night he came into my room and forced himself on me. I didn't dare scream and wake up my mom and sister.

"That wasn't the first time I had sex. Weeks before I'd slept with an eighteen-year-old boy who all the girls were crazy for, but I managed to charm him into inviting me to a movie. At fourteen, I looked eighteen. I was a very precocious girl. Afterwards, we had sex in his car and I disliked the experience and never wanted to see him again. But, when he told me he couldn't see me again because he already had a girlfriend, I felt humiliated and rejected. I kept telling myself I would not have wanted to see him again anyway, but the feeling of rejection did not leave me for a long time.

"After that night, my stepfather started to bribe me with gifts and shut me up with threats. He would say I should feel lucky he loved me, because I wasn't pretty or smart enough to attract boys my age. I couldn't tell my mother, because she wasn't showing much interest in me. I would dread the nights when he would creep into my room after my mother had taken a sleeping pill. I developed anxiety, claustrophobia, panic attacks...but the biggest phobia was my fear of birds, which made no sense.

"I ran away from home, but the police found me and returned me. At the age of seventeen, I met a twenty-two-year-old guy who had a job in a neighboring town, so I left my home town and moved in with him. He kept telling me how beautiful I was, but I saw no beauty in the girl with long black hair and blue eyes; I always felt my face was marred with a huge scar no one could see, not even I. I felt it crisscross my left cheek even though it was invisible.

"I kept attracting men by the droves and their attention would give me a sense of self-worth, but only for brief periods. Then I met a married guy who fell in love with me so madly he left his wife and two children. He was rich, gave his family lots of money so they were comfortable, but money is no substitute for a broken family. His wife found out my address and sent me a letter in which she cursed the slut I was. Her letter ended with, 'May you never find peace, you heartless slut, you merciless home wrecker.' I married him and we had two sons. I also worked hard at finishing high school with high grades and entered medical school. We had nannies and cooks and cleaning ladies so I could devote myself to my studies. He even paid for me to have a six-month internship in the US and perfect my English.

"I thought, then, I would finally be alright. But the need for love, attention, adoration and affirmation was still insatiable in me. I seduced my anatomy professor and started an affair with him. That increased my self-hate and I despised myself more than ever. My husband found out and divorced me, calling me the biggest piece of trash who'd walked the earth. Eventually, he and his first wife got back together. I finished med school, psychiatry, and went from one man to another. I even had an affair with a woman who tried to kill herself after I left her. I'm now with my third husband. The second one was a common-law relationship which lasted only two years. Now, my current marriage is breaking up because my husband can no longer tolerate my need to flirt and charm people, and like an extreme narcissist, live off the admiration. My children have also had some very bumpy times because of the emotional instability at home they feel."

"You are a typical Hungry Ghost, Jorunn," I say. "The love and admiration you attract is short lived and turns to ash. Without self-love, all external affirmation runs through your soul like water through a sieve. Nothing can ever be enough without an internal source of love."

"I want to save this marriage. My daughter adores her dad. He's a great guy who loves us so much. I've tried counseling, psychoanalysis, cognitive therapy, behavioral therapy. This is the last discipline I'm willing to try to see if I was cursed in a past life, if there's some kind of bad karma I'm expiating."

"As a psychiatrist you know well enough it is hard to heal completely from sexual abuse. It changes who you are, or were meant to be; it annihilates self-esteem, fills you with shame, guilt, and self-hatred, and the road to healing is long and difficult. Your defense and your method to find healing is to charm people and show them how lovable you are; however, during the process, you have hurt many people. That may have been your subconscious need for vindication." Leandra's voice is full of compassion. She obviously realizes Weylin was another one of Jorunn's objects of attention whom she successfully seduced.

Jorunn adds she can hardly wait to undergo regression and has high hopes of finding some answers to her hellish questions. It is already eleven o'clock, so we pay the bill and leave.

Once back home, I realize how much I miss Mia's presence. I want to propose to her as soon as possible. She went to New York to take a Kundalini yoga certification course and I can only think of her. I plan to ask Leandra to help me pick out a ring for her and suggest the best way to propose. I feel utterly clumsy and helpless when it comes to being romantic.

The next day, all participants are already in the conference room when I come in. We are supposed to start at nine and, half an hour early, everyone is sitting there waiting for me. Jorunn is dressed in a simple white tunic and black leggings. She looks pale. She must still be jet-lagged.

Before I regress her, I review the technique I'll be using to help her achieve a deep relaxation state. I answer a few questions and ask everyone to sit behind Jorunn. I put on soft meditation music and begin the session by directing her visualization. She seems to be resistant for the first ten minutes, then begins to relax. I instruct her to go to a past life where she expects to find most answers to the questions that arose in her current lifetime. Once she seems to have reached a point in time that holds some crucial answers, I instruct her to describe where she is. She starts speaking softly.

"It is summer. I'm sitting in a meadow. There are many varieties of flowers around me and I pick those closest to me and inhale their fragrance. Crickets are jumping through the grass. I don't like bugs."

"What is your name?"

"Jane."

"What are you feeling, Jane? Are you happy?"

"I'm crying, shaking."

"Why are you crying?"

"There's blood trickling down my thighs and I hurt between my legs. I'm going to have to wash myself in the stream. I must get to the water and cleanse myself. Blood is filthy. I am filthy."

"Is the stream close to you?"

"It is just behind the White Circle."

"What is the White Circle?"

"A circle of large, white stones. No one knows where they came from and why they are standing in a circle. People have celebrations there. I like the festivities. We play hide and seek there sometimes."

"How old are you?"

"Thirteen."

"Do you have a family?"

"Aye. Three sisters and a brother. And my parents."

"Have you reached the stream?"

"Aye. I'm sitting in the water. It's cool, and it's soothing the swelling between my legs. I think the bleeding has stopped."

"Why are you bleeding? Did you get your monthly bleeding?"

"Nay…it is not the monthly curse. I have been hurt…again."

"How did this happen? Did someone hurt you?"

"The man on whose land we live. My mother sends me to his house every week to clean, but I do not clean. He keeps me in his bedroom for two days and sends me back home with a basket full of food. We are poor. My father works on his land, and my mother stays home with my sisters and my brother. I am the eldest child."

"What does he do to you?"

"He touches me first and he kisses me, but his kisses are not soft. They bruise me and leave red marks on my skin, I try to hide them. He hurts me the most when he forces his way between my legs and I always bleed. He licks the blood like a beast, and that also hurts and scares me."

"Did you tell your parents?"

"Aye. My mother says we are so poor, and I am helping them have bread every day. I also get cloth from the master, and my mother sews clothes for us. I have two very pretty dresses. And he gave me pretty ribbons."

Jorunn is fidgeting in the chair and touching her face again.

"Jane, are you a pretty girl?"

The question makes Jorunn's eyes well up with tears.

"I thought I was pretty, but not anymore. My left cheek is…it's hideous and I keep my hair over my face to hide the ugly, ugly red scar."

"How did you get the scar?"

"The master has falcons. They land on his gloved hand when he calls them. He takes them hunting. If I let out screams of pain when I'm in his bed, he punishes me by releasing the falcons on me. They swoop over me, and chase me around the courtyard and I cry in terror. They scratched me with their talons, and I have the most horrible scar on my face, which can never heal. It runs across my left cheek like a red swollen snake, twisting and twisting, not knowing which way to go. It is mostly red, but has some white splotches in it. I feel so ugly I want to wear a hood at all times. The master doesn't mind my scar and tells me I'm still pretty. But then he laughs so hard he slaps himself on his knee, and I think he finds me very, very ugly."

"What are you doing now?"

"I'm still lying in the cold water. But I hear someone coming."

"Who do you see coming?"

"Jilleen."

As soon as she says Jilleen, I hear Leandra let out a gasp. I look at her as she covers her mouth with her hand. Her eyes are filled with astonishment and in her look the question is clear, 'How can this be possible?'

I continue with my probing.

"Who is Jilleen?"

"She's our priest's daughter. She is always happy. Everyone likes her. I am jealous of her happiness. She is often in the fields gathering herbs. I see her talk to animals. They like her. She's talking to me now, and touching my scar gently."

"What does she tell you?"

"She tells me she can heal my scar. I don't believe her. She will mock me like everyone else."

I look at Leandra and see her eyes widen in further disbelief. She is thinking the same thing I am. Could it be that Jorunn lived as Jane in the same past life Leandra had as Jilleen? Their fates have been intertwined and I can hardly wait to excavate more evidence of that.

"Go on, Jorunn...Jane. Tell me what happens between you and Jilleen."

Jorunn continues her narration in a small, quivering voice.

"She caresses my cheek and says she knows the herbs to help me heal. She wants me to look beautiful again. She takes my hand and leads me out of the water. She removes her shawl and wipes my legs. She sees a blood stain and asks me if it hurts between my legs. I am silent and cannot find my voice. I feel shame but I don't know why. I want to tell her about my pain and my ugly face and who did that to me while he was laughing at my fear, but I cannot speak. She looks so clean and so happy. She looks so free. We all see how much her father loves her. He holds her hand when they walk. He talks to her. My father never talks to me. My mother only wants to see what I bring back in the basket.

"She's taking me to her house. Her room smells of herbs, but mostly of honeysuckle. Her whole house has a nice smell. There are no smells of damp clothes, rotting vegetables and meat. I know Jilleen boils herbs and makes medicine of them. She likes helping people. Ailionora has been teaching her the craft, she tells me."

"Who is Ailionora?" I look at Leandra again; her jaw is dropping, and she's looking around the room as if expecting to discover some evidence of staging, of crookery on my or Jorunn's part. There are just too many coincidences to believe they are indeed only coincidences. The other participants are looking at us with questions in their eyes, realizing something unusual is happening.

Jane continues and says, "Ailionora is the village healer. Some say she's a witch. I'm afraid of her. She looks at me as if she knows my secret, my shame."

"What is Jilleen doing now?"

"She takes two small clay pots and tells me to lie down on a bench. She spreads something cold on my cheek and my cheek starts to burn. How can something so cold turn into heat? This must be witchery. She is also a witch. She tells me to put the ointment every day on my cheek and very soon the scar will become invisible. I do not believe her, but I take her gift.

"I go home and hide the pot in the garden and smear the herbal ointment on my cheek every night. Like a miracle, the red scar starts to fade. My mother notices and tells me my prayers to God have been answered, and God is making my face look beautiful again. I do not dare tell her it may be the Devil's and not God's work, because Jilleen must be a witch if she could make my scar disappear."

"What does the man you call master say when he sees your scar is fading?"

"He laughs and tells me he will have to turn his falcons on me again if I am disobedient. I do not dare speak, for fear he will hurt me again like that. And I bite my lip when I feel pain, and I do not scream for fear he will make the falcons scratch my eyes out. He continues to hurt me by spreading my legs wide and putting something long and smelly in me, a thing I see in donkeys and horses. That thing looks like a living creature.

"I hear women whisper about having to please their husbands, and I know that women do not like to do this. I hear my father panting like a dog behind a thin blanket that separates my parents' straw bed from us children."

Jorunn is silent. Hey eyelids are fluttering and she is clenching her fists. I instruct her to go to the time she is older and tell me what she sees. When she starts to speak, a tear rolls down her cheek.

"Where are you now, Jane?"

"I am in my house embroidering."

"How old are you?"

"Seventeen."

"Are you living with your parents?"

"Nay, I am married."

"Where is the master who hurt you?"

"He is still in his beautiful house. He has a wife and a son."

"Are you happy he can no longer hurt you?"

"He threw me out of his house. He told me I was too old for him. He said I was like a used rag. He never loved me. He liked my body for a while, but bodies change. He needed new bodies."

"How did that make you feel?"

"Angry and sad. I was happy he no longer wanted me, but I was also sad he did not. It made me feel ugly and rejected. I could no longer bring food back home. I also knew people talked about me. They said I was filthy. Jilleen was always kind, but I hated her. She is married but she is still free. She roams the fields and goes to see Ailionora, and she heals people and animals and people love her. My husband beats me and does not let me leave the house on my own. He says he does not trust me because I look at other men. I want people to like me. That is why I look at other men."

"Jane, why do you hate Jilleen if she has been good to you?"

Jorunn's voice is brimming with malice when she speaks, and Leandra's reaction to her tone is visibly visceral. I can see her recoil.

"Because she is a witch! Only a witch can live like that. She probably dances naked in the moonlight with other witches. Only witches nurse animals back to health. She once came for a visit and a storm started and lightning hit our apple tree."

"But she healed your scar."

"But I cannot have children. She must have cast a spell on me."

"Why would she do that?"

"Because she is a witch."

"I want you to move forward in time, just a few months. …Tell me where you are now?"

"On the bridge. I am standing behind my husband because I do not want her to see me."

"You do not want who to see you, Jane?" I ask.

"Jilleen. The inquisitor or the gaoler will throw her off the bridge to drown. They believed me when I told them she was a witch. Her husband will not be back for a long while, and he will never know I said she was a witch.

"She knew what the master was doing to me. I think she told him to stop his use of me. I saw her father, the priest, go into my master's house and talk to him. After that he threw me out. She hugged me that evening as if she knew what happened. I did not like being thrown out."

"But, he was abusing you and she saved you."

"She made me feel like a booted out dog. Like a kitten that gets thrown into the river to die. I was hoping the master would marry me. She ruined that. Now she will drown. Women do not know how to swim."

"What is happening now?"

"The gaoler pushes her into the water and there is a big splash. Now we are moving down the river bank, but it is hard to see if she has drowned because her body is not floating on the surface, and it is too dark, although the moon is bright and we carry torches in our hands. The willow trees make it hard to get near the river. The river is fast and deep. We start running and laughing. People are merry because they are safe and the witch is dead."

"Jane, could it be that she never did you any harm? Could it be that she meant everyone well?"

Jorunn's voice is bitter as gall. "People do not like me but they like her. When they look at me, they see the scars the master left even when there is no scar to see anymore. My husband does not let me talk to other men. He trusts me not. Jilleen's husband is a powerful chieftain, but he gives her freedom. I saw her talk to Kieran many times."

"Who is Kieran?'

When I ask that question I look at Leandra again. She is pale and her lower lip is quivering. She is wiping her eyes with a paper napkin. She looks at me with incomprehension, and moves closer so she can hear Jorunn better. I know exactly what she is thinking. Jorunn lived in the same past life as Jilleen and Kieran. Their interconnection spans centuries. With eyes still wide, Leandra is waiting for Jorunn's response to my question.

Her voice is now soft and sweet, imbued with a sigh of longing. "Kieran is…he is our neighbor. I watch him from my bower as he rides across his land. He is just a distant speck, but I still know it is he. One day at the market he talked to me. In his eyes I saw his desire for me. I spoke to him in my sweetest voice. I shook my hair, wanting him to notice its beauty. I gazed into his eyes and started giggling and telling him how much I admire his riding skills. I know he loves horses so I talked about horses, and about the last harvest that was bountiful, and I repeated words I overheard exchanged between my husband and some landowners. I wanted to sound wise.

"But then Jilleen walked by and his face blushed and she lowered her gaze. Jealousy consumed me and I wanted the witch dead. I swore I would find a way to rid our town of her. I told Kieran people were whispering behind her back that she was a witch who danced all night with the devil. I lied, and I wanted him to believe that lie, but he said he did not believe in witches. At that moment I wished I were a witch who could cast a spell on him so he would fall in love with me and never notice Jilleen again."

"Do you find Jilleen's body in the river?"

"No, it is too dark. I shout they should have thrown her in the river at dawn and not night when we could not see. We travel at least another half mile down the river and then the inquisitor yells we have to go back, and she must have drowned. We go back home and my husband asks me if I know who it was that accused Jilleen of witchery. He remembers how she healed his arm when an arrow hit him. I am seething with anger. He then says he fears revenge.

"When Jilleen's husband, Aidan, comes back from his visit to the king of England and finds out what happened, he may kill many people. My husband fears Aidan and wants to know who did this to Jilleen. He believes this was not about Jilleen being a witch. She was killed because some people must have wanted to hurt Aidan by killing her because he was feared and because he sometimes wielded his power mercilessly, protecting the interests of the king of England. My husband must never find out it was I who spread the rumors about her using spells and doing evil."

I glance at Leandra again. Her expression is still one of utter disbelief and shock. She is staring at me almost suspiciously as if I had staged this regression together with Jorunn. I shrug my shoulders, wanting to show her I am as incredulous as she. I ask Jane to move forward in time.

"Where are you now, Jane?"

"I am at a masked dance. Jilleen is here. No one understands how she escaped drowning, but no one dares to ask. In his fury, her husband ordered a few men hanged and it scared me to know that some of them were innocent. I lived in terror for a long time that my secret would be discovered and he would have both me and my husband put to death, but those who knew died by hanging.

"We all wear masks, but I recognize Jilleen's gait, and mostly, I recognize her by the way a man leans toward her to whisper something in her ear. It is Kieran sitting next to her and jealousy burns in me once again. I want him to love me and not her. The master adored me. He just did not know how to show it. Or, maybe by hurting me and frightening me with falcons, he was showing me how much I meant to him. He had his special ways of loving. I laugh and talk to many people at the ball. I want to feel close to everyone, to touch and suck on their souls. That fills me with the fire of life.

"When after dinner and some dancing I see Kieran alone, I approach him and tell him I recognize him. I tell him I am feeling dizzy and may faint, and ask him to accompany me outside into the garden. He obliges like a true gentleman. I walk with him among the rose bushes, but he keeps turning around and looking at the doors leading into the garden. Fury grabs my heart because I know his eyes search for Jilleen. I take his hand and place it on my chest and tell him I am in love with him. He removes it gently and tells me he is very flattered to be the object of my attention, and I am beautiful and desirable, but he respects my husband and would not want to insult him by behaving inappropriately toward his wife. I feel insulted and infuriated by his rejection. I want to slap him and bite him, and claw his eyes out, but I smile sweetly and say I must go to find my husband."

Jane is silent again. It is easy to recognize she was a deeply troubled woman in that lifetime, perhaps even bordering on insanity. Early childhood trauma can do that to people. I ask her again to move forward in time.

"Where are you now, Jane?"

"I am sitting by the river crying. I should not be crying because I heard people talk about Jilleen birthing a dead boy. God punished her for her witchery. I am crying because I am bleeding and cannot bear a child to my husband. He beds me rarely. I caught him in bed with a servant girl and I threw a log at her head. She bled all across the room and I kicked her out into the rain and hail. I even ran out trying to catch her and kill her with a knife but my husband caught me instead, and wrestled me to the ground. Afterwards, he laughed at me in his drunkenness and told me my violent temper amused him."

She is silent again. I ask her questions but she does not respond. Her eyelids are fluttering. After I ask her to tell me what it is she is experiencing now, her voice turns to a whisper.

"He is snoring loudly. I hate him. He wanted a lowly servant girl more than me. Saliva is dripping out from a corner of his mouth. His nightshirt is stained with wine. He reeks of sweat and wine. I never wanted to marry him, but my parents forced me. He did not want a dowry, and that is why my parents pushed me into this marriage. He had a limp from a battle wound and a scar on his face. Girls joked about him, and I joked with them. I never thought I would have to marry a man so odious. The master gave him a piece of land as reward for his loyalty in battle and made him a lower-ranked nobleman. My husband's father works for Aidan. I had no choice but to marry my husband. Jilleen told me her father never pressed her to marry Aidan, but she fancied him well enough.

"Watching my husband sleep, I am filled with revulsion. He is as disgusting as all men who keep us women enslaved. I want Jilleen's freedom, I want her life, and I want Kieran. Only a witch can live a life she wants to live. Only a witch can have such love in her life. I hate my life. I cannot accept it is the will of God that I subjugate myself to this horrible man who calls himself my husband. I almost wish a new war breaks out and he never comes back."

"Jane, tell me if you have seen Jilleen again."

She furrows her brow and starts speaking.

"She was not seen for weeks. One of her maids spread rumors she has been sitting in her window gazing at the fields in complete silence."

"Where are you now?"

"It is our harvest festival. The day is very warm. There is wine and ale, and merriment everywhere, all day and night. It is already night and torches are casting warmth all around. I am glad neither Jilleen nor Aidan is here. Kieran is here with his wife and sons. His eldest son is very tall and slim, just like him. His wife is pretty and merry. She has long brown hair and friendly eyes. She smiles at everyone kindly. He bows his head when he sees me. All night we drink and dance and I follow Kieran with my eyes. I want to catch him alone. I want him to be mine. Jilleen lost her baby and she lost Kieran.

"Ah, I see him go into a thicket and I follow him. I stop to let him relieve himself. Time passes slowly. As he is closing his breeches, I put my arms around him. He cannot see who it is. He staggers. He is drunk. Very drunk. He pulls me to the ground and lifts my skirts. The heat of rut goes through me like fire and I stifle my moans. I am gloating that I have captured him. I will not let him go. I recently bedded our stable boy, but there was not much satisfaction in it. I want Kieran to worship me. My husband has brought the servant girl back and forbidden me to speak of his infidelity. He threatened to throw me out of the house. He called me a barren bitch.

"But I have Kieran now. It is my revenge against Jilleen and my husband and the master who loved me not. Kieran is panting heavily and I am getting tired under him. I am afraid people might stumble upon us. Once he lies exhausted across me, I gently push him away and kiss his closed eyes. He is not opening his eyes and is breathing heavily. I cover his nakedness and get up, straighten my skirts, braid my hair and leave him. I ask him to meet me at the White Circle tomorrow morning. He does not respond. I leave smiling.

"The next morning I wait for him in the shadow of a stone and he comes. We talk for a while and then we make love on the ground on which he has laid his coat. It takes him a long time to appease his passion, and I feel tired and bruised from his weight but do not say so because I am happy he is mine now. I want to keep him so much that thoughts of poisoning my husband start obsessing me.

"Kieran has to go and he embraces me before he leaves. I wish he embraced me harder, I wish he told me he loved me, but I have to be patient. He is now mine." Jorunn has the look of a cat that got the cream.

I glance at Leandra and see her shaking her head in disbelief. I instruct Jane to go to the White Circle again and tell me of her meeting with Kieran.

"He said he might meet me today, but he fears being discovered by his wife. When he wants to ride out, his wife wants to come with him and he must find reasons why he needs to go alone." Jorunn's expression reveals concern and impatience.

"On the way to the White Circle, I see Jilleen in the distance and I follow her."

Jorunn's voice assumes a hissing quality now. She is obviously upset at seeing Jilleen walk in the same direction.

"She is walking toward the White Circle. She has started roaming again after her long period of grieving her dead son. I hope Kieran does not come today. I don't want them to meet. If he sees her, he may want her again. Her hair is flowing in the breeze. She is wearing a black dress. She stops from time to time to pick herbs. She touches trees and then embraces their trunks.

"She must be mad. She should have died in childbirth. When she enters the circle, she steps onto a stone and raises her arms toward the sun. I hide behind another stone and watch the witch. I want her gone before Kieran appears. Could she be meeting him here? I have not finished the thought when he appears on his white horse. At first it seems he would ride on, but he notices her, slows down and dismounts. When she sees him, she seems startled. She steps down from the stone and starts walking quickly away from him. He calls after her, but she does not stop. She was not meeting him. She is now running toward Glenda's Bluff."

"What is Glenda's Bluff, Jane?" I ask.

"It is the Bluff from which Glenda jumped to her death. Legend has it she threw herself into the ravine after her lover was killed in a war."

"What is Jilleen doing now?"

"She is standing on the edge, and gazing at the sun again. She seems to have forgotten Kieran wanted to speak with her. She is standing so close to the edge I expect her to fall into the abyss. Stones and earth can so easily crumble beneath her feet. Kieran is now approaching her on foot. I am standing out in the open, watching them, but he does not see me. Or he does not care to see me. He turns around once, and it is strange. He must see me, and yet there is no recognition in his eyes. He does not remember what we did a few nights ago. He nods his head in greeting and approaches Jilleen from behind.

"I come closer and hear him call out to her. She does not respond. She is gazing at the sun. His hand strokes her hair gently, and I see a dragonfly flutter away. She finally turns toward him and she is saying something to him, but I am too far away to hear. I see her hand touch his cheek gently, and then she moves away from him. It looks like she said goodbye to him, but he comes close to her again and speaks to her. He seems to be explaining something to her and she seems to be smiling patiently.

"At that moment a demon of fury possesses me. I come from behind a stone, charge at them like a bull and throw my body into them. She is so light I send her flying through the air. He falls to the ground close to the edge and I claw at his eyes. I hit and kick and scream with hatred against all men and all witches who make me feel small and unwanted. The stones are tumbling and rolling under us and we are falling, falling...."

Jorunn is shaking and I gently instruct her to come out of hypnosis remembering every detail. Once awake, she looks around, locks gazes with Leandra and bursts into tears.

"I killed two people and myself? Is that the sin I committed for which bad karma in the form of sexual abuse has followed me? It is no coincidence I came here to experience this. There was a mysterious force pulling me toward this workshop. But who is

Kieran? I don't know anyone like that. Could he be one of my ex-husbands or lovers?"

Leandra is silent.

"Oh my God! My fear of birds!" She touches her cheek and her hand is travelling up and down an imaginary scar. "I have never been able to stand close to any precipice. I have always been afraid of heights. David, can I stay an extra day to analyze all of this with you? And Leandra, I'd like your input, too. I can clearly see patterns of my trying to attract love, adulation, and adoration because of having always felt small, insignificant and rejected...and abused."

"Yes, of course you can stay," I say. Leandra is still silent and pale as alabaster. Jorunn turns toward the other psychiatrists and a loud session of psychoanalysis begins with everyone talking over everyone else in an attempt to offer interpretations of what Jorunn has revealed.

Dieter postulates that the cycle of abuse has perpetuated itself throughout incarnations as punishment for past life transgressions. He says she behaves almost like an energy vampire sucking on people's positive energies to fill a hunger and a void that cannot be filled. Jorunn looks offended when she hears the vampire analogy. He adds that now she has discovered the roots of her ornithophobia and acrophobia, it is to be expected she may be cured of them. Once you come face to face with your worst nightmares, the path toward healing should become illumined.

Giovanni contradicts Dieter, and accuses him of viewing Jorunn as a victimizer instead of a victim. How could he have even thought of comparing her to an energy vampire when she was only trying to survive the indignities of her abuse by turning to other people in search of love?

Dieter says her regression showed her as a scheming, pathological, malicious person, and abuse does not justify subsequent criminal behavior.

Giovanni disagrees vehemently, saying abuse destroys personality, and as a child victim, she had no coping mechanisms...as a child without any external support she was not able to make sense of her life, especially during the era of extreme superstition in which she lived.

I decide to leave them to dissect her past life and give Leandra a sign to follow me outside the room. We go into the hotel café and order coffee. We don't talk until we sit down.

"You must be as shocked at the connection between you and Jorunn as I am," I start. "We both know that unless you had told her about your regression therapy with me, there was no way she could have found out you were Jilleen. The only possibility would be that she somehow hacked into my computer, found your file, read it and decided to sign up for this workshop to play a prank on both of us. How possible or logical would that be? And what purpose would it serve?"

"David, I've never told anyone about the content of my sessions with you. This is simply more than unbelievable. The triangle in which Weylin, she and I have found ourselves, oh, this is too much to process…it just cannot be. The rational side of my brain is trying to tell me there must be some explanation that makes sense. We just don't see it. No one has anything to gain by inventing a story like this. And, she had no means of finding out what I revealed to you under hypnosis. Hacking into your computer is completely preposterous. We must not tell anyone; this must not reach our hospital administration, we'll be accused of quackery, witchery. What the hell just happened?"

And then she looks at me in astonishment and opens her mouth to say something, but loses her voice and coughs.

"What is it?" I ask, worried.

"Adrian volunteered to be your guinea pig." She is breathless when she says, "I have a strong premonition…something's telling me without any doubt—he also lived in the same lifetime as Kieran, Jane and I. You must regress him to that time specifically. It all connects. Maybe you were there, too. Maybe you were the inquisitor who saved me. No, you did not live in that lifetime with me. You were the doctor in England and your name was David. You were so kind to me as Juliet, and so helpful."

She is very excited and, in her agitation, knocks her cup over and spills coffee all over the table. Some of it lands on her lap and stains her beige pants, but she just dabs at the stain absentmindedly with a napkin.

"Promise me you'll use everything you know to regress Adrian to the same time, even though we don't know the exact year. We have names of places, so please mention Glenda's Bluff and the White Circle, and the names of people like Aidan. That's who he would have been if my instinct is correct. Those names might ring some distant bell to lead him back to that time. And, of course, I don't want anyone else to be there. Please text Adrian and remind him to come Thursday after lunch when we finish the workshop and after everyone else has left. Please, text him now."

I take out my phone and send Adrian a text. A few minutes later, he texts back saying he'd try to make it and hopes he can reschedule an appointment. I ask Leandra if she wants another coffee as she spilled most of her first, but she shakes her head.

Back in the conference room we find Jorunn, Dieter and Giovanni analyzing Jorunn's experience. She still appears shaken and distraught. At the same time, she is casting inquisitive looks at Leandra and there is a hint of anticipation and expectation in her eyes, but Leandra obviously has no intention of revealing the connection between them. It would be too surreal.

The rest of the afternoon we all spend discussing Jorunn's case and drawing parallels between her past and present life, her lack of self-love and self-worth stemming from childhood trauma. She is genuinely shocked at the revelation she has killed innocent people in one of her incarnations, and especially the woman who had always been so kind to her.

She breaks down in tears and tells us she has never liked herself less than today. I reassure her the revelations will initiate a healing effect and agree to spend an hour with her alone after the workshop. I agree reluctantly because it will mean getting home really late. Both Dieter and Giovanni want to be regressed and with the other three volunteers, tomorrow will be a full day of past life regressions. The Japanese colleague, who has been taking copious notes all along, remains silent.

Dieter invites us all for dinner, but I excuse myself and say that after my session with Jorunn ends I need to go home. Leandra accepts the invitation, but agrees to stay an extra hour with me and Jorunn, after Jorunn asks her to join us. Every now and then, Jorunn looks at Leandra with expectation, as if sensing a meaningful connection between the two of them. After Dieter and Giovanni leave the room, Jorunn has a meltdown.

Leandra hugs her, and tells her things can only get better now she has uncovered these important pieces of her life puzzle. When Leandra gently brushes away wisps of Jorunn's hair from her face and touches her left cheek with the utmost softness, in a half whispering voice Jorunn says Leandra's touch reminds her of Jilleen's gentleness. Leandra diverts the topic and turns to me, asking, "David, what do you make of this? After all, you have experience in this field, which we all lack."

I explain to Jorunn what, in my opinion, her revelations indicate and mean, but it is obvious she can clearly see that for herself, because she says, "Even though I was sexually abused, I was still devastated when the abuser no longer wanted me. I sought love and attention wherever I could find them. I realize how aggressive I was in that seeking. But to kill out of jealousy, out of feelings of rejection? No wonder I was punished by another abuser. Now I know I've experienced the same pattern in this incarnation, I wonder how many incarnations of a similar kind I've had. David, what can I do now?"

"You need to work through your pain, relive it, process it and release it. You need to forgive yourself, and most of all you need to become a friend to yourself. Become a source of love for yourself. Your self-acceptance will eventually diminish your neediness. You have as much experience and knowledge as I do, and this session only opened you up for a different kind of introspection. You will not find many of our colleagues who believe in past lives, but whether you believe or not, if this experience brings about change, if it lessens your pain, if it fills you with self-love, ultimately it will not matter if it is believable or not."

Jorunn turns to Leandra and asks point blank, "What was your experience like?" Jorunn seems to exude some certainty about Leandra's experience. I wonder if Leandra will lie or if she will acknowledge the uncanny bond between them.

"As I told you before, I did have a session with David and it seems I lived in England and Italy. The session revealed I was ditched by a man I deeply loved. An ordinary story in comparison to your tale of hurt, neglect and abuse. I did not arrive at any earth-shattering truths except, how easily I always seemed to believe in a fantasy of my own making."

Even though she tells the truth, that truth is a lie, as it has been taken out of a wider context, and out of her current life situation.

"I was curious about David's approach to treatment," Leandra continues, "but I don't feel skilled enough to apply it to my own patients." Now, the lie is naked, but Jorunn seems to be satisfied with the answers and starts sharing more details about her tormented life. When I look at my watch I see it is already seven, and I have three text messages from Mia I haven't answered. Jorunn apologizes for having kept us so long, and leaves for dinner with Leandra.

CHAPTER TWENTY TWO

Leandra

I'm so distracted at dinner I order mussels and eat a few without thinking. I had stopped eating them since experiencing food poisoning with mussels. So I offer them for sharing and my colleagues gladly accept. Jorunn is sitting next to me, and from time to time she hugs me and thanks me. She tells me I am special, and she knows and feels in her soul there is a bond between us. I'm hiding the full truth from her, but at the same time, I wish her all the best. I hope her demons leave her, I hope she saves her marriage and finds love and peace within. After an hour, I excuse myself, feeling drained.

As soon as I arrive home, the feeling of being alone becomes suffocating. The house looks dark and uninviting. If Adrian and I divorce, I will sell it and move into a brand-new penthouse, furnish it sparsely with modern furniture, perhaps have a white and blue, or yellow and blue color scheme, with a lot of glass objects to make everything look light and translucent. I laugh at myself and my frivolous thoughts. After a quick shower, I go to bed and pick up Herman Hesse's *Steppenwolf* from the nightstand. I'd read the book a long time ago, and have recently decided to re-read some of the classics.

I don't read longer than half an hour before I start feeling very sleepy. At the same time, I start shivering, and the chills become more and more intense until my teeth are chattering. I am running a fever. I stumble into the bathroom and take two aspirin, find an Alpaca blanket a patient brought back from Peru as a gift, and wrap myself in it under the duvet. The chills do not let up all night. In the morning, exhausted, I text David to tell him I will have to miss today's session because I am aching all over. He texts back, telling me to take it easy. I reply I'll come the next day to say goodbye to everyone and to attend Adrian's regression.

I spend the day in bed reading and sweating. Even though I am still shivering from fever, I find the strength to change the bed linens and take a shower. After sleeping for a couple of hours, I start feeling better. The next day is a blur of sleeping, sweating, changing the bed linen again and sleeping again. Around six in the evening, the doorbell wakes me. I drag myself to the door and when I open it, I see Mia standing there with a bag that seems to be full to the brim with food.

"David told me you were sick, so I've brought you soup, quiche, fruit and a piece of homemade cake. And I'm sorry to say, you have looked better."

What a wonderful woman, natural and spontaneous, charming and witty. I ask her in but she says she has to run to teach a class. She hugs me even though I shrink back and tell her she might catch the bug I'm carrying. She laughs it off saying her immune system is invincible.

My appetite is suddenly back. The soup is still warm and I eat it out of the plastic container. The quiche is divine and I finish half of it in no time. After dinner, I feel resuscitated and go for a walk around the block. Meeko follows me and a passerby comments he is an adorable cat.

That night I sleep deeply and in the morning I feel almost back to normal. I dress carefully, and try to hide the gaunt look on my face with makeup, but without much success. When I arrive at the hotel, David is wrapping up the session and answering the last questions. The Japanese colleague seems to speak for the first time saying that what he witnessed seems like a magician's illusion, but he has no reason to suspect deceit. He plans to invite David to Tokyo, all expenses paid, because he would like his colleagues to witness what he has seen.

Jorunn hugs us all warmly, and thanks everyone for offering their insight into her situation. She apologizes for having monopolized so much of our time and having compelled so much attention toward her case. She also says she feels optimistic about her future, and would like to see us all again.

I'm the last to say goodbye to her. After she hugs me for what seems to be the fifteenth time, she whispers, "I still believe there is a strong past connection between us. I hope we discover what it is."

"Jorunn," I say, "the present connection between us is one of love and friendship. Let that be the only one that counts. If our paths had crossed in a past life in whichever way, it has no bearing on this present life. And remember, we are all interconnected, but we do not always know in what ways. Let's stay in touch." Again, I feel tempted to mention Weylin, but decide against it. His importance in my life is waning more and more. Maybe there are no more lessons to be learned.

"You're right. Please come and visit me. Bring your husband, too."

"I'd love to visit Norway, and one day I just might pay you a visit. Life is surely unpredictable and takes us in so many unexpected directions," I reply.

When everyone leaves, David and I go for a light lunch. He is very satisfied with the outcome of the workshop. He tells me what Giovanni and Dieter's regressions revealed and how Dieter found out he and his wife were soul-mates in a past life and he was full of hope they would weather their marital crisis.

"David, are you sure you can guide Adrian back to the time I lived as his wife Jilleen?"

"I will do my best, but can't guarantee success. You also told me he was the type of guy who didn't believe in anything of this sort, so he may be resistant to hypnosis."

"He was that kind of guy, and I don't understand why he's now volunteered for this…maybe he hopes…oh, never mind."

When we come back, we find Adrian standing outside the conference room. The door is locked so David lets us in. Adrian asks me if I'm all right because I look pale. I tell him I was sick and he seems concerned.

When we enter David points to the chair he wants Adrian to sit in. Adrian looks comfortable in a pair of jeans and a pale green sweater of high quality, one I haven't seen before. The sweater flatters him, but is not something he would have bought for himself. A present from Ginny? I wonder.

David explains to Adrian the concept of hypnotherapy, how it works on some people but not on everyone, and how he will guide him back in time until he reaches a specific epoch. I expect Adrian to ask a few questions, but he just answers he is ready. David puts on a Mirabai Ceiba CD and the room starts floating on soft, mantric, chanting and hypnotic voices of a man-woman duet. The music transports me to a state close to meditation. It has an effect on Adrian because he appears relaxed. David gets up to dim the lights. My heart starts racing in expectation of the unknown. It is filled with an aching yearning for an answer to a question I cannot fully articulate.

David starts the session by guiding Adrian through the relaxation steps and visualization of a white, healing light. He then suggests Adrian access the time when he was a baby and then to move beyond that time and enter the realm of his previous lives. When Adrian seems to be regressed, David asks him to tell him where he is and Adrian's answer is he is an English officer in the First World War and his name is James. David and I exchange looks as this seems to be a reference to Juliet and James, but David gives me a sign indicating he will go further into the past.

He suggests to Adrian to leave that period and go back to the sixteen hundreds when he lived in Ireland and knew Jilleen. David mentions the White Circle and Glenda's Bluff, but these names stir no reaction in Adrian. After about fifteen minutes of probing, David guides Adrian through a state of trance by asking him to visualize doors with different inscriptions denoting the place, the time and well-known landmarks. Once he brings him to the door, the one on which the name Ireland is inscribed and the picture of the White Circle is depicted, David asks him to open that and walk through it. Adrian is still silent for a while, so David opens his mouth to guide him further.

Adrian startles both of us by saying, "I remember the White Circle. I mostly remember meeting her there."

"Who is it you remember?"

"Jilleen, my wife."

"How did you meet her? Tell me more about her."

"She captured my heart the first day I saw her roaming the fields with a wreath of daisies in her long brown hair. I feel my heart leap upon the sight of her, but I pretend I am in possession of all my strengths, my power, my pride, because as the future chieftain I must not appear too soft before the women folk. Mother tells me I should marry, and with a smile on her face, she lets me know there is no family into which young girls would wish to marry more eagerly than ours. She asks me to choose wisely, and invites to our house wealthy and powerful families who have daughters.

"I ask her to invite our priest and his daughter, Jilleen, and she looks at me suspiciously and says, 'I hope you're not falling under the spell of that strange girl. I cannot imagine anyone wanting to marry someone so untamed. No well-bred girl roams the fields and climbs the hills like she does. I have been told she gazes at the sun with her arms open and dances alone by moonlight.'

"I tell my mother she is a good girl, she heals people, everyone likes her and no one can resist her tinkling laughter."

"What does your mother say?"

"She says Jilleen roams the fields and forests like a wild beast...her temper flares up and she chastises men for killing beasts to prove their valor, she spends too much time with Ailionora, a witch. Women gossip about Jilleen, saying she will not make a good wife. She wants freedom to roam and gather herbs, and she loves books more than the company of people. She tells me Jilleen is unsuitable as a mate for a warrior and future chieftain. She also reminds me that as learned as he is, her father lives from our alms and cannot give her a dowry. A girl who reads, writes, and roams should be shunned.

"Just to catch a glimpse of her, I ride out every morning to the White Circle where she often sits gazing at the sun, reading the bible or some other book. I learned how to read and write, but was never interested in books. What I am interested in is justice. I want to be a just ruler."

"Where are you now, Adrian?"

"I am nearing the White Circle."

"Describe the White Circle."

"It is a circle of white, tall stones. There are four gates into the circle. No one knows who built this circle. We celebrate Beltane here and dance around fires. Jilleen comes here often. She is here now."

"What is she doing?"

"She is standing on one of the lower stones, a stone that seems to have fallen. With arms spread, she is gazing at the sun. A dog...no...it looks like a wolf is lying at the base of the stone. I am afraid it will hurt her and I want to kill it, but her hand is on the wolf's head. The wolf is now licking her hand and she is speaking to it. She is a strange girl, indeed. I move closer and the wolf catches my scent, snarls and runs away."

"What is she doing now?"

"She has heard my footsteps and turned around. She smiles at me. My heart is thumping."

"Tell me what happens between the two of you."

"We are talking. I tell her she is lovely…that God made her beautiful.

"'God made everything beautiful,' she says. 'God's beauty is in every leaf, flower, beast and brook. His voice is in the wind; his touch is in the moonlight streaming down the trees. Divinity is present in everything we see.'"

"What happens then?"

"She says, 'Your name is Aidan, isn't it? You did not always live with your parents, right? People say you were living in England where they trained you in the art of battle.'

"Aye, that is correct. I lived in England for two years. I came back because my father is getting old and he wants me to be the new chieftain. People talk about me, but I hear them talk about you, too. You can read and write."

'Yes, my father taught me everything he knew. There is magic in books…in them I find new worlds that excite my soul, worlds I knew nothing of. There is this world around us I love, but there is one inside me that the written word awakens and excites. It feels like a ray of sun touching my soul and then setting it on fire. That is how I feel when I read. And I crave more books. Will you bring me some books from England when you go there next time?'

"Aye, I shall bring you many books. People find it strange that you often wander alone. Shouldn't you fear encounters with wild beasts or evil men?"

'I am wary of evil men, but not beasts. Evil only lives in men, but not in animals. I know it, but I cannot explain it. I know how to protect myself, but I cannot tell you how. It is my secret.'

"Why do you come here, you smiling and beguiling wench?"

'These stones hide sacred fire. I can feel and touch the fire that comes from gods.'

"There is only one God."

'There are many. My father tells me I must never say that, but I trust you. I do not know why I trust you, but there is goodness in your eyes. You are not like other men even though you are more powerful than most, and they fear you. Word has reached us of your bravery in battle.'

"In a giggling voice she tells me all the girls talk about me, and dream of becoming my wife.

"Do you dream of becoming my wife?"

'I have never dreamed of becoming anyone's wife. I see too many wives live dolorous existences filled with hard labor, painful losses of their babies, suffering caused by their husbands who beat them and keep them subjugated. I have seen too many girls whose wedding May garlands turned to withered wreaths of bitter disappointment. So, my lord, I am not dreaming of marrying anyone. If I married you, would you allow me to come to the Circle to worship the sun, would you allow me to come here and dance in the moonlight?'

"I am a man of honor, and I am a man who always wanted a sword no one else had, and it was forged just for me. And I wanted a dagger with a blade to cut through stone, a horse that could withstand any battle without losing heart, and so I want a wife unlike any wife, but a wife to love me as ardently as I love her."

She says I do not know her well enough to love her.

"I want to know you. Can we meet here again? I want you to tell me about the books you read, and I shall tell you about my life in England and my plans for our country, my allegiances, my desire to have sons to teach to fight, hunt. I shall bring you books to read. The books we have that my father brought from England will be yours, and I shall buy you more books when I go away."

'I want children who will read and write poetry. I write poems,' she says.

"Her eyes sparkle and her voice rings with insouciance. Her green dress moves with her laughter and she looks like an enchanting creature of the world of the Fae.

I meet her at the Circle day after day. Every time I see her, my stomach swirls with excitement and my heart flutters like a caged bird yearning for freedom."

After Adrian stops speaking, David turns to me. I am crying silently, inconsolably. Sadness and sorrow flow from my eyes, soaking my silk top. David turns his attention again to Adrian and asks, "Adrian—that is, Aidan, where are you now?"

"I am waiting for her in the Circle. It is raining hard and the thunder and lightning are frightening my horse. She will not come in this weather and I should go home, but hold on. I see a shadow running in the rain toward me. It is Jilleen; she dared come in this weather. What a brave girl! My love for her chokes me. She runs into my embrace and I kiss her face, eyes, lips and her wet hair. She is shivering and gasping from the exhaustion of running. I shout through the thunder and rain, 'You shall be my wife.' She shouts back, 'I shall be your wife but I shall remain free.' I shout even more loudly, 'I shall never take your freedom away. You may live the way you wish, but you must also be devoted to me. I am not your master and you are not my possession. I want you to love me with a free and happy heart.'

"We are kissing and laughing and gasping and planning our wedding. She does not say she loves me, but smiles when I tell her how much I love her and how I never dreamed I could love so much."

Adrian is smiling reliving these ancient reveries and I cannot stop crying. So many things have happened to me in the last couple of days. My intuition to have David guide Adrian to the same incarnation I had lived in proved correct. Everything is falling into place; all the pieces of this mystery puzzle, called my life or lives, fit.

"Tell me more about your life together," David asks Adrian.

"My parents are not happy when I announce I'll be marrying Jilleen, but after spending one evening talking to her, they are charmed. My father jokes she must be a witch to sway his mind toward her so quickly. The wedding is a three-day festivity. Jilleen insists we distribute food to the poor as our wedding gift. The outpouring of blessings is overwhelming, but all I care for is Jilleen's smiling face. My mother takes me aside one day to tell me not to show so much feeling toward my wife as that is unbecoming of a man in my position. People must instead respect and fear me.

"During the day, I become more reserved, but at night, while moonlight floods our chamber, I make passionate love to my lovely bride and am overjoyed that after the first period of shyness, she starts to meet my fire with her own, with a ferocity I had never known before. When I learn I must go to battle, my heart breaks, looking at her distraught face. The first time I was gone for a whole spring. I led my men into fierce fighting after which we pillaged and burned and raped. I raped only to show the enemy I was the conqueror, and to prove to my men I was a God-appointed leader, but whether women came to me willingly or surrendered in fear, my pleasure was small. I wanted my wife, but did not dare mention that in front of my men, who would have laughed at me."

David suggests to Adrian he go to the time of his and Jilleen's wedding anniversary.

"Our hall is full of people. It is my fourth wedding anniversary, but we are not celebrating that. The celebration is in my honor. I am succeeding my father as chieftain."

"Describe the atmosphere."

"There is a din of revelry. Wine and ale are flowing and men's drunken behavior is chasing the women from the hall. Jilleen has also retreated to our chamber. Lately, the look in her eyes has become distant. She still roams the fields after she has put our two-year-old boy to bed for his afternoon nap. She is not present in our lovemaking and I catch her looking at the ceiling as if she is with me only in body but not in soul. I ask her if anything is the matter. I want her to be happy. She is my love. She does not wear the jewelry I bring her. She says she feels every piece is drenched in pain, blood, mortal fear and death. She says she cannot wear other people's death. Any other woman would be pleased with gifts of gold, but my Jilleen does not seem to be of this world. Again, I think it was the Fae who left her on her father's doorstep as a baby."

David again guides him to move forward in time and tell us what is happening. After a few minutes, he seems to access a memory that makes him flinch and flail his arms in great agitation and anger.

"She disappeared! Jilleen has disappeared! Our son is crying and wailing. He wants his mother. I send men everywhere in search of her. They interrogate people and find she was accused of witchery and thrown into the river to drown.

"I am mad with fury and pain, and intoxicated with revenge I shall kill the inquisitor, but firstly I have the gaoler hanged. I order a few other men and women hanged, those who had watched Jilleen being thrown into the river. People are hiding in their houses terrified for their lives. Why would anyone want to hurt Jilleen? Everyone loves her. She heals people and animals; she is an angel on earth."

David intervenes again and asks Adrian if he sees Jilleen again. Adrian's voice is filled with relief when he says, "Just as I'd lost hope of ever seeing her again, she appears in our chamber, waking me up. I fall on my knees thanking the Lord for this miracle, hardly believing she is not an apparition. I embrace her and our son with such might I am afraid I will crush their bones, wishing to protect them. She tells me about her ordeal and the way the inquisitor, her childhood friend, protected her. I remember him as a sickly boy playing by the river with other children. Even as a child, I felt I was meant to become a great warrior and refused to play with children who looked timid."

"What is your life like now?" David probes further.

"Our life has settled into its old routine. After a few weeks of staying home with our son, Jilleen again begins leaving the house to roam the fields. She says she has missed her freedom and needs to feel the earth breathe under her feet; she craves the sun and wind kissing her face and filling her with strength and power. I am afraid to let her go alone, but she reminds me of my vow to never curtail her freedom."

"Where are you now?" David asks after a few minutes during which Adrian is silent.

"We are at a masked ball at Lord Tyrone's house. It is a custom he brought back from his visit to Italy or, rather, one he enriched our Samhain festival with by the custom of wearing beautiful Italian masks, and not the usual ones representing evil spirits. Tonight, there are all kinds of masks and elaborate costumes. Some look like evil spirits and some are opulent costumes representing the Fae, or kings and queens.

"Jilleen looks ravishing as a dragonfly. I have never understood her fascination with dragonflies, but I have surprised her with a dragonfly brooch fashioned from gold and precious stones. I ordered it made because she refuses to touch any jewelry I bring back from my conquests. She is sitting close to someone. I do not recognize the man, but he seems to be leaning into her and touching her. I am jealous, but do not want to show it. I trust her virtue. I become alarmed when she disappears, but do not notice how long she is missing from the banquet room. The man who had been sitting on her right is also nowhere to be seen and I am filled with cold dread that they might be together somewhere in the gardens.

"I go outside and search frantically for her. I mistake other women for her and my head starts hurting from too many colors, too many costumes, too many masks which are starting to look hideous and menacing. I finally find her outside the manor. Her hair looks disheveled, and her dress is wet and full of leaves. She tells me she took a walk and fell into the brook at the end of the estate. I am astonished, and ask her why she went so far, but she replies quickly she needed to be alone as she felt she was suffocating among so many masks and heavy costumes. She says she is going into the house to ask Lady Tyrone to lend her a dry dress.

"I am about to reproach her for disappearing like that but change my mind. I wait for her outside. Very soon, I see Lady Tyrone storm out of the house with a look of madness in her eyes. Jilleen is trailing after her, and I notice her dress is still wet. I approach my wife and at the same time a blood-curdling scream makes me turn around. I cannot believe my eyes. Lady Tyrone is stabbing a woman to death. Then I recognize the woman. It is Morgana, Lord Tyrone's mistress, who is lying in a pool of her own blood on the ground. Screams erupt everywhere and without even thinking, I grab Jilleen and take her home."

I am in total disbelief when I hear Adrian recount in such great detail what I recounted to David during my own sessions. How can this be possible? Is it a conspiracy between Adrian and Jorunn to hack into David's computer, find my file and make idiots of both David and me? I immediately dismiss that as utter absurdity, but I am also unable to process what I have just heard and seen. But Adrian is talking again, and both David and I know what is coming. Aidan will lose Jilleen for good.

"When she tells me she is with child I am overcome with gratitude to our Lord. I want more sons to inherit my vast estate and to spread my influence. I want her to stay home and be safe. I do not want to let her out of my sight, but to no avail. She has the spirit of a wild animal called by some voice only she hears. Her owl hoots every night from a large oak tree below our bower and she goes to the bower and peers into the night. 'He's calling me,' she whispers. I ask her if it is the owl calling her, but she only says he does not allow her to forget him. I know not what she means, but believe carrying a child makes women think and say strange things. I wonder if she can be losing her mind. I want to know who it is that does not let her forget. If it is a man, I shall find him and rip his heart out."

David prods Adrian again to move along in time and bring us to Jilleen's delivery.

When Adrian starts to speak, I feel nauseated, distraught and filled with worry. He is doubling over in his chair and gasping.

"I am losing her...my prayers are unanswered...she is bleeding. I beseech the women, the midwife, to save her, but there is only more blood. I am going mad with pain. If she dies I want to die with her. I am kneeling at her bedside, holding her hand and praying to the Lord to save her and a miracle happens: She opens her eyes, but closes them again, yet she is still breathing. I look at the swaddling in the midwife's arms and she tells me our son is dead. I want to see the baby who almost killed Jilleen. He is so tiny and red and has wisps of yellow hair. Our firstborn has black hair like me. I order the women to take the baby out of the chamber and to call Jilleen's father to say a prayer over the baby before we bury him. May the Lord receive him with love! There will be more sons, but I cannot live without Jilleen."

Adrian is sobbing. His body is shaking and I give David a sign to stop the session. We have heard enough and there is no need to take him through the pain of Jilleen's death and his realization the woman he loved so much was unfaithful to him in more than one lifetime. Finding her, Kieran and Jane together at the bottom of the cliff may cause him to suspect her infidelity. But perhaps he never learned in that lifetime she was disloyal, or that she never loved him with the fiery passion she had for Kieran. He would have never found out the truth in this life had I not disclosed my secret so fortuitously.

David gently guides Adrian into the present moment. When he is fully back, he's still sobbing, remembering how he almost lost Jilleen.

"I feel it in my heart that I did lose her, but I cannot remember how," he says. Turning toward me, he says, "Yes, I know it was you. The reason I volunteered to be regressed is I hoped I'd find some answers. You were Jilleen. Did you love me then?"

"I loved you," I say. "You were the best husband any woman could have wished for. I was so lucky you wanted me. You have always been my pillar of strength; you were loyalty incarnate. No wonder we found each other in this lifetime, and who knows in how many more."

Adrian stands up and takes strides over to me. We hold each other in a long embrace. Adrian's shoulders are still shaking under the effects of the emotional earthquake he has experienced. I wipe his tears away and tell him, even though all of this seems to be surreal, impossible, fantastical, it has been a journey of self-discovery, and a rediscovery of each other.

"Did I always have to lose you?" Adrian asks me.

"You lost me only to find me again in this lifetime."

"But I lost you in this lifetime, too."

His countenance is filled with despondence laced with a flicker of expectation.

"Adrian, we are now at a crossroads. It seems I made poor choices in more than one lifetime. But I also made some good choices, and the best choice I have ever made was you in each and every incarnation. The reason I kept making bad choices is that until this lifetime, it seems I had not learned the lessons I was destined to learn. This session is irrefutable proof of our connectedness. Do you think you could give me another chance to prove to you I can be trusted?"

Adrian's expression is a mix of sadness, exhaustion, but also of hope.

"I'd like to give it a try, but I may be difficult to live with. I may snap and lash out at you during the moments when I remember what you did. I may hate you at times, I may not be able to trust you, and I may yell at you," he tells me.

"I will not expect much of you, and we may fail at this or we can make our bond unbreakable, in this incarnation. I never stopped loving you as my husband, friend and father of our children. I just forgot how to love you as a lover, but in that respect our marriage is no better or worse than many. We still have many years ahead of us to rebuild what I demolished."

His hug is firm. I look for David, but he is no longer in the room. He has done what he could for us.

That night, I fall asleep in Adrian's arms feeling more secure and sheltered than ever before. In my dream, I hear a whisper, 'Don't you ever forget about me.' I just smile, wrap my arms around Adrian, and fall back into a peaceful sleep.

THE END

Acknowledgements:

Had it not been for the immense encouragement from my family and friends, I may have never dispelled the gnawing self-doubt about my writing ability. I am forever grateful to my mother Masa Begovic for sincerely believing I wrote one of the most beautiful novels she had ever read; my husband Miro Vasilj for diligently saving all the versions of my manuscript, knowing how hopelessly disorganized I am; my son Andrej Vasilj for appreciating my input on his school essays and continuously prodding me to write a book; my sister Dr. Dijana Oliver and my uncle Dr. Hifzija Bajramovic for offering advice on the psychological building of my characters from the psychiatrist's perspective; my aunt Dr. Seka Bajramovic for her honest and insightful feedback on the manuscript; my friend Sanya Petrovic for reading the manuscript several times and offering structure related suggestions; my friend Mary Jo DiBiase for finding the manuscript "un-put-down-able," even in its rough form; my soul sister Julie Dubeau for her infinite love and belief that the book would be a success; my friends Milica and Victor Puljic, Kosa Pilic, Gordana Mrdja, Visnya Kapetanovic, Mira Vukovic, Lya Mountford and Heike Scheffler for acting as my Alpha and Beta readers and calling the novel riveting and mesmerizing; my friend Dr. Karen Dover for helping me finalize the back cover blurb; Dr. Tanya Bracanovich, Natasa Stojmenovic and Nancy Rossi-Capers for going out of her way to assist me in promoting the book; my fantastic editors, Kathleen Marusak and Lynne Street, for their invaluable polishing of the manuscript; my cover designer Bill Oliver for patiently producing several cover art versions; and last but not least, Rebecca Hart from Roane Publishing, for not only accepting the manuscript, but allowing it to break the boundaries of a typical romance. You have all made this journey unforgettable!

Printed in Great Britain
by Amazon